# THE MAKING OF A TUDOR

# THE MAKING
# OF A TUDOR

CAROLINE NEWARK

Matador
9 Priory Business Park,
Wistow Road, Kibworth Beauchamp,
Leicestershire. LE8 0RX
Tel: 0116 279 2299
Email: books@troubador.co.uk
Web: www.troubador.co.uk/matador
Twitter: @matadorbooks

ISBN 978 1800464 346

British Library Cataloguing in Publication Data.
A catalogue record for this book is available from the British Library.

Printed and bound in the UK by TJ Books Limited, Padstow, Cornwall
Typeset in 11pt Minion Pro by Troubador Publishing Ltd, Leicester, UK

Matador is an imprint of Troubador Publishing Ltd

*For Jackie Lane*
*who believes in magic*

# THE FAMILY TREE
# (SO FAR)

*Edward the First, King of England, married as his second wife, Marguerite of France, and had by her issue Edmund of Woodstock.*

*Edmund of Woodstock, Earl of Kent, Earl of Arundel married Margaret, daughter of Lord John Wake and widow of John Comyn, and had by her issue Joan of Kent.*

*Joan of Kent in her own right Countess of Kent, married Sir Thomas Holand, Lord Holand, Knight of the Most Noble Order of the Garter, to whom she bore issue Thomas Holand.*

*Thomas Holand married Alys, daughter of Richard Fitzalan, Earl of Arundel, by Eleanor, daughter of Henry, Earl of Lancaster, and had by her issue among others, Eleanor Holand.*

♥

*Eleanor Holand married Thomas Montagu, Earl of Salisbury, Knight of the Most Noble Order of the Garter, Count of Perche and Lieutenant General of Normandy to whom she bore issue Alice Montagu*

# LIST OF MAIN CHARACTERS

| | |
|---|---|
| Alice Montagu | daughter of the Earl of Salisbury |
| Her husband | Richard Nevill |
| Her mother-in-law | Joan, Countess of Westmoreland |
| Her father-in-law | Ralph Nevill, Earl of Westmoreland |
| Her sisters-in-law | Lady Percy |
| | Lady Mowbray |
| | Anne Nevill |
| | Cecily Nevill |
| | Margaret, dowager Lady Scrope |
| Her brother-in-law | William, Lord Fauconberg |
| Her aunts | Margaret, Duchess of Clarence |
| | Joan, Lady Bromflete |
| Her stepmother | Alice Chaucer |
| Her friend | Eleanor Cobham |

## THE ENGLISH ROYAL FAMILY

| | |
|---|---|
| The king | Henry V |
| His queen | Katherine of Valois |
| His brothers | Thomas, Duke of Clarence |
| | John, Duke of Bedford |
| | Humphrey, Duke of Gloucester |
| His uncle | Henry Beaufort, Bishop of Winchester |
| His cousin | Edmund Beaufort |

# OTHERS

| | |
|---|---|
| The king of France | Charles VI, "The Well-Beloved" |
| His queen | Isabeau of Bavaria |
| His son | Charles, the disinherited dauphin |
| His cousin | Philip, Duke of Burgundy |
| Countess Jacqueline | Philip of Burgundy's cousin |
| Lady Warwick | Isabel, Countess of Warwick |
| Guillemot | a maid to Katherine of Valois |
| Owen Tudor | a Welsh gentleman |
| Mistress Jourdemayne | a supplier of charms and potions |

# Prologue

*Troyes, a city in the Champagne region of France
under the control of the Duke of Burgundy.*

Outside in the soft summer twilight a nightingale is singing, joined in counterpoint from the courtyard below by the plaintive notes of a lone Welsh harp.

It is two weeks since the English king arrived at the gates of Troyes with the principal commanders of his army and an escort of two and a half thousand men. He was greeted by the duke of Burgundy and brought immediately to a formal meeting with the royal family where a veil was politely drawn over past disagreements, although some were heard muttering behind their hands of treachery and dishonour. But now with the treaty signed and the marriage celebrated, the truth is indisputable: here within the old palace of the counts of Champagne, the elect of God, Henry, King of England, regent and heir to the throne of France has come to collect his prize.

They said it couldn't be done and laughed at his arrogance, calling him the son of a regicide, marked by the Almighty for his father's sins. Even after his success on the killing field of Agincourt they said it was impossible and tried to subvert his plans with whispered threats of sin and eternal damnation. But as the French princes tore

ix

each other apart, drowning their fellow countrymen in a sea of internecine blood, some questioned whether the English invader was not perhaps the lesser of the two evils menacing France.

In his mind's eye he sees once more the walls rippling with banners of azure and scarlet and gold, the gloom within the cathedral church, the treaty roll, the pale face of the hapless king of France, broken, unable to comprehend how divine retribution has brought his kingdom to its knees. And hovering, like a guest come late to the feast, Philip, Duke of Burgundy: black-hatted, black-robed, black-hearted, selling the throne of France to an English king in revenge for his father's murder.

'She is afraid of you.' The words slide out of the darkness like a snake from under a stone. The duke uncoils himself from the shadows and murmurs, 'Her mother tells her you kill those you profess to love. You like to see them burn.'

Henry is not a man for regret but on rare occasions his sleep is disturbed by the smell of burning flesh, the crackle of flames, the searing heat, and screams which fill the air until nothing remains of his one-time boon companion but shattered bone and a smoking pile of ash.

'The man was a heretic,' he says coldly. 'I could no longer defend him.'

The duke smiles. 'Ah but, *mon cher,* your bride, she is a woman. She does not understand.'

Henry imagines the naked shoulders of his young wife, pearly white against the dark tresses of her unbound hair, the long slim body, the touch of her scented skin. Thrice a week avoiding holy days, his physician has advised but when asked if a single act of coupling each night was sufficient to achieve his purpose, the man looked askance as if he'd suggested sodomy.

At the wedding feast his bride did not once mention her brother, that scrawny adolescent disinherited by the treaty who dares to call himself his father's true and rightful heir. In truth, for a princess of the *fleur-de-lys* she has spoken very little. In the morning she will expect jousts and feasting, a day of magnificent festivities to mark their marriage, but she will be disappointed. He intends to have her accompany him and once the towns of Sens and Melun are taken and the road to Paris lies open they will ride together through the royal gate beneath the headless stone figure of St Denis and the citizens will cry, "*Noel!*" For is not he their undoubted saviour, the English king who has put an end to years of strife and near starvation and brought them peace?

Then he will take her back to England and have her crowned his queen.

# 1

## CORONATION 1421

My mother-in-law's voice contained all the chill of a raw winter's day and could not have been more unwelcoming.

'Did you know?'

There followed a prolonged silence while I debated which answer would cause the least amount of trouble. If I had learned anything these past months as a new bride in the Nevill household it was the wisdom of remaining quiet and unnoticed.

'I doubt she knew,' remarked my sister-in-law, the willowy Lady Mowbray, wife of the earl marshal, only recently returned from France. 'A dutiful daughter would have known but she is hardly that.'

'What have you to say?' said my mother-in-law.

'My father told me nothing,' I said in the smallest of voices.

'Ha!' exclaimed Lady Percy, wife of the earl of Northumberland and another of my mother-in-law's many daughters. 'Just as I suspected.'

Lady Percy had her mother's eyes, the noticing kind which see every little mistake a woman makes and more besides.

My mother-in-law was not a Neviil by birth, she was a Beaufort, a king's granddaughter, but today like every other day she was surrounded by Nevills: Nevill cousins, Nevill daughters, Nevill step-daughters and Nevill daughters-in-law. Even the young woman crouched at her feet making last minute alterations to the hem of her gown was a Nevill of sorts, the unfortunate result of one of her husband's past indiscretions. The castle at Middleham, where we spent much of our time, was strewn with Nevill bastards and my mother-in-law had at least two maids in her service who bore an uncanny resemblance to my aging father-in-law, Ralph Nevill, Earl of Westmoreland.

My mother-in-law's voice if anything grew more glacial. 'I presume my son has had words with you on the matter?'

I did not like to say that words were not common currency between my husband and myself. In truth, in the six months since our wedding day Richard Nevill had favoured me with barely a dozen and those mostly of the ordering kind. Our nocturnal business was conducted in silence and when we appeared in public he would politely offer his arm but otherwise I was ignored.

'Richard doesn't talk to her,' said Lady Percy.

'He talks to me more than he talks to her,' remarked Lady Mowbray. 'I swear I've not heard him address a single word to her.'

'My husband has spoken to me about my father's letter,' I said staunchly, determined to defend myself from this Nevill onslaught.

'I doubt that,' said Lady Percy. 'I was told he cursed you roundly before consigning the letter to the flames. Conversation was not mentioned.'

In essence what she said was true. Richard Nevill had burst into my room while I was dressing, ordered my maid out and then thrust the letter under my nose while shouting the foulest of insults imaginable. He had kicked a stool against the wall and swept my jewel box onto the floor, calling me a cunning little deceiver. I was a cheat, a fraudster; my father had tricked him in the most despicable of ways; the Nevills had been duped. The letter had then been torn into shreds in front of my eyes and thrown onto the fire so I was none the wiser as to what my father had actually done. Clearly some heinous crime had been committed but what it was I had no idea.

'You do realise why my son agreed to marry you,' said my mother-in-law, twitching the folds of her gown away from the inexpert fumbling of the seamstress.

'I am my father's only child,' I said with dignity, conscious of my ancient and honourable pedigree. My father, Thomas Montagu, was Earl of Salisbury and one of the king's most important commanders. He had fought at Agincourt when the English army defeated the flower of French chivalry and had been present at the signing of the treaty of Troyes when the king was made heir to the throne of France. My mother, who had distant royal connections of her own, had been immensely proud of him.

'Exactly!' said my mother-in-law. 'An only child, a sole heiress, a valuable commodity.'

'As I am still.'

'Not for much longer,' said Lady Percy with a smirk.

'Why not?' I said, panic-stricken. 'What have I done?'

'It is not what *you* have done but what your father has done,' said my mother-in-law. There was a pause which lasted too long to be comfortable. It filled the room with swirling menace and I knew something dreadful was about to be said.

'He has cheated us,' said Lady Percy.

'Your father,' said my mother-in-law, indicating with a wave of her hand to the whey-faced maid to fasten the jewelled collar around her shoulders, 'has informed us of his decision to remarry.'

'But that's impossible,' I gasped, remembering my father's distress at my mother's death. 'He swore his heart was broken and he'd never take another wife.'

'Apparently his heart has remarkable powers of recovery,' said my mother-in-law drily. 'His letter says he is to marry the widowed Lady Phelip.'

'A widow!'

An image of a grey-haired elderly body with a warm smile and plump cheeks flashed through my mind.

'A *young* widow, so I believe.'

'Not above seventeen,' remarked Lady Percy.

'Pleasing to look at,' smiled Lady Mowbray.

'Fertile,' said Lady Percy, grinning at my increasing discomfiture.

The cold horror of what might happen crept slowly towards me and my legs began to tremble. A young wife! Not above seventeen! A fertile wife! I knew only too well what that meant.

'She could have a child,' I gasped.

'She could have a son,' said my mother-in-law.

'But a son would...'

' ... disinherit you.'

'A son would get everything and I'd be left with nothing.'

'*Richard* would be left with nothing,' she corrected me. 'But it is far worse than that.'

What could possibly be worse than losing my inheritance? I had grown up knowing how precious I was to both my parents and how, as their only child, everything they possessed would one day come to me.

'My son did not marry you for your father's properties. Surely you knew that.'

I looked at her with blank incomprehension.

'Your father is Earl of Salisbury,' she said as if telling me something I didn't know, as if I was stupid. 'The title is ancient and is entailed which means that when he dies it will come to you. That is why my son agreed to take you as his wife, not for a paltry handful of manors. Now do you understand?'

I could not believe my father's treachery. We had knelt together in the Bisham chapel that winter, praying for my mother's immortal soul. He said she had been the best of wives, an incomparable companion in all his trials and tribulations. Irreplaceable. He had wept tears of genuine sorrow and I had wept with him. And now he was to betray her memory and marry again. He was going to rob me of the only prize I had brought to my marriage, the only gift which would satisfy my husband, who was not a man who liked to be thwarted.

'Leave it alone!' snapped my mother-in-law to the maid who was trying to adjust the jewelled collar. 'Why does everything have to go wrong today of all days and why have I been blessed with a half-wit for a daughter-in-law.'

So saying she swept out of the room with two of her step-daughters and a dozen flustered maids in tow leaving me alone with my sisters-in-law to face further humiliation.

'I'm not stupid,' I muttered. 'I'm not.'

'You mustn't mind our lady mother,' said Lady Mowbray, pretending a sisterly affection. 'She doesn't mean to be unkind but she's worried for Richard.'

'And about the widow,' said Lady Percy gleefully, adopting her usual position as the sister-in-law to point out my deficiencies as a new member of the Nevill family.

'We are all worried about the widow,' said Lady Mowbray. 'Who knows what she might do.'

'And how many sons she might whelp.'

'Is your mother acquainted with the widowed Lady Phelip?' I asked timidly.

'Certainly not!' said Lady Mowbray. 'I believe she is Master Thomas Chaucer's daughter.'

'Master Chaucer is a cousin of sorts to our mother,' explained Lady Percy.

'He is said to be influential in the parliament but we do not know him,' said Lady Mowbray as if sitting in the parliament was an unsavoury occupation, not something to be encouraged.

'I thought she'd be old?' I said mournfully.

'Foolish,' murmured Lady Percy.

'Very,' agreed her sister.

'And I do not see why my father needs to marry again.'

Lady Percy and Lady Mowbray exchanged sly looks.

'Perhaps he wants a wife to warm his bed,' said Lady Percy with a laugh.

'My father is old,' I cried. 'He cannot need a wife for that.'

'Our father is even older and still feels the urge,' she said with a shrug of distaste for Ralph Nevill's well-known liking of fornication. 'Besides, old or not I'm sure your father will do his duty by his new wife.'

'It's not as if the widowed Lady Phelip is uncomely,' said Lady Mowbray.

'Indeed no. And men in their middle years can be extremely foolish over pretty young women,' said Lady Percy mercilessly.

'Doubtless she'll give him children.'

'A son or maybe two.'

'Our lady mother has given our father five sons,' remarked Lady Mowbray.

'And theirs was a second marriage,' agreed Lady Percy.

'Five sons,' I said weakly.

'Of course a son would rob Richard of the Salisbury title.'

'We none of us expected such treachery,' sighed her sister.

'I fear Richard is already regretting his marriage to you.'

'But he will have his father's title,' I protested. 'Is that not enough?'

'Oh you *are* ignorant,' said Lady Percy. 'Did they not tell you? No, obviously not.'

'Tell me what?'

The sisters picked up their skirts and made ready to leave.

'Richard may be our father's favourite son but he is not the eldest,' Lady Percy explained. 'Our father had sons by his first wife and it is a grandson of his first family who will inherit. Richard will never be Earl of Westmoreland. And he is not best pleased.'

'No, not pleased at all,' echoed Lady Mowbray.

When they reached the doorway, Lady Percy turned. 'Is that your best gown?'

I touched the costly silk folds of my skirt. 'My second best.'

'Dear child! What are you thinking! Do you wish to disgrace your husband. This is the queen's coronation feast not a family supper. Make haste and change before our lady mother notices and tears the gown off your back. And have your maid do something with your hair. You cannot go to Westminster looking like that.'


Queen Katherine was far more beautiful than I expected. She had long gleaming dark hair framing a pale narrow face and even at this distance I could see her cheeks were flushed a delicate pink with the excitement of her coronation day. Her lips remained resolutely unsmiling as befitted a queen but her luminous dark eyes sparkled.

Everyone said the king was passionately in love with her. They said he'd taken one look at this exquisite daughter of France and was determined to make her his wife. Only my mother-in-law believed this was a fiction. She said he'd married the queen for who she was not for her more obvious charms. Their marriage, according to my mother-in-law who understood every aspect of her royal nephew's kingship, lent further legitimacy to his divinely sanctioned claim to the throne of France. It was, she said, a physical manifestation of the peace brought to a ravaged land by the English king and heralded the perpetual union of the two kingdoms of England and France.

I let my gaze drift across the hall. There was a time when my mother would have occupied one of the gilded chairs reserved for women of the highest rank, but today it was my mother-in-law and her elder daughters who were seated on the dais near to the queen.

As I slipped into my allocated place at the ladies' table I recognised with dismay the narrow hunched shoulders of my aunt, Lady Bromflete, and cursed my misfortune at being seated next to her.

'Niece,' she said, nodding a greeting and sucking in her painted lips. She ran her eyes over my gown, doubtless seeking a grease spot or a pulled thread. Remembering my mother's final pleas to be kind to her sisters, I asked politely after my aunt's well-being and that of her husband. Yet all the time I knew she was finding fault with me just as she had always done.

'I see the Beaufort woman is preening herself up there,' she remarked, looking towards my mother-in-law who had her head inclined gracefully towards the king of the Scots. This was a skill learned in the cradle by women like my mother-in-law. However disagreeable she could be in private, when on display she exuded an elegance which was both captivating yet dignified.

'I sat there once, y'know, at the high table,' complained my aunt. 'First lady in the kingdom I was; every honour heaped on my shoulders. Coffers overflowing with silks and furs. King Richard himself showered me with jewels. I could have been queen. I *should* have been queen. But look at me now?'

This was an old story with its familiar litany of complaints. My aunt had once been the duchess of York, married to old King Henry's uncle, but death, treason and a suspicion of her loyalties had reduced her over the years to this decidedly inferior marriage. I was rather surprised she'd been sent an invitation.

'She was born a bastard, y'know.'

'Aunt, please, hush! Someone will hear.'

'Calls herself a Nevill. She's naught but a Beaufort bastard.'

My mother had told me the story of the marriage between the proud duke of Lancaster and the beautiful Lady Swynford, and how their four Beaufort children, born out of wedlock, had been legitimized by papal decree. At the time it had been an enormous scandal and one which greatly offended not just my aunt but other senior ladies of the royal court who were forced to yield precedence to the lowborn duchess.

'The Beauforts were all bastards yet see how they prosper,' muttered my aunt. 'As for my poor boys – their endeavours came to naught.'

A single glistening tear rolled down her pink puffy cheek as she mumbled on about her York stepsons: one whose folly brought him to the traitor's block and the other who died at Agincourt. 'Tragedy,' she muttered. 'It was naught but tragedy.'

With relief I turned to the young woman on my other side and gave her an encouraging smile.

'Where is the king?' she whispered.

'He does not attend,' I whispered back. 'It is the custom. This is the queen's day, everything is for her alone.'

'How odd. But forgive me, I'm being rude. Let me introduce myself. I am Eleanor Cobham. My father is Sir Reginald Cobham of Sterborough.'

She seemed friendly enough so I inclined my head and replied, 'I am Lady Alice, wife of Sir Richard Nevill.'

'I know.' She gave me a conspiratorial smile. 'I asked the lady on my other side.'

I was unused to being sought out like this and felt strangely flattered.

'Is your husband in attendance?' she asked.

'Yes, he's a carver.' I nodded to where Richard Nevill stood by the top table, knife held ready, though in truth, being Lent, there was very little to carve other than an exceedingly large fish. This, I had been assured by one of the servers, was a porpoise.

'Handsome,' she murmured.

I looked again at my dark-haired husband dressed in his best blue and green doublet and scarlet hose. It had never occurred to me that Richard Nevill was handsome but he was not unpleasing to look at with his father's long straight nose and his mother's broad forehead. He stood nearly six feet tall, or so my sisters-in-law told me, as in his company I mostly kept my gaze lowered in the way of a dutiful wife and stared at his feet.

'Who is that?'

Eleanor indicated a bare-headed man standing in front of the dais facing the queen. He was dressed in a doublet of pale blue velvet embroidered all over with tiny ostrich plumes picked out in silver thread. His padded sleeves were slashed to show a vivid crimson silk and his pleated skirt, with its scalloped points edged in fur, skimmed his knees in the latest fashion.

'Humphrey, Duke of Gloucester,' I whispered. 'He is the king's youngest brother.'

'Interesting,' murmured Eleanor Cobham.

'He has a vast library of books,' I whispered. 'My

cousins say he is much admired by the common people of the city.'

Eleanor smiled. 'Married?'

I shook my head.

She raised a pair of delicate eyebrows. 'No? How surprising!'

When she smiled, Eleanor was beautiful. She had a pointed chin in a heart-shaped face with large slanting green eyes and lips which, as far as I could tell, owed their rose-pink colour to nature rather than some womanly artifice.

'He is said to be devoted to his brother because the king saved his life at Agincourt,' I ventured. 'Lord Humphrey fell and the king stood guard over him, fighting off the enemy.'

'Brave,' murmured Eleanor. 'I should like a husband like that; one who is courageous as well as wealthy.'

'Are you betrothed?'

'No, but Sir Reginald hopes I shall secure a position in some great household and thus find a husband. Would you recommend marriage?'

I blushed, thinking of all that marriage involved. 'A young lady has to marry.'

She laughed, showing a set of pearly white teeth. 'That is what my mother says.'

'And your father?'

'He would keep me at home if he could. He enjoys my company and is loath to part with me. What of *your* father?'

There was a pause while I considered my father and his latest perfidy. 'My father is to marry again,' I said in a small tight voice, the words sticking unpleasantly on my tongue. 'Soon I shall have a stepmother.'

'So I am too late,' she laughed. But when she saw my eyes fill with tears, the laughter died. 'I am sorry. I did not mean to distress you.'

'It's nothing,' I sniffed, blinking away the tears. 'It's just, I miss my mother.'

'Of course you do,' she said gently. 'However much I may disagree with mine I'd be greatly distressed if she was no longer sitting in her usual place in our parlour. How old are you?'

'Thirteen.'

'Very young to be without a mother. Do you have sisters?'

'No, I'm an only child. There is no-one else.'

Eleanor gazed thoughtfully across the room to where Richard Nevill was placing a generous helping of porpoise in front of Archbishop Chichele. 'Is your husband pleased at you acquiring a stepmother?'

I blushed with embarrassment, realising I had said too much to someone I had only just met. The subject of my stepmother and my threatened inheritance was not a subject to be bandied about in public and dissected over a dish of baked mullet. But Eleanor was kind. 'Don't worry,' she whispered. 'I shall tell no-one. Your secrets will always be safe with me.'

It was an odd thing to have said, as if she anticipated a closeness in the years to come, a time when as grown women we would exchange words of a private nature, the kind of confidences I might share with a sister.

There was a sudden blast from the trumpets at the far end of the hall and everyone turned their heads.

'Oh look!' Eleanor clapped her hands together. '*Sainte Vierge*! It's a pelican!'

The procession of young men in royal livery moved slowly up the hall to where my husband stood ready to direct them. On their shoulders they carried a vast silver platter with what had to be the culmination of many days work by the royal confectioners: a glittering white bird with a capacious golden bill settled on a nest of jewelled grasses. As they walked, the pelican shimmered and quivered as if alive whilst hundreds of tiny agates and emeralds gleamed and winked in the candlelight.

'What is that?' said my aunt, tapping me on the shoulder as she peered forward. 'Is it a heron?'

'No, my lady. I believe it is a pelican.'

'Oh vanity,' she muttered. 'Nothing but vanity.'

# 2

## EWELME 1421

A week after the coronation feast I was in my room, diligently mending the hem of one of my gowns when I received an unexpected summons from my mother-in-law. In her plans for her eldest son she had met with an unexpected setback but, undaunted, was already devising a ploy to outwit the enemy. If my father had not been straight with the Nevills in this matter – and she was certain he had not – he could hardly expect them to accept this abomination of a second marriage without mounting an assault on its foundations. The earl of Salisbury far away in France leading the king's army against the forces of the disinherited dauphin, was unassailable, but there was always the more proximate target, the weaker one, the widowed Lady Phelip. This was to be an elaborate game of deceit in which I was expected to play a central role.

'A first sight of a future stepdaughter,' purred my mother-in-law, savouring the words with a little smile on her bloodless lips. 'What could be more delightful? And there will be a great many things for you to discuss.'

Yes, my lady, I said doubtfully, wondering what I could possibly find to talk about with this woman who was stealing both my father and my inheritance.

'I have it on good authority that the dowager Lady

Phelip presently resides in her father's house at Ewelme, by Wallingford.'

I knew Wallingford. When I was a little girl my mother had once taken me there to see the castle where her grandmother, Princess Joan, had lived in her declining years but nobody had mentioned a place nearby called Ewelme or a widowed Lady Phelip. Perhaps they were mean folk who lived at Ewelme, people unworthy of anyone's attention. That was it. Yet my father would not have chosen a woman of low birth to replace my mother, that would have been unthinkable; unless, and I felt myself grow cold at the thought, he had somehow been bewitched.

My mother-in-law was still talking. 'You will write today. Ask if you may visit. Naturally I shall tell you what to say. Also a small gift for Lady Phelip, something suitable for a widow, not too extravagant, some little delicacy. And you may take one of my maids.'

Of course there was a hidden meaning to her words, one which she later spelled out in explicit detail fearing I was too stupid to understand what she wanted me to do. I was to discover my future stepmother's intentions with regard to this highly unfortunate marriage, a marriage which nobody wanted, apart from, one presumed, the participants.

Was she to live at Bisham after the wedding? Would my father continue with his military duties overseas? Would she perhaps travel to France to join him? And there was the more delicate matter of her personal health, not to mention her intimate relations with her first husband. Had they been satisfactory? My mother-in-law expected me to discover the likelihood of my future stepmother bearing a healthy child, a Montagu heir, a boy who would disinherit me and thus her own son. And what was worse, I had no idea how any of this was to be accomplished.

Edmund, the youngest of my Aunt Margaret's four Beaufort sons and the hero of my solitary childhood, had once said I was incapable of being a spy as every working of my mind showed plain on my face. Wanting him as a brother, I would follow like a trusty servant wherever he led, but Edmund was a harsh captain to his men. When planning a raid on his brothers' fortress in the bushes, he'd said that if I wished to be his second-in-command I must learn to dissemble.

If dissembling was to be the order of the day for this visit to Ewelme, and it seemed that it was, then I feared for the success of my endeavours. More and more I was beginning to wish I had never heard of the widowed Lady Phelip.

I set out in the cold of an early dawn with no sign of sun and a thin grey mist shredded in wisps above the dark surface of the river. Muffled church bells were ringing for Prime but the cluttered wharves and jumbled rooftops of the city were hidden from view and, as the oarsmen pulled away into mid-stream, even the towers of the royal palaces were barely visible.

On the journey I refused to think of the unknown woman I was about to meet or of Eleanor Cobham who had been so very kind to me at the coronation feast and who I would like to have as a friend. Instead I thought about my mother.

At every familiar bend in the river my memories unwrapped themselves, clutching at my heart and bringing tears to my eyes: my mother's private smile at the long-delayed letter from my father; the slanting sunlight catching her face as we sat together in the bower in the Lady's Garden; the touch of her fingers on mine when we wandered through Quarry Wood seeking windflowers for my hair; the whispered stories, the shadows dancing in the firelight and the howling winter storms battering the shutters as she held me tightly in her arms.

Those had been golden years when my mother and I had lived together at Bisham with just a handful of servants, waiting patiently for my father's return. Those were the years of my growing up, my education at my mother's knee, my learning to be a young lady and my belated acquaintanceship with my Beaufort cousins. Then my mother died and my father sent me to live with my prospective mother-in-law in readiness for marriage to her son. The golden years had ended.

I stared, surprised at how modest Master Chaucer's place at Ewelme was. Set back a little way from the road amidst green fields and surrounded by the familiar undulating chalk hills of my childhood, the house was a low two-storey affair with tiny windows and a central door. There were no turrets and just a single gatehouse, one that could easily be overrun by an enemy. The willow trees by the bubbling little stream were already in leaf and a profusion of lenten lilies grew up against the churchyard wall. The scene brought a lump to my throat as I compared its homely appearance to the bleak Yorkshire castles where my husband had taken me after our wedding and where we spent our summers.

I told my mother-in-law's two men to remain in the gatehouse, then walked across the courtyard towards the house with my mother-in-law's elderly maid following silently behind.

'Lady Nevill.'

She stood at the open door, a tall young women, reed-slender with a sinuous movement to her body and a calculating look in her eye. But her lips were smiling.

'I do not know what to call you,' I blurted out, unsure whether she was Lady Phelip or Mistress Chaucer or if she would expect me to call her "stepmother".

She didn't laugh, merely told me I might call her "stepmother" as the betrothal was formalized and she and my father were as good as man and wife. The church's blessing would take place when he returned to England.

I proffered the basket of sugared fruits which my mother-in-law had selected.

'Why, thank you,' she said in her cool quiet voice. 'I was not expecting such bounty.'

After I had been relieved of my cloak and my gloves, she led me through the low-ceilinged hall into a small parlour where a fire burned brightly in the hearth. The walls were covered with richly coloured hangings and, to my surprise, several books lay on a table together with evidence that my future stepmother had been busy writing.

She noticed my curiosity.

'Do you like to read?'

'Yes, I do. My mother-in-law has several books which we read aloud in the afternoons but I have none of my own, only the little one my mother gave me to help with my devotions.'

The silence was awkward while she watched me out of her calm grey eyes. She was narrow-faced like Queen Katherine, but with high cheekbones and a decidedly full underlip. I thought my cousin Edmund would admire her.

'My first husband gave me a book,' she said. 'He thought it a suitable gift for the granddaughter of a man who wrote verses.'

'Is it long since your first husband died?' I asked, wondering if she still mourned or if she was glad to be free of him.

'Yes,' she replied. 'More than five years. He travelled with the king's army to Harfleur where he fell sick and died. I was younger than you when I was widowed. We had only been married half a year. I barely knew him. Afterwards I was sent back to my father's house. Is that what you wanted to know?'

I could feel the heat in my cheeks as I realised she must have guessed I'd come to discover her secrets.

'Will my father return home soon?' I asked, overwhelmed with a sudden longing to see him, for him to tell me it was all a mistake and he had no intention of remarrying, not the widowed Lady Phelip or anyone else.

She looked at me for a long time saying nothing as if deciding what I should be told and if I could be trusted with her secrets.

'Your father has been reappointed lieutenant of Alcenon and the march of Maine by the king. Would you have him neglect his duties? He cannot come merely because it is your wish.'

'No, no, I realise that, it's just …' I stopped. This young woman, barely four years older than me, could not understand the acute need I felt for my father's presence, his slow smile and the touch of his hand.

'His letter arrived yesterday,' she said into the lengthening silence. 'It requested my father's help with the retrieval of the remainder of the Montagu inheritance from the Crown. He knows of my father's standing in the parliament and now that we are betrothed he wishes to assure himself of my father's support.' She curved her lips upwards, all the time watching my face, then added, 'There was, naturally, a private letter enclosed for me.'

The peace of the room was disturbed by a rustling in the corner as a little merlin on a perch settled deeper into its blue-grey feathers. A hound under the table raised his head at the noise and opened one eye but finding nothing amiss returned to his slumbers. The widowed Lady Phelip smoothed the folds of her skirt with her long pale fingers. I noticed how the glow from the fire made the soft green wool shine with a peculiar lustre.

She picked up a letter from the table and placed it in her lap. 'He spoke of his desire to make me his wife as soon as possible. He said if he could not come to me, would I make haste and come to him. And in case I was in any doubt as to his true feelings, he sent me a verse he'd written. Would you like me to read it to you? It is an expression of a man's love for a woman but I am sure he would not mind my sharing it. You are, after all, his daughter.'

Her gaze didn't falter as I struggled not to weep. My stalwart father had not been a man given to romantic sentiments or flowery avowals of love and I felt the betrayal of my mother in every word this woman said. He had never asked my mother to accompany him to France and had never once written her a verse.

'Do you know where my father is?' I asked stiffly.

'Of course I do. He is with the king's brother, the duke of Clarence. They are to move further into Anjou. It is what the king desires.'

I said nothing because what could I say. She knew everything about the king's cause in France and about my father's work there and I knew nothing. All I knew was that Charles, the so-called dauphin, who refused to recognise the treaty of Troyes, had fled from Paris with his supporters to escape from our armies. Nobody had mentioned Anjou.

'We could be friends,' she said. 'You are only a little younger than me. Thinking of me as your enemy will gain you nothing and will distress your father greatly. Is that what you want?'

'No, of course not,' I muttered, wrong-footed at every turn by this confident young woman who had set out to steal not just my father's affections but also my inheritance. We would never be friends. I hated her. My mother had preached the virtues of being kind but my mother had never met the widowed Lady Phelip.

On my return from Ewelme my mother-in-law's youngest daughters, Anne and Cecily, were waiting for me in the great hall of The Erber. They were engaged in a noisy game with Cecily's doll, two pegs and a length of wool but jumped up as soon as they saw me.

'What's she like?' said Cecily who at six years of age wanted to be first in everything.

22

'Is she beautiful?' said Anne who was a year older than Cecily and already betrothed to the earl of Stafford.

'Pleasing to look at,' I said, removing my cloak and handing it to the maid.

'What colour are her eyes?' Cecily was practically dancing on her toes with impatience.

'Grey.'

'Oh, how dull!'

'Does she sing as well as me?' asked Anne who was inordinately proud of her lovely singing voice.

'There was no time for making music.'

'Does she weep when she talks of her first husband like Lady Scrope does?' giggled Cecily.

The dowager Lady Scrope was a Nevill step-daughter, usually found hiding in a corner bent over a sodden piece of sewing. After seven months of widowhood she still wore mourning and was prone to wild outbursts of weeping which frightened the servants.

'She hardly mentioned him,' I said.

'That means she's in love with your father and she has forgotten the first one.'

'It means nothing of the sort,' retorted Anne. 'She might be too distraught over her loss even to speak of him. Widows are like that. Grief overtakes them and they lose their senses.'

'She was very young when he died, not much older than you, Anne,' I said.

Anne tossed her head. 'I should not forget,' she said stoutly. 'I should light candles and say prayers for the rest of my life. I might even take a vow of chastity.'

'Does she like you?' asked Cecily, intensely curious about my future stepmother. 'What did she say?'

'She said I was pretty.'

Anne giggled. 'Richard once said you were pretty but without your father's inheritance I think your prettiness will not count for much.'

'Is she coming to visit us?' asked Cecily, picking up her doll which had fallen on the floor.

'I doubt it,' I said.

'You know they're waiting for you in father's room?' said Anne, ignoring her sister. 'They'll want to know everything, absolutely everything.'

'So do we,' said Cecily.

I left them in the care of one of the nursemaids, still arguing about the respective merits of the widowed Lady Phelip and complaining bitterly at being excluded from a family conference. I ran up the stairs and hurried to my room in order to wash my face and change my water-splashed gown before facing my interrogation.

The Nevills were a fortunate family. They had chosen the winning side in times of conflict unlike my Montagu grandfather who had risen in rebellion against the king's father and paid for his foolishness with his life. By supporting old King Henry, Ralph Nevill had reaped the rewards of loyalty, The king's reign had brought him immense wealth which he had used to redesign his many houses so that now they resembled princely lodgings. The Erber on the banks of the Thames might be old and rambling but its rooms reeked of the ownership of a man with money to spend.

In Ralph Nevill's private chamber, tapestries and banners decorated every inch of wall. There was a single window, too far above the river for any loitering boatman to hear what was being said inside the room, and a heavy door guarded by a pair of Nevill men-at-arms. If nothing else the earl of Westmoreland was guaranteed privacy.

My belly lurched at the sight of my father-in-law who was a terrifying figure with his scarred face and grizzled beard.

'How long?' he asked his wife.

'A single night. I thought it best for an initial visit. It allows us to see how far they've gone in the matter.'

He grunted. 'And she knew why she was sent?'

'Yes, I made certain of that.'

'So, daughter?' He raised his battered old face to mine. He must have been nearly in his dotage and had lost some of his teeth but, like an elderly bear unconstrained by its chain, tearing my limbs apart in a rage would be easy. 'Is the Phelip woman to marry your father?'

'Yes, my lord,' I stammered.

'She said so?'

'Yes, my lord.'

He turned to his wife. 'We must find a way to stop this business.'

My mother-in-law, who was capable of dismembering me with no teeth at all, merely by using her nails, skewered me with her gaze.

'Are she and your father well acquainted?'

'I do not know, my lady.'

'She's not got much to recommend her,' growled the earl. 'Chaucer's rich, and influential in some quarters but that would hardly sway a man like Salisbury. Is she a handsome wench?'

My husband, who seemed to know about these things, remarked, 'I've heard say she is uncommonly beautiful.'

'Humph! I suppose Bishop Beaufort might be prevailed upon to intervene.'

Bishop Beaufort was my mother-in-law's brother but we rarely saw him. He was much too busy to visit.

'To what purpose?'

'To persuade Chaucer the marriage is ill-advised, put forward another candidate for his daughter,' he snarled.

'I doubt my brother will speak against Thomas Chaucer,' said my mother-in-law. 'The man is useful. Offending him would not be wise.'

The earl shifted himself as if sitting was a matter of discomfort. 'The contracts are not yet signed. No stone must be left unturned. I urge you to speak privately with your brother.'

'It is too late,' I blurted out. 'They are already betrothed. As good as wed.'

The earl swore under his breath and my husband's face paled.

My mother-in-law was as quick as a snake. 'All is not yet lost,' she said. 'She didn't give Phelip a child, did she?'

'Not that I've heard,' said my husband.

The earl stroked his beard and then barked, 'Well? What of Phelip?'

They all looked at me.

'She said her first husband died at Harfleur,' I stammered. 'They'd been married only six months.'

My mother-in-law leaned closer across the table. 'Did she say if they had lain together?'

My husband made a sound of disgust. 'By the rood,

mother! She'd have been a child at the time of Harfleur.'

My mother-in-law touched her son's arm. 'Some men have an appetite for young girls. Regrettable but true.'

'Did she give Phelip a brat?' The earls eyes were narrowed beneath his bushy eyebrows.

'I do not think so, my lord.'

'You saw no sign of one?'

'No, my lord.'

My mother-in-law looked at me thoughtfully. 'Nonetheless we must plan for the worst. Did she say where she will live after the marriage?'

I swallowed hard, trying to rid myself of the memory of what had been in my future stepmother's letter. 'If my father is unable to come home to England he asked her to travel to France.'

There was a pause while the three of them considered the importance of those words.

'So he's keen,' said my mother-in-law, sniffing in disgust. 'I think we can assume the earl of Salisbury will do his duty with some enthusiasm. And if the woman should prove fertile then all our plans will have gone awry.'

After my inquisition at the hands of my husband's family, I paid more attention to my mother-in-law who had shown little sign of the submissiveness I'd expected from the wife of an important man like my father-in-law. I had a suspicion that it was she who made family decisions, not the earl, which turned upside down my understanding of marriage and how a wife should behave. I watched her carefully trying to discern how she differed from other wives of my acquaintance but her secrets remained tantalisingly elusive, hidden behind the facade of an outwardly obedient Nevill wife. As a king's granddaughter she would have been a great marriage prize for the earl but that could hardly explain his deference. I was once a great marriage prize but my husband had never deferred to me, not once, nor was he likely to now that my father was marrying the widowed Lady Phelip.

My life at The Erber returned to the usual routine of daily instruction from my mother-in-law on the duties of a great lady who would one day be in charge of a vast household, and futile attempts on my part to improve my skill with the lute. If there was a spare moment to fill it would be filled by prayer. My mother-in-law was the most pious women I knew and we spent a great many hours on our knees and very few wandering through the woods picking windflowers.

I was informed that before he left Westminster the king had summoned a parliament for the day following May Day which meant that neither my husband nor my father-in-law would go north until after then. If Queen Katherine had remained in one of the royal palaces there might have been a little entertainment, but as it was there was nothing to think about other than my father's treachery.

While I brooded, the other Nevill women idled around the city visiting friends and awaiting the king's return. We received occasional snippets of news: the king was at St Albans, at Bristol and at Shrewsbury; he had been joined by the queen and was at Coventry where the city had given the royal couple handsome presents; he was at Leicester for the Easter festivities, then at Nottingham, at Pontefract and at York.

'Why does the king visit so many places?' I asked Lady Mowbray.

She laughed. 'To fill his coffers. If a man wants the king's favour he must pay for it. His father was just the same.'

'But why?'

'You ignorant child. For the war in France. What else?'

Of course. What else. For our king there was nothing more important than the completion of his destiny to rule over the whole of France and that, as I should have known, required hard English coin and an army of willing men.

My mother-in-law said nothing more about my father's forthcoming nuptials and I tried not to think about Ewelme but my nights were beset by troubling dreams. I would wake with my cheeks damp with tears and the fear that I would never be Countess of Salisbury as my mother had been and my husband would despise me because I had failed in my duty. No amount of skill with the lute or submissiveness on my part would make up for such abject failure.

# 3

## COUNTESS JACQUELINE 1421

One bright morning I awoke to find the city alive with rumours about the arrival of Countess Jacqueline, a cousin of the duke of Burgundy. Gossip from the taverns flowed into The Erber like a running stream and by noon the servants were saying the lady was an heiress, and beautiful, with many rich manors in the Low Countries. The Nevill steward added to my sum of knowledge by telling me that the countess had been invited to England by none other than the king. Naturally people wondered why the king was not here to greet his honoured guest but it seemed the lady would be entertained instead by the king's brother, Humphrey, Duke of Gloucester, who was certain to mount a fine display.

Since daybreak wagons had been seen taking supplies of food and firewood into the duke's London residence, and the goldsmiths and embroiderers in the city reported a sudden increase in trade. The first firm news I had of this exciting new visitor was an invitation for the Nevill family to a welcome feast for the countess of Hainault to be hosted by Lord Humphrey in his house at Castle Baynard .

I'd seen Castle Baynard many times. It stood below St Pauls directly on the waterfront with the river lapping at its walls. Two massive towers reared up out of the water like great stone monsters waiting to devour the barges which disappeared beneath an ancient portcullis into a yawning gateway. But the grim exterior of Lord Humphrey's town house hid a softer world, one of candlelit warmth and fashionable elegance. As we entered, the sound of sweet music filled the air and the smell of crushed rose petals drifted upwards from the rushes strewn on the floor, reminding me achingly of Bisham.

The hall was crammed with people, a melee of shimmering silks, rich brocades, and men wearing headdresses in the latest Burgundian fashion. To my delight the first person I met was Eleanor Cobham.

'Lady Nevill,' she said, greeting me with a small curtsey and an incline of her head.

'Mistress Cobham; I didn't dare hope you were still in London.'

'The hunt for a husband is never-ending,' she said in an amused voice. 'I think I might still be here at Christmas.'

I would have liked to throw my arms around her and give her a hug but had to satisfy myself with a broad smile. 'May we sit together or must you be with your mother?' I asked, hoping for her company.

'My mother is at home in Sterborough,' she said with a small lift of her eyebrows. 'I am here at my brother's command. He serves Lord Humphrey.'

'Then there is nothing to prevent us from being together. My mother-in-law is seated near Countess Jacqueline and my sisters-in-law are with their husbands so I am all alone.'

'You are not with your husband?'

I blushed. 'No, I believe he is with his father.'

31

At the tables there was no division between men and women so we squeezed ourselves onto a bench between the fat wife of a Suffolk knight and a small dark man with a beard the colour of a raven's wing who said he was an illuminator from Genoa and wondered were we ladies interested in books.

'What d'you think of her?' whispered Eleanor.

'Who?'

'Countess Jacqueline of course.'

The visiting countess was a plump rosy-cheeked young woman with an abundance of fine fair hair caught up in netted cauls who seemed far more interested in the gallant Lord Humphrey than perhaps an honoured guest of the king should be. She wore a gown of startling crimson brocade and a short jacket of pale green velvet heavily encrusted with pearls which I would dearly have liked to own.

'Lord Humphrey is paying her a great deal of attention,' I remarked.

'I think she is eyeing him every bit as much as he is eyeing her,' said Eleanor, her voice as smooth as butter on a knife.

'I thought she was married.'

'She is but it is a bad marriage,' whispered Eleanor. 'They dislike each other. She wants rid of him.'

'Can she do that?'

'Oh probably. She looks a determined sort of woman and determined women usually get what they want.'

I stared at the firm round chin of the countess and noticed how, although she leaned provocatively towards Lord Humphrey, smiling and laughing and presenting him with a view of her splendid bosom, she allowed no liberties. His attempt to take her hand was coolly rebuffed and when he tried to feed her a morsel of partridge from his plate she politely declined.

'My brother says she is seeking an annulment,' said Eleanor quietly.

'Is that possible?'

'She and her husband are cousins. There's a problem with the dispensation for their marriage.'

'How does your brother know such a thing?' I asked in amazement, wondering once again at the breadth and depth of Eleanor's knowledge. She was only a young woman from a little manor in Surrey, not one of the king's envoys with an army of spies at her command.

'People talk,' she said casually. 'If a man keeps his wits about him he can discover all kinds of secrets. Now, tell me about you. Have you visited your new stepmother?'

Of all the people I knew, Eleanor was the one person who would understand the horror of my visit to Ewelme. She would sympathise with my predicament.

'Yes, I have.'

'And what is she like?'

'Young, four or five years older than me.'

'Pretty?'

'My husband says people speak of her as beautiful.'

'Clever?'

'Much cleverer than me.'

'I think you underestimate yourself, my dear Lady Nevill.'

'I'm not clever in any way,' I said, twisting a piece of silk on my skirt into a tight little ball. 'She spoke of places

I've never heard of and she knows everything there is to know about the king's plans for his French campaigns.'

'And now you know too because she's told you. After your visit you are wiser than you were before. That is how a woman learns, by listening to others.'

'But nobody talks to me,' I burst out, sounding, even to myself, like a petulant child.

Eleanor laughed kindly. 'Your stepmother talks to you, and your mother-in-law. And your husband – does he not talk to you?'

I blushed and bent my head so that she couldn't see my face. 'No,' I said in a whisper.

'Not at all?'

'No.'

She paused for a moment watching my blush deepen as I felt more and more uncomfortable. Since the horror of my father's letter, Richard Nevill had only twice come to my bed and if anything the silences between us had become deeper and more ominous. Now he didn't even thank me. He behaved as if I was a maidservant to be used at will, not a beloved wife. And worse; other than when he came to my room carrying a candle with his cloak thrown carelessly over his nakedness, I hardly saw him. Once or twice in the hall at dinner and occasionally at a family supper when he was forced by politeness to sit next to me, but we never spoke. It was obvious he was avoiding me which was no way to treat a wife.

'It will get better,' Eleanor promised. 'You are very young. You cannot expect a grown man to take much pleasure from a thirteen-year-old girl. What conversation could he have?'

'I wish I was like you,' I said longingly. 'I wish I knew what to say to people. I annoy my husband and anger my mother-in-law, and my sisters-in-law make fun of me. And now I'm to have a stepmother who makes me feel stupid.'

'And you are miserable because of all this.'

'Yes,' I said bitterly. 'If my stepmother has a son it will be the end of my husband's hopes of being Earl of Salisbury and he says it is *my* fault.'

'Of course he does. Who else can he blame? A man will always lash out at whoever is closest to him when things go wrong. It is how men are made. But you need not despair. Since we last met I've thought about your problem and believe I've discovered someone who may be able to help.'

'You have!' I said eagerly. 'Who? How can they help?'

She put a finger to her lips to indicate I should be quiet. Then she smiled. 'I shall tell you when I know more but in the meantime you must be patient.'

'Oh I shall,' I said. 'I promise I'll be exceedingly patient but I beg of you not to forget me.'

She gave me the most lovely smile: slow, sweet and with a depth of warmth. 'Of course I shall not forget you, dear Lady Nevill. I count you as one of my friends.'

'And I you,' I said eagerly. 'And please, call me Alice.'

'It will be my pleasure, dearest Alice, but only if you agree to call me Eleanor.'

I beamed at her and then turned to my other side to do my duty by the fat wife of the Suffolk knight. The woman was curious about my headdress, a new confection of pale-coloured silk and twists of wire and wanted to know where she could purchase one like it. I exchanged pleasantries

35

about Suffolk and what she found to do amongst the fields and marshes, and when I grew bored, I turned back to Eleanor and spent the rest of the meal pointing out people I recognised.

'The king's brother, John,' I said, indicating the beak-nosed duke of Bedford who was watching his younger brother's antics with disapproval.

'Is he married?' asked Eleanor.

'Not yet.'

'Odd,' murmured Eleanor. 'Two brothers, both grown men and both unmarried. Does the king not care to arrange marriages for his brothers?'

'My mother said the king prefers to put his brothers to work. Perhaps he thinks a wife will distract them. And wives can be costly.'

Eleanor gave an amused laugh. 'A hard taskmaster.'

'The king believes time is a precious gift from God and should not be wasted.'

'He regards marriage as a waste of time.'

No,' I said doubtfully. 'Not if it serves a higher purpose.'

'Like his own marriage.'

'Yes,' I said happily. 'Like his own marriage. He married Queen Katherine to fulfil his divine destiny. It was God's plan.'

'I wonder if the king regards Countess Jacqueline's marriage as one which serves a higher purpose.'

I giggled at the irreverence of the joke and looked around the hall for somebody else to show to Eleanor.

'That is Richard Beauchamp, Earl of Warwick, one of the king's finest soldiers; very well liked,' I said pointing out one of my father's friends. 'Three daughters.'

'No sons?'

I shook my head.

'And the voluble cleric?'

I looked over to where my mother-in-law's brother, Henry Beaufort, Bishop of Winchester sat, towering over everyone else with his magnificent bulky presence. I'd heard my sisters-in-law say the bishop was not a friend of Lord Humphrey so I was surprised he'd been sent an invitation. But Edmund said men like to keep their enemies close and in that way watch what they are doing.

'The bishop has been out of royal favour,' I said confidentially to Eleanor, repeating what I'd heard in my mother-in-law's rooms. 'He was to be made a cardinal but that did not please the king. He refused the bishop his cardinal's hat. I thought it would be an honour for the king to have an English cardinal.'

Eleanor gazed thoughtfully at the bishop's beautifully embroidered robes and the way he commanded every conversation at the top table. My Aunt Margaret, whose first husband had been the eldest Beaufort brother, said the bishop was fearsomely well-educated, exquisitely charming and always got his own way.

'Too powerful perhaps?' mused Eleanor. 'Too ambitious? Kings dislike clerics becoming over-mighty. I'll wager he's rich.'

'He is. My mother-in-law says the war in France would founder if it were not for the bishop's help,' I whispered. 'She says parliament is against the raising of more taxes. They are not convinced the war needs to be prolonged. They approved of Agincourt because there were profits to be made but they cannot see the sense in pushing further into France.'

'So the king has turned to the bishop for a loan.'

I shrugged. 'I suppose so. I'm afraid you must think me very ignorant. I don't understand how parliament can refuse to do what the king wants. But I have very little understanding of such matters.'

'Nonsense!' said Eleanor. 'You understand far more than you think and you know more than you imagine. You are half way to becoming a very knowledgeable young woman.'

I laughed at her compliment, pleased there was one person who did not think me stupid and as the warmth spread I realised that for the first time since coming to live in my mother-in-law's household I had a friend, a true friend.

Later, after the feasting there were acrobats and fire-eaters and a troupe of Russian dancers with swords. By the time Eleanor and I parted company, we had arranged to meet the following week at Sir Reginald Cobham's lodgings near St Paul's by Ludgate. An afternoon to myself with just a Nevill maid and a couple of elderly men to guard me should prove easy to arrange and I was certain no-one would notice my absence.

Once back at our house as I cast about for a suitable excuse to leave the safety of The Erber, my confidence disappeared. A visit to a young woman whose family was unknown to the Nevills and of no particular advantage to the family, would not, I knew, meet with my mother-in-law's approval so I would need to be clever. That evening I examined the possibilities: my Aunt Margaret was in France with her husband the duke of Clarence and my Aunt Joan had crept away to sulk in Sir Henry Bromflete's lair in the north so neither of them would serve as an excuse for a visit and I could think of no-on else. I wondered if I dared ask my husband for permission to take an afternoon's ride alone with only a small escort for company but was uncertain if he'd agree.

For two days I watched him closely to see if he was in a mellow mood as I knew a man should not be approached when feeling ill-tempered or unwell. I'd never studied Richard Nevill before having been too nervous to do more than steal a quick glance in his direction when the situation required. But as I watched, I realised that Eleanor was right, he *was* good-looking. Most of the time his face bore a rather grim expression with his mouth turned down at the corners as if nursing some private grudge and although a wife should not criticise her husband, I did wish he would smile more. If he smiled he might even be considered handsome.

'Peace, Richard!'

I raised my head at the sound of my sister-in-law's voice coming from behind a half-open door.

'Don't talk to me of peace. I don't need a lecture from Henry Percy's wife.'

'Richard, there's nothing to be gained by railing against what cannot be changed.'

My husband must have been striding up and down the room because I could hear the heavy tread of his boots and the pause as he spun on his heels.

'It's not *your* husband who'll lose his earldom,' he growled. 'Henry Percy will always be lord of Northumberland whereas I shall be lord of nothing while that little turd at Raby struts over what should be mine.'

The "little turd at Raby" was my father-in-law's eldest grandson, a young man I'd never met and who for the past month had been the focus of my husband's ill-temper.

'He is your nephew, Richard. None of this is Percy's doing.

'Everything in the north is of Percy's doing. If I turn my back for one instant his greedy hands are all over something of mine. He covets my office of warden of the west march and now he's planning an alliance with the little turd.'

My sister-in-law gave a deep sigh. 'The boy is family.'

'He's a thief. He'll steal my father's title which should come to me.'

'The title is entailed. It is the law. Our father's other family will always come first. Your "little turd" will one day be earl of Westmoreland and there is nothing you can do about it.'

'We'll see about that! And whatever happens I'll see he gets nothing else: not a single castle, not a single manor, not a single inch of Nevill land. I'll 'have him out of Raby on his fat arse before he can take his oath.'

I heard the rustle of Lady Percy's skirts and stepped back quickly into the shadows before I could be discovered eavesdropping.

'There's still the Salisbury earldom. That may come good,' she said.

I flinched as something heavy hit the door with a resounding crash.

'Holy Mother of God! Stop behaving as if you're still in the nursery, Richard.'

My husband swore loudly.

40

'I know you only married the girl for the title but what's done is done. Go and be a pleasant husband; she looks in need of someone to be kind to her.'

'What use is she to me?'

'The same as for any man. I thought all men liked thirteen-year-old virgins.'

'Young girls are not to my taste.'

'Then send her to Middleham and amuse yourself elsewhere.'

I put up my hand to cover my mouth. Middleham! Shut away in that dreadful bleak northern castle with no-one but servants for company. My husband would appoint some elderly Nevill crone to keep an eye on me and I'd die of cold and loneliness and boredom and never see Bisham again.

Two nights later, after completing his duty, my husband remained lying beside me in silence.

'My lord?' I whispered into the darkness.

He moved his head on the pillow. 'Yes?'

'Are you angry with me?'

The sigh was that of a disappointed man.

'No, I'm not angry with you. Go to sleep.'

It wasn't much of a conversation for a wife and her husband to be having after seven months of marriage but perhaps in time we might do better. He had said nothing about sending me to Middleham but to ask a favour of him at that moment required more courage than I possessed. I would have to find another way to arrange my visit to Eleanor.

In the end it was the widowed Lady Scrope who solved my problem. I stumbled upon her sitting in her favourite corner looking so mournful that only a woman with a heart of stone would have passed by without a word. I dipped a curtsey and asked if I might join her. Her eyes widened in surprise at someone seeking her company and when she gave a grateful smile I realised that she too must be lonely.

I sat down on the bench and wondered what to say.

'You are Richard's wife?' she began, somewhat unsure of exactly who I was.

I managed a little smile. 'Alice.'

She nodded. 'I remember. Your mother died.'

My eyes filled with tears at the mention of my mother but Lady Scrope was very understanding and patted my knee. 'Come my dear. You mustn't weep. I of all people know how cruel it is when someone you love is called to God. You think your heart is damaged beyond repair. But you must have faith. One day you will stop grieving. The sorrow you feel will pass and when it does you will have memories of your years with your mother to soothe you.'

'Did you love your husband?' I asked timidly, still being of an age where love in marriage was an ideal to be pursued.

'He was a good man,' she said quietly.

'And now you are alone.'

She gave a wan smile. 'I have his children, two boys, three and two years of age.'

I recalled seeing two little boys playing in the nursery but had not connected them to Lady Scrope. I did not know her well enough to ask if she planned to remarry but thought it likely as I believed her only a little older than Lady Percy. Naturally her prospects depended on the settlement from her first marriage and if it was enough to attract a husband.

'And you?' she asked. 'How do you find marriage?'

I twisted my hands awkwardly in my lap and when I made no reply she said, 'The Salisbury earldom?'

I nodded.

'I heard. Bound to cause trouble. Second marriages always do.'

'My husband is disappointed in me,' I said miserably, remembering the torn letter and the hurled insults and the long cold nights when he failed to come to my bed.

There was a pause while she considered that word – disappointed.

'It is not you who has disappointed Richard, it is circumstance. And not for the first time.' She smiled, a misty look in her eyes as if reminiscing. 'A long time ago when he was put up on his first pony, Richard crowed how he was the eldest son, boasting like small boys do. The horror when he discovered our father had another family with older sons and he would never be the heir!'

It was odd to think of my husband as a small boy but even the king was once a child.

She put her hand over mine. 'Is he unkind?'

'Not unkind, just angry. He shouted at me.'

She gave a short laugh.

'And Richard can certainly shout. It is his grandfather's temper. The old duke had men quaking in their boots yet my stepmother speaks kindly of him.'

It was not much comfort to know that my husband's temper was a peculiarity of family like red hair or big noses.

'Will he forgive me?'

'None of this is your fault,' she said gently. 'He knows that. You must be patient. Give him time.'

I wondered how much time Richard Nevill would need and whether I'd live to see my rehabilitation in his eyes.

She regarded me closely. 'What do you do with yourself when you're not at my stepmother's beck and call? Have you friends?'

I hesitated. 'I have one friend but I do not think ...' I stopped.

Lady Scrope, for all her weeping, was a shrewd woman. She understood my difficulty at once. 'You fear my stepmother would not approve?'

'Eleanor is not quite ... not the kind of ...'

She laughed. 'You mean her family is not sufficiently wealthy.'

I nodded. 'Her father is Sir Reginald Cobham but it seems all he has is a single manor down in Surrey. Eleanor must make a good marriage.'

'Like all young women. Where did you two meet?'

'At the queen's coronation feast.'

'Is she still in London?'

'Yes.'

'But you do not visit.'

'My mother-in-law would not permit it.'

Lady Scrope leaned forward and whispered, 'Your mother-in-law need never know.'

My eyes widened and my mouth dropped open at this suggestion of rank disobedience. Lady Scrope seemed a most unlikely stirrer of rebellion but I was fast learning that appearances could be deceptive.

'Is it possible?'

'Certainly. If you wish to escape I shall tell my stepmother I've asked you to accompany me to the House of the Blessed Mary. Which day would you like to visit your friend?'

# 4

## MISTRESS JOURDEMAYNE 1421

The dowager Lady Scrope and I made our way along the Cheape towards St Paul's by Ludgate. The air was sweet and I waved merrily to the street traders thinking what a pleasant place London was in the springtime. For the queen's coronation the townspeople had strewn the streets with branches of greenery and hung their houses with carpets and silks; even now they wrapped ribbons round their upper windows and continued to tuck sprigs of blossom into their caps. A woman with a basket of new-laid eggs called out a greeting when she saw the Nevill livery and by the time we reached the lodging house of Sir Reginald Cobham off Bread Lane we had attracted a small procession of ragged urchins hoping for an afternoon's employment.

'I shall return for you in three hours,' said Lady Scrope as she turned her horse and prepared to ride back towards Aldgate. 'Enjoy your visit!'

Sir Reginald's house was small and dark and I quickly adjusted my assumptions about the state of his finances. He had to be even poorer than I'd first thought. But the upstairs room where Eleanor awaited me was clean and well appointed with a faded wool hanging, a board, a small table and three stools.

She rose with that peculiar grace which she must have learned from her mother and made me a perfect greeting. I smiled shyly in return. It was odd to see Eleanor somewhere other than in a grand setting. She looked the kind of young woman who should have been born to a higher estate, not merely the daughter of an impoverished knight. Perhaps her mother's family were of consequence.

She was extremely hospitable and offered me a cup of ale and some little cakes.

'I had them from the baker on the corner,' she admitted. 'His wife makes them from her husband's left-over dough. She is a very enterprising woman.'

'They are lovely,' I said biting into the soft warm bread flavoured with cinnamon and stuffed with currants.

She watched me eat until there was nothing left, not even a crumb, then we exchanged our gossip and speculated on the relationship between Lord Humphrey and pretty Countess Jacqueline. It was all very pleasant.

'You remember I spoke about someone who might help you,' she said once we'd finished giggling over the countess's attempts to hold Lord Humphrey at bay. 'Are you prepared to meet with her? I doubt she's the kind of woman you're used to but I've been assured she is trustworthy.'

'She cannot come to The Erber,' I said quickly. 'My husband would hear of it from the servants. He'd want to know who she was. What could I say?'

Eleanor laughed. 'Of course she'll not come to your husband's house. You will go to her.' I must have looked doubtful because she added quickly, 'We shall go together.'

The thought of a clandestine visit with Eleanor was intriguing, almost sinful, and I felt a little flutter of excitement.

'It would not be wrong to go, would it?' I asked anxiously, thinking of Bishop Beaufort and his thunderous warnings to my girl cousins about the dangerous world outside the confines of their mother's house.

'No,' said Eleanor, reassuringly. 'What could possibly be wrong about visiting a woman to ask her advice?'

'Is that what she does – gives advice?'

'That and other things.'

'I'm not sure,' I said, suddenly nervous of this unknown woman and the advice she might give.

'Stop worrying,' said Eleanor gaily, calling for the maid to bring our cloaks and gloves. 'If we mislike the look of her we shall run back here and hide.'

I gave a nervous giggle wondering where a young woman could possibly hide in Sir Reginald's meagre lodgings.

Shrouded in our hooded cloaks we followed the instructions Eleanor had been given, but as the streets became narrower and the overhanging houses shut out more and more sunlight I began to feel afraid. Unlike the neatly swept surroundings of The Erber where tenant shopkeepers prided themselves on clean entrances to their premises, here there were puddles of filth and piles of rotting debris blocking our path. Men in dark coats loitered on the steps of a tavern and from inside one of the houses came the sound of a woman's scream. An apprentice, shouting obscenities, passed us at a run and a moment later crashed into a man carrying two pans who knocked the lad to the ground and began beating him about the head.

We turned the next corner and there to my relief was the house where Eleanor's mysterious acquaintance could be found. It was only a little house with shuttered windows and a jutting upstairs storey but unlike its neighbours, looked reasonably well-kept. Eleanor knocked and the door was opened by an old woman who after enquiring as to our business, invited us in. We bent our heads and stepped into a low dark interior. We followed the old woman into another room at the back of the house where an open door led out into a yard. She bade us wait while she fetched Mistress Jourdemayne.

'Mistress Jourdemayne?' I whispered to Eleanor.

'She is the woman we've come to see.'

What was odd about the room was that it did not have the look of either a parlour or a kitchen. There were a number of jars standing in ordered rows on a board. They were about the size my mother used for preserving damsons but I could see no reason for there being so many unless the garden boasted several damson trees.

All of a sudden the room grew dark as a woman's figure appeared in the doorway to the yard, blocking out the light. She was small and neat with a clean cap on her head and a grey woollen gown covered by a large coarse apron. For a moment she said nothing but I could see her rapidly estimating the value of my fur-trimmed cloak, my embroidered gloves and the toes of my costly riding boots. Once the calculation was made she dropped a deep curtsey and asked what she might do for two such noble ladies. She spoke like a countrywoman with a soft burr in her voice and seemed most unsurprised by two strangers arriving unexpectedly at her door. I noted she did not ask who we were. Perhaps she considered having knowledge of our names would be unwise.

'We have need of someone with a useful skill, Mistress Jourdemayne,' said Eleanor. 'A friend told me you were once kind enough to help her. She recommended your services.'

The woman looked at Eleanor, then moved her gaze across to me. Unlike most common women she did not lower her gaze in front of her betters but continued to stare as if assessing me for some purpose or other. I felt a familiar warmth creep into my cheeks and knew I was blushing.

'What is it you be wanting?' she asked me. 'A young man to fall in love with you? Is that it?' She laughed, a not unpleasant low gurgling sound. 'You be bonny enough, young mistress. You don't need my help. I'll wager he's half way to being in love with you already.'

'Oh no,' I replied quickly. 'It's not for me. I'm a married woman.'

She smiled. 'And did love stop at the church door?'

I didn't know what to say as there was no love between Richard Nevill and me, not then or at any time before or since we'd arrived at the church door.

'It's not for that purpose we've come,' said Eleanor coming to my rescue. 'I know you're skilled in the making of love potions but I've been told you also help women who find themselves in difficulty.'

'I may do,' said Mistress Jourdemayne obliquely. 'It depends on who's asking.'

'It is my friend and I who need your help, nobody else. And in case you're concerned, we've told no-one about our visit.'

The woman thought for a moment before speaking again.

'I possess a little skill in such matters.'

'Herbs?' said Eleanor. 'My friend spoke of a concoction of herbs.'

'I have many herbs, some be for one purpose, some for another. Bishopwort, rosemary, sage, wormwood? What is it you be wanting, mistress?'

She stared at Eleanor but I had an uncomfortable feeling that every word she spoke was intended for my ears, not for Eleanor's.

'Want a child? Raspberry leaves will do the trick. I'll warrant your mother took raspberry leaves to get you. But there be other herbs which serve as well.'

She turned and looked at me again. 'You be very young to wish for a child. Be you certain that's what you want?'

I was unable to speak. I knew my nocturnal encounters with Richard Nevill were for the purposes of making a child but I'd never truly considered such a thing might happen. What he did to me hidden behind the curtains of my bed was too brief, too impersonal and much too unloving for us to be blessed with a child.

'What if you should want to prevent a child?' said Eleanor.

'Ah, mistress, the church do tell us that be a sin.'

'And you? Do you believe it's a sin?'

'I do my best to help any woman in distress, mistress That be all I do. Sins cannot be laid at my door. I plant herbs and make potions. I be a good god-fearing woman. Ask anyone.'

This did not satisfy Eleanor and she pressed the

woman for more. 'But there *is* a remedy for a woman who wishes to prevent a child?'

'There might be.'

'What is it?' Eleanor was impatient to know.

Mistress Jordemayne took one of the many little jars on the side board. She set it on the table, removed the cover and reached inside. I craned my neck to see what it was she had in her hand. It looked like dried leaves of some plant or other.

'This will prevent a child.'

Eleanor made to take the leaves but Mistress Jourdemayne had already dropped them back into the jar. 'Don't be too hasty, mistress. What if the woman be already with child?'

Eleanor shook her head. 'Then it's too late. The remedy won't work and I shall have wasted my money.'

'No,' smiled Mistress Jourdemayne as if explaining matters to a child. 'If the woman be with child and she drinks a concoction of your making, the child will be washed away in a stream of blood. That, mistress, would be murder.'

'Holy Mother of God!' Eleanor hastily crossed herself.

I clamped my hand over my mouth as vomit rose into my throat and a sudden pain caused my belly to cramp.

'I cannot do this,' I whispered to Eleanor.

'Is there no other way?' she asked, eying the rest of the jars.

Mistress Jourdemayne gave an enigmatic smile as if she held a raft of secrets known only to herself. 'There be always other ways.'

'Something softer, something less violent?'

'You mean charms, words whispered by moonlight. You be thinking of magic.'

'You know about magic?' Eleanor was intrigued. I could tell from her breathless voice and the way she leaned in close, whereas I was in a state of utter terror.

'I know many things.'

'Another way to prevent a child, a way which involves the words whispered by moonlight, a way of magic?'

I pulled on Eleanor's sleeve. 'Please, let's go, Eleanor. This is too dark. I don't care for it.'

'Don't be such a ninny,' she hissed. 'D'you want to stand by and do nothing while your stepmother steals your inheritance?'

'No,' I said lamely. 'But not like this.'

'*This*,' said Eleanor firmly, 'is your best chance. It may be your only chance. Think of your mother,' she added cunningly. 'She'd want you to have your inheritance. She'd not want you supplanted by some other woman's whelp.'

I clutched at the edge of her cloak like a child clinging to a nursemaid's apron. 'Please, be quick.'

'Mistress Jourdemayne,' Eleanor said with all the firmness of a merchant bargaining in the marketplace, 'if I give you this, will you tell me of the other way?'

The glint of silver in Eleanor's hand was sufficient to loosen the woman's tongue and with the coin laid on the table she proceeded to tell us what we needed to know.

'A newt, gathered when the moon is on the wane. Bury it deep beneath the threshold of the house where the woman bides.'

'Is that all?' Eleanor sounded disappointed by the simplicity of the remedy.

The woman gave her a sharp look. 'There be words you must say, mistress, but you needs be careful. Words should not be used lightly.'

'But words are just that – words. What harm can they do?'

Mistress Jourdemayne laughed. 'You'll find out. There be some words which have a power beyond the understanding of man, beyond what the mortal eye can see and the ear can hear; words which can heal a man's wounds, words which can destroy. It's a foolish woman who meddles in the ways of magic.'

She reached into a small wooden box beside the jars and drew out a scrap of faded parchment. There was something written on it. She folded the parchment carefully and handed it to Eleanor. 'Here you be, mistress but remember what I said.'

'If we do as you say, the woman will not get with child?'

'She will not.'

I thank you Mistress Jourdemayne,' said Eleanor taking my arm. 'If we have further need of your services we know where to find you.

'You'll likely not find me here. At Eye near Westminster I have my garden and most days I tend my herbs.'

As I lowered my head to pass under the doorway she laid her hand on my arm. 'Young mistress, take care.' Then she muttered something which sounded horribly like a curse.

The words frightened me so much I pulled away and practically ran back through the dirt and the puddles of the narrow street until I reached a patch of sunlight.

'What did she say?' I gasped as Eleanor caught up with me. 'Why did she curse me?'

Eleanor laughed. 'That was no curse. *Si non casta non tamen caute*. Do you not know your Latin?'

'A little,' I said, wishing I'd paid more attention to my cousin's tutor.

'If not chastely at least with care – she imagines you deep in a love affair and was advising you to take precautions.'

'Precautions? What kind of precautions?'

'The kind a woman takes when she does not wish to conceive a child with her lover.'

I was shocked. 'But I'd never do such a thing. I'm a married woman. To take a lover would be wrong. Perhaps her warning was meant for you.'

Eleanor laughed. 'Oh no, for I'm always careful in everything I do.'

By the time we got back to Sir Reginald's lodgings, I'd thought of a dozen reasons why Eleanor's plan was impossible.

'I cannot bury a newt myself,' I said. 'Lady Phelip would wonder what I was doing. Besides, I have no idea what a newt looks like.'

Eleanor laughed kindly. 'Little ignoramus! Have you never seen one? Slippery little rascals. The lads at Sterborough use them for sport.'

'Where would I buy one?'

'You don't buy them, you find them in the fields, in the ditches and the ponds.

'I cannot go wandering off across the fields poking in ditches. What would my mother-in-law say?'

Eleanor tutted. 'You are finding problems for yourself, Alice. It's really quite simple. When the moon is next waning ask one of the boys in the stable yard to catch you a good specimen. Don't ask one of the older men, he'll most likely tell your husband. Pick a fresh-faced lad who'll enjoy the attention; he'll imagine he's in love with you.' She smiled as if this was an everyday practice down in Sterborough.

'But when I have the newt, what do I do then?'

Eleanor sighed. 'Do I have to hold your hand all the way? Wrap it in a piece of cloth. Go and visit your stepmother and take the lad with you. Get *him* to dig the hole and bury the newt. Just remember to murmur the words written on the paper over the creature before you part with it.'

'You make it sound simple,' I said, wishing Eleanor could travel to Ewelme in my stead.

'It is,' she said giving me a quick kiss. 'Everything is simple when it's something you want.'


Once Lady Scrope and I had parted company in the hall at The Eber, I passed my cloak and gloves to the maid and prepared to creep unnoticed up the stairs. But my plans were thwarted when I found young Anne Nevill sitting on the bottom stair.

'Richard is looking for you,' she said taking note of the mud on my boots.

Immediately I felt like a thief discovered making off with his ill-gotten gains. My husband could not know where I'd been. Apart from Lady Scrope I'd told no-one about my friendship with Eleanor Cobham and would have faced the fires of purgatory rather than admit to a visit to Mistress Jourdemayne with her pots of herbs and mysterious incantations. It was impossible he knew unless he'd had me followed. But I'd seen no-one. Yet this was a husband with a temper, who was angry with me and might, with a snap of his fingers, send me away to Middleham.

I ran quickly along the gallery to my room planning to wash my face and remove my dusty gown before seeking him out. But I was too late. Richard Nevill was standing in the middle of the floor gazing at the red brocade gown I'd tossed carelessly onto my bed. He turned when he heard my footsteps. He wasn't smiling.

'My lord.' I sank down in a respectful curtsey wishing he'd not taken me by surprise. 'I'm sorry I was not here to greet you. Lady Scrope and I …'

He shook his head impatiently. 'Never mind that. I have bad news for you.'

I caught my breath.

Bad news must mean bad news from France. There was no other kind of news to be had. It was endless sieges and bloody battles and always, people dying.

'My father?' I whispered, fear squeezing my heart so that I could hardly speak.

He stepped forward and took my hands in his. I felt a little jolt of surprise at the touch of his fingers. One part of me was thinking, how warm and solid his hands are, how comforting, how strong, while the other part was overwhelmed by the horror of what he was about to say.

No, not your father.' His voice had lost the hard edge it usually had when mentioning my father. He hesitated as if wanting to say something else but was unsure of the words. I waited while he stared at my flushed cheeks and dishevelled appearance, at the tangles of hair which trailed across my face and the foul-smelling splashes on the hem of my gown. For a moment I wondered what it would be like to have Richard Nevill run his fingers through my hair and carefully remove my gown from my shoulders. But of course that would never happen.

He shook his head as if suddenly remembering what he'd come to say.

'The king's brother, the duke of Clarence has been killed.'

The duke was my Aunt Margaret's second husband, stepfather to my Beaufort cousins. He'd had little time for us younger children and by the time Edmund, Meg and I were old enough to make ourselves known he'd joined the king's expedition to France and was seldom seen in England. I wondered if I should say I'd pray for him.

'It's a disaster but there's something else I must tell you,' said my husband. 'Our Beaufort cousins have been taken prisoner.'

This time my heart leapt.

'Our cousins?'

'John and Thomas.'

My legs trembled beneath my skirts and under my ribs I felt a sharp pain. 'Edmund?'

My husband frowned. 'No, not Edmund. The duke would not have him riding into battle. He's too young.'

I breathed out. Edmund would not have agreed. Two years ago he'd considered himself old enough to take up arms and in Aunt Margaret's private garden had given me a dazzling demonstration of his skill, all quick movements and vicious thrusts with his sword.

But John was only seventeen and Thomas a year younger. I could not imagine either of them held captive by an enemy. The last time I'd seen them they were still boys playing at fighting.

'What will happen?' I asked timidly. 'Will they be kept in a dungeon? They won't be killed, will they?'

He looked at me as if I was stupid for asking. 'How would I know? A ransom perhaps or if they're lucky an exchange of prisoners. But John is the earl of Somerset; he's valuable to our enemies and they'll not sell him cheap.'

Baugé was the name they gave to the battle and the considered view of the Nevills was that a moment of audacious folly on the part of my aunt's husband had been responsible for the catastrophe.

'Found himself outnumbered and facing a Scots army led by Lord Buchan,' growled my father-in-law, who'd been to Westminster for news. 'A wiser man would have waited for reinforcements before attacking but Clarence was ever one eager for personal glory.'

My mother-in-law was vocal on the continuing treachery of the Scots in allying themselves with the so-called dauphin. Tears had already been shed in private for her Beaufort nephews and we'd been twice to the chapel to pray for their safe return.

'I shall speak to my brother,' she said firmly, sniffing and dabbing her cheeks. 'The bishop will know how to arrange money for their ransom and see them brought safely home.'

'Will they come home soon?' I whispered to Lady Mowbray.

'No,' she said tersely. 'The enemy will want more than the king can afford. They'll want the duke of Orléans.'

The enormity of the ask took my breath away. The duke of Orléans was the king's most valuable prisoner, an implacable enemy of our ally, the duke of Burgundy. He'd been captured six years ago at Agincourt and paraded through the streets of London like a trophy. Sometimes he was housed in the Tower, occasionally at Windsor and at other times in the great northern fortress of Pontefract. It was said that he lived in luxury, waited on by French servants with books and music to wile away the hours but he would never be released. My mother had told me that the duke's removal from the arena of conflict was necessary for the king to achieve his divine destiny: the conquest of all France.

It was for the king's continuing success that my father was fighting. It was acknowledged that following the disaster at Baugé it was my father's genius that had allowed the remnants of the broken English army to reach Normandy without further loss. With the rivers in full flood and an enemy flushed with victory snapping at their heels, it had taken my father's resolute brand of courage and skill to march three thousand Englishmen to safety. I was immensely proud to be the daughter of such a great man and wished my mother was still alive to hear the praise heaped on his shoulders.

Of course there were other casualties at Baugé as well as the king's brother. My mother's cousin, John Holland, earl of Huntingdon was a prisoner and doubtless in the same dismal situation as my Beaufort cousins, waiting to see if the enemy would agree to a ransom and hoping the amount they wanted was not beyond his ability to pay. And there was another loss, one which touched the Nevill family. Lady Umfraville, one of my mother-in-law's many Nevill stepdaughters, had lost her husband. Perhaps she would now join the dowager Lady Scrope in her corner where together they could whisper of their losses and weep.

On an overcast day in the middle of May when the sky turned black with rooks and the ground was damp beneath our feet, my Aunt Margaret returned with the body of her husband. The duke's black-draped coffin was followed by a dozen liveried torch bearers, hundreds of black-robed members of his household and my cousin Edmund as the sole representative of the duke's legitimate family. The king and his remaining two brothers joined the procession on its way to Canterbury where the duke was laid to rest next to his father, old King Henry. It was an unbearably sad occasion.

'He was his father's favourite,' murmured Lady Scrope wiping the wetness away from her cheeks. 'How often a man prefers the younger to the elder and how often it tears a family apart, setting brother against brother, uncle against nephew.'

She might as well have been talking about my husband and "the little turd" at Raby rather than the king and his brother, Thomas, late duke of Clarence.

Once the dismal duty of burying the dead was over, we returned to London where the king began making arrangements to go back to France. To my surprise the queen was not to accompany him but would remain at Windsor where the king's brother, the duke of Bedford, would be in charge of her comfort. The opinion of the Nevill women was that she was carrying the king's child and this change of plan was a precaution to keep both her and the child safe. Lord Humphrey, we learned, was to leave with the king. At the farewell feast, if the king's eyes had not been so firmly fixed on his campaign in France, he might have observed a certain sadness in Countess Jacqueline, an occasional tear brushed away from her eye, but perhaps I was the only one who noticed.

And with the parliament risen and the king's business done, it was time for the Nevills to travel north. I'd wanted to see Eleanor again, to call on my Beaufort cousins and write to Lady Phelip asking if I might visit but my mother-in-law said there was no time for running around, only for making ready for the journey. Middleham beckoned once more.

# 5

## BIRTH 1421

The rain fell in torrents on the courtyard walls at Middleham and I wondered why the North was so wet: wet, cold and stormy. Crops had been battered to the ground, the harvest ruined and at every place we'd stopped on our journey, people were angry and fearful. What could a man do if there was nothing to eat and no work to be had? How could he feed his family when what he'd sown in the spring was washed away by the rains? And following hard on the heels of hunger would come sickness. It didn't matter how many lengthy prayers were said or holy pilgrimages undertaken, how many soothsayers were consulted or sinful men redeemed – death and misery were certain to return.

Denied solutions from their priests, Nevill tenants came flocking to Middleham looking for answers. Day after day our hall was filled with farmers and blacksmiths, millers and shopkeepers, widows and petty merchants; anyone who thought their lord might help. My husband rode far afield with his father visiting Nevill manors across the North, listening to complaints and adjudicating in disputes between neighbours. On one occasion they were absent for two weeks at Carlisle where, as warden of the west march, my husband had business ensuring the garrison was properly armed and supplied.

We were unable to go hawking on the moors, which Lady Percy had assured me was one of the delights of Middleham, and riding out in the driving rain was no pleasure. So we reverted to our usual round of sewing, making music, reading and prayer, made all the less enjoyable when accompanied by the sound of rain lashing on the newly installed windows. It was cold, damp and uncomfortable and by October I was so miserable I could have wept.

'Did I hurt you?'

I was so surprised to hear my husband's voice coming out of the darkness I almost failed to reply.

'No, my lord.'

'So why are there tears in your eyes?'

It was strange enough for my husband to be still lying beside me but for there to be words between us was unheard of. He never spent the night in my bed. Once he'd done his duty he slid out from under the covers, threw his cloak over his shoulders and disappeared.

'I did not mean to weep,' I stammered trying to brush away a telltale wetness.

For a long while he said nothing more but I was certain he was looking at me though what he could see in the gloom I couldn't imagine.

'How old are you, Alice?'

'Fourteen, my lord.'

'When I was fourteen my father took me on service to the west march. It's a wild place, at constant risk of incursions by the Scots.' He gave a sigh as if remembering when he was young like me. 'He told me it was time I became a man.'

I tried to envisage a place that was wilder than the

moors around Middleham. Perhaps there were forests on the west march, forests with wolves and wild boar. Or perhaps there were bogs.

His voice sounded as if he was smiling. 'Don't worry. I'm not taking you to the border. We're returning to London. And now that you're fourteen we are to have our own lodgings at The Erber, our own establishment of which you shall be mistress. But you will have to stop weeping. Do you understand?'

'Yes, my lord,' I whispered, wondering how soon we'd be leaving and if it could possibly be tomorrow.

'So no more tears.'

'No, my lord.'

'And you will run our household diligently?'

'Yes, my lord.'

'And economically?'

'Yes, my lord.'

'And perhaps you might try to smile occasionally.'

'Yes, my lord.'

I would have danced and smiled and sung gleeful melodies if he'd wanted me to. I would have gathered up my belongings and run back to London on my bare feet at that moment if I'd been permitted.

'And Alice.'

'Yes, my lord?'

'In private, when it is just you and me, I should like you to call me Richard. Can you do that?'

I gave him a wide smile. 'Yes ... Richard.'


We were supposed to quit Middleham on the next Thursday but had to wait a whole week while runners were sent on a last minute errand to Sheriff Hutton and my father-in-law concluded some intricate business with his son-in-law, Lady Percy's husband. Then a message arrived from Raby which had to be dealt with and which caused my husband to fall into a very black mood and I did not dare think of singing or dancing or of calling him Richard.

We returned to London, to a new way of living. To be truthful it was like playing house. I walked from room to room marvelling that this was mine to command, touching the tiny gold flowers powdering the walls, the sides of every narrow arched doorway, the oddly shaped panes of coloured glass, the sloping sills below the mullions and the magnificent fireplace with its huge stone mantel. I spent hours planning which hangings to have in the hall and where I should place my chair in the upstairs solar.

At the beginning I was nervous of my responsibilities but my husband had chosen an experienced Nevill steward who took command of the indoor servants. I lost count of the number we had hurrying in and out of the hall with dishes of food and flagons of ale, and the dozens more who cleaned and swept and struggled up stairs with baskets of wood and pails of hot water for my comfort.

I had a maid of my own, a small boy for running errands and an elderly groom to look after my horse. The silky grey mare had been a gift from my husband upon our return and I was so surprised I could hardly find words to thank him.

'I cannot have my wife riding around on an old nag,' he said, smiling at my obvious pleasure.

If he'd not been my husband, if he'd been my cousin Edmund, I would have flung my arms around his neck and kissed him but instead I dropped an awkward curtsey and said a few words of thanks in a prim little voice.

I was also given two young girls to instruct who regarded me with the same awe and respect which I'd once accorded my mother-in-law, a fact which pleased me greatly. They were daughters of men known to my husband, girls who needed to learn the ways of a noblewoman's household so that in time they could make good marriages. They were pleasant enough but I found them remarkably ignorant.

The grandeur of my new surroundings so overwhelmed me it was hard to believe I could go out without asking my mother-in-law's permission. I received a weighty lecture from my husband on the dangers of London's streets and how I must be accompanied at all times. He required to be told where I was going and afterwards where I had been but there was still a delicious feeling of freedom in knowing I could order my horse and go more or less where I pleased. In the first week I sent a note to Sir Reginald Cobham's lodgings but to my disappointment was told that the family had left and nobody knew where the daughter had gone.

Of course my mother-in-law made frequent visits of inspection and my sisters-in-law liked to see what I'd done so they could criticise. Even Lady Scrope deserted her favourite corner and came poking around asking was I anxious for company.

'Oh but you have made your rooms quite beautiful!' she exclaimed in a genuinely admiring voice.

'Thank you,' I murmured politely.

'I remember when I was first married how difficult it was,' she said confidingly. 'I think my husband's servants thought me very stupid.'

'I know what you mean,' I agreed. 'Making sure all the little rituals are properly performed and servants don't forget anything. My maid muddles the strict order for rising and at supper yesterday our steward had to reprimand one of the servers for standing too close to my husband.'

'But your mother will have trained you well.'

I gave a rueful grin. 'My mother's servants were not well supervised. She said her years in Devon with no servants had made her lazy.'

'No servants! Surely not?'

'They had one maid, a woman for the cooking, an elderly man and a boy for the horses.'

The dowager Lady Scrope looked disbelieving. 'How did she manage?'

'I don't know but at Bisham we kept a very lax household. My father was always complaining.'

She sniffed. 'Husbands are like that.'

'Do you miss your husband?' I asked, curious to know what kind of marriage hers had been.

'Yes,' she sighed. 'He was a kind man. I'd very much like to marry again but my father is too busy with Richard's problems and my stepmother cares only for finding a husband for Cecily.'

'Oh, Cecily!' I said, rolling my eyes heavenwards.

'I know,' laughed Lady Scrope. 'She is impossible. The child should be in the nursery where she belongs.'

'What if they don't find you a husband?'

'I dare not think of it. I've no desire to be my stepmother's poor companion for the remainder of my days but what else can I do? Richard has control of my son's inheritance so there's nothing there to attract a future husband and my own dower is miserably small.'

It was a bleak assessment of her prospects. I felt truly sorry for her. If the earl failed to arrange a suitable marriage for her she would remain tied to my mother-in-law for the rest of her life.

It was a cold December that year with a heavy frost each night and by morning, icicles hanging from the gatehouse roof. I was snuggled deep under a pile of heavy furs when a loud peal of bells from the church at the corner of The Erber, woke me. I sat up still shrouded in bedcovers and untied my nightcap. Then I realised I could hear more than one ring of bells, peal after joyful peal ringing out across the city. And in Advent! Perhaps the king had won another glorious battle. Another Agincourt!

I jumped out of bed and ran to the door, ignoring the icy cold and forgetting to call for my maid. Down in the hall someone was shouting and from outside in the street came the noise of men cheering. Perhaps my father had taken the king's army to a great victory. I could see him: he would have led from the front because he was the bravest of men.

As I stood on the threshold in my nightshift peering warily down the gallery I saw my husband leaping up the stairs two at a time, Before I could retreat to the safety of my room he had seen me and came running.

'What is it?' I asked.

He grasped my hands. 'A son! The queen has given birth to a son!'

I blinked in surprise. What about the cheering? What about my father's victory on the battlefield?

'A son?'

'Yes. A son for the king, an heir for England. What better news can there be. A boy born on the feast day of St Nicholas. A strong healthy boy.'

I felt a slight tug as if he wanted to sweep me off my feet and into his arms but instead he let go of my fingers and smiled into my eyes.

'Are you not pleased?'

I gave him my very best smile. 'I am greatly pleased.'

His gaze dropped to where my belly was hidden by the folds of my nightshift. 'Perhaps in time we too …'

I blushed wildly, overcome with embarrassment at my tumbling hair, the lingering smell of night-time warmth and the sight of my bare toes peeping out from beneath the hem of the nightshift. A husband should not see a wife like this. Naturally he wanted a child but that was not a subject for the bright light of day. I lowered my gaze to the floor and muttered that I was certain our marriage would soon be blessed.

'Every man needs a son,' he said seriously.

I nodded and murmured, 'Yes.'

Yet even while agreeing with my husband, I knew the same rule was not to apply to my father. My father was a great war hero, a man like other men, but if my husband had his wish my father would never be blessed with a son, he would never experience the joy felt by the king when told the news.

With the king in France and the queen still confined after the birth of her son, there were no royal festivities that year but one morning soon after the feast of the Epiphany

I was informed that as my husband's wife I might attend the ceremony at Windsor for when the queen returned from the service of her purification in the chapel. I thought it a great honour but the women who frequented the company of my mother-in-law smiled behind their hands and murmured they'd heard there was a problem.

'A problem! How is that possible?' enquired my mother-in-law, icily.

Apparently. after much confusion it was admitted that nobody, from the archbishop down to the most minor cleric, knew how things should be done. There must be rules, on that everyone was agreed but exactly what they were nobody knew. No-one could remember a child being born to a king in their lifetime. The queen dowager, Joanna, shut away at Leeds, had given old king Henry no children, and King Richard's two queens had both been childless. Ancient documents were consulted and Bishop Beaufort had the best minds in the country scour every college library for clues, but all in vain. A coronation would have proved easier. Ample evidence existed for the solemn ceremonies, the order of service and necessary rules for feasting afterwards. Also many people remembered not only the king's coronation but that of his father.

'It must be nigh on eighty years since my own father was born,' mused my mother-in-law. 'And he was King Edward's third son.'

'Perhaps The duke of Bedford could ask the French queen how it's done,' suggested Anne pertly. 'Queen Katherine's mother must surely remember.'

But Queen Isabeau was not to be consulted. After agreeing to pass the throne of France to the English king and his heirs, her reputation as a queen and a mother was tarnished. With one stroke of a pen she had disinherited her son, the so-called dauphin. I'd heard whispers about her conduct within her marriage but that was all it was, only whispers, nothing proved and probably invented by her enemies.

After several frantic weeks of discussion, The duke of Bedford, Archbishop Chichele, and Bishop Beaufort, together with the chief officers of the Crown, issued a set of instructions which were to be obeyed to the letter. Invitations were sent out and in mid-January we gathered at Windsor to greet Queen Katherine and her baby son.

The senior men of the queen's household looked magnificent in their glittering new outfits while the queen herself shone with the inner joy of a woman who knows she has achieved everything that was expected of her: a son for her husband within eighteen months of their marriage. It was no wonder she radiated happiness.

'Is he not a darling?' Countess Jacqueline held baby Henry in her arms, gazing like a besotted lover at the queen's son.

'He is heir to the throne of England,' said my mother-in-law, feeling the need to impress on this foreign woman the importance of the child's position. 'In time he will inherit the dual crown of England and France.'

'But look at his eyes, how dark, how serious. And that sweet little mouth.' Countess Jacqueline turned to me. 'Do you not agree, Lady Nevill? It is Lady Nevill is it not?'

'Yes, my lady.' I sank into a deep curtsey, surprised at her interest in my opinion. 'He is the most beautiful baby in Christendom.'

Countess Jacqueline reluctantly surrendered baby Henry and his billowing white shawl to the arms of the chief nursemaid who was hovering anxiously nearby, frightened her precious charge might be dropped.

'You have none of your own?' enquired the countess.

'No, my lady.'

'Lady Nevill.' She leaned closer so that my mother-in-law couldn't hear. 'When all this gaiety is done, I wish to speak with you in private. I shall send one of my women to bring you to my rooms.'

'Me?'

She gave a roguish grin as if she was arranging a sinful assignation. 'Yes, you, Lady Nevill, no-one but you. Most definitely not your husband, or your oh-so-worthy mother-in-law, or any of those sisters-in-law who trail around after you, hissing in your ear. Just you.'

She swept away in a cloud of musky perfume, leaving me standing there open-mouthed, wondering what she could possibly want. But as I watched her disappear followed by her train of ladies, my astonishment grew even greater.


'Why did you not tell me?' I said to a beautifully gowned Eleanor Cobham when later she came to fetch me. 'I nearly fainted when I saw you walking two paces behind the countess.'

'It was an opportunity.' She smiled her familiar sweet smile. 'There was no time for writing letters or sending messages even to someone as dear to me as you. My father wanted a great household for me and who has a greater household than Countess Jacqueline? Do you know how many beds the king has given her?'

I shook my head.

'Forty! And an allowance from the exchequer. Can you imagine the splendour of her apartments? I shall do very well here. I might even find myself a rich husband.'

I trotted at her heels through the warren of spacious chambers increasingly amazed at the magnificence of the king's castle at Windsor. It made The Erber look like a provincial merchant's house, not the princely lodging I had once thought.

There was no denying Countess Jacqueline had one of the most prestigious sets of rooms in the castle, certainly superior to my mother-in-law's. Comfort and luxury positively oozed from every corner of her chamber: couches cushioned in white satin and draped in topaz coloured silk; new hangings ablaze in vibrant reds and greens, and dominating one wall a huge fireplace with a green marble surround, carved into intricate boughs of leaves and strange woodland creatures.

Once she had me seated she picked up a silver dish from the gilded table at her side and offered me a sweetmeat. Then we exchanged a few meaningless pleasantries before, like a seasoned hunter, she cut straight to the chase.

'Mistress Cobham tells me you are an only child. Is that true?'

I blinked at the directness of her question.

'Yes, my lady.'

'And your father, he is rich?'

'Yes, my lady. I suppose he is. He is the earl of Salisbury.'

'So you are an heiress.'

I nodded. 'Yes, my lady.'

'And being an heiress, your father married you carefully, I'm sure. Am I correct?'

'Yes, my lady. He married me to the son of the earl of Westmoreland. He told me it was a good marriage for both families.'

Countess Jacqueline screwed up her face and gave a little sniff as if wanting to disagree with my father's assessment.

'How long have you been married, Lady Nevill? You seem very young.'

'Sir Richard and I have been married for a little more than a year.'

'And are you happy in your marriage?'

I hesitated which made her laugh. 'Say no more, Lady Nevill. I, of all women, understand.'

I wasn't sure what it was that she understood any more than I could fathom what it was she wanted from me.

'Mistress Cobham tells me your father has plans to remarry.'

I gulped at Eleanor's indiscretion. How careless to have prattled about my father's secrets! And why had she told the countess?

'Yes, my lady. He is to marry the widowed Lady Phelip.'

The words almost stuck in my throat and I swallowed hard. Each time I thought of my father's betrayal of my mother, I wanted to weep.

'And the widow is young and comely so I hear.'

'Yes,' I whispered.

Countess Jacqueline regarded me without smiling. There was no way she could fail to notice how my lips trembled and how tears were gathering on my eyelashes.

'She will give your father a son,' she said with admirable bluntness. 'And you will lose your inheritance.'

Dumbly I nodded. 'Yes.'

She leaned forward and tapped me sharply on my arm.

'You are like a piece of manchet bread soaked in milk, Lady Nevill: soft and sweet and fit only for the mouths of little children and toothless old women. What is it that you intend to do about this widow whose child will steal your inheritance? Do you intend to sit there and weep?'

I sniffed miserably. 'I do not know what I can do, my lady.'

'You think you are powerless?'

I nodded.

'Listen to me, Lady Nevill, and I shall tell you a story. My first husband was a prince of France. You'd have thought a man like that to be untouchable. But he was greedy and his enemies did not think they were powerless. They noted his excessive liking for sweet pastries and hatched a diabolical plan. They fed him poison and he died. He was eighteen years old. Would you dare to do such a thing?'

My eyes widened at the horror of what she was suggesting.

'That would be a sin,' I gasped.

'Like I said, Lady Nevill, you are too soft. You have yet to accustom yourself to the harsh realities of this world. Is it not a sin for one woman to steal from another? Remember what the scriptures teach us about the narrow gate to eternal life. The question for you is: which sin is the greater. Which sin leads to the narrow gate and which to the wide gate and man's eventual destruction. Pray if you like, Lady Nevill, pray, as I am certain your king does but observe also that your king is not weak. He is not soft and sweet like milk-soaked manchet bread. He knows what God wants from him and he is not afraid.'

'But the king is a man,' I cried. 'I am a woman.'

I sat there with my head lowered, too nervous to get up and leave yet afraid of what the frightening Countess Jacqueline would say next.

'I too was an only child, Lady Nevill, an heiress, just like you.'

'I did not know, my lady.'

'Of course you didn't. Why should you. I was only a little older than you when my first husband died. Two months later while still in deep mourning, my father also died and I found myself surrounded by those who wanted what was rightfully mine. I had to fight for my inheritance, Lady Nevill. I had no experience of being a ruler, no-one had taught me.'

'And you had no husband to guide you.'

'As you say, I had no husband. But my cousin of Burgundy, seeing some advantage for himself, swiftly married me to his nephew, my cousin of Brabant.'

This cousin must be the husband she wanted rid of so I said carefully, 'Did that not please you?'

She pulled back her pretty pink lips and showed the points of her sharp white teeth. 'I hate him. He has given away everything that was mine. First he mortgages my counties of Zeeland and Holland to my father's brother who always believed they should be his. Then he pledges Hainault to my cousin of Burgundy in exchange for a paltry sum of money to pay off his debts. I will not stay married to such a man.'

I was shocked by her display of visceral hatred. 'But he is your husband, my lady. What is yours is his.'

'Pope Benedict will give me an annulment.'

She sat back, flushed from her attack on her husband and regarded me steadily. 'Now you see what can happen to an heiress?'

'Oh yes, my lady, I understand but my situation is very different. My husband would never betray me the way yours did.'

She laughed. 'You think not? Your father did.'

She put her head on one side and narrowed her eyes, as if measuring me for some unknown purpose, wondering if I was worth the money she'd laid out on me. I remembered my grandmother looking at me that way before complaining to my mother about my conduct.

'And now Lady Nevill,' she said smoothly, 'it is time for you to make payment. I have told you my story. I have given you valuable advice to help you hold on to what is yours. In exchange you will tell me about your mother-in-law, Lady Westmoreland and her brother, the fat bishop. I think that a fair bargain, don't you?'

I nodded, much too scared to do anything else.

The countess rested her elbow on the arm of her chair, cupped her chin in her hand and said lightly, 'Their father was the king's grandfather, was he not?'

So this was to be our bargain. In return for her confidences I would tell her what she could not discover from other people.

'Yes, my lady,' I said slowly, taking great care which words I used. 'John of Gaunt, the great duke of Lancaster, a son of old King Edward.'

'I see.' She stared at me gravely. 'One of my ladies tells me Lady Westmoreland's mother was a peasant woman.'

I gave a nervous giggle. 'Oh no, my lady. Not at all. Lady Swynford was not a great lady but she was in no way a peasant woman. I believe she was a knight's daughter. The duke loved her. He married her and made her his duchess.'

'So the story that Lady Westmoreland and Bishop Beaufort are baseborn is false?'

I hesitated for a moment. This was difficult and I was not quite certain how to answer without slandering my mother-in-law and the bishop. 'Their birth was made legitimate, my lady. The king and the pope decreed it should be so. My lady mother said the duchess's four Beaufort children were treated by King Richard as if they were true-born.'

'Do they aim for the throne?'

I was so shocked I nearly fell off my chair. 'In no way. The Beauforts have no ambitions in that direction. They are loyal.'

She put her head on one side and looked straight into my eyes. 'Are you certain? That is not my experience of men. Or of women.'


'She expects me to poison my stepmother,' I whispered to Eleanor as we made our way back through the outer chambers. 'She doesn't even consider it a sin.'

Eleanor shrugged. 'Perhaps it is not.'

'Eleanor!'

'Not every death can be counted as a sin otherwise how could men ride into battle.'

'That is different. My father explained it to me once. It is a way to determine God's divine will. But to poison another woman!'

Eleanor signalled to the guards to open the door. 'Then you'd best be quick and follow Mistress Jourdemayne's advice. Visit your would-be stepmother or your husband might write to Pope Benedict asking for an annulment.'

Was that a joke. I never knew with Eleanor. Was she serious or was I meant to laugh. Before I could ask she gave me a little push through the doorway, turned and walked back the way we'd come, her heels tapping lightly on the tiles as her fur-trimmed brocade skirts swirled elegantly around her legs.

# 6

## THE BARGAIN 1422

The widowed Lady Phelip was as coolly welcoming as she had been the first time, kissing my cheek and bidding me come in out of the rain. We sat in the parlour at Ewelme with the little merlin and the elderly hound asleep in their allotted places. Two books lay on the table beside a pile of manuscripts, and the gown worn by my future stepmother was the same green woollen gown from my previous visit. A stranger could be tricked into thinking nothing had changed, that we were the same women we'd been last spring with the same hopes and dreams. But I knew better. Everything had changed.

'I am pleased to see you before I depart, Lady Nevill. It was good of you to come. '

'You are leaving?' I felt a surge of panic at the thought of her running off to be with my father.

She smiled. 'Soon the queen will return to France to be with the king. I shall travel with her. Your father is impatient for us to be together and begin our married life.'

I swallowed hard. I'd been foolish to imagine there was plenty of time to lay careful plans. Both Countess Jacqueline and Eleanor had urged boldness in my dealings with my future stepmother and they were right. By delaying a month I'd nearly missed my opportunity.

With my husband's agreement I'd brought with me the stable boy who helped care for my horse. He was only a little lad but eager to help and after a week of my attention and a few days outside the city walls scouring the fields for newts he was pale and sick with a puppy-like devotion. In the privacy of my room I had consulted Mistress Jourdemayne's scrap of parchment but was not at all sure what the little squiggles meant. I'd turned the paper this way and that but the writing was odd, not like a proper script at all. There was no-one to help decipher the words and it was well nigh impossible to guess at their meaning. I spent hours murmuring unfamiliar sounds until the girls began giggling in corners at my strange behaviour and asked what I was doing.

Now that I was here at Ewelme I too wondered what I was doing. I knew this was wrong, I knew it was a sin but every time I looked at the widowed Lay Phelip and imagined her in my father's arms, I realised I had no choice in the matter. "Think of your mother," Eleanor had urged.

On the second evening after an early supper my future stepmother said she wished to write a letter.

'Would you mind if I walked in your garden?' I asked politely, thinking this would be the perfect opportunity to carry out my plan. 'The rain has stopped and I shall not mind being alone, to be truthful, I enjoy peace and quiet.'

She raised her eyebrows. 'Indeed? I had marked you down as a young woman to take pleasure in dancing and music, not a lover of solitude.'

'I was often alone at Bisham when I was a child,' I said lamely.

'Ah yes, Bisham.' she said, rolling the word lovingly on her tongue. 'I do believe I shall enjoy living at Bisham. Of course there will have to be changes. Your father says he will place a sum at my disposal and I may do as I wish with the rooms. He is very careful of my happiness and wants me to have whatever I desire most.'

'And what is that?' I said, stung into an unwise reply.

She smiled. 'What every woman desires: a husband with ambition and a son in the cradle. And the riches which go with a good position. I'd not want to be impoverished. I'm sure you wish for the same.'

At the moment I would have wished her dead but bit my tongue on the thought. To ill-wish someone dead really was a sin.

The maid brought my cloak and excusing myself, I went outside to survey my surroundings. The gardens at Ewelme were laid out with pebbled paths edged with low box hedges and patches of untidy trailing plants which seemed at odds with the orderly life of Lady Phelip. Perhaps it was her father who enjoyed riots of greenery or perhaps their gardeners were idle. The sun had set in a watery sky and already the air had assumed that indefinable quality of dusk, a stillness, as if the world was slowly sinking into slumber.

Once out of view of the house I slipped round to the stable-yard where I found the boy. He was carrying an armful of hay for my horse but stopped when he saw me approach.

'M'lady.' He scrabbled at his hood, dropped the hay and flushed a bright red.

I felt like cuffing him for his stupidity but instead smiled encouragingly. 'You have it safe?'

He nodded. 'Yes, m'lady.'

'Where is it?'

He retrieved a small sack from a peg on the stable wall and stood holding it in his hands with an infatuated look on his face.

'Here, m'lady.' He proffered the sack as if expecting me to open it.

'You must do it,' I said. 'A lady cannot put her hands into a dirty sack.'

He reached inside and produced the disgusting bundle of the dead newt. At least I hoped it was dead and wasn't going to slither away as soon as he unwrapped the layers of cloth.

'Let me see it.'

It was worse than disgusting and I jerked my head away. I wasn't sure as to the order of this supposed magic charm but thought it best if I were to breathe the words over the creature and then leave the boy to bury the pale shrivelled body somewhere outside the entrance to the house.

'Make sure you bury it deep,' I instructed him. 'And be certain nobody sees you. Do you understand?'

'Yes, m'lady,' he muttered, looking at the toes of his boots, the tips of his ears pink with embarrassment.

'If you do this well, I shall be pleased with you.'

'Yes, m'lady.'

I steeled myself to bend over the ragged cloth bundle and whispered Mistress Jourdemayne's strange words into the evening air. I hoped they would wrap themselves tightly round the dead body of the newt giving it supernatural powers.

I knew nothing of magic except that it was the province of witches and sorcerers and was deemed dangerous, but this seemed harmless enough, except, of course, to my future stepmother. As Eleanor kept reminding me, the purpose was to blight the woman's womb so that she would not conceive a son, and this way was most definitely kinder than Countess Jacqueline's suggestion of a dose of poison.

I told myself the widowed Lady Phelip and I had struck a bargain: she was free to entrance my father, to lie with him and turn his thoughts away from my mother and me, but in return she must forego the blessing of a son. She would long to conceive a child but would remain barren. The king might have been blessed with a son but she and my father would never know that joy.

Standing in the shadowy stable-yard at Ewelme with the spring darkness fast approaching, the bargain seemed perfectly fair. I almost persuaded myself I was doing her a favour.

'It was not a pact with the devil,' I said to Eleanor in a firm voice. 'Others might think so but I know better.'

She patted my hand. 'The devil had nothing to do with what you did. It's not as if you were raising hailstorms or causing madness in cattle. Any sensible woman would have done the same. I'm certain your mother would have approved.'

'Do you think so?' I said doubtfully, remembering my mother's insistence on kindness as a guiding principle in life. Fearing God and being kind to your fellow man, was the central tenet of her belief and I wasn't at all sure that she would have viewed my measures against the widowed Lady Phelip as a kindness.

'Think of it as a love charm,' said Eleanor.

'Like sleeping with may blossom under your pillow to discover which boy you're going to marry,' I said eagerly. 'All girls do that. Besides I shall know if God approves my actions.'

'How so?'

'If she fails to bear a son it will be a sure sign of God's pleasure.'

I folded my arms around my waist in defiance so that Eleanor would not suspect the niggling doubts plaguing my conscience. I knew I was playing a dangerous game but it was one I had to win if my marriage to Richard Nevill was to succeed. If I brought him the coveted earldom of Salisbury he would surely learn to love me.

But in the darkness, sinister voices whispered in my ear. What if the curse I'd laid on Lady Phelip's womb caused her great harm? What if she died? What if as she lay dying she called out my name and cursed me for all eternity? What then? In the bright light of day I could dismiss those as night-time fears for I was only fourteen and had no idea of the danger I was in.

That year the long sunny days made our summer visit to the Nevill castles of Sheriff Hutton and Middleham a joyful round of hawking, hunting, picnics and country games. We paid friendly visits to our neighbours and entertained lavishly. I observed how the local tenantry regarded my husband as his father's acknowledged heir and wondered about my father-in-law's plans for his other sons and grandsons. There would need to be good marriages for all of them but heiresses were few and titles did not grow on trees; men either inherited them or married them. What if they did neither?

One evening my husband, surprised me as I sat having my hair brushed by my maid. He came through the doorway, unannounced, a jug in one hand and two goblets hooked on the fingers of the other. The air was still warm from the day's heat so the sight that met his eyes was of me on a stool wearing nothing but my nightshift and a shawl thrown loosely over my shoulders. For a moment he just stared, then with a quick movement of his head sent my maid scurrying away while he set the jug and goblets on the table.

'Wine?'

'Thank you,' I said, wondering were we to have a second supper here in my room. At that very moment a boy might be hurrying up the stairs with a plate of little delicacies.

'Here!' He put the goblet into my hand. I cradled the metal in my lap as if it were a small child needing warmth.

He dragged up another stool and sat down beside me. I was unsure if this was a prelude to a gentle reprimand, some failure on my part to behave like a proper Nevill or if he wished to change the routine of our occasional night-time encounters. When we'd moved into our own lodgings he was unusually tolerant of my mistakes but since coming to Middleham he clearly expected more of me than I was able to give. In front of my mother-in-law I became clumsy and under constant scrutiny by Nevill women made me tongue-tied lest I say the wrong thing.

'You spoke with William this morning,' he began.

William was my husband's younger brother, recently married to the Fauconberg heiress. I liked him, he was unfailingly cheerful and treated me the way a brother should.

I watched my fingers, not wishing to look at my husband. 'Yes,' I said quietly, wondering what William had told him.

'Some tale of a prior who sat on top of a barrel.'

I smiled. 'There was a flood.'

'And that was it? Nothing more?'

'No.'

I recalled the tale I'd told of the brothers at Bisham who, one year when the river flooded, took refuge in the priory undercroft. Seeing several sturdy wine barrels stored in a corner, they'd climbed on top of them, pulled up their tunics and kept their feet dry. It wasn't much of a story but it had amused my brother-in-law.

My husband frowned. 'William says he wishes his own wife was like you. He says I am a fortunate man.'

'Your brother is very kind.'

William's wife was not a young woman able to tell stories. She'd been brought to Middleham after the wedding but the visit was not a success. She sat in my mother-in-law's room dribbling from the corner of her mouth and said not a word, just stared slack-lipped at the hangings on the wall. I tried to be charitable because it was not her fault she was simple-minded.

'It puzzles me. Why do you talk to William but not to me?'

What could I say. Because I'm not nervous of William. Because your brother speaks to me as if I am a person with

88

something to say. Because I know you only married me for the Salisbury earldom and I'm frightened I'll be put aside if my father has a son.

When I said nothing he sighed. 'Alice, we are husband and wife. Husbands and wives talk to each other. They discuss small matters of mutual interest. They confide in each other because they are friends. Do you not wish us to be friends?'

'Yes, I do wish it,' I said quietly.

'Then let us agree that when I'm at home, each evening we shall sit together and talk. Nothing more. I shall make no demands on you.'

'But …'

'What?'

I bit my lower lip. 'The other.'

For a moment he looked perplexed. Then a slow smile. 'Oh, you mean, *that* other.'

'Yes.' I blushed.

'Does it distress you?'

I shook my head. 'No,' I whispered. 'Not at all.'

Even though I was not looking at his face, I felt the warmth of his gaze.

'Perhaps twice in the week?'

I lifted my gaze to his uncompromising stare, wondering if he regarded our nocturnal business as duty or pleasure.

'Alice?'

'I would like that,' I whispered.

And so our marriage took a step forward into a future I could not yet imagine.

# 7

## DEATH 1422

Each day at dawn a soft golden light spread slowly across the eastern horizon, warming the stone walls of Middleham and gilding the stubble in the newly harvested fields down by the river. The moors were purpled with heather and above us, stretching from horizon to horizon was a canopy of the palest of pale blues. I was happy in my indolence and felt as if this lazy summer idyll would last forever. On the eve of the feast of St Matthew a party of more than thirty of us rode out early for a day's hawking, making our way along Coverdale and up onto Gammersgill moor. It was late when we returned home for a celebration feast, flushed with excitement and a good day's sport.

'A toast to Richard,' said my father-in-law raising his cup. 'Best catch of the day.'

'The honours go to Gavina, my pride and joy; and to Con of course,' said my husband with a nod to his falconer who sat on the lower benches. 'There's no-one else I'd trust with my precious darlings.'

It was one of my husband's finer qualities, this willingness to share his successes. I hoped one day he might share a victory with me. Matters had improved since the evening he'd come to my room and despite my clumsiness, we were more at ease with each other than before.

With wild cheering and the noise of table-thumping,

no-one noticed the arrival of a dust-covered man dressed in black. He stumbled up the hall and threw himself on the rushes at the earl's feet, holding out a letter. I could see exhaustion on his grimy face and the slumped shoulders and shaking hands of someone who'd had a long hard ride and wondered what had happened.

There was a moment of complete silence while the earl broke the seal and slowly read the letter. His face turned ashen. He grasped the hand of his wife and turned to her with a look of utter horror, almost unable to speak.

'Harry!' he gasped, gobbling in the back of his throat.

She snatched the letter from his hand and ran her eyes down the page. 'Holy Mother of God!' she whispered, by now almost as white-faced as the earl.

'What is it?' said my husband, leaning towards his parents.

My mother-in-law passed the letter. My husband's hands trembled when he saw what was written and in silence passed it to his brother, William, who sat at his other side.

The hall was hushed. Everyone was waiting as the earl rose unsteadily to his feet. I could see tears in the old man's eyes and knew he was about to say something truly dreadful.

'I do not know how to tell you this,' he said, his voice cracking as he spoke. 'Our sovereign lord, King Henry, is dead.'

There was a sharp intake of breath from around the hall and several men cried out, 'No!'

'He died on the last day of August just past, in France at the palace of Vincennes. That is all I know. May God have mercy on his soul.'

My father-in-law sat down abruptly as a swell of talking swept along the tables. From the women's benches came the unmistakable sound of sobbing.

I sat completely numb. How could the king be dead. He was a man in the prime of life with a beautiful wife and a baby son. He was at the height of his powers, the victor of Agincourt, heir to the French throne. How could he be dead. Someone must have made the most terrible mistake.

Later I sat with Lady Scrope and the younger children in the private parlour listening to the Nevill men arguing in angry raised voices. Chaos was about to engulf England and none of them knew from which direction disaster would come or what form it would take. And none of them could agree on what to do.

'Lord Humphrey will try for the throne,' said William bluntly. He had no liking for the king's youngest brother.

'No he won't,' growled the earl. 'Bedford's older and legitimacy is what the Lancastrians crave above all else.'

'Well it won't be March,' said my husband. 'He's naught but a cockscomb, a preening bag of useless bones.'

'Clear line of descent from King Edward, though,' said William, considering the claim of my Mortimer cousin, the earl of March.

'Through a woman!' roared the earl. 'Who'd accept that? Besides he don't have the support.'

'Bedford then.' agreed William.

'I wish Robert were here,' cried the earl. 'He'd know the legality of it.'

Robert Nevill was my mother-in-law's second son,

destined for a bishop's mitre and reputedly the cleverest of the lot.

'Well he's not here,' said my husband shortly. 'He's at Beverley.'

My mother-in-law leaned forward and tapped the arm of her chair in exasperation. 'By the rood, husband! Have you all forgotten Harry's son?'

'He's a babe,' spat the earl. 'No-one wants a babe. March might be a disaster but a child would be a catastrophe.'

'King Richard was a child.'

'That was different. He was near full grown. Besides who's to say Richard was not a catastrophe.'

*'Woe to thee O land when thy king is a child and thy princes feast in the morning,'* murmured Lady Scrope.

'What did you say, daughter?' snarled the earl 'You prating scriptures again?'

'Not much hope of a feast here,' whispered Anne.

My husband kicked his stool away. 'Body of Christ! Why are we wasting time while Percy is making plans to take back what he sees as his?'

'Didn't work selling him our sister, did it?' muttered Edward, the youngest Nevill boy, earning himself a hearty cuff from his next eldest brother, George, who'd kept studiously quiet throughout the proceedings.

'Our first duty is to protect the border for the king,' said the earl stubbornly, 'not go rushing off to London.'

'We have no king!' shouted William.

'Our first duty is to our family,' said Richard firmly. 'We must protect our own interests.'

'Well said, my son,' said my mother-in-law. 'It is what I have always believed – family first.'

'The border is well-protected but they'll be tearing each other's throats out at Westminster,' said my husband patiently to his father. 'Unless you want a Percy candidate on the throne and all your work these past twenty years undone, we'd best be on our way. We need to have our voices heard. And that means going south.'

They argued furiously about men who were loyal and men who were false and what to do with those suspected of treachery or double-dealing. As my husband's voice grew harsher and his reasoning more vehement I realised I didn't know him at all. I'd thought him a civilised man who might value me because our marriage would bring him a parcel of fat southern manors and an ancient title. But I was wrong. Being the earl of Salisbury's daughter would not be enough, title or no title. If I wanted to survive in his dangerous new world I would have to earn my place as a Nevill wife.

My husband had no need of a sweet young woman raised on milk-soaked manchet bread. He needed a wife to follow him blindly in everything he did, who would never cease striving to advance the cause of the Nevill family. I would have to be obedient to him in every respect: surrender my body, my heart and my soul and never look back. As my mother had once told me: in marriage there can be no one for you other than your husband; you have placed yourself in his hands and you must pray God guides him to be gentle with you.

My father-in-law and his sons quit the castle of Middleham before dawn with flaring torches to light the way and close on three hundred armed men for protection. They rode out under the gatehouse into the night like a ghostly procession of the devil's host with long dark cloaks wrapped tightly over armour and hidden weapons at the ready. They feared attack on the road and were taking no chances.

'What a coup it would be for Henry Percy to capture a Nevill son,' remarked Lady Scrope. 'An excellent bargaining tool.'

'What about us?' I cried in horror. 'What if we are attacked?'

'They'll not bother with a parcel of women. Besides we have two hundred men to guard us and our wagons,' she said soothingly. 'You've no need to worry.'

But I did.

All the way on our journey south we heard people crying how a country without a king was a country in danger. In houses and monasteries they talked of little else. King Henry had given them victory abroad and peace at home. Now they feared a return to violence. Scots would roar down from the border, stealing their cattle and carrying off their grain. Flemings would creep in under cover of darkness to rip the cloth from their looms. And what if God did not protect them when the French came burning their towns like they'd done in their grandfather's day. The king's death was a sign of God's displeasure. Why else would it have happened.

Men hid weapons in their beds and frightened groups of travellers attached themselves to our party for protection. By the time we reached the outskirts of London, every village was seething with rumour and people were arming themselves with whatever they could find. We were told Bishop Beufort had gone to Windsor where the queen's innocent babe slept peacefully in his cradle. But for what purpose? He'd been joined by Archbishop Chichele and some lords who'd been resting in the vicinity. Lord Humphrey, the child's uncle, returned from France, had been seen hurrying to his ducal barge with a face like stone. A journeyman carpenter at Tottenham swore he'd had sight of old Bishop Langley riding towards the city gates like a man possessed of the devil. It was rumoured that stashed in the bishop's saddlebags was the great seal of England.

It was common gossip in the streets that the lords and the bishops had gone to Windsor to decide what should be done and who should do it, but that did not necessarily mean the rumours were true. Wives worried for the safety of the queen's babe while husbands worried for their livelihoods. With no king on the throne and the duke of Bedford and the great men of England fighting in France, the sense of impending disaster was everywhere.

My mother-in-law told us how in the early days of Richard's reign, when he was only a boy, bad decisions led to open rebellion and many deaths. She said that if the queen's child lived it would be many years before he could rule. Arrangements must be made without delay to stop the country from sliding into lawlessness. And our lands in France must be protected. Only then could men turn their minds to the question of who should rule.

'They swore fealty to a baby!' said Anne, wide-eyed upon hearing the news brought back from Windsor by her father.

'He's not a baby, he is our king,' remarked Lady Scrope who looked as if she might start weeping all over again.

'But who will decide what's to be done?' wailed Anne.

'Will it be the queen?' whispered a subdued Cecily.

'No,' said Lady Scrope wearily. 'It will not be the queen. She's only a woman. I expect there'll be a regent, and a council to help with decision-making.'

'Will our father be on the council and make decisions?' said Anne.

'How would I know. You'll have to ask your lady mother.'

But my mother-in-law knew no more than we did.

My husband returned to our lodgings most nights, exhausted and despairing. He spent each day with his father and brothers but had little to report. He would come to my bed and lie beside me, more for comfort than anything else. Once I laid my hand on his arm and he didn't push me away. Instead he sighed deeply and rested his head on my shoulder.

'I don't know how we'll come out of this,' he said, half to himself.

'You won't lose what you have, surely?'

'Percy will push for himself and it's he who will sit on the council, not me.'

I didn't dare ask why Henry Percy was to have a seat on the council and not my husband. As joint defenders of the border it seemed to me that they should be of equal importance.

'My father is too old for a fight,' he sighed, untying the ribbons of my nightcap. 'I thank the saints for my uncle, the bishop. Without him we'd be lost. It's like a bear pit at Westminster and we've barely begun.'

News of the death of Charles, the half-mad king of France, travelled with the English party bringing King Henry's body home for burial but to the people of London it was an inconsequential death. They wept as the hearse carrying the royal coffin passed through the city streets and they wept again at Westminster as a knight wearing the dead king's crown and armour rode up to the high altar to be ritually stripped. Then the body of the victor of Agincourt was committed to the ground and lowered into eternal darkness. If he had lived two more months he would have been proclaimed King of France, instead this honour would fall to the little son he had never seen.

Once the formalities were finished, the eulogists silenced and the rivers of tears wiped clear away, the wrangling began over who was to control the baby king and rule in his name.

'Lord Humphrey believes it should be him,' remarked my husband next evening. 'He wishes to be regent.'

'Was that the late king's wish?' I asked politely. I knew the late king's will was being discussed before parliament sat but was unsure if the contents were known to my husband.

'Lord Humphrey says it is what his brother wanted. *Tutela* was the word he used but that is too foreign a word for most Englishmen and there are many who believe Lord Humphrey should not have the power.'

'Is that what it is, a question of who has power over the queen's child?'

My husband looked at me approvingly. 'That is very perceptive of you, Alice. Yes, it's a battle for pre-eminence. Whoever has authority over the child will wield the power of a king. Naturally Lord Humphrey believes it should be him.'

I thought of the greedy eyes of Lord Humphrey feasting on the person of Countess Jacqueline. I wondered was his appetite for power as great as that for the desirable countess.

'Will he prevail?'

My husband smiled. 'You've asked the wrong question.'

I thought for a moment. 'Is he the hungriest?'

He gave a grim laugh. 'Well said! Lord Humphrey is certainly hungry for power but so also is my uncle, Bishop Beaufort. And in all this we mustn't forget the duke of Bedford. He may be absent overseas but he's the heir and no-one can afford to ignore his wishes.'

I knew nothing of the duke of Bedford other than that the late king trusted him with the care of the kingdom of France.

'Do you know his wishes?'

He smiled. 'That his brother be kept under control.'

I considered the elegant Lord Humphrey and wondered if he would tamely accept a tether. And if so, who would be his keeper?

'What of the others?' I asked. 'What of Archbishop Chichele and Bishop Langley and the men lately returned from France? And what of your father and Henry Percy and your sister's husband, Lord Mowbray?'

'They will takes sides.'

'Whose side are we on?'

He smiled at my use of the word "we". 'The Nevills will support Bishop Beaufort. He's my mother's brother and will help further our cause. There's nobody I'd trust more.'

I considered the frightening figure of the portly bishop and hoped my husband's trust in him was not misplaced.

'What if the sides cannot agree?'

The firelight flickered as a sudden draught caught the flames and my husband's shadow leapt up the wall and merged with the darkness in the corners of the room..

'That is not a question you want answered.' he said shortly, stroking my cheek with the fingers of one hand.

'Would we be in danger?'

'Very probably.'

Yes, I thought. Ambitious men jostling for power in a rudderless world with no-one prepared to give way. I could almost smell the danger.

'You need not worry,' he said, pulling me close until I could feel the heat of his body on mine. 'You are my wife and I shall keep you safe.'

# 8

## AFTERMATH 1422 - 1423

The short days of Advent were cold and dark. Eleanor and I sat together in an outer room of Countess Jacqueline's apartments in the palace of Westminster, supposedly waiting for the countess to reappear. In truth we were relating juicy bits of gossip to each other.

'Shall I tell you a secret?' said Eleanor with a sly little smile.

'Is it worth hearing?'

'Oh yes, you will most definitely enjoy it.'

'Very well; tell me.'

'Who do you think comes riding into the courtyard most afternoons and doesn't depart again until late in the evening?'

I considered the possibilities but each one seemed more unlikely than the last.

'I have no idea.'

'Lord Humphrey.'

I gasped. 'Truly?'

She nodded her head, little gleams of light dancing in the depths of her eyes.

'They are friends?'

'Oh, more than friends.'

'Intimate?'

Eleanor put her head on one side, considering the

question. 'That depends on what you mean by the word. Certainly intimate in their conversation. He whispers in her ear and pays her the most outrageous compliments. He kisses the tips of her fingers and the inside of her wrist and moves his mouth slowly up her arm until the brocade of her sleeve prevents further ingress. Then he places his legs so they press against hers and leans so close you'd think he intends to gobble her up.'

'*Sainte Vierge!*' I whispered.

'And in case she needs a reminder of his interest, when he is absent he writes verses praising her eyes and her lips and her bosom and sends gifts of the kind only a lover would choose.'

'And she?'

'Oh, she is kind to him and permits the occasional kiss but not the freedom of her body.'

'Will she?'

'What do you think? If you were her, would you allow the gallant Lord Humphrey to carry you off to bed?'

'He is very handsome,' I said, smiling at the thought.

'He is indeed.'

'And a royal duke which is most certainly to his advantage.'

'Undoubtedly.'

'And wealthy.'

'Mmm.'

'So?'

'Oh Alice! What does the Countess Jacqueline want above all else?'

I wrinkled my forehead as I considered the question of what a woman wants. Love? Wealth? Position? I thought back to our conversation at Windsor and what the countess had told me about her inheritance.

'She wants a champion to win back her lands, the ones her husband gave away,' I said triumphantly.

Eleanor leant forward and whispered, 'Husband no more. She has her annulment from Pope Benedict.'

'She's free of him!'

Eleanor sat back and regarded me critically. 'You are being extremely stupid today.'

'Oh! She wishes to marry Lord Humphrey.'

'Precisely.'

'And he? Does he wish to marry her?'

Eleanor nodded her head. 'I think so. He is not a man who enjoys defeat at the hands of a woman. The longer she says no, the more he wants her. She's clever and knows exactly how to play him.'

'What if he is called back to France?'

'He is the king's chief counsellor. His duties are here. I wager you they'll marry before the summer.'

That evening after supper my husband and I were sitting by the fire in my room before retiring. This had become an enjoyable ritual at the end of each day. He would come and take a cup of wine with me and tell me of his doings. Three times a week he would take me to bed, climb in beside me and once the curtains were drawn, the candles extinguished and the servants departed, do his duty as a husband. He was gentle with me and liked to whisper inconsequential nothings into my hair as he took his pleasure. Now that I knew him better I found the whole experience delightful but was unsure if

I should let him know how much I enjoyed what he did so said nothing.

After he'd described a conversation he'd had with his uncle, the bishop, I plucked up courage and told him I had some information I thought he should hear.

'And what have you heard today that's so important?' he teased.

'Lord Humphrey and Countess Jacqueline are to marry.'

He spluttered into his wine. 'Who told you that?'

'A young woman in the countess's lodgings.'

He wiped his mouth with the back of his hand. 'I think your young woman is misinformed; the countess is married already.'

'It is said she has obtained an annulment.'

My husband fingered the stem of his cup while he considered this latest development in the countess's marital affairs.

'The marriage would be ill conceived; King Henry would not have allowed it.'

'But he is dead so there's no-one to stop them. Besides, couples often marry without their king's consent.'

'True, but this would be an unwise marriage. Burgundy has an interest and he's our ally. I hope Lord Humphrey knows what he's doing.' He downed his wine and replaced his cup on the table. 'When will this proposed marriage take place?'

'By the summer so I've been told.'

'Perhaps Lord Humphrey will think better of his folly before then.'

As the wind howled beyond the walls of The Erber, the fire issued a small puff of smoke and a splatter of rain hurled itself against the window. My husband took my hand in his and carefully raised me from my chair and into his arms. Summer seemed an impossibly long time away.

A week later In the pale grey hours of the afternoon, I had a visitor. It was nearly six month's since King Henry's death and after our muted Christmas festivities I'd had little company what with the snow and ice and freezing cold. Even my mother-in-law kept to her rooms and rarely ventured forth. But now a thaw had set in and our yard had turned into an unsavoury stewpot, the streets beyond our gates were awash with snow melt and the Thames had become a raging flood.

The dowager Lady Scrope came in, red-cheeked and damp, pulling off her hood and shrugging herself out of her cloak.

'Lady Margaret!' I exclaimed with pleasure.

She kissed my cheek and, holding my arms, scrutinised my face.

'Are you unwell, Alice? You have no colour.'

'Not unwell,' I said carefully, 'just a little indisposed.'

She dropped her gaze to where my hands had crept protectively over my belly and raised a single eyebrow. 'How long?'

'Two weeks.'

'And what do you think about it?'

'Nothing yet.'

Of course that was untrue, I'd been thinking of little else.

'Have you told Richard?'

'Oh no,' I said quickly. 'It's much too soon to be certain and I'd not want to disappoint him, not when I've caused him so much disappointment already.'

Remembering my duties as lady of the house, I summoned my maid and poured some spiced wine.

'I have news for you,' said Lady Scrope, settling herself close to the fire and watching the contents of the cup seethe as I thrust in a hot poker. 'From your aunt.'

'You've been to the convent at Syon!' I said, surprised, passing her the cup.

She dabbed her mouth delicately with a napkin. 'Not the dowager duchess. Your other aunt, Lady Bromflete. She made herself known to me and sent you her greetings.'

'A pleasure for her, I'm sure. But for you?'

Lady Scrope laughed. 'She waxed long on the glories of her past and the iniquities of her present position but I bore it bravely. I fear she's a bitter woman.'

'Once first lady in the land and now all but forgotten. It must seem cruel.'

She smiled. 'Your aunt may no longer be at the centre of events but she's not ignorant. She gave me a piece of news which will amaze you.'

I leaned forward, eager to hear something to brighten my day and divert my attention from the queasiness in my belly.

'Lord Humphrey has married Countess Jacqueline.'

I blushed slightly. 'Yes. I knew it was to happen.'

'You never said!'

'It was told to me in confidence.'

'And your lips were sealed?'

'Naturally,' I said. 'I would never betray a lady's secret.'

'I shall remember that,' she laughed. 'When I have a secret worth betraying I shall know who to tell.'

I doubted Lady Scrope would have many secrets but I smiled politely and turned the conversation to stories of her childhood in the nursery at Middleham which she'd shared with other Nevill children including Lady Percy and my husband.

By the time the warm days of June arrived, England had become a tranquil place. Whatever disagreements there had been, were settled. Lord Humphrey was protector in England, the duke of Bedford was regent of the kingdom of France and there was a council of great lords to make decisions relating to the governance of the realm which curbed Lord Humphrey's power and satisfied his brother. The baby king remained with his mother at Windsor under the guardianship of the duke of Exeter and in the special care of Sir Walter Hungerford and Lord Fitzhugh. And I had at last told my husband I was carrying our first child.

In one of the many pleasant rooms of Baynard Castle the newly married Duchess Jacqueline, surrounded by bolts of cloth and piles of furs, was reading a letter from her mother.

'Oh no!' She clutched the letter to her bosom and screamed with laughter. 'I must tell Lord Humphrey.'

She jumped up and beckoned for her women to follow. 'Come quickly!' she cried as she hurried through the room, scattering servants and paying no attention to the dozens of people waiting to see her.

Eleanor grabbed my hand. 'She means you.'

Baynard Castle was a rambling old fortress full of stairways and odd little recesses and it was hard for me to keep up with the others. I had only come to bid farewell to the duchess and to Eleanor before I travelled north to Middleham for the birth of my child but I was intrigued to discover what had been in the duchess's letter.

Lord Humphrey's apartments were guarded by two men-at-arms who stood back when they saw Duchess Jacqueline coming.

'My lady, he's with his tailor,' gasped Humphrey's squire leaping to his feet as we entered the ante-chamber. 'He's in a state of undress. It's not seemly.'

The duchess ignored him and burst into the room leaving her women hovering in the doorway.

'My lord, look!' She thrust the letter towards her husband who was most certainly not as I usually saw him. There was far more elegant leg on display than was proper and his fine linen shirt was unlaced and his doublet unfastened. He was contemplating his reflection in a mirror but turned at his wife's entrance. The tailor stayed where he was, crouched on the floor at the duke's feet clutching a box of pins.

The duke gave a broad grin. 'What have we here? Have you brought a dozen lovely nymphs to help with my disrobing, my lady? How thoughtful!'

Duchess Jacqueline was not to be diverted. 'Humphrey, my lord, see what my mother says. Your brother has married a sister of my cousin of Burgundy. Oh the poor man! They're plain as owls. All of them. What a dreadful life he'll lead.'

Lord Humphrey stretched his broad shoulders, keeping half an eye on Eleanor as I tried to hide myself behind her skirts. I hoped no-one would gossip. I could not have my husband knowing I'd been in the ducal apartments, particularly with Lord Humphrey in his present state of undress.

'I knew he had it in mind,' drawled Lord Humphrey. 'He promised Harry he'd take one of them. So he's actually done it, has he?'

'Yes, look here.' She moved as close to him as was decent considering the circumstances and held the letter under his nose. 'Anne. He's marrying Anne.'

'If he's taking Burgundy's sister he's secured another link in the chain binding Burgundy to the alliance. But this is not good news for us, my lady.'

'You think your brother will interfere with our plans?'

'He will certainly not approve of them.'

'What plans?' I whispered to Eleanor.

'Lord Humphrey is raising an army,' she whispered back. 'He wishes to reclaim the lands the duchess has lost.'

'Eleanor, that cannot be so. What of the duke of Burgundy?'

'Oh we all know Burgundy will take up arms against Lord Humphrey. He won't want his grasp on the region loosened. He'll see Lord Humphrey as a threat.'

'But Burgundy is our ally. My husband said when the so-called dauphin murdered Burgundy's father there was no-one Burgundy loved more than the king of England. He'll never fight an English army.'

'He will if it threatens the expansion of his powers.'

'Surely the duke of Bedford will stop him.'

Eleanor shrugged. 'That depends on which is more important to Bedford – Lord Humphrey's pride or England's alliance with Burgundy. And talking of pride – how is Sir Richard?'

I smiled in a rare moment of total happiness. 'As you would expect.'

'Content?'

I remembered how Richard Nevill had looked at me long and hard and told me what a clever wife I was, and how afterwards he'd gone to tell his mother.

'He is certain I shall give him a son.'

The two of us were silent. I knew Eleanor was thinking of that other man far away across the Narrow Sea who also wanted a son from his wife. With God's blessing Richard Nevill might get what he wanted but we both knew my father would always be denied a child because of what I'd done. And that made me uneasy. I'd heard nothing from my stepmother apart from a brief note a year ago. Neither she nor my father had written since their wedding and I seldom thought about either of them in case I should start weeping.

She was not a boy, she was a girl. She had great dark eyes and a smooth cap of fine fair hair and although the women exclaimed how beautiful she was, how bonny, how healthy, I knew I had failed. My husband was surprisingly kind considering how much he had wanted a son, kissing me tenderly. He gave me a necklace of tiny garnets to show his pleasure, a poor substitute for the rubies he'd planned to bestow on me if our baby had been a boy. My mother-in-law was brisk, saying I had done well but Richard would expect a son next time.

'Pay no attention,' said the dowager Lady Scrope, wiping my forehead with a cloth scented with rosewater. 'There will be other children. You are still young.'

'She shall be called Joan,' said my husband firmly when I asked if our daughter might be named for my mother. 'She is a Nevill child and will carry a Nevill name. I'm surprised you should ask. I thought you understood the importance of being a Nevill?' He frowned as if he couldn't understand how I could be so foolish as to imagine things would be different.

In the peace and quiet after his departure when there was nothing to be heard but the snuffling of my daughter in the cradle and the calling of skylarks from the high moors, there lingered a distinct aroma, not of rosewater but of failure. I thought of my mother who had given my father only one child and wondered if that would also be my fate, forever remembered as the Nevill bride who had failed in her duty to her husband.

In November, with the border quiet, the Nevills returned to London and my husband returned to my bed. Our little daughter travelled with us, swaddled tightly and cared for by a wet nurse and a girl who I was sure was too young and too clumsy to take charge of my beloved daughter. My tightly bound breasts ached and I felt bereft but as my mother-in-law explained with little sympathy, it was time for me to do my duty. This was why I had been chosen as a Nevill wife – to give my husband children, not to play at being a nursemaid. Any half-witted girl could rock a cradle or swaddle an infant but only a wedded wife would have the honour of bearing a Nevill heir.

My mother-in-law visited more regularly now there was a Nevill grandchild for her to admire and when Christmas came I noticed how my position was enhanced. I was moved higher up the table, seated in a more comfortable chair with softer cushions and given special mentions. I became "dear Alice" or "my dear daughter-in-law" as I sat quietly basking in her approval.

'You'll never guess what?' said Anne as she thrust her New Year's gift into my hands.

'Anne!'

At the sound of her mother's voice, Anne lowered her head, gave me a small bob and a grin and slid back to her appointed place. I smiled at my mother-in-law, remembering the days when I was newly married and frightened of her sharp tongue. She had not changed but I had. I was not longer just a wife, I was a mother, the mother of a Nevill daughter.

Cecily sat at her mother's left hand with a smirk on her face. She was nearly nine and growing into a slender golden-haired beauty. Unfortunately she was only too aware of her blossoming good looks and tended to the sin of vanity.

The dowager Lady Scrope leaned over and whispered in my ear. 'My father has bought the wardship and marriage of the York boy.'

I thought for a moment. As far as I knew there were no York boys, they were all dead: dead and buried.

'Which one?' I asked, curious as to who she meant.

'Young Richard. His mother was a Mortimer.'

Now I remembered. My cousin the earl of March, had sisters. The boy's mother must be one of them.

'And his father?'

'Your aunt, Lady Bromflete's, York stepson. Not the heir. The other one. He plotted against the late king and was beheaded as a traitor. The boy is his only son.'

112

'And lives under the shadow of his father's disgrace.'

'Not at all. I believe he has been raised in a good Lancastrian household.'

'Is he for you?' I said, hoping my father-in-law had at last bestirred himself and found a husband for Lady Margaret.

She smiled ruefully. 'I think not. The uncle died at Agincourt so the boy is duke of York. He will be for Cecily.'

'You are more deserving than Cecily,' I said, genuinely sad for the one true friend I had in the Nevill household.

'I doubt my stepmother would agree. She has worked hard to get grand marriages for her children. And what could be grander than this?'

I put my hand over my mouth and gave a little squeak. 'Mercy! Cecily will be a duchess. She will outrank us all and we'll never hear the end of it.'

The dowager Lady Scrope laughed. At the sound my mother-in-law looked over at us and frowned.

# 9

## SHROVETIDE 1424

In the midst of Shrovetide feasting, the hall in the bishop of Winchester's magnificent palace at Southwark was crowded with dozens of Beauforts and Nevills, all drinking, laughing and making merry. It was an unusual time to celebrate a wedding with forty days of denial and meatless dinners lying ahead, but that morning, my Beaufort cousin, Joan, had married the Scottish king, James. A truly remarkable triumph for the Beauforts.

'He was constrained in his choice,' remarked my mother-in-law with the air of a woman torn between joy at her niece's success and fury that her youngest daughter's marriage would not attract the same degree of awe.

I raised by eyebrows in surprise. 'Surely not.'

'My dear Alice, the Scottish king has been our prisoner since before you were born. Naturally if he wants his freedom he must marry where he is bid. Joan may think she is the wife of his choosing but she has deceived herself.'

I looked across the room to where the happy couple were engaged in conversation with Lord Humphrey and his wife and wondered if deception was not an integral part of a good marriage. We all had secrets, even me.

By late in the afternoon, Lord Humphrey and Duchess Jacqueline had left with their entourage, the dishes were cleared away, the elderly dowagers had drifted into the great parlour to nod over plates of sugared biscuits and goblets of sweet white wine, while the young people were gathered in knots to flirt, exchange gossip and make plans. The groom, whose consumption of wine had been liberal, had been borne away by Bishop Langley, leaving the bride in the care of her family.

'Dear God but I'm tired of weddings,' said Edmund, smiling into my eyes.

He took both my hands and in full view of everyone pulled me close.

'Dearest Alice.' He placed his lips on mine: firm, warm and oh so seductive.

I was surprised by the tug of a familiar feeling that I'd once identified as love.

"Why can I not marry Edmund?" I'd asked my mother. She was gentle but firm. "Because you are your father's only child, heiress to the Montagu lands and title, and Edmund, however pleasant a young man, is a fourth son and not for you."

Marriage was never mentioned again but feelings do not disappear simply because they are unacknowledged and my affection, as I wisely chose to call it, for my cousin, had continued for many years.

'Edmund,' I said, primly. 'I am a married woman.'

Across the room my husband was watching and I was unable to prevent a flush from rising into my cheeks.

'And does marriage agree with you, pretty cousin?'

The taste of him was sticky on my lips as I swallowed hard and brought my scattered thoughts to order. 'It does.'

Edmund leaned far too close for my comfort. 'Does he treat you well?' he murmured.

'Why would he not,' I replied. 'Richard Nevill is a good man.'

'Leave her alone, Edmund,' said Meg, giving her brother a sisterly pinch on the arm.

'I wonder where our worthy uncle is,' said Edmund searching the room for the bejewelled bulk of Bishop Beaufort.

'Planning your future, I'll wager,' said Meg. 'Because you, dear brother, are the only Beaufort available for him to meddle with now that he's got Jo married.'

'And one day you'll have your Courtenay heir,' I teased, reminding her of her nine-year-old betrothed.

Edmund sighed. 'D'you know, there are times I envy my brothers in their captivity.'

I smothered a smile. 'What about you Jo? How do you find marriage?'

'I wish he'd stop sending me verses,' Joan grumbled, smoothing the rich cream panels of her satin gown. 'Every day there's another one. Half of them I can't understand.'

'Oh happy the wife whose husband pens words to her beauty after the wedding day!' said Edmund with a sly glance at me.

'Not happy at all,' snapped his sister. 'All that business about the cultivation of wisdom and Mistress Fortune pinching his ear. I've never heard such nonsense.'

She reverted to pulling at the stitches of a tiny gold lion embroidered on her crimson jacket.

'People say he's got talent,' remarked her brother.

'He is a self-indulgent scribbler.'

'Why is she making such a fuss?' I whispered to Meg. 'Surely being a queen is every girl's dream.'

'James is being returned to Scotland. It has been agreed. He is leaving together with his English queen and Joan is *not* pleased. Has your husband not told you?'

'Yes, he has. Richard is escorting them north to Durham and I am to go with him.'

Meg looked closely at my face. 'Durham's not Scotland, you know.'

'I know that, but …'

'What?'

'I think he plans to take me to Middleham for the summer.'

'You *think*! Has he not told you?'

I shrugged. 'He tells me very little.'

'How odd. James tells Joan everything, even which birds sing outside his window.'

'And does Richard write you pretty verses, my Alice?' enquired Edmund with a look of total innocence on his face.

'The Nevills are not the kind of family who write verses,' I said coolly.

'A family of action not words, you mean. Stab a man through the heart rather than parley; steal a kiss rather than woo a girl honestly; and if all else fails and lust overcomes you, throw her over your saddle rather than ask her father's permission for marriage.'

'Is that some kind of play on words?' said Joan crossly. 'Because if so I don't understand it any more than I understand my husband's.'

Edmund laughed. 'Have no fear, your grace. Your Scottish subjects will make you welcome and speak beautifully in perfect English for your delight.'

'How much are they paying to get him back?' I asked, wondering if the sum was sufficient to pay the ransom for John and Thomas.'

'Thousands,' said Edmund. 'But the council said it wasn't enough; insisted they took Joan as well.'

'Beast!' said his sister giving him an un-queenly shove.

At that moment there was a small cough. I looked round to see one of the bishop's servants at my elbow.

'Bishop Beaufort awaits you in his private room, Lady Nevill.'

'Me?' I said in surprise.

'Yes, if you please, my lady.' The man gave a little bow and waited for me to make a move.

'What have you done?' hissed Meg.

'Nothing! I've no idea why he wants me.'

'I'd be careful if I were you,' murmured Edmund. 'Our uncle likes to make mischief.'

I followed the servant through one room into another and across a courtyard to the bishop's private apartments. It was a palace fit for a prince: every space beautifully decorated with painted walls and tiled floors. One room was lined with black-robed clerks engaged on the bishop's business and in another, three of the bishop's servants were making an inventory from a chest of some man's goods.

We climbed a staircase and walked along a wide gallery to a door where two liveried guards stood with halberds crossed as if expecting an enemy to attempt an entrance. They stood aside and I stepped into a room of such splendour I gave a little gasp. Edmund had once said his uncle lent money where there was gain for himself and here there was enough wealth to fund a small war.

Tall windows of translucent glass, costly tapestries, and polished boards covered with woven silk rugs and everywhere the gleam of silver.

The bishop sat behind a table of carved oak. I'd not seen him this close before but he was as I had imagined: heavy-set, a broad face with fleshy jowls and a calculating mouth much like my mother-in-law's. He wore his episcopal robes as if born to them, as if he went to his bed wearing them, even bathed in them. His hands were oddly pale, his fingers long and well-manicured with his bishop's amethyst ring gleaming on his right hand.

I dropped into a deep respectful curtsey.

He accepted my greeting with an incline of his head and a satisfied smile. 'Sit, Lady Nevill. Make yourself at ease.'

I murmured my thanks and perched on the edge of an elegant gilded chair.

'You must be wondering why I've summoned you, Lady Nevill.'

'I am yours to command, my lord bishop,' I said humbly, wishing I was with my cousins.

He nodded. 'Your husband, my sister's son, speaks well of you but, naturally, he is disappointed, Your marriage has not brought him the rewards he believed would be his or the benefits he was promised.'

'I was not to know, my lord.' I spoke quickly and almost tripped over the words. 'My father swore he would not take another wife.'

'It is not for a daughter to criticise, Lady Nevill,' the bishop said gravely. 'A daughter must honour her father.'

'No, my lord. Forgive me. I meant no disrespect.'

'What has happened is regrettable but the damage has been done. However it may be mitigated if you do your duty as a loyal wife. You would not wish to see your husband suffer.'

'No, my lord,' I murmured.

'I can help him, Lady Nevill. I have influence as I'm sure you are aware. I have many friends on the royal council, men who owe me favours, men who see it as in their best interests to promote my candidate when there is a difference of opinion on some matter. The council can often be swayed if it is made clear it is to their advantage. Do you understand?'

'Yes, my lord.'

'But if I am to help your husband, you too must play your part.'

'Anything, my lord. I will do anything to assist my husband.'

He smiled. 'Good. I have a small commission for you, nothing too arduous. It concerns the dowager Queen Katherine, mother of his grace, the king. She has been in deep mourning this past year which is only to be expected. My nephew's death was a great shock but one which, with God's help, she has borne bravely.'

I murmured how we had all grieved with her grace over the loss of King Henry.

The bishop touched the heavy gold cross he wore at his neck and briefly closed his eyes, his lips moving in prayer.

'Her grief must be set aside, Lady Nevill,' he said, his hooded lids lifting. 'She must think of her son, the little king. It is not right for the boy to see his mother forever in tears. It will induce in him a melancholic disposition which will not serve him well.'

'No, my lord.'

'So, Lady Nevill, as to your small commission. In the royal household her grace is amply served by many worthy women, from those who bear her company to those who care for the little king. But she is in many ways, alone. Her husband is dead, her father is dead and her mother does not visit – for which we must be grateful. She has left her family but has yet to make England her home. As a woman I'm sure you understand her predicament. She needs a friend, Lady Nevill, a true friend, and I think you are the woman to befriend her.'

'Me?' I squeaked in alarm. 'But, my lord, I am far beneath her. She is a king's daughter …'

'And a woman alone.'

By now my heart was racing at the thought of treating the queen dowager as a friend.

'She doesn't know me,' I protested feebly.

'All to the good. You carry no unpleasant reminders of the past, a past tainted by tragedy. You will be a breath of springtime; you will being her back to health and happiness.' His smile widened making him look almost fatherly. 'She is in great need of resurrection, Lady Nevill.'

'Surely her grace has no wish to befriend someone like me. I have no idea how she lives, what she does, how she behaves.'

The bishop's voice was gentle, almost soothing. 'Lady Nevill, her grace is a woman and a mother. *You* are a woman and a mother. What more is there to say. Are not all women sisters under the skin, handmaidens unto God and subject to His Holy Will.'

'So I have been taught, my lord.'

'Then you will do as I ask.'

Truly there was no possibility of refusal. One didn't refuse the bishop of Winchester when he gave you a commission; you accepted the burden with humility.

'Shall I live under her grace's roof?' I asked, thinking of my baby daughter and my husband.

'No, that will not be necessary. You are required merely to visit, to entertain her grace, make her laugh.'

Laugh! How could I make the king's mother laugh when her life was destroyed and could never be remade.

The bishop pulled a written document from the pile in front of him and perused the contents. 'At present her grace and the little king are at Kennington. Tomorrow she will receive the king and queen of Scotland prior to their departure. The following day I shall pay a visit. I propose to take you with me.'

'Oh, but I cannot.'

'Cannot?' He raised his eyebrows.

'Forgive me, my lord, but I am to accompany my husband to Durham. He is to travel with King James and my cousin on their way north to the border.'

He waved his hand. 'Do not concern yourself. I have spoken with Sir Richard. He is content for you to remain here at my disposal. He is full of gratitude at this mark of the queen dowager's favour towards his wife.'

I smiled shyly as if overcome with the honour whereas inwardly I was quaking with fear.

'And Lady Nevill.'

'Yes, my lord.'

'I trust you have made your greetings to your kinsman, the earl of March.'

I blinked in surprise at his mention of my Mortimer cousin. In the hall, the earl had given a perfunctory brush with his lips to my cheek but his eyes and his attention were elsewhere.

'Yes, my lord, I have.'

'Then all is well. Before the year is out the earl will leave our shores for Ireland. The council wishes – how shall I put it – they wish to be rid of him. He is a foolish young man and has greatly alarmed others with the size of his retinue. He lodges here within my palace. I could have saved him but, you understand, I chose not to. So Ireland it is. A most unpleasant place: a bog-ridden rat hole. Half-tamed savages and no company for a civilised man.'

I had no idea why he was telling me this except to demonstrate the extent of his power. With a wave of his hand he could have saved my cousin from his unenviable fate but had declined.

He sat where the candlelight framed his head in a golden halo, watching me carefully.

'It is never wise to offend those who have power over you, Lady Nevill. I hope you understand.'

'I should be careful if I were you,' said Eleanor from her position perched on top of one of my chests. I'd sent her a note telling her my news and she had come rushing over to The Erber to give me advice.

'Of what?' I said, taking my blue brocade gown from the fumbling fingers of one of the maids and showing her how to fold it properly. 'Like that, and don't forget to layer everything with lavender.'

'Of the bishop.'

'Why? He is my mother-in-law's brother. He has our best interests at heart.'

'You're such a child, Alice. D'you know why the earl of March was sent to Ireland?'

I picked up two fur-trimmed jackets trying to decide which one to wear the next day.

'Something to do with the size of his retinue.'

'Is that what the bishop told you?' She took the jackets out of my hands, threw one to my maid and handed the other back to me. 'That one. Now, listen to me. One of the earl's kinsmen is to hang next week. It was a plot. The man was to kill Bishop Beaufort and Lord Humphrey, steal the bishop's money and make a king of the earl of March.'

I gasped. 'My cousin would not involve himself in a treasonous plot.'

'How would you know? How does a woman know anything about a man?'

'My husband has said nothing.'

'Perhaps he knows nothing. Understand this, Alice. If the bishop has asked you to befriend the queen dowager you can be certain it is more to his advantage than to anyone else. He is a devious man.'

'He frightens me.'

'Good! If he frightens you, you will take care.'


The lone figure waiting on the landing pier at the bishop's palace, staring moodily into the muddy shallows, was Edmund.

'What are you doing here?' I asked as he extended his hand and helped me out of the boat.

'Playing at being nursemaid.'

'I don't need a nursemaid,' I said, shaking the last drops of water off my cloak.

'No, but my uncle, the bishop, does.'

I giggled. This was an old joke According to Edmund, when the bishop was a youthful scholar he'd got a young woman with child and had been paying ever since for the child's upbringing. It was a scurrilous story and probably untrue but as Eleanor said, with men you never knew.

Edmund tucked my hand into the familiar crook of his arm and together we wandered slowly back along the pier.

'Are you coming to Kennington?' I asked.

'I am. You don't get to have all the fun.'

I frowned. 'This isn't fun, Edmund; it's work. Your uncle has given me a commission.'

'And he has ordered me to keep an eye on you. I am to help you bring the bloom back into the cheeks of the lovely Katherine.'

I gave him a quick nudge. 'You'd better not speak of her like that in front of your uncle.'

He shrugged. 'It's odd. He never bothered with me before. I was the youngest son, unworthy of his notice but now, with Hal dead and John and Thomas stuck in a French prison, everything has changed. He took a candle and looked into my face. I saw him wondering what use I might be to him.'

'Well, candle or no, if you're coming to Kennington you can be of use to me because, I tell you, I'm frightened out of my wits. I have no idea what I should say.'

'Don't concern yourself,' he laughed. 'My uncle will do the talking. Just be your usual pretty self. I must say, Alice, motherhood suits you. You've a bloom you never had before. Is Richard pleased with his daughter?'

'He'd have preferred a son,' I said lightly.

At that moment, as if summoned, a procession appeared from within the shadows of an arched entrance to the lower buildings of the palace. Bishop Beaufort walked slowly down the path towards us dispensing blessings to those who crowded the foreshore in the hope of seeing him. Edmund bowed and I sank down, waiting for the bishop's servants to help him aboard the barge. He sat on an elevated throne beneath a golden canopy while Edmund and I sat quietly on hard wooden benches well out of his hearing.

'The best that money can buy,' whispered Edmund.

The gilded barge with its intricate carving was more magnificent than any I'd seen apart from the great royal barge and as we travelled the short distance to Kennington with the bishop's standard fluttering on the prow, I thought how pleasant it must be to have both wealth and power. On the Southwark shore people cheered as we passed but from the wharfs and quaysides of Dowgate there was no cheering.

'The city is Humphrey's fiefdom,' whispered Edmund. 'The Londoners love him and have no time for my uncle.'

A foul smelling effluent from the mayor's new city latrines at Vintry was washing out with the tide but thankfully the oarsmen kept close to the opposite shore.

'It's no worse than the privy pit at Bisham,' laughed Edmund as I screwed up my face. 'Pinch your nose and you won't even know it's there.'

# 10

## KENNINGTON 1424

When my great-grandmother, Princess Joan, was alive, the royal manor of Kennington had a reputation as a place of unrivalled happiness. Processions of mummers and minstrels from the city came dancing across the bridge with their pipes and tabors to perform for the royal bride and each evening there was a new and extravagant entertainment. There were orchards and vineyards and wonderful gardens, planted for her delight, every inch designed with his wife in mind by her second husband – or was it her third? My mother was rather vague about the number of my great-grandmother's marriages. Each time she retold the tale of the beautiful Joan of Kent, particulars changed, details were altered and aspects transformed until the story became so muddled I stopped trying to make sense of anything. All I knew was that Kennington had been one of the princess's favourite residences.

The approach from the river led us past a trellised walk and a series of tiny arbours with turf benches where a lady might take her ease. A gap in a yew hedge offered a glimpse of pebbled paths and a white marble fountain bowl surrounded by the wintery remains of a bed of herbs. In summer the terraced banks would be ablaze with flowers and instead of leafless trees there'd be greenery. But today a sense of sadness hung in the air, a sadness which grew steadily more intense the closer we came to the high walls and silent courts of the palace.

We were greeted by Sir Robert Babthorp, steward of the royal household, who escorted us through a succession of lofty chambers to a private room where the widowed Queen Katherine was waiting. She appeared diminished, no longer the radiant wife and mother of the Windsor celebrations, just a tiny figure surrounded by green velvet cushions. I could see at once that she'd been weeping. There was a telltale puffiness beneath her eyes and a slight reddening of her eyelids. But her smile was composed and I doubted if either the bishop or Edmund saw anything amiss. Women were far more noticing of other women despite what men might believe.

The queen dowager exchanged formal greetings with the bishop, then it was my turn to be presented. I dropped into the deepest curtsey I could manage hoping my shaking knees would not betray me and when I rose up she was smiling.

'Alice, Lady Nevill, wife of my nephew Sir Richard Nevill whom your grace will have met yesterday,' said the bishop in the oily tones he used when speaking to women. Edmund said his uncle regarded all women as less able to understand the complex utterances of men and therefore in need of especial soothing. 'Lady Alice has been most anxious to meet your grace.'

I was immediately stricken with panic and afterwards had no recollection of what I said or what the queen dowager replied. Fortunately, before I could make a complete fool of myself, I was drawn discreetly backwards to allow Edmund to be presented.

'I'm well used to royal dowagers,' he had confided to me on the barge when I'd admitted to being nervous. 'I used to go with my uncle to visit King Harry's stepmother, Joanna, in her prison at Leeds. She was very dull but I put myself out to be charming.'

I watched with envy as he charmed the queen dowager but Edmund was an adept at weaving webs with charming pleasantries; he always had been.

The bishop glossed over any awkwardness which might have arisen by praising the royal household and asking if the little king was at his lessons.

'My lord bishop,' said the queen dowager with a sliver of pride in her voice. 'You will be amazed at his progress. Mistress Astley declares his *Pater Noster* is a wonder of clarity. And he clamours for more. She says she has never seen a child so eager to embrace God's teachings. I believe he has a true gift for piety.'

'Like his father, may God have mercy on his soul,' said the bishop reverently.

'Are we to see his grace?' enquired Edmund.

As the queen dowager turned, her face lit up. She truly loved this child. I could tell. I understood what the bishop meant when he told me we were both women and both mothers. I recognised the mother in Katherine even if I felt no communion with the queen.

He came in like a child dragged away from a favourite game, frowning at those responsible for the interruption. He was a tall child for two years old, well-formed with a solemn expression. But if I'd expected a miniature copy of his father I was to be disappointed. Except for the burnished copper of his hair, little Henry was in every way his mother's child.

129

The nursemaid, who I assumed was Mistress Astley, let go of the boy's hand and gave him an almost imperceptible push on the shoulder. He took two steps forward and said in a clear high treble, 'Gweetings, my lord bishop.' He glanced at Mistress Astley who gave a small nod of approval.

Bishop Beaufort removed his hat and knelt down, bare-headed, in front of his king. The child put out a small white hand which wavered slightly as if he had forgotten its purpose, but the bishop placed his own large hand underneath and lowered his head to kiss the child's fingers.

'Your grace,' he murmured.

The child withdrew his hand and patted the bishop's head.

'Gwey,' he said after some thought.

I could sense Edmund grinning at my side.

'Indeed, your grace,' said the bishop. 'Doing God's work gives a man grey hairs before his time and I have laboured long and hard for the Almighty and for His blessed servant, the king of England.'

The child' eyes widened. 'Henwy is king.'

'King of England and King of France, your grace.'

'Fwance?'

'France is your other kingdom; across the Narrow Sea.'

'He is yet to learn the parts of his kingdom,' said the queen dowager apologetically. 'He is still very young.'

'And yet to form his words correctly,' remarked the bishop. 'I trust his nursemaid corrects him. A king must learn to speak clearly no matter that he is a child.'

I glanced at the queen dowager and sensed her desire

to sweep her son into her arms. Her lips trembled and her body quivered like a leveret hidden amongst summer grasses. Edmund must have noticed because he asked if he might speak with the king, if her grace would permit. Her gratitude was palpable.

Edmund knelt and the child eyed him warily. This was someone he didn't know, an intruder into his small world. The bishop was familiar if not loved but the little king wasn't sure about Edmund. Then to my surprise, before anyone moved, he began to laugh. It was a delightful sound coming from so serious a child. He put out his fingers and touched Edmund's face.

'More,' said the child.

Mistress Astley moved forward but was checked by the bishop's warning hand.

'You approve of my nephew, Edmund, your grace?'

'Come wiv Henwy.'

'I think it is time his grace returned to the nursery, Mistress Astley,' said the queen dowager, anxious for her little son and aware of the ever-present need to protect him.

The nursemaid bent and whispered something into the child's ear. He eyed his mother and made her a wobbly bow. Unable to hold on to her reserve a moment longer, the queen dowager swooped down, placed her fingers on her son's velvet sleeve and planted a kiss on each fat little cheek. Henry the king wiped away the kisses with his hand and turned to his nursemaid.

'What did you do?' I whispered to Edmund as the slow procession of child and nursemaids disappeared through the doorway to the king's apartments.

'This,' he said, giving me a huge wink.

I felt a tremendous urge to giggle but, aware of the bishop's watchful eyes, managed to keep my face still.

In the end it was a happy visit. We ate a private dinner with the senior men of the household where the bishop talked business with Sir Robert, and Edmund entertained the widowed Queen Katherine to a catalogue of amusing stories while I sat marvelling at how my life had come to this. Only three years ago I had sat on the lower benches at the coronation feast and admired the distant figure of Queen Katherine, never imagining that one day I would sit at her table.

Once the last dish was cleared away there was a little music and then the queen dowager invited me to accompany her.

'My women say it is too cold to be outside,' she said, 'but we could walk in the cloisters. It is peaceful and one of my favourite places.'

In the chill air of the cloisters our breath streamed out in clouds of thin white mist. The winter sun which gilded the walls and little turrets of Kennington had failed to reach into the depths of this courtyard where the air was cold and the low box hedges touched with frost. I was thankful I had worn my blue jacket with the fur trimming which Eleanor had selected and had also brought my warmest cloak.

Once I recovered from my terror of saying the wrong words, I found the queen dowager an easy companion. She asked about my daughter and spoke to me of her pride in her son but beneath everything I sensed a layer of sorrow.

Her days rested on a bed of tears and unlike the dowager Lady Scrope there would be little hope of another husband to enrich her life.

'Maître Beaufort,' she said, pronouncing Edmund's name the French way which made him sound very exotic. 'The bishop tells me the young man is his nephew.'

'Yes, your grace. Master Beaufort's father was the earl of Somerset. He died many years ago.'

'Yet Maître Beaufort carries no title.'

'No, your grace. He was not the heir. His brother John has the earldom.'

'Ah yes. I had forgotten.' She shook her head. 'Baugé where my husband's brother died. They told me Somerset was taken prisoner. Is he freed?'

'No, your grace. I believe both he and his brother, Thomas, are still held by your grace's brother.'

Doubtless it was painful for her to think of her brother pretending to be the king of France which of course he was not. I wondered if I should say something or if I should wait for her to speak. It was difficult to know as nobody had told me what was polite when dealing with a woman like the queen dowager.

'Maître Beaufort is your cousin?' she said just when I thought she had tired of me as a companion.

'Yes, your grace,' I said eagerly. 'Our mothers were sisters. He and I shared a nursery when we were children. He is like a brother to me.'

'You have no brothers of your own?'

'No, your grace. I have neither brothers nor sisters.'

She wiped away what might have been a tear and I saw her gloved hand move to the jewelled clasp at her neck.

'I pray for my brother,' she murmured. 'I pray that he may be returned to God's forgiveness.'

I could hardly say that murder was beyond forgiveness. Everyone knew the dauphin had ordered the killing of the old duke of Burgundy. Even the queen dowager's mother had disowned her son as a peace-breaker and cold-blooded killer. With no other royal sons left, the half-mad king of France and his nephew, the young and grieving Philip of Burgundy, had agreed that the dauphin should be disinherited and the crown given to the English king who would marry the French king's daughter. It was the intransigence of Katherine's brother which had plunged France into turmoil when there could have been everlasting peace under the reign of the one true king. He was no better than those men whose heads decorate the gatehouse of London's bridge but I thought it unwise to say so.

When we reached the archway leading out of the cloisters she turned, gave a small sad smile and asked if I would visit again. It sounded less like politeness, more a plea for company.

'I should be honoured,' I murmured.

'And I should be pleased.'

# 11

Next day I took a boat upriver to the peaceful convent at Syon where my Aunt Margaret lived in her widowhood. The years she had spent in Normandy with her second husband, the duke of Clarence, must have given her an intimate knowledge of Queen Katherine. She was the only person I knew who could give me good advice.

The room where my aunt received me was small with plain whitewashed walls and the tiniest of fires. Apart from a display of books, richly illuminated and bound in the softest of leather, there was nothing here to lighten the austere surroundings. The place did not look much like a dowager duchess's residence, more like a convent cell. But this was what she had chosen and perhaps after a lifetime of luxury she craved a simple life.

'You think she should remarry?' she asked with a wry smile.

'I think she is lonely.'

'That is possible.'

'Should not all widows remarry if they can?'

'You think *I* should take another husband? Would you have me be like my sister who looks set to end up with a grocer.'

I grinned. Months of seclusion away from the world had not blunted my aunt's sharp sense of humour and certainly Lady Bromflete's rapid descent through four husbands had been spectacular.

'I think you have had enough of marriage and seek a higher purpose.'

'You are right. Here at Syon I have time to study and talk with the brothers. I find it necessary to contemplate my end. I have lost two husbands who cared for me in their different ways and I did my duty by both of them but now I believe I better serve God's purpose in prayer than by using my talents to satisfy some little man's self-importance. And having once been a duchess, I have no desire to become a grocer's wife.'

'My friend, the dowager Lady Scrope believes there is no life for a woman other than in marriage.'

'Lady Scrope? Is she is young?'

'A little older than my husband.'

'Then certainly she should remarry.'

'She has been four years without a husband. Her father does nothing for her.'

'Then she should find a husband for herself.'

I laughed at the idea of the dowager Lady Scrope trawling through London looking for a suitable husband.

'But not a grocer.'

My aunt laughed. 'I think she might aim a little higher.'

'And what of the queen dowager?'

'Ah yes, poor Katherine. Such a tragic life. Hungry for love and God knows she got little enough of that from her mother. Isabeau's hands were steeped in blood and what she hadn't stolen from the royal treasury to give to her lovers she used to enrich herself. But Harry needed her help.'

It was as the bishop had said when he'd thanked God that the queen dowager, Isabeau, had not come visiting: a poisonous woman and a poor mother.

'Katherine deserved better,' sighed my aunt. 'She imagined Harry in love with her. She told me he sent horns and pipes to be played for her at sunset, called her his angel, gave her gifts of jewels and caged nightingales. She believed this was a sign of his desire but he'd have taken her whatever. It wasn't her he wanted but the keys to the kingdom of France.'

'I thought he loved her,' I said simply.

'So did she but he was a cold man and perhaps did not live long enough to disabuse her of her folly.'

'Was it folly?'

'I think so. Harry was not an attentive bridegroom. The morning after their wedding, instead of the joyful celebration proposed by the Burgundians, he dragged her off to war, to Sens and Montereau and all the way to Melun. She spent her days huddled with her women in a pavilion listening to the distant sound of cannon fire and her nights in the arms of a man whose greatest joy came not from her but from the bloody slaughter of his enemies. Harry saw himself as God's own soldier and Katherine as a necessary tool of war.'

'She must have thought it odd.'

'She told me his love for her was too violent for them to be apart but in truth he was using her to bring her treacherous countrymen to heel. What Frenchman would dare take up arms against his anointed king? And if the *roi tres-chrétien* was rolling mad and unfit to be put on display, at least Harry had the daughter. Katherine would do for him what her father could not.

I shivered at the thought of sleeping with a man fresh from the battlefield, marked with gore from the men he'd killed. At least the castle at Middleham was a peaceful place and Richard Nevill never involved me in his wars with the Percys and the little turd at Raby. Any skirmishes were entirely his own affair, nothing to do with me.

'Now,' said my aunt, settling back in her hard wooden chair. 'I have told you about Katherine, you must tell me about your daughter.'

Five days later to my profound discomfort I found myself making my way to the royal palace at Eltham, again in the company of Bishop Beaufort and my cousin, Edmund. Knowing what awaited us, I was more nervous this time than when we'd travelled upriver to Kennington on the bishop's barge.

Eltham was the favoured residence of the little king's grandfather, so the bishop informed us as we rode along the country lanes from Greenwich – eminently suitable for the queen dowager and the child.

'A joyful place,' he remarked to Edmund. 'Excellent hunting.'

'Eel stew today, Uncle,' grinned Edmund as we clattered across the bridge. 'Feasting's over. Forty days of carp and tench await us without so much as a whiff of roasted venison.'

The bishop didn't smile but neither did he chastise Edmund for lack of seriousness. Maybe he'd developed a fondness for my disrespectful cousin.

The queen dowager was waiting for us, a high spot of colour on each cheek and a welcoming smile on her lips.

'Lady Nevill,' she said with genuine warmth. 'I have been eager to see you again.'

It was only a week since we'd last met so I was taken aback by her enthusiasm. Perhaps the bishop was right and she truly *was* lonely.

'And you have brought Maître Beaufort with you. *Quelle plaisir!*'

This was a different Katherine from the sad widow of Kennington. The fur trimming at her neck disclosed a tantalising glimpse of black kirtle and her richly patterned gown was further enhanced by discreet panels of deep crimson brocade. Here at Eltham, despite the rigours of Lent, she glowed.

She paid great attention to the bishop's lengthy address but when he consulted his beads, her eyes slid sideways to where I stood beside Edmund. Her pale hands were crossed at her throat and I noticed a slight tremor when the bishop spoke of her late husband.

After exhortating Sir Robert Babcock to see that the household make proper preparations for the holy days of Easter, the bishop asked for a private conversation with the queen dowager. In a great swirl of costly cloth and bowing heads, they disappeared into a private chamber leaving Edmund and I to amuse ourselves.

'Well?' he said, taking my arm and leading me to one of the window embrasures where there was a low padded seat.

'Well what?'

'We are making progress.'

I removed his fingers from my sleeve and sat down.

'You mean *I* am making progress. This has nothing to do with you, Edmund. The bishop gave this commission to me.'

He picked up my hand and held it tightly. 'Don't you enjoy my company, dearest cousin. I know Katherine does.'

'Edmund, hush! Someone will hear you. Have you no manners? You mustn't talk about her like that, it's not right. She's the queen dowager and deserves your respect. I'm surprised your uncle brought you. If I was him I'd have left you at Southwark.'

He slid his other hand up my arm. 'I fear it will be a long time before you're a bishop, Alice. Your thoughts alone would make such an elevation impossible.'

'You know nothing of my thoughts.'

A slow smile spread across his face. 'D'you remember the den we made in Quarry Wood?'

'Yes,' I said shortly.

'I thought perhaps you'd forgotten.'

He had caught me out by mentioning the woods at Bisham and the time when we were young and he was the only boy I wanted.

'I am a grown woman and don't care to recall the past.'

'Liar!'

I remembered that day in the woods: the carefully constructed hiding place of bracken and fallen branches, the feel of his bare skin on mine, the soft touch of his lips, the foetid warmth and an awareness that our friendship was changing into something dark and dangerous. I had scrambled up from the carpet of leaves and run home to my governess. And when I saw him at supper, I had blushed.

I opened my eyes as wide as I could and stared him straight in the face as if he was a low-born menial. 'I would be obliged if you'd let go of my hand, Master Beaufort.'

With his gaze fixed on mine, he slowly raised my hand to his lips, turned it over and planted a soft kiss on the palm. He folded my fingers carefully over the kiss then placed my hand gently in my lap. My eyes grew hazy with an unexpected rush of desire.

'Please, don't.' I whispered, trying not to think of the weakness of my defence against my cousin's trespass. It was a week since Richard Nevill had left for the North and I felt his absence every night in the coldness of my bed.

We visited Eltham three times more before Easter and on each occasion I felt myself drawn closer to Katherine. It was as if she was the sister I'd longed for, the sister I'd never had. We walked, we talked, we sewed and we prayed together, but it was not until the third visit that she began to confide in me.

A sun the colour of buttermilk lurked shyly behind the clouds but the air was warm enough for us to walk across the bridge to the private gardens. Katherine placed her foot on the first of the wooden planks and hesitated.

'I am frightened,' she said quietly.

I looked around in alarm but we were quite alone. Apart from a trail of women a dozen paces behind us and the distant men who kept an eye on the queen dowager whenever she stepped outside the confines of the palace, there was no-one.

'You are perfectly safe, your grace,' I said. The walls of Eltham are well-guarded. Besides, who would want to harm you?'

She smiled sadly. 'Yes. England is a peaceful place. Here you have no wars, your great men do not tear each other apart and your people fear God and love their king. Harry told me it was so.'

She'd not once called him Harry when we were alone. I knew a wall had been breached bringing us closer together.

'You have no need to be afraid,' I said quietly.

She stopped and turned to me, her huge dark eyes luminous with unshed tears. 'They are going to take him away from me.'

For a terrible moment I thought someone had dug up her dead husband's body and hidden it in her bedchamber. Then, chiding myself for such foolishness I realised what she meant.'

'I do not think they can do that, your grace. You are his mother.'

She gave a nervous laugh. 'They mistrust me. They think me unfit.'

'You are not unfit. You are a good mother.'

'The council are angry because he cannot speak clearly and the bishop says he is to have a governess.'

So this was the outcome of the bishop's visit to Kennington – a governess for Katherine's son. He would soon be three years old so perhaps it was time. It was not as if he had a father to give him good guidance.

'I'm sure they are acting in the king's best interests, your grace,' I said gently. 'The council would not do otherwise.'

'But he is such a little boy. This woman, this Mistress Butler, she is to be given the right to chastise my son. She will beat him and he is only a baby.'

By now tears were running down her cheeks. I longed to take her in my arms the way I would a friend but it was not for me to determine the limits of our closeness.

'Your grace,' I began.

She grasped my sleeve and pressed herself against me. 'Katrine,' she whispered. 'Call me Katrine. It is the name he gave me and there is no-one left who remembers. I've tried to be good, I've tried to be strong but it is such a long time to wait.'

'To wait for what, your grace?'

'For death.' She smiled though her tears. 'I want to lie with him again, to feel his body next to mine.'

'Forgive me your grace, but it is not for any of us to choose the hour or the day. God determines our earthly span.'

She raised her face to mine. 'I was his Katrine.'

Bishop Beaufort had been right; she *was* a woman alone.

I patted her shoulder awkwardly and placed my other hand on hers. I felt most uncomfortable clasping the queen dowager in such an intimate way but she clung to me like a child clings to its mother.

'They will not take the king away from you, your ... Katrine. Not yet. When he's older, when he is seven years of age, but not yet. And I do not think Mistress Butler will beat him. He's too sweet a child for that. She will be charmed by him as we all are.'

She sniffed, disentangled herself and attempted to wipe traces of tears from her cheeks. Her hands were narrow and her fingers slender like those of a royal lady but she rubbed her face in the way of a grubby child trying to rid herself of tell-tale smudges of dirt.

'You are kind,' she whispered.

It was easy to be kind to a woman like Katherine who, with a little care, blossomed like a lily.

I thought of how things were done at The Erber, with my own child, my little Joan. Perhaps in France, in royal palaces, children were raised differently, possibly kept for years at a mother's knee but Katherine would have to learn our ways.

'If the late king, your husband, had lived he would have the ordering of your son,' I said slowly. 'This is no different. The council are not cruel men, they have the king's best interests at heart. They want what is good for him. As mothers we long to keep our children close but it is our duty to see they are prepared to take the place in the world that God has ordained for them.'

'Your cousin, Maître Beaufort says he will teach him to wrestle this summer,' she said, with a valiant attempt to smile.

I laughed. 'The king will enjoy that. Edmund loved wrestling when he was a small boy.'

'The bishop would prefer him to be at his prayers,' she said doubtfully.

'The bishop is not his mother. Nor, I believe, is he in charge of his education.'

'Harry's brother, Lord Humphrey, says he will give my son a wooden sword.'

'And a pony?'

'Oh no! Not a pony. He might fall.'

This child was so precious I could imagine him stifled, wrapped in velvet rugs to keep him safe. He would be kept forever on his knees or at his lessons, hovered over by tutors and priests, denied the rough and tumble of a childhood which had made men of my boy cousins. For if this royal child died, God forbid that he should, there would be no-one else but the duke of Bedford and Lord Humphrey to keep the country together and that thought did not bear thinking about.

We walked across the bridge into a trellised walk but with spring a long way off and no sign of budding leaves, the carefully clipped branches were bare.

'Do you miss your husband, Lady Nevill? When he is absent?'

I thought of how on that first visit to Eltham Edmund's closeness had made me tremble simply because I was without Richard. 'Yes, your grace. I do.'

She sighed. 'I too miss my husband. We were together such a little time and the winter of my grief stretches out into an eternity.'

I hesitated to say anything in case she began weeping again. It would be two years this summer since she became a widow and there were days when she seemed consumed by her loss.

'I fear I am sinful,' said Katherine softly.

'No, your grace,' I replied stoutly. 'That would be impossible. Why would you think it?'

'Ah, Lady Alice. You would champion my thoughts even when you do not know them.'

I bent my head and bit my lip but this time the words came straight from my heart with no calculation. 'Your grace, Katrine, you were a great queen and you are a wonderful mother to your child. I am certain your thoughts are perfect in every way.'

She smiled but her eyes were sorrowful. 'You sound like my chaplain.'

We walked on, no longer in close proximity, no longer

Katrine and Alice who shared intimate secrets, but the dowager Queen Katherine and her companion, Lady Nevill who watched their words lest they were overheard and misconstrued by others.

There was no-one to turn to but my aunt and as soon as we returned to London I took a boat upriver to Syon.

'She fears she is sinful which is why I've come to you. Do you think it possible she has sinned? She was talking of her husband and became very distressed.'

My aunt twitched her mouth in a half-smile. 'There are a dozen ways a woman can sin but for a widow there is a particular sin. You are a married woman, Alice. You should understand.'

'But she does nothing which would lure her into sin. She leads a blameless life, caring for her child.'

'Oh Alice! Think! You know what marriage entails. A man does not have to love a woman to satisfy her carnal needs and I imagine a forceful man like Harry made Katherine yearn for conjugal closeness, a closeness of which she has been cruelly deprived. She is emerging from her grief and is doubtless aware that the longings she has are wrong but she has neither the means to satisfy them nor the courage to take up a penance.'

I knew a great deal about conjugal closeness but my aunt was slyly suggesting that Katherine was carnal by nature.

'You think her sinfulness that of thought not deed?'

'A wrongful act conceived in her heart is a sin.'

'I cannot believe anything bad of her.'

'She will be carefully supervised. No man will be

146

allowed close to her, not while she has the child in her care. The council will have surrounded her by those loyal to Harry's memory. No man would dare touch her even if she made an invitation.'

'Her household is very small. It consists mostly of the little king's nursemaids.'

My aunt laughed. 'No wonder she frets.'

'What can I do? The bishop has given me this commission and to be truthful I am frightened.'

She patted my knee in the way my mother did when I was small. 'Be a friend, that is all you can do. If Katherine has lustful thoughts there's little to be done but occupy her so that her mind does not fall into sin. You might suggest a penitential scourge. I've met women who achieve great relief from self-mortification.'

I shuddered at the idea of Katherine's smooth pale skin torn and bleeding. It was a horrible thought and I put it straight out of my mind.


The days grew warmer and Richard Nevill, returned from the North with stories of excited receptions by the Scots for their king and his English queen. With luck, he said, the peace accord would hold and we'd no longer need to watch our backs. We could concentrate our efforts on completing the late king's vision of God's purpose for a true union of the two kingdoms of England and France.

I was pleased to see him and surprised at the warmth of our reunion.

'I think we should visit our properties in the South this summer,' he said, running his finger under the edge of my embroidered nightcap. 'Would you like that?'

147

I could smell the rosewater on my neck and wondered if I had used too much. Eleanor said the whores at Southwark practically bathed in it. Did Richard Nevill notice my careful preparations or how I shivered as he began to untie the ribbons and release my hair? With the cap laid aside he carefully kissed my forehead, my eyelids, my cheeks and my lips. I had been told that what passed between us was duty but it felt more like Heaven and I didn't want him to stop.

'Yes,' I whispered into the warmth of his mouth. 'Yes please.'

I wasn't sure which I was agreeing to and which I wanted more – the promise of a summer without visiting the gloomy stronghold of Middleham where my mother-in-law reigned supreme or the solid weight of my husband's body on mine. I was swimming in a pool of golden sunlight with warm water lapping at my shoulders and hoping the dream would never end.

# 12

## ELEANOR 1424

Bishop Beaufort excused me from my duties for the summer. He said the queen dowager would not expect me to wait upon her when my presence was required in the country. It was well-known that the Nevills journeyed to Middleham every year once the roads were clear, and there were times, he slyly suggested with a joining together of his long pale fingers and a lowering of his powerful voice, when the needs of a husband must come first. But if it should so happen that I found myself near the royal palaces then I was most welcome to arrange a private visit, provided of course I kept him informed. I was not to go without his permission.

But my summer was not spent at Middleham and I found time between the inspection of our Hampshire manors and a lengthy expedition into the West Country to pay two short visits to Katherine. As the bishop had instructed, I informed him of my intentions and each time found I was accompanied by my cousin.

'Is Edmund Beaufort also charged with befriending the queen dowager?' said my husband sourly as he toyed with his food the day following my second visit.

'Your uncle, the bishop, insists I cannot go alone,' I said apologetically.

'He thinks you feeble?'

'He is careful.'

'What's he up to?' Richard Nevill picked up his cup and peered into the depths as if seeking an answer to his question.

'He says my visits are to your advantage.'

'Not my uncle – Edmund! He sniffs around you like a mange-ridden dog with an itch.'

'Edmund Beaufort is my cousin, my lord.'

'And mine! But even a cousin can play you false as you should know, my lady. He is not to be trusted and I don't like you being in his company.'

Although my husband's word was law in our house, the bishop was more powerful still and could command me how he liked so having said his piece, Richard Nevill left me alone. He didn't come to my bed and at dinner made a great show of ignoring me which made me feel extremely foolish. The young women in my chamber noticed his neglect and wondered in hushed voices what I had done. Surely a husband should be pleased with a wife who was welcome in the household of the little king and his mother? Why would her husband not visit her? Their insinuations were hard to bear but I had no answer.

It was unpleasant being at odds with my husband so I worked hard to please him and at some point on our journey he stopped sulking. As we rode together through the soft mists of Somerset with the morning sun warming our backs and the sound of birdsong echoing amongst the trees, I even dared to believe he truly cared for me. He liked me well enough, I knew that, but there was none of the tenderness I had expected in marriage. When he was mellow he would invite me to sit with him and would talk of his plans for our manors, showing some pleasure in my company but mostly he ignored my presence preferring to talk business with our hosts.

My father had been generous in the matter of my dowry and from the number of places we stopped at I guessed the Nevill settlement had also been substantial. It seemed my husband and I were rich landowners which was odd because no-one had told me. As he was not his father's heir I had expected Richard Nevill to be favoured with a few of his father's lesser properties but there was no denying the size and wealth of the manors we visited.

We returned to London as the last of the harvest was being brought in. The barns were full, the fields bare of crops and the orchards stripped of every last piece of fruit. As we crossed the bridge from Southwark towards the welcome sight of London's smoking chimneys, we found our way blocked by an apple cart. Shopkeepers were shouting noisy protests and while the carter's eyes were elsewhere a swarm of small boys had climbed on the cart intent on stealing his produce.

'The city gets worse each year,' remarked my husband as we pushed our way through the crowd. 'Perhaps we should think of building outside the walls. I hear Lord Humphrey has his eye on the duke of Exeter's house at Greenwich.'

'Why would the duke of Exeter give up his house?'

'He is sick. If he dies Lord Humphrey will claim the house as his.'

'I thought Lord Humphrey had plans to go overseas?'

My husband laughed. 'He does and my uncle, the bishop, is more than a little content. With Lord Humphrey away, he sees his way clear to rule the council. He's been made chancellor and who can benefit from that but us?'

My husband didn't wait at The Erber to greet his baby daughter or his mother but left straightaway for Westminster. It was my duty to enthuse over little Joan's progress and to make my mother-in-law welcome.

'The duke of Bedford and your father have won a tremendous victory, Alice,' she said, kissing me on both cheeks and for once failing to cast her eyes around the room to check on the proper workings of my household. 'The rebel French and the earl of Buchan's army have been defeated.'

'Hardly anyone survived,' remarked Lady Percy, who had returned from the North with her husband and was today visiting her mother. 'Buchan was butchered. The report says it was a killing field, just like Agincourt.'

'Ten thousand dead,' whispered the dowager Lady Scrope as if afraid the bodies might rise from the ground and crawl into my chamber, dripping blood and crying out for their mothers.

'Hacked to pieces,' chirped Cecily who harboured no such fears.

'How would you know?' hissed Anne. 'You weren't there.'

'The duke of Bedford wore a blue velvet robe emblazoned with the red cross of St George within the white cross of St Michael,' purred my mother-in-law happily. 'A message to the man who calls himself *le roi tres Chrétien* but is too much of a coward to lead his men into battle. Two saints, two kingdoms. What could be clearer?'

'It is revenge for Baugé,' announced Lady Percy.

'And Paris remains ours,' smiled Cecily.

I remembered my Aunt Margaret telling me how four years ago she had ridden into Paris at Katherine's side, when the crowds had cheered for the English king and his French queen. Would they cheer the man who called himself king of France if he should ride into Paris? My aunt said all the citizens wanted was peace, a proper peace under the English king. War meant hunger and shortages, profiteering and killings, and fear that God had turned His back on their city.

'Will our cousins, John and Thomas, be set free?' I asked, wondering if Aunt Margaret had heard the news.

Lady Percy laid her hand gently on mine. 'We have heard nothing, Alice. The English army is not seeking out the enemy so it may be that our cousins will have to stay where they are a little while longer.'

They called the battle, Verneuil, and everyone said the cause of the queen dowager's brother, Charles, "the ill-advised" was doomed. His little court was filled with rogues and evil-doers. He had lost his best commanders and his Scottish allies and there was no-one left to bring him salvation. He would never be king and it was only a matter of time before his friends would desert him, his resistance would crumble and the whole of France would be ours.

I settled back into our routine until one dark afternoon in November a message came from Eleanor. She needed me and said it was urgent so as instructed I ventured out wearing a dark hooded cloak with my hair tucked up under a plain white cap. I had removed my rolled headdress with its pale blue veil and looked like any ordinary townswoman.

'Quick! Over here!' Eleanor grabbed my arm and pulled me into the shelter of the wall where we couldn't be seen.

I shook myself free. 'What are you doing? Why aren't you with the duchess?'

'Because I need you to bear witness.'

'To what?'

'Never mind. Just follow me. And be quiet. There are ears everywhere.'

A thick wet fog had drifted up from the Thames hiding whatever lay ahead, making it impossible to see anything but the leather of our boots and a few inches of muddied path. We edged forward in silence, past the solid bulk of an old stone tower rearing up into the mist, past a locked gate and some empty barrels until we reached an open door. Beyond the door was darkness. On our other side, behind a long narrow building which, from the stench, might well have been where Duke Humphrey kennelled his hounds, was the river. I could hear gurgling and sucking as the tide pulled relentlessly at the walls of Castle Baynard.

Eleanor put her fingers to her lips and stepped through the doorway. I looked behind me but could see no-one so I, too, slipped inside. For a moment I could see a faint glow from a wavering taper before the flame was hidden by a hand. The room felt cold and damp and the only sound was our breathing and the thumping of my heart within my breast. I clutched at the folds of Eleanor's cloak, afraid of the dark, of the silence and whatever lay behind the light.

Slowly, with nothing having been said, a figure detached itself from the shadows and the taper was held up, illuminating the space between us The figure was that of a woman. She pushed back her hood and to my surprise I saw it was Mistress Jourdemayne, the woman who'd sold me the charm I'd used to blight my stepmother's womb. I shrank back as if contact with her might harm me in some way.

She smiled.

Greetings, lady,' she said in her familiar country burr with its peculiar ups and downs. 'Been busy since last we met, I see. Little one in the cradle.'

I gasped. How did she know? I'd often wondered if she dabbled in magic and this confirmed my suspicions.

She laughed. 'Never fret, lady. Next one will be a boy.'

Knowing things without being told and foretelling the future were sure signs of a woman who practised witchcraft. This was no placing of may blossom under a girl's pillow at night, this was something dark and forbidden and dangerous.

She laughed, more of a hen-cackle than a pleasing sound. 'Oh don't look like that, lady. I've not used the powers of the evil one. It be no secret that Nevill got hisself a girl child and your lord's a lusty young man, so my customers say, so 'tis a fair guess you'll have a boy afore long. 'Tis not magic, just a woman with an ear for gossip. And as you know, people do dearly love to talk about their betters.'

Eleanor placed her hand on my arm to stop me from running.

'Do you have it?'

The woman eyed Eleanor with a hint of amusement. 'Impatient, mistress?'

'Last week you promised it would be ready. You're nearly too late. If you'd waited three days more I'd be gone and your silver gone with me.'

Mistress Jourdemayne planted her feet a little more squarely on the ground and looked around for somewhere to place her taper. On a ledge was the remains of a pricket candle. She put the taper next to the wick and waited while the candle fizzled and finally caught alight.

'There,' she said, pinching out the taper.

''If you do not have it,' said Eleanor making to leave, 'then I am wasting my time.'

'Oh, I have it a'right, mistress, but are you sure this is what you want?'

'Of course I'm sure.'

'You don't wish to change your mind?'

'I'd not be here if I'd changed my mind. Give it to me.'

'Patience, mistress. This cannot be hurried. Like all charms it can be dangerous as your pretty young friend here will soon discover.'

I felt my belly quake. She was speaking of some future danger. Not one past and known but one yet to come. Every time I thought of the spell I'd worked upon my stepmother I felt uneasy, fearing that one day I'd have to pay for what I'd done.

'Eleanor delved into her purse and I saw a glint of silver. 'Stop trying to frighten a young woman who's done you no harm and give it to me.'

Mistress Jourdemayne reached under her skirts and, to my surprise, produced a ring. I recognised it as Eleanor's, one her father had given her, a pretty trinket but of no value.

Mistress Jordemayne held the ring up to the candlelight and spoke in a low soft voice as if in a trance.

'When the moon was waxing, when the powers were at their strongest, this offering was dipped in blood: the blood of a chicken whose plumage was white as bone, and the blood of a cockerel whose feathers were black as the coals of Hell. Secret words were spoken, words that you'll never know and never hear.' Her voice passed through the silence like the sharpest of knives, the whisper of a deadly blade. 'When you wear this ring, you will be irresistible. Any man who looks upon you will see a fair and delectable body and will stop at nothing to take you for his enjoyment. The energy of this charm is so powerful that he will be helpless in the face of his lust.'

'And I?' Eleanor's voice was cool but her breath was coming short and I knew she was excited at the thought of what this meant.

Mistress Jourdemayne chuckled. 'Oh you, mistress! You'll be a slave to your own desires but you know that already. You'd not have sought me out if all you'd wanted was a simple potion to attract a green boy. As I said to you last time, this is a dangerous business and you'd do well to be careful.'

'Eleanor,' I whispered. 'What are you doing?'

'Nothing you wouldn't do, Alice, so be quiet.'

I turned away, unwilling to watch Eleanor complete her transaction. I heard the chink of coin, the rustle of cloth and a long drawn-out sigh from Eleanor's lips. The next moment, the light was extinguished and I felt

Eleanor's hand push me back towards the doorway. Mistress Jourdemayne slipped away into the shadows until there was nothing left of her but a pool of darkness and a sour smell of decay. A moment later I was outside on the narrow path, retching onto the ground.

'Whatever is the matter with you?' said Eleanor, grabbing my arm and trying to hustle me along.

'That woman,' I gasped. 'I don't trust her.'

'You trusted her before. You told her your problem and she gave you what you wanted.'

I wiped my hand across my mouth, trying to rid myself of the taste of Mistress Jourdemayne. 'I wish I'd never seen her.'

Eleanor placed her hand on my sleeve and pushed me hard against the wall.

'Duchess Jacqueline was right,' she hissed. 'You are utterly feeble. If Mistress Jordemayne had not shown you what to do and if I hadn't practically stood over you while you did it, your stepmother would be breeding sons. Your father would have his heir in the cradle and your husband would have no further use for you. We've not only saved your inheritance but also your marriage.'

'Richard Nevill cares for me,' I protested.

'Richard Nevill cares for what you can bring him. Don't fool yourself into thinking it's your pretty brown eyes he wants. He wants what he was promised. It was why he married you. For mercy's sake, Alice, it's time you realised that men care about only two things: wealth and power. Everything else can be bought, including a willing woman.'

She put an arm round my shoulders and gave me a

quick kiss. 'Don't fuss. It's all finished now and I'm leaving for Dover in three days. I'll not see you for a while.'

I dried my tears and tried to smile. 'Lord Humphrey has his army?'

'Yes and the duchess is whipping us into a frenzy. She's determined he'll succeed and she will have her lands so everything has to be packed and transported onto the vessel taking us to Calais. Her household has increased tenfold, like a neglected bed of nettles. When she first came to England she had hardly anyone, now she has cooks and pantlers and grooms of the ewery, grooms of the buttery, a steward, a clerk of the wardrobe, a half-dozen musicians, two pages and a laundress.'

'And they are all travelling with you?'

'*Bien sûr.*'

'And your ring?'

Eleanor smiled, her eyes dancing mischievously. 'What about my ring?'

'You have someone in mind?'

I could see her wondering how much to tell me. Of course she had someone in mind but I doubted she'd tell me who.

'When I have him netted, I shall tell you.'

'Not before?'

'No.'

'Why not?'

She laughed. 'I'd look a fool if after all this he didn't desire me.'

'I won't tell anyone,' I protested.

She kissed me again. 'Run home to your husband, Alice. If there is an opportunity I shall write. Otherwise

I shall see you when we return in triumph with trumpets blaring and flags flying.'

'You *will* come back?' All of a sudden I realised how lonely I'd be without Eleanor and how much I'd come to rely on her for advice.

'I promise,' she said.

'I pray you keep safe,' I said, close to tears.

'I pray you remember what I told you about the bishop.'

She led me back to the yard where a Nevill groom waited with my horse.

'Hurry,' she called as I wound my cloak more securely round myself and turned my mount's head to the gate. 'The fog is getting thicker. Soon you'll not be able to see the future in front of your face and with no future, what will you do?'

# 13

## NATIVITY 1424

On a grey morning in the middle of Advent my husband tossed a note my way with a curt, 'I suppose I have you to thank for this?'

I blinked in surprise when I saw what was written.

'Nobody said.'

He looked disbelieving. 'It might be nobody said because this was the queen dowager's idea, done without knowledge or consent of the council.'

'Are the Christmas celebrations at Eltham a matter for the council?'

'When it touches the king's person, of course they are.'

'But your uncle rules the council. Surely he'd not object?'

'He'll be angry if he was not consulted. I'm surprised you are being so obtuse.'

These days I felt I was dancing on a bed of thistles to the tune of Bishop Beaufort's pipe. Everything I did was done at his behest and there seemed no way of freeing myself from his iron grip. Then I looked at my husband and realised I would do anything to gain and keep his favour, even obey the orders of his uncle. I was Lady Nevill now, no longer little Alice Montagu, the girl who played in the woods at Bisham. My mother had been taken by God and my father by the widowed Lady Phelip. Richard Nevill was all I had and without him I was nothing.

'The company will be small,' apologised Katherine when I saw her a week later. 'Just a few friends. Despite what Mistress Butler says, the king is too young to enjoy a large gathering. Last year Lord Humphrey came for the festivities but this year both royal uncles are overseas.'

'Lord Humphrey is busy securing his duchess's lands,' I observed.

Katherine winced as if Lord Humphrey's business of waging war in Hainault was not to her liking.

'Harry would not have approved.' Her voice was sharp. 'Humphrey is setting himself against my cousin of Burgundy and that cannot end well. But it is not my affair. Nobody asks for my opinion so I say nothing. Except to you, dearest Alice.'

'Then my lips are sealed and I'll not speak of it.' I placed a finger over my lips and smiled.

'And now,' said Katherine, 'we will speak of happier things. Sir Robert tells me he has organised a band of London players for the Nativity celebrations.'

I clapped my hands. 'I hope they bring dragons. Those were my favourites when I was a little girl. All that wiggling and roaring and billows of smoke. Do you think the king will enjoy them?'

Katherine laughed. 'I'm certain he will. And there will be my musicians. We shall have a merry time although sometimes I wonder if it is wrong to be joyful.'

'It is never wrong to find happiness in God's creations,' I said stoutly. 'May I know who else is invited for the festivities?'

'Archbishop Chichele will visit but he is an old man and feels the cold in his bones. He won't like being away

162

from the comforts of his palace. Bishop Morgan and of course, Bishop Beaufort but I doubt they will stay long either. They have other duties. Sadly Lord Fitzhugh has been unwell and is unable to travel but I hope the earl of Warwick will bring his new countess. She is his cousin's widow, Lady Worcester. Have you met her?'

I shook my head. 'I have heard of her. A fortuitous second marriage. The earl will make her a fine husband.'

'From what I know of him, I agree. She is indeed most fortunate. Harry left his son in the earl's care so he visits often and when we're together we speak of the days of my marriage which is a great comfort to me.'

Two women; both widowed that long hot summer nearly four years ago and yet for Lady Worcester there had been a fresh start, a new husband, perhaps a second brood of children, while for Katherine there would be nothing but long dreary years of widowhood spent watching her only child grow further and further from her care until she was of no use to anyone anymore. She would retire to some lonely manor far from her son's court, her income halved, her household reduced; she would be unseen and unvisited. It was a dismal prospect for a young woman.

'Maître Beaufort will be with us.' Her voice remained calm but I noticed a fine sheen of moisture on her upper lip and a flicker of something odd in her eyes. She lowered her lashes so they brushed her cheeks and except for two tell-tale spots of colour, I might have thought I was mistaken.

Throughout the autumn and early winter I had observed a flowering of happiness in Katherine. She tried to disguise it, perhaps thinking others would not approve, but I had come to know her well. When we were alone I called her Katrine and she called me Alice. I had begun to think of her as a friend, a friend who was set far above me, but a friend nonetheless.

Twice I had told Edmund I no longer needed his company on my visits but each time he shrugged and said his uncle was of a different opinion. And I had to admit he made Katherine laugh.

Richard Nevill and I arrived just in time to see the last boughs of greenery being brought into the hall where crimson ribbons were wound round doorways and tied to the rails of the galleries. Tendrils of ivy snaked their way into every corner and bunches of holly hung precariously from the high beams. With Katherine's fool sitting astride in the manner of a crusading knight, the massive Yule log was heaved and dragged to the hearth where it was rolled on top of a bed of glowing embers. The fool leapt off, shrieking that he was being roasted by the flames of Hell which made everyone laugh. It was a happy start to this most joyful of seasons.

I loved the aromatic scent of winter greenery almost as much as I loved the smell of spit-roasting meats wafting up from the kitchens. I could hardly wait to taste the dishes the cooks had prepared: the spiced sauces, the orange wafers, the figs in small ale and the marchpane sweetmeats. Of course this would be nothing compared to Katherine's coronation feast but it was better than a dish of boiled eels.

We had a truly wonderful time. At midnight on the Eve of the Nativity, Archbishop Chichele celebrated Mass with the whole household on their knees. The king was brought from his bed by his nursemaid and given to the earl of Warwick to carry for the occasion. The child was wrapped in a cloak of cloth of gold and blinked at the glow from the hundreds of candles alight in the chapel. His attention was caught by the little thatched stable where wooden figures of the Virgin and Christ Child were surrounded by a group of sturdy shepherds dressed in sheepskin. Someone had attempted to fashion a lamb but it looked more like a bundle of fur with no legs. The king stretched out his hand but the earl wisely carried him away so that temptation was no longer within reach.

'Is that an omen?' whispered my husband. 'Royal desire will be thwarted by the noble earl of Warwick.'

I smiled. 'Perhaps it shows an eagerness to be a shepherd to his people.'

After a day of feasting we said farewell to Bishop Morgan and Bishop Beaufort who were returning to London to be with the archbishop at his palace at Lambeth. The requirements of office lay heavily on their shoulders, explained my husband's uncle as he took his leave of the queen dowager.

With the restraining presence of bishops gone we settled down to livelier pursuits. It was a long time since I enjoyed Christmas celebrations as much I did that year. There was storytelling and music and the usual games of hoodman blind and hide and seek designed to include the little king. I was ordered to hide in the corner with my face to the wall and my husband to contrive a secret place behind a log basket. When Edmund crawled under one of the trestle tables and then jumped out, the king laughed so much his nurse became quite agitated.

'Again!' he crowed.

Edmund obligingly crawled back beneath the table where a cascade of snow-white napery hung down, completely covering him.

'I have him,' cried little Henry attempting to drag Edmund out from his hiding place. 'He is mine!'

'I shall always be yours, your grace,' said Edmund, allowing himself to be subjugated by one small royal foot planted firmly on his chest.

'Be careful, Henri,' said his mother. 'Do not hurt Maître Beaufort.'

'I have him,' cried the child. 'He is my prisoner.'

'Even prisoners should be treated kindly, your grace,' explained the earl of Warwick. 'A king should show mercy.'

'May I not pierce him with my sword?'

Edmund raised his clasped hands. 'Spare me, your grace. Treat me well and I shall crawl all the way to the end of the hall on my knees.'

'I think it is time his grace returned to the nursery,' said Mistress Butler, appealing to Katherine. 'He is over-tired and shortly it will be the hour for his prayers. If your grace will permit, I shall remove him before he over-heats himself. We do not want tears.'

Katherine hesitated.

'Edmund Beaufort should have a care,' whispered a voice in my ear. It was the new countess of Warwick.

'My lady?'

'Do you not see where this is leading?'

I frowned, uncertain what she meant. 'My cousin is playing with the child.'

'That is what it looks like but we know, because we are both sensible women, that looks can deceive. Things are not always what they seem.'

'What else would you think he is doing?' I asked.

'Fishing in forbidden waters and that is a foolish venture for one in his position.'

'What position would that be?'

She smiled and clapped her hands at the king's perfect farewell to his mother.

'A young man with a reputation to make. Youngest son. No land, no title, dependent on the goodwill of others. It would be a most unwise move to acquire the enmity of those who might misconstrue his intent.'

'Lady Warwick,' I said. 'I truly do not know what you mean.'

She gave me a long appraising stare. 'Oh, I think you do, Lady Nevill. I think you know very well what I mean.'

She drifted away. I stared across the room to where Edmund stood brushing the dust from his knees. He was laughing. This past year he had grown and was almost as tall as my husband. His shoulders were slim but he had the look and stature of a man. Somewhere, the boy I'd played with at Bisham had been mislaid. Since that day we'd rowed upriver to Kennington he had changed. I realised with a shock that he was no longer a childhood friend with whom I could share a joke or whisper secrets; he had crossed a line to join the ranks of young men who were to be given my obedience and respect. It was an unsettling feeling and not one I much liked.

Once the last of the procession of nursemaids had disappeared in the direction of the royal nursery,

Katherine's musicians took up their instruments and Sir Robert Babcock called for dancing.

'In the French style?' enquired the earl of Warwick. 'What say you, your grace?'

Katherine coloured and shook her head. 'I prefer English tunes, my Lord Warwick. Let us have an English carol.'

My husband grasped my hand and led me into the circle before there was any chance of Edmund claiming me for his partner. My other hand was held by a nervous young man from Katherine's household and opposite us Lady Warwick and Sir Robert were engaged in a heated argument about the steps.

'To the left, my lady,' said Sir Robert. 'It is always the way.'

'Not at Caversham.'

'Widdershins, Lady Warwick!' called Edmund leading Katherine into the circle. 'Here we carol with the warmth of the sun and I have the fairest lady of all to light my way.'

' Maître Beaufort,' said Katherine, blushing furiously. 'You praise me more than is my due.'

'That would be impossible, your grace,' said Edmund with a smile.

'What a *gentil chevalier* our Beaufort cousin is becoming,' remarked my husband quietly. 'I'm surprised he doesn't grovel at her feet and offer to lick her slippers.'

I caught Lady Warwick's eye and remembered what she'd said. To my relief, at that moment the leader of the musicians raised his hand and the carol began.

There was no question I preferred our energetic English country dances to the slow formal *bassedance* with its intricate steps and ponderous music. In the carol we could sing as we danced, smile as we lifted the hems of our gowns and skip and trip as we circled faster and faster until we collapsed, giddy with laughter. Three times we followed the music and three times we avoided disaster but on the fourth, Edmund faltered, tripped and fell sideways, ending up in Katherine's arms. He extricated himself and apologised but the damage was done and Katherine quickly excused herself and retired to her chair where two of her ladies fussed over her and asked was she hurt. I imagined the shock of finding Edmund's muscular young body pressed on hers, the feel of his arms beneath his satin sleeves, the scent of his skin and the touch of his fingers as they clutched at her waist.

With the ring broken we left the floor to Katherine's harpist, a dark-haired Welshman with a voice like an angel who played and sang beautifully.

'Still wondering, Lady Nevill?' murmured Lady Warwick as she settled on the seat beside me.

'It meant nothing. It was an accident.'

'Possibly? Or maybe it was carefully contrived to look like an accident.'

We sat in silence listening to the music but I kept my eyes on Edmund.

'In your stable yard do you have cats?' enquired Lady Warwick.

'Naturally.'

'Have you observed how they play with a mouse? Slowly, carefully, one silent paw advances. Sometimes the movement is so slight you'd think the cat was making no progress. But behind those yellow eyes is the thought –

just a little bit closer and a little bit more. The mouse is oblivious to its fate. It sees the cat and is transfixed by its sleek beauty and shining feline grace. It cannot see the pointed teeth and hidden claws and has no idea of the danger.'

The days rushed by too quickly. The Childermass feast and the excitement of Sir Robert's London players gave way to the annual gift-giving ceremony with its own unfolding dramas. Mistress Butler's team of flustered nursemaids found difficulty in restraining the little king who was more impressed with Edmund's gift of a child-sized wooden shield than with the costly ring given him by Lady Warwick's husband. His mother's illuminated psalter was received with a solemn face, a dutiful kiss and a few halting words of thanks. But my husband had chosen wisely, a pair of tiny bronze knights on horseback which enchanted the boy and even caused him to set aside the favoured shield.

I received from my husband a jewelled clasp for my gown and from Katherine, a little silver cup embossed with images of fabled beasts. Being a youngest son with no fortune of his own, Edmund's gifts lacked magnificence but more than made up for this in their singularity. I received a tiny enamelled butterfly while Lady Warwick was given a squirrel in a cage which caused her husband much amusement. To Katherine, Edmund presented a box within which was cunningly secreted another smaller box and then another until in the final box – ? We all waited, our heads craned, intrigued to see what was inside. But Katherine quickly closed the lid, her cheeks aflame.

'I thank you, Maître Beaufort.' She raised her eyes to look at Edmund but said nothing more.

'What was inside?' I whispered to Lady Warwick who'd been at Katherine's shoulder throughout the ceremony.

She pursed her lips. 'A button.'

'A button?'

'Yes. Have you not noticed your cousin is missing a button from his doublet. A pearl. One of the many which decorate his sleeve.'

'I don't understand.'

'Don't you? Well, perhaps the Twelfth Night revels will aid your understanding, Lady Nevill. I'd not like you to remain in ignorance.' She gave me a sideways smile before gliding away in the direction of the group of women surrounding Katherine.

A pearl button? I was puzzled. Was there some hidden meaning in the gift? My husband had given me a ring set with a single pearl on the day we wed as a tribute to my purity. It was, I was told later, a common enough gift to a bride on her wedding morning. And certainly Katherine was a symbol of purity. Despite having borne a child, she appeared quite untouched as if the earthly demands of a husband had never sullied her virtue. I knew what childbirth did to a woman. Since Joan's birth I had felt more rooted to the ground I walked upon, a member of that vast congregation of motherhood who shared the secrets of their bodies. I might yearn for past freedoms but my husband's avowed intention to create a Nevill dynasty of his own ensured that childbirth would from now on be an integral part of my life, or so I hoped.

Before Twelfth Night and the attendant revels could burst upon us, my husband received a summons from his uncle. Bishop Beaufort required him to return to Southwark without delay. No reason was given and I wondered what was of such importance as to disrupt our festive season.

With a grim face, Richard supervised the hasty packing of his chest while I hovered dutifully at his elbow. Our close proximity, squashed into this tiny chamber each night, had brought us an intimacy we'd not experienced for some time. On waking each morning I'd found pleasure in his warm male presence in my bed every bit as much as I enjoyed what had passed between us in the dark.

Once the chest was roped and carried out by two of his men, my husband turned to where I stood and grasped my hands.

'I do not like to be apart from you,' he said, echoing my own feelings. 'I know the queen dowager needs you but I am uneasy at leaving you.'

'It is only three more days,' I reassured him. 'Then she will release me and I can come home.'

'I shall send an escort.'

'There's no need. My cousin will bring me back.'

Richard Nevill's grip tightened. 'I shall send an escort.'

Of course he would. Like Lady Warwick, my husband instinctively mistrusted Edmund.

'If that is what you wish,' I said meekly.

'It is.'

I felt a surprising sense of loss as he rode across the bridge into a frosted dawn. Somehow with his departure the gathering lost its glittering magnificence and our festivities were muted as if seen through darkened glass.

Even the riotous revels of Twelfth Night where everyone whooped and laughed and danced and sang, failed to excite me. Without Richard at my side I had a sense of foreboding, of some unforeseen danger lurking on the periphery of my vision.

By the time the last practical joke had been played and my cousin had made his final appearance dressed as a dragon in archbishop's robes, Katherine gathered up her laughing ladies and prepared to leave. Throughout the ridiculous activities of the day she had maintained a remarkable composure and Edmund had kept his distance. There were no more unfortunate stumbles, no pretence at losing his footing and collapsing into the queen dowager's lap and no whispered asides or inappropriate gifts. Lady Warwick was wrong. There was nothing more to Edmund's behaviour than the high spirits of a exuberant young man.

In my chamber I issued instructions to my maid to start packing my gowns. I had no inkling at what hour my husband's escort would arrive in the morning but whenever it was I must be ready. The girl muttered under her breath as she worked and rather than listen to her endless grumbling I decided to take a final walk in the cloisters to breathe some cool, clean air before saying my prayers and climbing into my cold bed.

A couple of old women were gossiping in a corner of the hall but the servants were already folding up the napery and readying the trestle tables for the morning. With no difficulty I found the door which led to the garden where only two days before I had walked with my husband. The cloisters were silent but through the gloom I could just make out Katherine's hooded figure on the far side of the garden. With her slender figure and her slightly hesitant way of walking I knew it was her and was about to step forward when a hand clamped itself on my wrist.

'Don't!'

It was Edmund, his voice breathing in my ear. I tried to pull my arm away but he encircled me with his other arm and pulled me against him so that I couldn't move. My back was tight against the figured damask of his doublet, my head held uncomfortably against his shoulder.

'Be quiet!' he whispered as I opened my mouth to protest. 'Or I'll put my hand over your mouth.'

'You'd not dare.'

'Wouldn't I?'

He would. Edmund had always done what he wanted and tonight's Edmund was not my merry little playmate from the past but a man with his own plans.

'Why are you here?' I whispered.

'Same as you.'

'Which is?'

'Waiting for someone.'

'Who?'

He turned me round and touched my lips with his, not really a kiss, more of an acknowledgement of our kinship. 'Go to bed, Alice. This is none of your business.'

I pulled my face away. 'This most certainly *is* my business. The bishop gave me a commission. I was to befriend Katherine and that means having a care for her and her reputation.'

'What do you imagine I intend?'

His voice was harsh and I noticed how the torchlight reflected in his eyes made them glitter. In the shadowy confines of the cloisters all he needed was a hooded cloak and a wicked blade to complete the illusion of danger.

I opened my mouth but found I was unable to say what I was thinking.

He gave a low laugh and smiled. 'Do you imagine I intend for Katherine what you'd like for yourself? Is that what disturbs you, little cousin?' He placed his lips to my forehead. 'It's been a long time since that summer in the woods, hasn't it?' he murmured, running his fingers down the curve of my throat.

'Leave me alone, Edmund,' I said, horrified at how my body responded to his caress. 'Caring for Katherine is *my* commission.'

'You're wrong, Alice,' he whispered into my hair. 'This is not your commission. My uncle does not wish you to move closer to Katherine. He has no interest in what you do here or how you do it.'

'What d'you mean?' I protested, stung into retaliation. 'Of course he does. It was the bishop himself who impressed on me the importance of my role in Katherine's life.'

'He needed your compliance so he made you feel important. But I repeat, this is not your commission.'

'It was given to me from the bishop's own lips'

'Be advised by me, little cousin, this is *my* commission.'

'*Yours?*'

'Yes. Did you imagine it otherwise? Did you truly believe my uncle sent me to be your nursemaid? How innocent you are. Understand this, Alice. You are here to give *me* the cloak of your blameless reputation. See how virtuous you are, quivering under my fingers like a fledgling bird. I offer you my arm and everyone thinks

175

I am taking care of my cousin in her husband's absence. Nobody notices what I do because all eyes are on you.'

'I don't believe you.'

'Ask my uncle if you doubt my word. But I'd counsel against it. He's not a man to take kindly to interference by a woman.'

Even thinking about Bishop Beaufort made me cold with fear, recalling what he'd done to my Mortimer cousin the earl of March. The bishop was not a man to have as an enemy.

'What does your uncle want? Why all this subterfuge?'

'It is not for me to divulge the bishop's plans nor is for you to question them. This is men's business, Alice. You have no part in it, not tonight or any other night. Now go!'

Unwilling to stay and listen to how I'd been duped, I left him in the peace of the cloisters. I should have stayed to protect Katherine but I was frightened. As I stumbled back to my room in tears, I thought of Lady Warwaick's words and knew that Edmund was wrong. At least one person had noticed what he was doing.

Next morning I sought a private audience with Katherine to make my farewells. She may have been the queen dowager but she was also my friend and I grieved at having to leave her. She was dressed in one of her more sober gowns, a high-necked damson brocade, patterned in black and trimmed with sable. The nativity celebrations must have wearied her as there were purple shadows beneath her eyes and she looked tired. There was no way I could ask her outright if she'd met Edmund in the cloisters, all I could do was offer an oblique warning.

'I would beg you to be careful,' I pleaded as she clasped my hands in hers.

She gave a little smile and a shrug. 'Of what? I thought we agreed that England is a peaceful country at ease with itself. Surely there is no-one who would wish harm to the king's mother, and if they did, the gates are well-guarded and Sir Robert assures me there are always men outside my door.'

'There are many kinds of danger for a woman like you, Katrine, and not all come from armed men bursting into your chamber. Some dangers arrive well-disguised with gifts in their hands and smiles on their faces.'

She laughed. 'Oh Alice, your words are as difficult to understand as the archbishop's sermons. I believe his ramblings are due to the burdens of old age, but for you, that is no excuse. Tell me of what I should be afraid?'

'You are very beautiful, Katrine.'

She laughed. 'Oh now I know you're being foolish, my friend. I am not blind. When I look in my mirror I take note of the hollows in my cheeks and how my mouth is too wide and my eyes too large. But I tell myself it is vanity to wish to be other than I am. In no way am I beautiful.'

'There are men who think otherwise.'

She sighed, the smallest of exhalations as if remembering a time that was past and gone, when her life was different.

'It is natural for men to praise a queen and speak kindly of her crimson lips and her ripe beauty but they are only words. They tell me the king of the Scots writes verses to his wife but I wager she values his caresses more than his stumbling attempts at poetry.'

I smiled, remembering Jo's wedding day tirade against her husband's verses. 'That is very true.'

'When Harry was alive I received men's approbation and murmurs of how they would worship at my feet, and have me recognise their unworthiness, but they have forgotten me now that Harry is dead. There is no advantage for a man in praising me' Her voice faltered and her lips trembled slightly. 'I fear that whatever beauty I possessed in the eyes of others has faded. My lips are dull, my eyes dim and soon I shall be nothing but a black-clad widow reduced to living a life in the shadows.'

'Katrine, you know there is one man who wishes to make you forget Harry and bring you out of the shadows.'

She gave a tiny gasp and her right hand flew to her throat, to the jewelled clasp at the neck of her gown. 'No, you must not say it. *Sainte Vierge! C'est impossible,*' she whispered to herself.

She had no need to ask who the man was. She knew. She had known from that first meeting at Kennington almost a year ago.

'It cannot be,' she whispered. 'It will not be permitted.'

She raised her eyes to mine. Her eyelashes were bright with unshed tears and her cheeks as pale as the frosted grass in the park beyond the little wooden bridge.

'Do you know what they say of me across the Narrow Sea, Alice? That I betrayed my own people. That when Harry took me to his bed I surrendered not only my body but also the kingdom of France.'

'You know that is not true. It was God's will.'

'That is what Harry said. He told me he and I were God's instruments and that by giving myself to him I was fulfilling God's divine purpose.'

'So you can be at ease. There was no betrayal.'

I could tell she was not reassured, that her nights were full of terror at all that she'd done. It was no matter that she'd married at her family's command, giving herself to her husband in the way of an obedient wife, she was still haunted by the fear of God's displeasure.

'My son is all that matters now. He is all that remains to me of Harry and I shall do my duty as God intends.'

'And do it well,' I agreed, noticing how her hands would not stay still. They fluttered in her lap, twisting and turning, her fingers pulling at her rings as if she would cast them aside and throw them onto the floor.

Then all of a sudden, she jerked up her head and regarded me defiantly. 'It is more than two years, Alice. Two years! Harry was my husband, my lord, my life. I loved him to the point of madness but we were together such a little time and he left me too soon. It has been two long years of weeping and loneliness and I am weary of it all.'

'Would you seek to end your loneliness?'

'It is impossible. You know it is.'

'But what if *he* does not? What if *he* is determined?'

Her eyes darted from side to side as if seeking a means of escape from this enemy who pursued her, an enemy both devious and unswerving in his resolve to make her his. Katherine was like a fragile moth drawn inexorably to the flame of a candle, mesmerized by the glowing light, unable to resist, while all the while knowing the danger. A flame may give light but it can also consume the unwary.

'I am armed with prayer,' she said, looking for all the world like a wounded deer beseeching its captor not to slit her throat. 'I have the Holy Virgin to protect me from

179

falling into sin. I have vowed to remain true to Harry's memory.'

I put my arms round her and we stayed like that for a long moment.

'I know you will be strong,' I said, touching her fingers. 'And I shall pray for you. I regret I must leave you but my husband's men are here to escort me back to London.'

'You should go. In this life a wife must obey her husband.'

I knew I was abandoning her when she most needed my protection but there was nothing more I could do. I'd warned her to be on her guard and hoped she would heed my warning. But as I left her sitting alone, a small vulnerable figure lost in the midst of her glittering splendour, I felt like the worst of traitors.

In the courtyard I found not only my Nevill escort mounted and ready to leave but also Edmund who was talking to one of the men. I guessed he'd been waiting for me. When he saw traces of tears on my cheeks he raised a finger to my face and carefully wiped them away.

'I dare not hope those are for me.'

'They are not,' I said bluntly.

'For sweet Katherine?'

For some reason his light remark, typical of the young man he'd become, annoyed me. 'This is no joke, Edmund.'

He gave a wry smile. 'You are right. It is not. It is very far from being a joke. Did you truly imagine for one moment that it was?'

I ignored him and walked over to where one of the grooms stood ready to help me mount but at the last moment I turned back.

'I warn you, Edmund, when I return to London I shall make it my business to visit Bishop Beaufort.'

'In which case, give my uncle my dutiful greetings. Tell him his matter moves apace.'

'What matter?' I said sharply.

He laughed. 'Have a pleasant journey, Alice. Tell Richard I have looked after you very well.'

And with that he waved the groom aside and lifted me up into my saddle.

# 14

## SOUTHWARK 1425

Frost had given way to thaw and the woods around Eltham dripped in relentless misery, matching my feeling of despair. By the time we reached the outskirts of London everything was enveloped in a vast pavilion of grey fog and as we made our way towards the bridge even the river was barely visible. Once we passed through the gates into the city the stench of smoke became unbearable, swirling out of every alleyway, making it hard to breathe as if the sky itself was pressing down.

At The Erber, my women brought me inside and hurried me to my chamber where they stripped off my damp clothing and made me warm myself by the fire while the nursemaid brought my daughter to greet her mother. Joan was nearly eighteen months old, a dumpling of a child, happier sitting on a convenient lap or on the floor than in toddling around like other small children. But she was quick with words, having already mastered "Mama" and "Papa" and "Gramercy". She also showed an intense interest in food. I unwrapped a napkin and held out a cinnamon wafer I'd brought her from Eltham. She eyed it suspiciously.

'Would you like this?' I said temptingly.

She nodded. The nursemaid tapped her on the shoulder as if to remind her of her manners.

'G'amerthy, Mama.'

'Very good, my darling.'

I bent down and kissed her plump little cheeks and stroked her fair curls.

A knock was followed round the side of the door by the head of my husband's youngest page announcing that Sir Richard would be visiting shortly. I promptly ordered my daughter returned to the nursery, the room tidied and some wine brought.

My first impression was that Richard Nevill looked extremely pleased with himself and as he asked no questions about Edmund's part in my departure from Eltham, I assumed his visit to Southwark had brought good news. He sat down on the stool beside me and took my hands in his. I noted how large and capable they were compared to Katherine's slender fingers which always seemed weighed down by the burden of her rings.

'I am to be given the lordship of Pontefract,' he said with undisguised pride in his voice. 'Are you pleased for your husband, Lady Nevill?'

I gave a little gasp at this unexpected advancement of my husband's career. Pontefract was the gloomy dark fortress a day's ride from York where King Richard had died and where the duke of Orleans was often found scribbling away at his verses. It was a rich prize.

'I am very pleased for you, husband.'

'This was the reason my uncle recalled me from Eltham. He wanted to tell me what had been agreed. He said it was an honour well deserved.'

'It is,' I said, wondering how much of my work for the bishop had been instrumental in achieving this great prize. 'Did Lord Percy think the honour would go to him?'

My husband laughed. 'Henry Percy expects every honour to go to him. He has not forgiven us Nevills for benefitting from his father's fall. If he had his way we'd be kicked back to where he believes we belong, fit only to lick his boots. He regards us as common upstarts compared to the glorious Percys of Northumberland with their ancient title.'

I laughed with him, thinking how much I enjoyed making Richard Nevill happy and hoping the news from Normandy would be silent for many years to come on the subject of my stepmother's health.

Next day with my husband's blessing I travelled across the river to Southwark. The word from the bishop's servant in answer to my request for a meeting was that the bishop was extremely busy but could afford me a short interview if I came in the early part of the afternoon. Once again I entered the great arched gateway and walked softly through the magnificent chambers and courts of the bishop's palace marvelling at the grandeur of his surroundings. He lived in greater state than the queen dowager and the little king and there was more overt evidence of wealth here than in Lord Humphrey's fortress at Castle Baynard. Even Duchess Jacqueline's womanly touch with brightly coloured silks failed to equal the softness and richness of the bishop's luxurious furnishings at Southwark.

He eyed me as if I were a juicy piece of prey, watching each slight movement of my hands and the way I perched uneasily on the edge of one of his gilded chairs. I barely dared breathe in case he swooped down and snapped me up in his claws, those long slender talons, so much at odds with the rest of his portly frame. Since the Christmas festivities he had acquired another pouch of dimpled flesh beneath his chin, one which swayed when he talked.

'You have come to thank me, Lady Nevill.'

'Yes, my lord. From the great honour given to my husband I presume you are satisfied with the service I have given her grace, the mother of the king.

'She speaks well of you.'

'She is very kind and I consider it a great honour to have served her. And you, my lord,' I added hastily. 'But …' I hesitated, nervous of telling him I no longer wished to be associated with Edmund's scheming.

The bishop raised an eyebrow. 'Is there some difficulty, Lady Nevill?'

''A small matter.' I stumbled, unsure what to say even though I'd rehearsed my words most carefully.

'Sufficient for you to seek this audience.'

'Yes, my lord.'

'Speak then, Lady Nevill, or I shall think you struck dumb.'

'It is my cousin, your nephew, Edmund Beaufort.'

'Edmund. Ah yes, my nephew, Edmund. Has he not looked after you? I chose him with great care, Lady Nevill. I knew there had once been a small matter of some, what shall I say, *tendresse*, between you. I thought his presence would make your task more comfortable.'

I blushed wildly, wondering who had told the bishop of my girlish infatuation for my cousin, hoping he'd not heard about that summer's day in Quarry Wood.

'My lord, it is not my wish to speak ill of my cousin or of any man.'

'Then perhaps it is better you say nothing, Lady Nevill.'

A wiser woman than me would have heeded the warning in those few scant words but at that moment my fears were not for myself but for Katherine and in my desire to protect her I tumbled headlong into a hidden pit of sharpened staves.

'I cannot return to the queen dowager's company so long as my cousin is present,' I blurted out before I could ponder on the wisdom of what I was saying.

One of those silences which seemed not only endless but spiked with danger slid around the room, filling every crevice, every tiny gap behind the tapestries, threading its way through the folds of rich red curtains and creeping along the polished surface of the bishop's table until I was near to suffocation.

The bishop's voice was oily. 'Last time we spoke, Lady Nevill, I impressed upon you the inadvisability of displeasing those who have power over you. It seems you have not learned that lesson. So let me remind you.'

He flexed his fingers and spread them on the table in the way a woman does when she wishes to study her nails. The amethyst ring gleamed, a worthy complement to the rest of his jewel-studded splendour.

He did not raise his voice but gradually the words became more and more threatening.

'It may surprise you to hear that I know all there is to know about you, Lady Nevill,' he said. 'There is nothing that happens in your family, in your chamber, in your lodgings or in the whole of England that I do not know. Information is brought to me in the same way that other men receive God's air to breathe. I am kept informed as to the state of your soul, the state of your marriage and the state of your linen. There is nothing about you, Lady Nevill, that I do not know. And if you do not believe me then let me advise you that I know every detail of your friendship with Mistress Cobham.'

I blinked in surprise. Holy Mother of God! How did he know that!

'I know about your clandestine visit to the woman, Jourdemayne. What was it? Four years ago?'

I gasped. How did he know? It was impossible. I'd told no-one, and Eleanor and I had been scrupulously careful. No-one had followed us to the house in that narrow street near St Pauls.

'I know why you went there that day and I know what the woman said to you. There is no reason to look so surprised, Lady Nevill. I told you, I know everything.'

I opened my mouth and then quickly closed it again.

'Would you care to tell me what you did with the advice she gave you or shall I remind you?'

'I meant no harm, my lord. Truly, I meant no harm.'

'I doubt your noble father's new wife would agree with you.'

Holy Mary Mother of God! Ewelme! He knew about my visit to the widowed Lady Phelip. I was being stripped naked and my sins exposed. Soon my innermost thoughts would be laid bare before the bishop, drawn out like entrails, one loop at a time, ready to be picked over and the choicest bits consumed.

'My lord!' I cried. 'I was but a girl. Just a foolish girl. I'd no thought for anything other than a desire to please my husband.'

'You chose to turn your back on the teachings of the Church. Instead of filling your heart with the glories of God the Father, of Christ Jesus His son, and of the Holy Spirit, you sought out that which was evil. Whatever it was you intended, it is well known that evil may not be done so that good may come of it. You were not just foolish, you were wicked.'

By now I was almost incoherent with fright but the bishop's voice continued, never varying in pitch, always the same low reasonable tone: insistent, probing, accusing. I was sinful. I was wicked. I was undeserving of God's good grace.

'You not only sinned, you involved others in your sinfulness. You enticed those who were ignorant of your true nature, those whom you had a duty to protect.'

'There were no others, my lord. I swear to you.'

'That poor boy from your husband's stables, the one you inveigled into helping you.'

'He was a servant.'

'He was one of God's creatures. You corrupted him. An innocent boy, barely more than a heartbeat away from his mother's skirts. I can tell you, Lady Nevill, that when he cried out in pain it was with a child's voice.'

'Please, my lord. I meant no harm.'

I dropped to my knees, sobbing. He raised himself up and moved to where I was crouched on the floor, standing over me like some fearful monster.

'It was for my husband,' I cried. 'I did it for him. Not for me. I wanted nothing for myself.'

He moved his foot so that it was close to my fingers, so close I could have reached out and clutched his white silk stockings. Wanting to abase myself utterly, I lowered my face and kissed the smooth red leather of his shoe, accidently grazing the edge of my mouth on a silver buckle.

'As a woman, your thoughts should be pure,' a voice from above me said severely. 'You should have opened your heart in humility to the Holy Virgin, the Mother of Christ, and allowed Her to advise you. But that is not what you did. You chose instead to listen to the words of a woman who uses talismans, who dabbles in the ways of the evil one and who is known to consort with those who would seek to subvert God's word. Do you know what the punishment is for a woman caught in the devil's grasp, Lady Nevill?'

I leaned forward and again pressed my lips to the toe on his shoe. 'I pray to be forgiven,' I sobbed. 'I meant no harm. You must believe me. Please.'

He removed his foot with a small sound of disgust and returned to his seat.

'Get up, Lady Nevill, and stop snivelling. You are not a child.'

I hauled myself back onto the chair and crouched there unable to stop weeping. I tried but tears kept coursing down my face.

'Our late king, may God preserve him in Heaven, was determined to root out heresies in whatever form they should be found, even amongst those who were closest to him. It grieved him greatly yet he consigned more than one of his comrades to the flames.'

Oh Holy Mother of Christ!

'You should pay attention, Lady Nevill. I explained to you the last time we met how I could have saved your kinsman, the earl of March, but chose otherwise. He had become a nuisance; so I let him be sent to Ireland, a fate some consider even more calamitous than to burn. You, however, Lady Nevill, have been of use to me this past year. But if you should no longer be of use then I shall cease to protect you. And if you think my judgement harsh, you should contemplate the law's punishment for heretics.'

I shuddered.

'Yes, Lady Nevill – heretics. Those whose belief in the sacraments is not orthodox, who deny the efficacy of prayer to the Virgin and the Saints, who would look other than to God to understand His mysteries. You should ask your friend, Mistress Cobham; she will understand. Some years ago the husband of one of her kinswomen was burned at the king's command. She will have intimate knowledge of the smell of roasting flesh.'

I remembered little else of that afternoon. I was weeping uncontrollably as someone bundled me unceremoniously out of the bishop's presence and left me sitting on a servant's bench where the guards eyed me with contempt as if used to weeping women leaving the bishop's chamber.

Later I crouched in the boat, crying softly. The oarsman took no notice, muttering to himself about the cold and why anyone would want to go to Southwark on a day like this when sensible folk were wrapped up warm by their firesides, not freezing to death on the river.

I was foolish and should have been more careful. I believed my arrangement with my stepmother that evening at Ewelme had been a simple matter between me and God but the truth was, you cannot bargain with God.

In the bishop's words – evil may not be done so that good may come of it – and while I was weaving my compact with the widowed Lady Phelip, the bishop had been busy taking notes.

I wanted to crawl into a corner and weep for my stupidity but of course that was impossible. I was the lady of the house and had duties to perform. If my women noticed my red-rimmed eyes and the way I looked over my shoulder at the slightest noise, they said nothing, though one of the young girls in my care did ask if I felt unwell. Knowing it was useless to confide my fears to any of my sisters-in-law who would be shocked to the very core of their orthodox Nevill-trained consciences, next day I asked my husband for permission to visit my aunt.

It was cold on the river and the deserted cloisters chilly, but this time my aunt's room at the convent at Syon was welcoming with a fire piled high with apple boughs and two sconces of wax candles.

'Alice!' she exclaimed as she folded me into her arms. 'What a pleasure! I was only thinking of you yesterday, remembering the nativity celebrations at Bisham the year before I married Harry's brother. Your mother offered me sanctuary for the season. How old were you -five?'

I kissed her, feeling myself enveloped once more in her love and compassion.

'Now, come and sit here, beside me, and tell me your problems. You do not have the look of a merry young woman so I presume you are in some difficulty.'

Instead of sitting, I walked over to the small reading desk next to the cupboard where she kept her books. A beautifully bound copy of the *Dialogue of Divine Revelation* lay open on the stand.

'You have been busy.'

'Ah Alice, idleness is the enemy of the soul. Holy reading brings me peace. Catherine of Sienna has much to say to a woman like me and if this, my small fire, should kindle greater understanding then I shall consider myself blessed.'

'You have friends here?' I enquired.

'Did you imagine me friendless?'

I shook my head, unable to look my aunt in the eye in case she should see what I wished to keep hidden..

'Yes. I have friends. We discuss our readings and thus gain greater understanding of God's great mysteries. But I doubt you came here to ask about my social life. Is something amiss? Is it Katherine?'

I hesitated, fingering the buttons at the wrist of my left sleeve.

My aunt patted the stool next to her. 'Come here, Alice. Or I shall have to order you the way I did when you were little.'

Reluctantly I trailed across the floor and subsided onto the stool at my aunt's knee. She stroked my cheek the way she had when I was a child.

'My dear, tell me what is the matter. Something troubles you, I can see it in your eyes.'

Now the moment had come I found I found myself unable to tell my aunt what I'd done that evening at Ewelme. The words stuck in my throat. Instead I told her about Katherine, how I feared she was in danger of yielding to her baser instincts. I described her refusal to accept what I perceived as real danger, her determination to remain faithful to her dead husband's memory.

'But?' said my aunt,

'She trembles. She is attracted but she is aware that any move on her part would be regarded as sinful not only in the eyes of God but in the more proximate eyes of the council and she'll not risk losing her son. She fears being labelled an immoral influence on the little king yet her skin flushes with something more than pleasure in a man's presence.'

'And the man involved?'

I bit my bottom lip and hesitated.

'Edmund?' she said.

'How did you know?' I gasped. 'I've said nothing.'

My aunt smiled at my naivety. 'I may live within the precincts of a convent, Alice, but I have visitors and, like you, they tell me things. Sometimes things I'd rather not hear.'

'Lady Warwick.'

'Yes, Isabel Warwick. Like you, she is worried and she asked my advice. You would be surprised how many people ask for my advice.'

'I pray you will advise me for I am sorely muddled.'

'That is because you feel Katherine is your responsibility. She is not. It may be the bishop has placed too much weight on your shoulders. I know it is said no burden is too great for man to bear but the bishop is devious. For thirteen years he was my brother-in-law and I know his character well. He doubtless selected you for this particular task because he saw in you a young woman who would bend rather than break.'

'I think I am already broken.'

My aunt laughed. 'You are stronger than you think, my dear. Now, listen to me. If my son chooses to make sheep's eyes at Katherine and she allows him certain liberties of a personal nature, it is none of your business. Katherine was born a king's daughter. She was a king's wife and is now the mother of a king. She may toy with Edmund to satisfy her womanly vanity but she will never forget who she is. It would be impossible for her to consider intimacy with a man whose blood is less sacred then her own. Believe me, nothing can come of this.'

'What if Edmund thinks otherwise.'

She smiled. 'Edmund is not stupid, Alice. An illicit liaison will not benefit him. He would be damned in the eyes of the council for bringing shame upon the mother of the king. Such behaviour would put an end to all his ambitions and you know he is ambitious.'

'You think on his part it is an idle fancy?'

'Possibly, but whatever it is he will be careful. He will do nothing to jeopardise his career. Remember, he is my youngest son and has no expectations so must court the favour of others.'

'Blind folly?'

She laughed. 'I think not. Edmund has his eyes wide open. He may appear impulsive, even reckless, but he is neither. Everything he does is done with calculation. He was exactly the same as a boy. Now, tell me what else is bothering you. I doubt you came here to tell me about my son. So, what is it?'

I considered what I knew of my aunt and how much she had changed these past few years since being widowed for a second time. She was a truly devout woman who would shrink from any contact with a heretic so it would be impossible to tell her what I'd done. I'd been stupid but the stain was of my own my making and my aunt would not hesitate to condemn me just as the bishop had done. She would not wish to see me burn but she would have my sins washed clean behind convent walls, some strict order of nuns. She would recommend incarceration for the good of my immortal soul and I'd never see my daughter or my husband again. To share my fears with my aunt might put me in even greater danger.

'I cannot tell you,' I muttered.

She said nothing, merely watched me, waiting for me to change my mind.

'Very well,' she said eventually. 'If you do not trust me then there is nothing more I can do to help you. But perhaps you will take advice from Catherine of Sienna who counsels every woman to build a cell inside her mind from which she cannot flee. Think on her words, Alice, and you will realise you cannot hide from yourself or from God. To believe otherwise is foolish. Now come and kiss me before you go and we will say a prayer together.'

On my journey back to The Erber I refused to think about what my aunt had said. Instead I thought of the little cap I was embroidering for my daughter, wondering if I should use rose-pink silk or coral. When unwanted thoughts slid back into the corners of my mind I thought about which dishes we would eat if we held a feast, and if our cook could be persuaded to try his hand at hen-brawn ground with rice and milk of almonds which my mother-in-law said was delicious. I filled my mind with a multitude of trivial thoughts so that I did not have to consider what might lie within the cell Catherine of Sienna would have me build inside my mind. Huddled in my winter cloak I barely noticed the royal palaces slip by and only when alerted by a little jolt as the barge nudged the wooden uprights of the pier, did I realise I was home.

Upstairs in my chamber I found the dowager Lady Scrope, seated near the fire, watched by one of my maids who was supposed to be mending a sheet.

'Lady Margaret!' I exclaimed. 'Forgive me, I was visiting my aunt. I did not know you were coming.'

She sprang out of her chair and forgetting her manners, grasped my hands.

'You must help me, Lady Alice. My stepmother would not understand but you will, I know you will.'

'Understand what?'

She looked round wildly as if expecting my mother-in-law to leap out from behind the bed curtains. 'You see, I have never done such a thing before, never. And I don't know what made me. It's not as if I do not know right from wrong, far from it. But you'll not tell, will you? You told me once you could keep secrets. So you'll not tell.'

Her eyes were wide with fear and her hands were shaking convulsively. I sent my maid running for the little bottle of valerian, my trusted remedy for shock, and pushed Lady Scrope gently into a chair.

'Dear Lady Margaret,' I said. 'Please tell me what has happened.'

'I didn't mean to drop it,' she said. 'Truly I didn't. I know it's the kind of foolish game an ignorant young woman might play, but not me. In truth, I was not aware I'd dropped it until he handed it back. When I saw it in his hands I didn't know what to say. It wasn't as if he was anyone I knew.'

'Who? And what did he have in his hands?' I said, thinking how difficult it was to discover exactly what was agitating her.

'My glove of course. What did you think it was? One of the grey ones with gold stitching on the back. A gift from my stepmother. It was the first time I'd worn them. And to be so careless. How could I have been so careless.'

She looked at me beseechingly. 'I never speak to strangers but it would have been rude not to thank him.'

'It would,' I agreed.

'Then he introduced himself so I felt obliged to tell him who I was.'

'Who was he, this good Samaritan?'

She blushed and then the colour drained from her face leaving her cheeks as white as the snowdrops found in early spring. 'William Cressener,' she whispered.

'Sir William?' I enquired, already knowing the answer.

'No, he is a gentleman.'

'Did you tell him who your father was?'

'Yes, and he told me about his father who has been dead these twelve years gone. He was such pleasant company. We stood at the foot of the church steps and I said I could tell he was not a Londoner and he laughed and said, no, he was a Suffolk man, from Sudbury.'

One part of me was intrigued to think of Lady Scrope conversing with a complete stranger in a London street in the middle of the afternoon. But part of me was horrified. 'Did your servants not escort you away?'

She blushed again. 'I told them to stand back.'

'Surely you knew it was very irregular?'

'Oh yes, I did. But you must understand, I wanted to stay. I wanted to stay all afternoon and listen to him tell me of the silk weavers' houses and the slow-moving river and how the college at St Gregory's has made the town rich.'

'And he?'

'I asked if business had brought him to London and he said his business was done. He was on his way to the wharf to find a ship to take him home. So I said should he not hurry and he smiled at me and said … oh Lady Alice, you will never guess what he said.'

This story was taking an age to tell but there was no hurrying Lady Scrope who was clearly relishing the reliving of her sinful afternoon.

I smiled as kindly as I could. 'Tell me.'

'He said, was I not warm from the heat of the sun.'

'Lady Margaret! It is wintertime, there is no sun.'

'Is there not? I didn't notice. I said yes, I was warm and he offered to fetch me a cup of ale. Of course I should have refused, I know I should. The earl of Westmoreland's daughter does not go drinking in ale houses with perfect strangers but he didn't feel like a stranger. It was as if I'd always known him and he was a friend. No, more than a friend.'

I arched my eyebrows questioningly.

'Oh Lady Alice, I have truly never felt like this before.'

'It is a form of sickness,' I said reassuringly, taking the little bottle of valerian from my maid and pouring a few drops into a cup and adding some ale. 'Here, drink this. It will make you feel better. Later your physician can mix you a potion and the tremors and the tightness in your breast will disappear, believe me. Then you can forget this man.'

She sat up, her back as stiff as a rod.

'You misunderstand. I do not wish to forget him. I wish to remember.'

'But Lady Margaret, nothing can come of this and if your father or my husband were to find out they'd be greatly displeased.'

'That is why you must tell no-one.'

I sighed inwardly – more subterfuge, more secrets!

'Lady Margaret, please, I beg you, forget this man and pray no-one tells your stepmother.'

She rose to her feet and looked round the room as if she'd never seen it before. She was speaking as if half-asleep and in a dream. 'He escorted me back to our gate. He said he could not leave me unattended in the streets, it would not be right. When we parted he said he was going home to wait and when I asked what was he waiting for. Oh Lady Alice, guess what he said.'

I shook my head thinking Lady Margaret had taken leave of her senses.

'He said, "You". That was all. Just, "You." Then he walked away and disappeared. I felt cold. It was as if all the warmth had gone from the day.'

She knew the rules as well as I did. A marriage must be of benefit to the bride's family and there could be no benefit to the Nevill's in allying themselves with a gentleman of small means from a little town in Suffolk. Even though she was a widow, Lady Margaret would do well to heed her father's advice in the matter of her remarriage. I hoped she would forget this impertinent man and I trusted he would not be so foolish as to pursue her. It was just as well his ship would be sailing on the early morning tide and she'd not see him again.

I only wished my own problems could be so easily resolved.

# 15

## CASTLE BAYNARD 1425

In the dark days of that endless winter Richard Nevill was absent somewhere in the north, inspecting his new castle and attending to whatever business fell to the lord of Pontefract. His letters said little of his actual doings but I could imagine him proudly ordering new fortifications, inspecting the garrison and dispensing justice in his firm Nevill way.

I had wanted to accompany him but with unusual gentleness he'd said, 'Not this time. The ride is too hard for a woman, even one like you. The roads are atrocious and there's water everywhere. You must stay here with our daughter where you will both be safe.'

And so I remained at The Erber, missing my husband but available for summoning at will by the bishop. On three separate occasions he sent orders for me to accompany Edmund to Hertford but the visits were not a success. I hardly saw Katherine and when I did she was either distant, hiding behind a mask of chilly aloofness, or else panic-stricken, drawing me into her private chamber where she would clutch at my hands and weep.

Everything around her was changing. She was distraught at the thought of the coming separation from her son. The little king was surrounded by sober priests and women appointed by the council and it had become obvious that whatever authority Katherine had once had over him was being eroded daily by Mistress Butler.

'I have done nothing of which I am ashamed,' she wept. 'Nothing! Yet they will take him away from me. It is as if I am no longer his mother.'

I murmured soothing words trying to explain how it was the same for every mother of sons. how boys must learn to be men, but she chose not to listen.

For comfort she turned elsewhere and once the business of the day was done I would see her walking with Edmund, trailed as always by her dutiful maid, little dark-haired Guillemot. I had no faith in the ability of a maid to protect Katherine from Edmund's insidious charms despite the apparent propriety of the situation. Guillemot worshipped the ground on which her mistress trod and would willingly have died to make her happy. I'd already warned Katherine of the danger my cousin posed to her person and to her reputation and she knew Bishop Beaufort had his eyes on everything she did. But there were others who were also taking an interest.

'Have you noticed them together?' Lady Warwick's whisper was just loud enough for me to hear amidst the chatter of women. 'She glows in his presence like a pearl bathed in candlelight.'

I refused to look but afterwards was haunted by her words.

As Edmund and I made the uncomfortable ride back to London along the valley of the River Lea there were few signs of spring even though April had already arrived. Rows of drooping willows lining our path stood with their feet in water like small children sitting by a stream.

From the moment we left Hertford Castle Edmund had carried on a one-sided conversation, talking of nothing in particular, relating snippets of gossip about people we both knew. But I refused to be drawn and had remained stubbornly silent.

'The news from Ireland will have gladdened your mother-in-law's heart,' he remarked.

Grudgingly I asked, 'What news?'

'Our cousin of March is dead.'

'*Requiescat*,' I murmured, sad for my disgraced cousin whom I barely knew but unable to think what his death had to do with my mother-in-law.

'Young York is his heir. The boy's mother was March's sister.'

Of course! The York boy who now resided in my father-in-law's household and was formally betrothed to Cecily. It was no wonder my mother-in-law had been purring with pleasure this past month. When the boy came of age, he would be one of the wealthiest young men in England.

'I wonder who will lay claim to the boy's allegiance?' remarked Edmund as if it was a matter of complete indifference to him who would corner and catch the young duke of York. 'My uncle or Lord Humphrey?'

'The duke is overseas.'

'Not for much longer, I'll wager.'

And as always Edmund was right.


'Lord Humphrey is back,' remarked my husband as his valet struggled with the fastenings on his master's doublet.

'Duchess Jacqueline?' I asked.

He shrugged. 'I believe not. I was told matters had not gone well for Humphrey's little war and his wife has chosen to remain in Hainault.'

'If I was her I'd have followed my husband.'

'I'm sure you would,' observed Richard dryly. 'But the duchess wants her lands back and she'll not achieve that by feasting on roasted peacock at Castle Baynard.'

The valet stepped back to survey his handiwork, tweaked a furred hem and bowed to indicate he was content.

My husband turned and held out his arms as if wishing to embrace me . 'What d'you think?'

I clapped my hands together. 'You look wonderful. Every inch a Nevill.'

'I should hope so,' he said, waving for the valet to fetch his cloak. 'And what about you, Lady Nevill?'

He lowered his gaze to my waist and the familiar sensation of failure gnawed at my belly. Our reunion on his return from the north had been joyful and that first night he'd whispered how much he had missed me. But if I could deliver neither a son nor a title for my impatient husband I feared his attention would drift elsewhere. Eleanor had said it was what men did when they were disappointed in their wives.

I watched him set off for the parliament at Westminster and wished he would let me accompany him. He had a room in the royal palace and sometimes did not come home at night.

It was early in the afternoon when the little page who ran messages raced up the stairs and into the solar. The steward kept telling him not to enter a room like a cantering horse but the boy seemed incapable of learning.

'A very grand lady, m'lady,' he said, beaming widely.

'Her name?' I asked, thinking I'd have to get rid of him if there was no improvement.

'Mistress Cobham,' said a familiar voice from behind the boy's back as Eleanor paused on the threshold.

I have to admit that I squealed with pleasure. 'I didn't know you'd returned,' I cried, grasping her hands and giving her a kiss. 'They said you were still in Hainault.'

'You think I am an apparition?' she laughed.

'I think you are the most welcome visitor imaginable.'

She held me at arms length and looked me over as if inspecting me for imperfections.

'And you, Lady Nevill, are as slim as a willow wand. I expected to see burgeoning growth. Has Sir Richard not been doing his duty?'

I blushed. 'He is very attentive.'

She kissed the tip of my nose. 'So he should be. You are a pearl of a wife.'

It was only then that I observed her new jacket of the softest, richest mulberry and the exquisite enamelled pendant hanging round her neck.

'Eleanor, you look wonderful. Where did you get that pendant?'

'A gift,' she said lightly.

'From?'

There was a slight pause before she answered. 'A person of my acquaintance.'

'A man?'

'Possibly.'

'Do I know him? Is it the man you spoke of?'

'Yes,' she said with a long drawn-out sigh of contentment.

I gave her a quick kiss. She was so clearly happy at whatever had happened in Hainault that I was happy for her too.

'Who is he? Has he spoken with your father?'

'Not yet.'

'But he will.'

'I am quite certain someone will speak with my father and when they do my father will be overjoyed.'

'You are being very mysterious. Is he someone in Lord Humphrey's retinue? I do wish you'd tell me his name.'

'Probe all you like, my friend, but you'll not unearth my secret. You will have to wait. There are feasts at the end of the parliament and you will see him then.'

I sighed. 'I suppose I must be patient but I think you are very mean.'

She smiled. 'Let me tell you a snippet of gossip. I heard it from one of the ladies in Hainault who'd been in Paris.'

Eleanor's snippets of gossip were always scandalous so I called for wine and sent my curious women away to sew in the furthest part of the solar so that Eleanor and I could be alone.

'Come and sit near the fire and tell me everything,' I said, drawing my stool closer.

'A few months ago The duke of Burgundy hosted a great banquet at the Hotel d'Artois in Paris,' she began. 'A marriage between the master of his household and one of Queen Isabeau's ladies. And who do you think was there?'

I shook my head. I knew little of Burgundy's friends.

'The English earl of Salisbury and his new countess.'

I gasped. 'My father!'

'The same. And one hears that the beauty of the earl's wife was the cause of much attention, particularly from the noble duke.'

I scuffed the floor with my toe and thought back to the young woman I'd last seen three years ago at Ewelme. Perhaps dressed in silks and brocades with a careful application of face paint she might look beautiful but nothing like Katherine's luminous beauty. 'Some men are attracted to those kinds of looks, I suppose,' I muttered.

'Greatly attracted it would seem. It is said the noble duke of Burgundy did not content himself with open admiration, he made an attempt upon the lady's virtue.'

'No!'

'Oh yes!'

'A seduction?'

Eleanor smiled slyly. 'A little less subtle. It is said he had the lady in a violent embrace with his hands all over her person when her husband walked in.'

'Mother of God! What happened?'

'A furious row. And your father removed himself and his wife from the duke's company. He has sworn to have his revenge upon Burgundy.'

One part of me rejoiced at my stepmother's faithlessness. No man puts his hands on a woman without encouragement and in those circumstances no man could fail to realise how inferior his second wife was compared to his first.

A little worm of hope was wriggling. 'Perhaps my father will set her aside.'

'Unfortunately for you, Lady Nevill, I think not. My informant reports that the earl was intent on taking his wife straight to his bedchamber to show her who was the better man. The whole of the Burgundian court was convulsed with laughter over the affair.'

However much I hated my stepmother I could not bear the thought of my father's humiliation.

'The duke of Bedford is furious,' remarked Eleanor

'At the insult to my father.'

'No, silly. At the risk to the alliance. It is not wise to have one of England's leading commanders at odds with our chief ally.'

It was the same as always, everything must be sacrificed for the unity of the two kingdoms. My father's pride meant nothing compared to the importance of England's alliance with the duke of Burgundy.

'Tell me something more joyful,' I said.

'No, it's your turn. How is the queen dowager? And have you outrun the wily bishop?'

For a few moments I'd forgotten my worries but one question from Eleanor and they came flooding back.

'I am caught in a trap,' I said miserably. 'You are the only person I can turn to, so please, dear Eleanor, advise me what to do. He knows.'

'Who knows?'

'Bishop Beaufort.'

'And what is it that the bishop knows?'

'About us. You and me. And our visit to Mistress Jourdemayne. He knows everything. He threatened me, called me a heretic, said I would burn. But I swear I am no heretic. Oh Eleanor, what shall I do?'

The expression on her face barely changed but her eyes darkened and her lips became a thin hard line .

'What did you tell him?'

'I cannot remember but I said I was sorry, I was just a girl at the time, that I'd meant no harm.'

'When was this?'

'Shortly after the end of the Nativity celebrations.'

'And he has done nothing since? Not had you taken into the Tower for questioning?'

At the thought of the Tower my belly lurched. The Tower was the stuff of my childhood nightmares, a place which swallowed you up. Edmund said there were dungeons in the Tower where men had iron pincers to extract the nails from your fingers and hammers to crush your bones. If you went into the Tower you never came out,

'No,' I gulped.

'If he questions you again you must be contrite. Say you will be guided by him. Abase yourself. Then come and talk to me. Meanwhile, say nothing to anyone else.'


My husband fingered the invitation which had just arrived by the duke of Gloucester's messenger.

'I wonder what he wants?'

'Should he want anything?' I asked.

'Lord Humphrey may be generous but he does not count us Nevills as friends. He knows we support the bishop, yet he invites us to his feast.'

'Is Bishop Beaufort his enemy?'

'Yes and Lord Humphrey cannot win this particular fight.'

'I was not aware there was a fight between the bishop and Lord Humphrey. I thought their differences were settled.'

He sat down beside me and took my hand in his. He enjoyed instructing me as if I was a child of seven and I must say I enjoyed it too. I liked having him sit close, so close I could inhale the scent of him. Unlike men who used perfumed oils on their skin Richard Nevill had a very distinctive smell of male sweat and fresh linen mingled with the tang of polished leather.

'They are fighting for control of the king,' he explained. 'The boy is young and everyone knows young children can be moulded. Why else would God have made them the way they are – feeble and ignorant. Lord Humphrey desires to have the boy to himself. He believes it was his brother's dying wish.'

'And the bishop disputes that?'

My husband smiled. 'The council disputes it. From the very beginning they have said Lord Humphrey has no right to govern through the child.'

'If he did, could he be trusted?'

'No, he is too ambitious. He'd make the boy into a puppet with himself as master puppeteer. There'd be a chain round the child's neck which only Lord Humphrey could jerk, and jerk it he would.'

I doubted I'd trust the bishop either, not now I knew the lengths to which he'd go to get what he wanted. I was frightened of him and thought him every bit as ambitious as Lord Humphrey and equally as dangerous. They were like two dogs fighting over a scrap of meat dropped in the mud, destroying what should be nurtured.

The duke of Gloucester's feast took place on the Thursday following the end of the Easter parliament. Preparations were already well under way for our removal to Middleham for the summer but my husband refused to leave before the duke's lavish entertainment. Lord Humphrey was as well known for his open-handedness as for his long-running feud with the bishop and, as my husband explained, when wine flows men's tongues loosen and information can be gathered. He had no need to tell me that I, too, must keep my eyes open and my ears alert for any gossip from the women, anything which might be to the Nevill family's benefit. This was a lesson I'd already learned.

In the room set aside for ladies to repair the ravages of journeying to Castle Baynard, I found Lady Warwick. She was taking her ease in one of those odd little recesses to be found all over Lord Humphrey's house but rose when she saw me approach. She had been at Caversham these past three months and looked radiant.

'A boy,' she whispered in my ear. 'We named him Henry, in honour of our king.'

'Oh Lady Warwick! Your husband must be pleased.'

She beamed. 'I think he'd have offered me the whole of England if it had been within his power.'

From his first marriage, Lord Warwick had been blessed with nothing but daughters so it was no wonder he was pleased with his second wife. But Isabel Warwick was not unkind and noticed my barely concealed envy.

'Don't be downhearted, Lady Alice. You are young. There is plenty of time for you to give Sir Richard a son. I counsel patience.'

We walked together through the fragrant chambers of

Lord Humphrey's house towards the hall. She gave me one of her sideways glances as if there was a morsel of gossip to share. 'Such a shame we'll not see Duchess Jacqueline today,' she murmured.

'Has she still not returned to her husband?'

'No, she is in Mons. But we must not fret about Lord Humphrey. My husband tells me he is having a little amusement in the absence of his duchess.' She lowered her voice. 'Some woman he brought back with him from Hainault.'

I recalled Eleanor's description of Lord Humphrey's amorous dalliances with the Lady Jacqueline before they were married and was not really surprised. It was well known that the noble duke kept a woman for his personal enjoyment hidden away in his house at Hadleigh far from his brother's prying eyes.

'We'll not have to meet her, will we?'

Lady Warwick laughed. 'What do you think this is, Lady Alice – a bordello?'

'No, but my friend Eleanor says …'

Lady Warwick placed her hand on my sleeve. 'Look! There she is! Over there, standing by Lord Humphrey. D'you see her? The woman in green.'

The shock hit me like a bucketful of cold water thrown straight in my face. Beyond the blazing reds and golds, half-hidden by a moving swirl of coloured brocades, stood a slender young woman in a fur-trimmed gown of green velvet. She was bathed in a circle of light from a great sconce of candles. It was Eleanor.

'Apparently she was one of the duchess's women,' continued Lady Warwick, her words a blurred echo in the background while my mind skittered around trying to make sense of what I'd just seen. Eleanor and Lord Humphrey! The woman I called my friend was the duke of Gloucester's whore. And she'd not said a word. How long had this been going on? Had the charmed ring she'd acquired from Mistress Jourdemayne been intended to lure the duke?

She had fooled me. There was no mysterious other man, no member of the duke's retinue who would make a formal approach to Eleanor's father to suggest a marriage contract. It had been Lord Humphrey all along, right from the beginning. I thought back to Katherine's coronation feast when I'd told Eleanor about the man in the blue doublet and how even then she'd been intrigued. Was that when it had started? This incredible plan to trap a royal duke in her coils?

'Such behaviour makes a wife look closely at her own women,' Lady Warwick was saying. 'Luckily my lord has no interest in such dalliance. He is a devoted husband. Of course she'll regret it. Lord Humphrey will play with her for a season and then it will be over. He will return to his duchess and the harlot will be discarded. It is always the same.'

But Lady Warwick had no knowledge of Eleanor Cobham. Lady Warwick's husband might do business with Lord Humphrey in council meetings and reckon he had the measure of the man; and Lady Warwick herself might share intimate conversations with the duchess, noting her determined chin and sense of purpose, but if I were a woman who liked gambling I'd put my money on Eleanor Cobham and not on Duchess Jacqueline.

Of course Eleanor knew full well that I'd seen her and next morning I received a note asking me to visit.

'It will make no difference,' she said, smoothing the edge of her furred sleeve and treating me to one of her sly little smiles.

'How can you say that!' I cried.

'Why should it? You are still Lady Nevill and I …'

'*You* are Lord Humphrey's whore.'

She did not flinch merely ushered me through the archway into a tiny private courtyard garden and closed the gate carefully behind us. 'Not a word I'd use but if you wish to insult me, it is your privilege.'

I was immediately stricken with guilt and clutched her arm. 'Forgive me, Eleanor, I do not mean to be rude, truly, but why are you doing this? It's very wrong, you know it is. And what about the duchess?'

'Ah yes, poor Jacqueline. Such a stupid woman. She has only herself to blame. She had no idea how to look after Lord Humphrey.'

'He is her husband. It is not her duty to look after him. He has valets and body servants by the dozen for that.'

'But how much more pleasant to receive a woman's caress. Her hands are softer, her voice more soothing and, when he has rested, only she can give him the satisfaction he craves. Lord Humphrey is a man who requires attention.' A very slight flush crept across Eleanor's cheeks which made her look younger and even more beautiful. 'Does Sir Richard not enjoy your personal attentions? Or are you too busy composing lists of your wrongdoings for the bishop, to notice what your husband needs?'

Eleanor could be very cruel when she chose and always knew exactly where to aim the point of her dagger.

'My husband has no complaints,' I said stiffly.

She laughed. 'Neither did Lord Humphrey until I showed him what I could do.'

'Eleanor!'

'I could teach you if you like.'

'My husband has been well rewarded by the council,' I said, feeling heat rise in my face. 'He has no need of whatever practices you use on Lord Humphrey to give him pleasure.'

She seized my hands and swung me round to face her. 'Little fool! D'you truly imagine the world revolves around a group of greedy old men? D'you think their ideas are conjured out of thin air?'

'They are well advised,' I protested.

'And who advises these men do you imagine?'

I shrugged. 'Men who are clever with words and understand the world, I suppose.'

'The words which really matter are those a woman whispers into her lover's ear, the promises she makes of the man he could be with her at his side.'

This was not the Eleanor I knew, the young woman who had gazed in admiration at her betters at Katherine's coronation feast.

'He will be tired of you by Christmas,' I said flatly.

'I think not.'

'Lady Warwick says he will.'

Eleanor put her knuckle to her mouth as she stifled a laugh. 'Lady Warwick! D'you know what they say about Isabel Warwick? That she cannot tell one husband from

215

the other. Two cousins, both with the same name. First one in her bed, then the other and no embarrassing misremembering in the throes of passion.'

'She is a very pleasant woman.'

'Pleasant! Who wants to be pleasant? How much better to be exciting, to be desirable. How much better to be irresistible.'

She ran her hands over her hips and down the length of her thighs where the dark green cloth clung to her slender body. 'How much better to be me,' she whispered, as if inviting me to join her in some devilment.

'But Eleanor. What of the future?'

She cupped my face in her hands and looked deep into my eyes. 'The future is taking care of itself. I have it all arranged.'

Once back home at The Erber amongst the familiar trappings of my Nevill existence, I knew that what I'd seen and what I'd heard were not matters I could keep from my husband however much I might wish it.

'You know her?' Richard Nevill was incredulous.

'I have met her a few times.'

'And you didn't think to mention it?'

I shifted my feet like a naughty child and waited for the fury to break over my head.

'She was one of the duchess's women. I didn't think it important.'

He wiped his forehead with the back of his hand and swore softly under his breath.

'How could you think that having access to the duchess's private chamber was not important. Do you not realise that men like Lord Humphrey tell their wives everything.'

I stared at my hands and considered how little Richard Nevill told me. Perhaps I was not considered much of a wife and so not worthy of anyone's confidences.

'Forgive me. I didn't think.'

'Obviously not. Is she a friend?'

Of course Eleanor was a friend but it would be unwise to make much of it. A Nevill wife did not consort with a whore, even the whore of a royal duke.

'I suppose you might call it friendship. She has been kind to me on one or two occasions.'

I could not tell my husband of the length and breadth of Eleanor's kindnesses because meetings with a woman suspected of witchcraft who encouraged me to dabble in magic spells and potions had got me into enough trouble already.

'Good.'

'Good?'

'Yes. We need to discover what is in Lord Humphrey's mind and who better to find out than the woman who shares his bed. Is she clever?'

'Yes, I believe she is.'

'A clever whore? How unusual, they're mostly stupid women. But if she is as clever as you say you must be on your guard. So listen carefully and do exactly what I tell you. You've not done much for me since I married you. It's time you made yourself useful.'

He had no idea how much those words hurt – you've not done much for me. He had no idea what I'd done for him. He had no idea of the risks I'd taken and the dangers

I'd put myself in. He would never know because I could never tell him. In his eyes I was simply a failure as a wife.

And so began a long summer of deceit. I lied to Eleanor, I lied to Katherine and I lied to my husband. The only person I could not lie to was Edmund because he knew me too well. I tried to keep out of his way, still angry at his behaviour at Eltham. but whenever I thought myself alone, which was a difficult feat in the crowded houses I frequented, Edmund was always there.

'I still love you, Alice,' he whispered in the shadow of a wall at Windsor where he'd followed me. The heat of the day meant the walk by the wall was deserted except for a single guard leaning against a jutting-out part of the tower some distance away. There was no breeze and I could feel beads of sweat trickling down my back.

He slid his arm round my unresisting waist and pulled me against him. I was unsure if the hammering under my ribs was caused by fear or desire but despite knowing what he was doing was dreadfully wrong, I was unable to make myself walk away. I loved Richard Nevill but he didn't know me, not like my cousin knew me. Edmund would always be there for me, whatever I did, whatever happened but if Richard Nevill knew what I'd done I feared he might cast me aside.

'Edmund, please …' He stopped my words with his mouth, a mouth at once so achingly familiar and yet so excitingly strange. His kisses were different from my husband's, sweeter, more tender, more searching and yet amidst the waves of sensation sweeping through my body an unbidden thought came creeping – perhaps Edmund was also lying.

# 16

## RABY 1425

In the autumn of that year my father-in-law, Ralph Nevill, died. He was an old man and had been sick for some months so his death was not unexpected. His chaplain said it was a good death although, to see my mother-in-law's ravaged face and the visible grief displayed by the men of the earl's household, it was hard to agree. The confines of The Erber fell silent apart from the tolling of a bell, the sobbing of women and the rustle of black silk gowns hastily pulled out of chests where they'd lain smothered in lavender since the last death.

Beyond our walls the growing dispute between The duke of Gloucester and Bishop Beaufort was threatening to erupt into violence but while armed men massed on the streets of London in support of Lord Humphrey, and the bishop's palace at Southwark resembled a fortress more than an episcopal residence, the Nevill family quit the city for the long journey north to Raby where the earl was to be buried.

Behind the hearse which carried the coffin rode my husband and three of his younger brothers. I travelled in my mother-in-law's litter and following us were the senior members of the earl's household and his squire leading the earl's favourite warhorse.

'My gown is the deepest of blacks,' whispered Cecily.

'This is not a competition, Cecily,' I remarked, thinking how much I would like to slap her face. Since her betrothal to the York boy, Cecily believed herself superior to everyone, barring her mother, and was becoming increasingly insufferable.

'When I am a duchess I shall have a dozen black gowns stitched ready for these sad occasions of which I expect there will be many as you're all very much older than me.'

'Be quiet!' hissed the dowager Lady Scrope. 'Our father is dead and your lady mother is grieving. Nobody wishes to hear your voice.'

Cecily opened her mouth to reply but caught sight of my frown and closed it again. She sat stroking the fur trimming on her jacket, murmuring quietly to herself, doubtless counting imaginary numbers of sable backs.

The journey was long and wearisome. At Sheriff Hutton we were joined by my husband's brother Robert who'd ridden from Beverley and by his sisters: Lady Mowbray, Lady Percy and a newly married Anne, Lady Stafford who threw herself into her mother's arms and wept. As we progressed towards Middleham people turned out in their thousands with tears in their eyes because here in the North the earl had been greatly loved. Men and women stood in silence as we passed and at every halt we were joined by my father-in-law's tenants who were to ride with us to Raby.

I had never seen a more magnificent place than my late father-in-law's great castle of the North. The vast sweep of the surrounding hills and the towering grey walls of Raby Castle caused shivers to run down my spine and as we crossed the moat I understood at last why my husband wanted this place and why he would do anything to prevent it falling into the hands of the "little turd".

The great iron portcullises had been raised to allow us entry but there was an uncomfortable feeling that we were interlopers, only here on sufferance, certainly not valued members of the Nevill family.

'I was born here,' whispered Cecily as we passed into darkness beneath the enormous gatehouse. 'My lady mother said.'

'So was I,' sighed the heavily veiled dowager Lady Scrope, her words wiping the smile off Cecily's face.

Our coming was expected and the other Nevill family – my father-in-law's first family – was out in force in the Great Hall as if to show us who was now in command of Raby. I was unsure who they were but assumed the tall young man at the front was my husband's "little turd". Named Ralph for his grandfather, the young man had all the height and dark good looks of a Nevill and every bit as much surly aggression as my husband. If this had not been a funeral I was certain they'd have been scrapping on the floor amongst the rushes or, more likely, drawing swords in the yard.

My mother-in-law, as always, took charge, treating the castle as her domain, ordering the servants and commenting unfavourably on the mourning gowns of her Nevill step-daughters. I was introduced to a Lady Hauley, a Lady Lancaster and a Lady Dacre, a trio of women with my late father-in-law's eyes above a softer, kinder mouth, who curtsied and called my mother-in-law "lady stepmother". Lurking at the back of the group, as if unwilling to make herself known was a hesitant woman who was my mother-in-law's daughter from her first marriage now married to a

Nevill. To one side, away from the men, the dowager Lady Umfraville clasped Lady Scrope to her breast and they both began to weep all over again.

In icy silence my father-in-law's sons and grandsons escorted his body to the family church at Staindrop, below the walls of the castle. The coffin would rest there for several days and nights, surrounded by a hundred beeswax candles and twenty black-clad weepers. While the men were away we women sat awkwardly together in the upstairs solar listening to readings selected by my mother-in-law and making half-hearted attempts at conversation. Since everyone claimed ownership of my father-in-law's memory and my mother-in-law was determined not to yield an inch, the gloomy reminisces were brief and frequently interrupted by her steely voice saying, 'You are mistaken. It was not like that.'

Three days later they buried him but the obsequies were barely complete when the shouting began. Men from both families were closeted together with my mother-in-law and elderly Bishop Langley in what had once been my late father-in-law's room of business. From the sound of raised voices I knew there must be some disagreement. When I tiptoed down the stairs to discover if I could hear what was being said, I found myself confronted by my husband's "little turd". He was standing on the bottom step, effectively blocking my way.

'Cousin,' he said, with a slight twitch of his mouth which a kinder person than me might have interpreted as a smile.

'My lord,' I replied. 'I am no kin of yours, other than by marriage.'

Now the smile broadened, displaying a fine set of teeth, his lips pulled back in a slightly feral grin. 'So they've not told you?'

'Told me what?'

'That we are cousins, you and I. Cousins germane.'

'My lord, I think you're mistaken.' I could not imagine being a cousin of this rather unpleasant young man.

'No, Cousin Alice. No mistake. Our mothers were sisters. My mother, Elizabeth, was the daughter of Sir Thomas Holand, earl of Kent and his wife, Alys, daughter of the earl of Arundel. I think you will find that your mother was also their daughter.'

I felt my mouth drop open and heard him laugh at my astounded face.

'I urge you to remember that blood kinship, Cousin Alice, while your husband is stealing my inheritance and cursing the day I was born. Remember it is your own mother's nephew he is attempting to disinherit.'

I shook my head in disbelief. 'Nobody told me.'

He shrugged. 'Perhaps it is of no importance. Raby is mine, the earldom is mine and nothing that witch of a Beaufort woman does can take it away. My grandfather promised he'd see I was well provided for and he was always a man of his word. Now that my prospects have improved I shall marry. Perhaps after Christmas you and your husband would care to join us at Raby for the nuptials?' He laughed. 'Although I doubt the news will bring Sir Richard much joy.'

'Who are you to marry?' I asked politely.

He leaned closer so that the little sparks of malice in his eyes danced as if they were alive. I could smell his breath. 'Henry Percy's sister.'

I gasped. This was a calculated insult and my husband would be furious.

'In the meantime, my little Nevill cousin, fare thee well. My two brothers and I wish *you* no harm, whatever we may wish for the rest of your husband's family.'

By the end of the evening it was obvious that discussions had gone badly.

'We are leaving,' announced my husband in a hard clipped voice. He was flushed and angry and looked as if he was aching to hit someone so I kept well out of his way despite longing to know what had been said downstairs.

'We are going to Middleham,' whispered Cecily who seemed overawed by her brother's fury. Earl Ralph doesn't want us here. He says Raby is his and he will decide who may visit.'

'Is it true?' I whispered to my husband once we were in bed.

'Is what true?'

'That your father's grandson, the new earl, will get Raby?'

He laughed as he eased his leg over mine and began nuzzling my neck. 'My mother would not have let my father to do anything so foolish. She arranged matters to her own children's advantage, which is how it should be. We can do nothing about the earldom which is entailed but Raby is part of my mother's dower and will in due course come to me. As will Middleham and Sheriff Hutton. All the little turd gets is Brancepeth. Have you seen it? A crumbling ruin barely worth rebuilding.'

One castle seemed very little when my father-in-law's

grandson was now Earl of Westmoreland, a man who would need property to support his dignity.

Between kissing my mouth and lifting aside the folds of my nightshift, my husband whispered into my ear, 'Kirby Moorside and a few manors in Lincolnshire. Nothing of value and nothing I want. Not for now!'

My mother-in-law had, it transpired, been remarkably astute. Since the earliest days of her marriage she had persuaded the earl to divert his vast wealth into her hands and thus into the hands of their children. What he'd done was perfectly legal but had left the children and grandchildren of his first marriage with almost nothing. If I had not cared so much for my husband, I'd have felt a pang of sorrow for my new-found cousin, banished from Raby to the distinctly less glorious castle of Brancepeth, with barely enough money to keep a cow let alone a household fit for an earl.

It was a sombre Christmas at Middleham. There were no travelling players and precious little in the way of entertainment and to my dismay I learned that my mother-in-law had granted my husband a lease of the castle. From now on Middleham would be our main residence.

'What about my friends?' I said, trying to sound calm and reasonable. 'What if the bishop should wish me to visit the queen dowager? How shall I manage? What about my aunt in her convent at Syon?'

I thought of the bleak dark moors and the endless torrents of rain and despite my best intentions felt my bottom lip begin to tremble. I was a grown woman, no longer a child, yet perilously close to weeping.

Richard Nevill pushed me down into a chair and pulled up a little stool and took my hands in his. 'Alice, you should be thinking of me, your husband, and of our child, not your aunt or your friends or even the queen dowager. You are my wife. That means living in one of the Nevill houses and, apart from Raby, Middleham is the finest. Why would you not be happy here?'

It was impossible to explain to my husband that I would not be happy at Middleham because it wasn't Bisham. It was a simple as that. There was none of the soft warmth of my childhood home where sunlight filtered though the beech leaves in Quarry Wood and I could run barefoot across the meadows to the church by the river to visit the old priest who fed me strawberries and told me I was my father's precious child.

'Can we not stay at The Erber?' I asked.

'When I need to be at Westminster we shall lodge there but my duties are here in the north, you know that.'

'And if the bishop requires me to visit the queen dowager?'

Richard Nevill kicked a branch further into the hearth with his boot. 'If we are invited to royal celebrations then of course we shall go south. I have no wish for you to be miserable, Alice, but you must remember you are a Nevill now.'

He was right. Of course he was. I was nineteen years old and had been married for more than five years and was the mother of a Nevill daughter. I had no right to be snivelling, behaving like a spoiled child who wanted something she couldn't have. I had to learn to be more of a Nevill and cease looking over my shoulder at the Montagu girl I'd once been. It was no wonder he found me something of a disappointment, I was a disappointment to myself.

To my great relief our stay at Middleham was cut short by a summons from the bishop. Lord Humphrey was out of control and the bishop had written to the duke of Bedford in Rouen asking him to return and intervene. The bishop's letter to my husband required him to be at Southwark as soon as possible for a gathering of the bishop's supporters. Gleefully, I supervised the packing of my chests and even managed an unseemly little hop and skip as I crossed the inner courtyard on my way to see my mother-in-law to tell her we were leaving.

Once installed at The Erber, the steward was impatient to tell us the news. In our absence there'd been much unrest in the streets, he explained, and a near riot on the bridge. Lord Humphrey had been denied entry to the Tower by the constable so the good duke and his armed supporters in the city had stormed onto the bridge where they'd faced a great force of men from the shires commanded by young Edmund Beaufort.

'Course 'twas the bishop ordered it from his inn at Southwark,' said the steward confidentially. 'He don't hold with Lord Humphrey's high and mighty ways. Not that Londoners think Lord Humphrey anything but a proper royal duke. They love him, God bless them. There's men out there who'd lay down their lives for Good Duke Humphrey. And then there's the apprentice boys. Always up for a fight they are *and* they've no love for the bishop, neither. Nor the merchants. They'd planned to throw the bishop into the river if they got their hands on him.'

'Surely not?' I gasped.

'Aye, m'lady. Said the bishop could swim with his wings.'

My husband laughed. 'How did it end?'

'Ah my lord, men were saying the bishop and Lord Humphrey would've spit roasted each other if the archbishop hadn't come between them and quietened them down. Don't know who called his grace out from his hole at Lambeth but afore the day was out he had Lord Humphrey and young Beaufort kissing his cross and swearing to put up their swords. They was like brothers.'

My husband snorted. 'I hear the duke of Bedford has returned from France.'

'Aye my lord. 'Twas said the bishop sent for him. He were that afeared of what Lord Humphrey might do. Course now Bedford's back, all's gone quiet. He's got that look about him, Bedford does, makes a man right scared to open his mouth for fear he'd put his fist in it.'

'My husband stifled another laugh. 'And Lord Humphrey?'

'Rode into the city at his brother's side but from the look on their faces I doubt there was much brotherly love on offer.'

Having gleaned what information he could from the steward about other Nevill interests in the city my husband left me to sort out my women and see to our child while he disappeared in the direction of the yard to deal with whatever difficulties awaited him there, still chuckling over his uncle's wings.

As soon as everything was straight and we'd eaten and enjoyed a good nights sleep under our own roof, I was set to work. Bishop Beaufort and his supporters needed to know what Lord Humphrey intended to do next and I was ordered to act as their intelligence gatherer.

'The bishop has agreed you are to go to Castle Baynard to see Lord Humphrey's new woman,' said my husband with a slight curl to his lip. 'Distasteful, I know, but my uncle stressed the importance of you doing your duty. Do you understand?'

Of course I understood. The bishop's eyes would follow me as I entered Lord Humphrey's fortress and in the enemy camp there'd be other eyes and other ears, men and women paid well for their information. As the bishop had once told me, he knew everything that went on in the city and I'd do well to remember what he'd said.

'You will take the Nevill barge,' continued my husband. 'At a time like this I'd rather you were on the water than in the streets. It's not far. The men can keep an eye out for troublemakers on the shore and you can land within the castle walls. But whatever happens, remember you are working for the bishop. My uncle needs good information so do not disappoint him.'

He watched me carefully as I put on my warmest cloak and selected the gloves he'd given me at the Nevill gift-giving ceremony, soft red leather lined with fur. 'Keep yourself safe,' he said and then added with a glimmer of a smile, 'and warm.'

Castle Baynard dozed like a sleeping monster in the pale winter sunshine. its huge grey towers surprisingly benign. I was met at the quay within the watergate by a liveried servant who, from his obsequious manner, was clearly expecting me. He led me through a maze of tiny chambers and up a winding stone stairway to the room where I'd last seen Duchess Jacqueline shortly before she left for Hainault. Today Eleanor was in residence but instead of sitting sedately at her embroidery surrounded by her ladies as the duchess might have been, she was standing alone at a table turning the pages of a book.

'Oh it's you,' she said carelessly. 'I was wondering when you'd turn up. Come to see if I've been cast aside yet, have you?'

'No. I've just returned from burying my father-in-law. I wanted to find out how you were.'

She whirled round, stretched her arms wide and gave me a brilliant smile. 'Voilà! As you see, still in favour and much desired. He cannot do enough for me.'

That was certainly true. I tried costing her garments but gave up when I noticed the sable trim on the hem of her skirt. My mother had once told me how many sable backs it took to trim a gown and I'd been horrified then and I was horrified now. The cost to Lord Humphrey of dressing Eleanor must be enormous. She wore only two pieces of jewellery: an enamelled pendant with strange markings on a large black stone, and a heavy gold ring with a small ruby cluster. Set against the figure-hugging jacket of tawny velvet and the dark folds of her crimson gown, they gave her a mysterious, somewhat exotic, air.

'I hear there's been trouble,' I said, remembering my mission.

'A little, but my lord got the better of the bishop which is why the old man sent to France for reinforcements. But if he thought Bedford would help him, the bishop has forgotten the ties of blood. Bedford will huff and puff and tell Brother Humphrey he's overstepped the bounds of his authority by challenging the bishop. But the bishop will lose the fight.'

'How can you be so sure?'

'Because I have reminded my lord how Bishop Beaufort tried to deprive old King Henry of the governance of his realm and the rumours of how he plotted to have King Harry killed.'

'Eleanor! Those were malicious lies. You know they were. There's not an ounce of truth in any of them.'

'Possibly, but not everyone will think so. There is enough doubt in the matter for the council to wonder if the bishop is a suitable man to be chancellor. And when they discover, as my lord and I have made sure that they will, how the bishop has been diverting into his own coffers, monies intended for the Crown, they will demand he is removed from office. And once that is done the way ahead will be clear.'

'Clear for what?' I asked.

Eleanor laughed. 'Has Sir Richard not told you? I'm sure he has and when you go home you'll have something new to tell him and he'll be pleased with you. You see, I know why you've come, Alice.'

I flushed, wishing things could be as simple as they'd once been, untainted by this feud between Lord Humphrey and Bishop Beaufort. I wished we could be back to the beginning of our friendship when we'd sat side by side at Katherine's coronation feast.

Eleanor patted my hand. 'Don't be downhearted. We're friends still, are we not? Come and see what I've found.'

She turned one of the pages of the book but I was unsure what I was looking at.

I pointed. 'What are those strange drawings? And those little circles with squiggles inside?'

Eleanor raised her eyebrows as if in surprise at my ignorance.

'Those are the celestial bodies seen in the sky. D'you not recognise them? If you know how they move and how they co-join you can understand the forces which influence our destiny.'

'Surely the bishops disapprove of books like this and discussion of such practices?'

She laughed. 'There any many practices of which bishops disapprove but I'm sure even Sir Richard has transgressed on occasions. Has he never visited your bed on a Friday? Or on a Wednesday? Has he never removed your nightshift and enjoyed you naked?'

I peered more closely at the book to hide my embarrassment. I most certainly did not want to think of what Richard Nevill and I did in the privacy of my bed with the curtains drawn, not when here with Eleanor.

The drawings on the pages were not like the stars I saw from the roof leads at Middleham when I stood there longing for Bisham, wondering if my husband loved me and, if he did, would he love me still if I failed to bring him his earldom.

'Where is the sun?' I asked, frowning. 'And the moon?'

Eleanor laughed. 'I thought you might be interested but I think maybe it is too difficult for an untrained mind like yours. I thought you were clever enough but perhaps you should run home to your husband and child and leave all thoughts of the future to me.'

I did not care to be insulted but had to remember why I was here.

'Does Lord Humphrey know you read books like this?' I said stiffly.

She tapped the end of my nose with her finger. 'When a woman finds a man whose intelligence matches her own, she'd be a fool to lose him. Of course he knows. The books are his. He has hundreds of them. Men come from far and near bringing him writings they think he might enjoy. And as well as collecting books he commissions translations and employs a master illuminator from Antwerp to copy ancient texts. Here, let me show you his work.'

She picked up another book and opened it at the first page where a king with a golden crown and a long white beard. dressed in a dark blue robe, was holding in one hand an enormous blue orb covered in tiny silver points. The brushwork was exquisite.

'See!' said Eleanor, smiling. 'The heavens – held in one hand.'

When I returned to The Erber I was told my husband had gone to Westminster. In his stead I found the impatient figure of the dowager Lady Scrope, tapping her shoe and biting her lip.

'Lady Margaret,' I said with genuine pleasure. 'What are you doing here? I thought you were at Sheriff Hutton.'

She took my hands and leant forward to kiss me. 'I have come to say farewell.'

'Greetings and farewell, all in one day? When will you return?'

She hesitated. 'I shall not return.'

'But for how long?'

'I shall never come back to The Erber. It would be impossible.'

'But why?'

Her face became one huge smile and she looked happier than I'd ever seen her. Gone was the weeping, the sniffing and the tear-stained face; instead she looked radiant.

'William Cressener and I were married this morning. We are returning to Suffolk. Our boat leaves on the afternoon tide.'

I was stunned. 'But that's impossible. You cannot be married.'

'I am.'

'Does Richard know?'

'I've told nobody. But I shall write. As soon as we're settled in William's house I shall write to Richard and to my stepmother.'

'But your children?'

She gave a little shrug as if to rid herself of any lingering maternal feelings she might have for her two Scrope boys.

'They are in Richard's care. He will look after them. They do not need me any more not the way William needs me. Oh Alice, pray for my happiness. I never thought this day would come. I thought I was destined to be a widow for the rest of my life. But if I could hold this moment in my heart forever, I swear I'd want for nothing more.'

She told me she'd waited until her father was safely buried, then made her decision. She had written to this man she barely knew and told him she was ready to marry him if he still wanted her.

She beamed. 'He was in London before the ink was dry. He had the priest paid and the banns called. It was a very quiet ceremony.'

'Do you mind? Did you not want a large celebration with your family and friends?'

'No, I wanted William.'

Now it was my turn to cling. I could not imagine life without Lady Margaret. She had been weeping in corners for so long I'd not even noticed when the rooms at The Erber had fallen silent. She had been kind to me when the others had not and now she was going away, leaving me behind and I knew I'd never see her again. In marrying William Cressener she had cut herself off from her family. Even if she wished to visit she would not be welcome, my husband would make quite certain of that. She was no longer a Nevill, she was the wife of Master Cressener and the Nevills with their castles and manors and numerous offices from the Crown did not consort with men like that.

# 17

## LEICESTER 1426

It was raining when we left The Erber on the first part of our journey north. Perhaps it was wrong but I'd said nothing about Lady Margaret to my husband. Sooner or later he'd discover the facts of the Cressener marriage for himself without any assistance from me and I dreaded to think how angry he'd be. He was angry enough about our own marriage and my father's so-called treachery but at least I was an earl's daughter not some petty country gentleman's son with no wealth and no connections. The dowager Lady Scrope's marriage to William Cressener was of no use to the Nevills and Lady Margaret would suffer for her choice of husband, however much she protested her love for him.

My husband wished to return to Middleham as soon as possible but naturally could not leave until the parliament was concluded. Lord Humphrey had refused to go to either St Albans or Northampton so the parliament was to be reconvened at Leicester. Nobody was pleased about this because delay meant proceedings would spill over into the fasting season of Lent. There'd be no great platters of roasted meats on the tables merely fish disguised in a hundred different ways: baked in cream, jellied and coloured with columbine flowers or seethed in ale and decorated with whelks. However cunning the cooks, and I had to admit some cooks were exceedingly cunning, it was impossible to hide the lack of meat.

'I'd shove his royal face in the mud given half a chance,' muttered my husband as his groom struggled to pull off his master's boots. 'There's work to be done in the North and it's taken nigh on a month to arrange this cock fight. All due to Lord Humphrey's intransigence.'

With the duke of Bedford back from France to fulfil the role of protector, this parliament was to be the final reckoning between Lord Humphrey and Bishop Beaufort. By the end it would be clear whose hand would steer little Henry until the boy reached his majority. Guiding the boy meant guiding the kingdom so the position carried with it enormous power.

With such high stakes, tempers were starting to fray; snarling and bickering and small fights breaking out in every quarter. To prevent bloodshed, swords had been forbidden within the walls but I'd seen grooms in the courtyard openly carrying bats and men sneaking past guards with what looked suspiciously like clubs hidden beneath their cloaks. In dark corners of the castle insults were hurled and oaths sworn and more than one man had been set upon and injured by his master's enemies.

'Perhaps the duke of Bedford will have Lord Humphrey sent back to Hainault,' I said hopefully.

My husband gave me a withering look. 'Humphrey has no appetite for being made to look a fool a second time. Besides, Bedford won't let him go. The council might agree a small force to aid Duchess Jacqueline but we cannot afford to offend Burgundy. He is necessary to our success in France. I'd have thought as your father's daughter you'd be better informed.'

With the men in the Great Hall for the reconvening of the parliament and most of the women summoned to wait on the queen dowager, the rooms in the castle were eerily quiet. I wandered through one vast chamber after another wondering why Katherine had not asked for me. Had I offended her in some way? It seemed I was unwanted by both my husband and by the queen dowager, who had once said she regarded me as a friend. I wrapped my arms around myself to ward off the morning chill as my melancholy deepened. In despair I stared at the stone flags beneath my feet.

Suddenly an arm was raised barring my path. I looked up. It was Edmund. I was not greatly pleased to see him as we'd parted on bad terms last summer after yet another quarrel.

He grasped my arm and pulled me into a small alcove where we were hidden from public view.

'Let me go!' I hissed. 'I'm not one of your servants.'

He glanced up, checking that he couldn't be seen, then kissed me hard on my mouth.

'I don't do that to my servants,' he said, smiling as he drew away.

'You disgust me,' I said, wiping the back of my hand across my mouth.

He laughed. 'Where have you been, Alice? I've missed our fights.'

'Burying my father-in-law,' I said crossly.

'Of course. The ever-dutiful Nevill wife.'

I glared at him. 'How else should a wife please her husband than by being dutiful.'

'I can think of a dozen ways.'

He smiled, giving me ample time to imagine those other ways.

'My husband will be here shortly,' I said.

He laughed. 'Oh Alice, you are a dreadful liar. We both know Richard Nevill is far too busy to come to your aid. It's like bear baiting in the Great Hall. You can hear the hounds baying half-way across Leicester.'

'If he finds you here …'

'But he won't.'

I did not care to examine too closely my feelings for my cousin or why I allowed him to seek me out. A wise young woman would have screamed if detained by a man in this way, but I had remained silent. Not only did I not cry out, I barely struggled. Our being together like this was wrong. I knew Richard Nevill would be angry and rightly so. Edmund and I were no longer the boy and girl we'd once been, playing innocently in Quarry Wood, but the memory of first love lingers long after the flame has died and no matter how much I wanted him to leave me alone, part of me enjoyed the reminder of those days when I was young and in love, when life stretched ahead of me and anything seemed possible, a time before I was tempted into sin by Eleanor and Mistress Jourdemayne, a time before Bishop Beaufort discovered what I'd done.

'Why are you here?' I asked at last, breaking the silence. 'I thought you'd be dancing attendance on Katherine.'

'Tut, tut! A young man in the queen dowager's chamber! That would be most unseemly.'

'It's not stopped you before.'

'Ah but now the royal uncles are prowling and Katherine must be above suspicion.' He shrugged. 'She sent me away. She cannot have temptation within reach or she might forget herself.'

'She would never forget herself,' I said staunchly.

He put his mouth to my ear and whispered. 'She already has.'

Was he joking? I was unsure.

'I do not understand you, Edmund. Why are you doing this? What do you hope to gain?'

'The love of a beautiful lady.'

'Katherine is not free to love.'

'You think not?'

'We both know she is not.'

I recalled the agony of Katherine that Christmas at Eltham, fighting valiantly against her base desires, tempted by my handsome cousin's attentions but knowing the danger of entangling herself with any man.

'When Harry died his brothers placed her in a gilded cage,' he said slowly. 'And in case she should tire of her sorrow, they locked the door and threw away the key.'

'Now you are being ridiculous.'

'It has been three years of suffering. She is like a martyred saint nailed to the cross of Harry's memory.'

I looked around the empty room at the soaring beams and painted walls and knew that what he said was true. Unlike Isabel Warwick, content within her new marriage, there could be no second chance of happiness for Katherine. The royal uncles and the council would keep her on her knees in that gilded cage until she was of no further use to anyone but God. Yet Katherine was not like my aunt at Syon who had found solace in prayer and contemplation as she approached the end of her days. Katherine was young. She was beginning to emerge from her personal grief and needed a purpose to her life.

'What do you intend, Edmund?'

'I thought to offer myself as a pleasant diversion. I think she should fall in love with me.'

'You seem remarkably adept at making women fall in love with you,' I said tartly.

'Ah yes, but with Katherine it's different.'

'Of course it's different. She's not like other women. She was born the daughter of a great king and for two years was a beloved queen, bowed to and feted. Royalty is bred in her bones. No matter how hard you try and however much she may be tempted, she will not allow herself to fall in love with you.'

'She lets me kiss her.'

'That means nothing. You kiss your sisters. You kiss me. You kiss a great many people.'

Edmund moved closer and with his fingers tilted my chin, forcing me to look into his eyes.

'Not in the places where I kiss Katherine.'

I caught my breath as a sliver of fire shot through my veins. He wanted me to ask, he was daring me to ask. We both knew that words spoken between us were secrets shared but I also knew the danger of secrets

'I don't want to know,' I whispered.

'When we are alone,' he said so quietly that I could barely hear the words, 'I kiss her lips, her eyes and her lovely long neck. I taste her on my tongue. She purrs like a cat bathed in sunshine, all soft sleek fur and heavy limbs. Sometimes, if she is feeling kind, she lets me kiss the curves of her beautiful breasts.'

I stood perfectly still while Edmund traced a line with his finger just above the tight bodice of my gown where my skin lay exposed to view. My belly tightened and my mouth was so dry I was unable to speak. If there were voices in the castle they faded to nothing. All I heard was the sound of our breathing and the slight rustle of my gown as Edmund pressed me back against the wall.

'One day she let me lift her skirts.'

I twisted my head to one side and tried to push him away. 'I don't want to hear any more.'

He laughed deep in his throat. 'There's no more to tell. Just the sound of approaching footsteps.'

'Guillemot?'

'Who else.'

'What of Katherine?'

'Ah Katherine!' He paused as if overcome by the memory of what had occurred between them. 'Flushed, eyes hazy with desire, gown disordered as if she'd been tumbled on the bed. If there'd been more time she would have let me have her. I was that close.' He held up his thumb and first finger an inch apart to show me how near he'd come to dishonouring the widowed queen of England.

'I warned her,' I said flatly.

He grinned. 'I know you did. She told me. She says I am much too dangerous to be allowed near her and the council will have me sent away. But she tells no-one what we do. She pushes me away with one hand and yet pulls me ever closer with the other.'

'You are describing a woman on the rack of her desire.'

'It is most certainly desire. Oh God, yes! The liberties she allows me, the pleasure she takes in what we do. But it's not love. If it was love she would tell me. Women do. They say the words but she says nothing.'

I thought of Richard Nevill and the complex emotions he aroused in me. I practised the wifely duties of obedience and submissiveness, while knowing something was missing, something I had yet to identify. I yearned for a closeness he neither wanted nor offered.

'Perhaps she is afraid.'

'Of what?'

'Of you.'

He laughed. 'I'd not harm her.'

'Men often harm those who love them.'

He put his head on one side and said gently, 'Richard Nevill?'

I blushed and said nothing.

'You love him?' He sounded disbelieving.

I nodded, barely trusting myself to speak.

'And he?'

I sighed. 'I think not. He is kind to me but … things are not what he expected when he married the earl of Salisbury's daughter.'

'He's a fool,' said Edmund. 'I would have married you.'

'And I would have married you but my mother said it could not be.'

He grinned. 'My stepfather said if I meddled with you, he'd tie me to a cartwheel and thrash the life out of me.'

'So you stayed away.'

'No. That was before our afternoon in Quarry Wood. I reckoned you'd be worth a thrashing.'

'Oh Edmund!'

He put his mouth on mine once more and this time kissed me gently, a bittersweet kiss of farewell.

'What will you do now?' I said, removing myself from his arms, the imprint of his kiss still burning my lips.

He smiled. 'Perhaps I shall become an adventurer, out for what I can get; a pirate looting a town before sailing off with a few captive slaves. I shall take what I want then walk away leaving the lady behind.'

'While you make off with her heart.'

'How accurate you are, my dearest, dearest Lady Nevill. Each arrow true to its mark.' He grinned. 'But I think I'd better leave you before someone spots us talking together and tells your husband. I'm not sure Richard Nevill approves of me in any way and if he finds me kissing his wife and talking of love we might end up brawling on the floor and that would never do. Take care of yourself my sweet and lovely Alice.'

He turned and walked away leaving me pondering what he'd just said. Why did he kiss me and make me believe he wanted more when he knew I belonged to another man? And why was he trying to get Katherine to fall in love with him when he knew the danger for both of them. I remembered what my aunt had said. She was his mother and surely knew him better than anyone. Everything Edmund did was done with calculation, she'd told me, and yet trying to persuade a young woman not free to love, to abandon her moral principles and put herself in danger from universal condemnation was a most uncalculated act. It was an act of stupidity and Edmund was not a stupid man.

None of it made any sense.

In the Great Hall, the parliament dragged on interminably. With the little king perched high on his throne like a tiny doll, the archbishop recited a lengthy denial given on oath by Bishop Beaufort, a denial that he had ever attempted to deny the king's grandfather the governance of his realm or plotted to assassinate the king's father. The speech was received in stony silence and if the bishop thought his words would save him he was to be disappointed. The commons expressed their disquiet at dissensions amongst the lords and demanded reassurances. They wanted an end to fighting and looked to the duke of Bedford to deliver what they wanted. So it was no surprise when the bishop was forced to resign as chancellor. Instead, the great silver seal of office was given to the archbishop elect of York, John Kemp, and everyone agreed that the bishop's days of power and influence were over.

I wondered if Eleanor had heard the news and if so, was she cheering the downfall of Lord Humphrey's great enemy. She was nowhere to be seen and for all I knew might still be at Castle Baynard. I doubted Lord Humphrey was foolish enough to have installed her close by as word would surely reach the ears of his disapproving brother and at this fraught moment, with so much at stake, Lord Humphrey needed to be seen in a favourable light.

'Have you heard?' said a smiling Lady Warwick, sidling up to me shortly before supper. In truth, waddling would have been a better description, as she was heavy with another child and no longer the elegant woman of last autumn.

'Heard what?'

She lowered her voice. 'The commons have presented a petition which will, I think, interest you, Lady Alice.'

Her eyes were dancing but I had no idea what relevance this mysterious petition might have.

'Another request for one of Bishop Beaufort's loyal followers to be removed from his office?' I suggested.

'No, nothing like that,' she laughed. 'This petition asks that the widow of a king be allowed to remarry as she wishes.'

I gasped and my hand flew to my mouth.

'I thought you might find that intriguing,' she went on, clearly pleased with the effect she'd created. 'There'd be a fine to pay of course but that is only to be expected. Fines for marriages are commonplace.'

This was not possible. Everything I knew about Katherine, everything she'd said in the years I'd been her friend, told me she'd never marry a man who was not her equal and Edmund was very far from being her equal. But if not Edmund, then who? She'd shown no marks of favour to anyone else.

'I doubt if the instigator was the queen dowager herself,' said Lady Warwick, reading my mind. 'She'd not lower herself to involvement in anything so crude.'

So who could be behind this petition? Certainly not the speaker of the commons, a reliable Derbyshire man, known to the Nevills. Then I remembered my husband saying, the speaker had a connection to his uncle, the bishop. Lady Warwick watched me closely while I tried to solve this puzzle.

'Your cousin, Edmund Beaufort, will doubtless be pleased,' she said as if enjoying my only too obvious discomfort.

'I wouldn't know, Lady Warwick.'

'Oh come, Lady Alice. Bishop Beaufort's marks are all over this attempt to have his family move closer to the throne. You know they are.'

'I know nothing of the sort,' I protested.

She shrugged. 'It is no matter. Bedford and Gloucester will not allow such a thing to be brought into law and with the bishop out of favour there is no-one else to champion your cousin's cause. Edmund Beaufort may keep his intentions well-hidden but we all know what he wants.'

'Lady Warwick, I think you misunderstand my cousin. He admires the queen dowager enormously but he has no designs on her person.'

I crossed my fingers as I told the lie and prayed God would forgive me.

Lady Warwick laughed. 'You really do go around with your eyes closed, Lady Alice, don't you? If I were you I should open them quickly before it's too late.'

'Too late for what?'

'Ambitious men can be dangerous and Edmund Beaufort is an extremely ambitious young man.'


As Lady Warwick predicted, the petition was thrown out. Both royal dukes were utterly opposed to such a preposterous suggestion. It was possible they were unaware of Edmund's interest in Katherine but I suspected Lady Warwick would have alerted her husband and he would most certainly have told the duke of Bedford. And as if to rub the bishop's nose in his spectacular downfall from power and the collapse of his schemes, the council granted him leave to go on a long-delayed pilgrimage. They wanted him out of England.

I breathed a sigh of relief at the thought of his departure – no more terrifying interviews with me down on my knees begging for mercy and no further danger of imminent arrest. I'd only been a girl when I'd followed Eleanor's lead in an ill-advised attempt to secure the Salisbury inheritance for my husband. Now that I was older and wiser I could see how foolish I'd been. I regretted what I'd done but no amount of regret banished the uneasiness which overwhelmed me every time I thought of Bishop Beaufort and his threats of punishment.

# 18

## GREENWICH 1427

The old house at Greenwich was a peculiar affair, neither fortress nor palace nor simple hunting lodge, more a wealthy gentleman's house with funny little turrets and crooked windows. It was the favourite residence of the youngest Beaufort brother, the duke of Exeter who had fallen sick on his return from France and come to Greenwich to die in the place he loved best. He had lingered for several months giving the family renewed hope that God would spare him for further military duties but on the darkest night of the year he had made his final confession and died quietly with very little fuss.

Despite the oddity of the house and some clear signs of decay I considered its situation perfect for an ambitious man. It lay on a wide bend of the Thames a few miles downriver from the city and the palace at Westminster, and a short ride across the heath from the royal palace at Eltham. The possibilities of such a place were endless.

With a sigh I turned from my contemplation of the river to talk to my companion. It was more than a year since I'd last seen Eleanor and far from being downhearted, as Lady Warwick had once predicted, she was looking remarkably pleased with herself.

I, on the other hand, needed comforting and Eleanor was not a comforting sort of person.

'How did Sir Richard take the news?' she enquired with a smile.

'Very well, considering.'

'Considering?'

'He wanted a son.'

'Of course he wanted a son.'

'But Cecilia is a sweet baby.'

'Sweet or not, she's not a boy. And I hope you don't scowl like that when you're with your husband or he'll seek out some other woman for his enjoyment and that way you'll never get a son.'

All through the summer and into the autumn I had been confident I was carrying a boy but when the baby was born I found God had decided that a second daughter was what I deserved and remembering my foolish behaviour with Edmund at Leicester I knew I had been justly rebuked. When the midwife told me she was a girl, I burst into tears and it had taken a visit from Richard to stop the weeping. He had taken me in his arms and told me how clever I was to give us a sister for our little Joan.

'I so wanted to give you a son,' I had sobbed, overwhelmed by disappointment and the rigours of childbirth.

'Sons will follow. We're young. There's plenty of time.'

But time had brought yet more upset. The following day news had arrived at Middleham of the Cressener marriage and I doubted if even a trio of sons would have pacified Richard as he raged at his half-sister's foolishness.

'Humphrey and I plan to create a pleasure garden here,' said Eleanor, smiling as she surveyed the wide expanse of greenery which led down to the anchorage by the water's edge. 'That stretch of woodland will be for our deer park and when we've finished rebuilding the house, we shall entertain.'

'Entertain!'

'Of course! The king is too young to be of interest to anyone so people in want of diversion will flock to our court. We shall invite great scholars and poets to read and debate their works. The greatest painters and illuminators and musicians will fill our halls and soon Bella Court will be talked of far and wide.'

'You speak as if you were Lord Humphrey's wife not just his whore,' I said sharply.

'It is only a matter of time.'

I grimaced. 'How long is time? Jacqueline is still young. Do you intend to wait until she dies of old age or are you planning to help her on her way?'

I was too slow. I failed to see Eleanor's hand until I felt the sting of a slap on my face. I stepped backwards, covering my cheek with my fingers.

'Don't you dare say that!' she hissed. 'I have no need of poison to rid my lord of an inconvenient wife.'

'So you admit she *is* his wife. Earlier you swore she was not.'

I watched as she got a grip on her temper. Eleanor's little storms never lasted long but while they raged, they were dangerous. I rubbed my burning cheek and wondered if she attacked Lord Humphrey with her nails the way she did me and if he enjoyed the fight. Some men, it was said, liked a physical skirmish with their wives, believing it lent piquancy to their marriage, heightening their enjoyment of the marital act. Not my husband, of course; he was much too polite to strike me and I had no interest in attacking him.

Eleanor sighed and took my hands in hers. 'Alice, I know you do not understand theological arguments even though I have tried many times to explain them to you, but understand this: soon Pope Martin will rule that Jacqueline's marriage to her cousin of Brabant was valid therefore she was not free to marry Lord Humphrey. Their so-called marriage was no true marriage at all.'

She turned away from me and gazed out across the river to where a couple of heavy-laden ships had taken advantage of the incoming tide to make the journey up to the pool of London. At the water's edge ducks dabbled in amongst the reeds and above us, a flock of seabirds wheeled and dived in ever decreasing circles.

'Eleanor, he will not marry you,' I said. 'Men do not marry their whores, it is a known fact. What will you do when he casts you aside? It has been two years and Lord Humphrey is not known for constancy.'

She smiled like a contented cat. 'He will be constant to me. I know it. And by next spring we shall be married and I shall be Duchess of Gloucester.'

'You seem very sure?'

'I am.'

'But you bring him nothing.'

She gave a little throaty laugh. 'Lord Humphrey already knows what I can bring to our marriage. He'll not want to lose me, you can be quite certain of that.'

Eleanor always seemed certain of everything and time and again she'd been proved right. I knew I should not doubt her but I did. She never discussed the gifts

Lord Humphrey gave her but I hoped she was careful to make provision for her future like any prudent woman. In Eleanor's position, it would be wise to purchase a small property and set money aside for when she was no longer wanted by her lover because without the security of marriage a woman would be left with nothing.

'Have you heard the news?' she said as we wandered back towards the house.

'What news?'

'Your father is returning to England. He has been asked to raise reinforcements for the duke of Bedford.'

A great leap of excitement was followed by the sober realisation that my father would doubtless be accompanied by my stepmother, and she was the last person I wanted to see.

'Is he coming soon?'

'Probably. He has been made a member of the council so his return must be imminent.'

'And my stepmother?'

Eleanor gave a gurgling laugh. 'Oh Alice! The matter of a wife is of no interest to the council. But I know what you're asking. You want to know if she'll arrive with a bulging belly ready to give birth to a Salisbury heir.'

I flushed at how easily Eleanor could read my thoughts.

'I should like to know,' I said primly.

She gave me a little push. 'From what I hear, the existence or otherwise of a Salisbury heir is not for the want of trying. Since that bit of trouble in Paris, the earl has kept his wife close and his dislike of the duke of Burgundy has grown by the day.'

It was a month later when I met my father again, at a feast held in his honour at Castle Baynard. It was eight years since I'd last set eyes on him but I recognised him immediately. His lean angular face was leaner than ever and his eyes, whose colour changed as frequently as clouds roll across the sun, still searched restlessly round the room for something he couldn't quite find. I wanted to cry out, "I'm here, my lord father! I'm here!" but of course I did no such thing. I greeted him courteously as a daughter should, and afterwards we embraced and he kissed me on the lips. He was perfectly polite but treated me more like a valued acquaintance than a beloved daughter. His furred robes disguised his leanness but as he clasped me to his breast I was crushed against a hard bony frame. Holy Mary! I thought. She's wearing him out!

He was pleasant to my husband, talking to him of the difficulties of recruiting sufficient men to satisfy the duke of Bedford's needs, but I was disappointed. I had expected more. I had hoped for some recognition of my husband's position as a possible future earl of Salisbury, some warmth for the man who was his daughter's husband and father of his two granddaughters.

In the meantime I found myself forced to make conversation with my stepmother. She maintained the cool, calm composure I'd got to know well at Ewelme and I tried not to think of the duke of Burgundy's hands probing under her clothing and lifting her skirts. With her cold nature it was impossible to imagine her allowing any man such liberties, even my father, and yet Eleanor said my father kept her close which could only mean one thing.

She smiled at me. 'How are you stepdaughter?'

'Well, I thank you, lady stepmother.'

'And your mother-in-law, the dowager countess?'

'She finds consolation in prayer.'

'And in her grandchildren, I would imagine?' My stepmother raised her eyebrows questioningly.

'She is devoted to our daughters.'

'But would be more devoted if one were a boy.'

Luckily I remembered Lady Warwick's words.

'It is early days, my lady. I am still young. I'm certain I shall soon give my husband a son.'

She placed a hand protectively on her belly. 'That is what I say.'

'We are in God's hands,' I said piously, wondering was this all a pretence.

She gave a little wince.

'Is something amiss, my lady?'

Her fingers caressed her belly. 'It is nothing, just a nip of pain. You must have experienced such things when you were carrying your child. I'm sure you understand.'

Of course I understood. She was telling me she had a child in that flat belly of hers and she was certain it would be a boy. I felt sick at the thought. If her baby was a boy, all my efforts would have been in vain. The child would inherit and Richard Nevill would be furious. I would get the blame although I'd done everything within my power to prevent this catastrophe from happening.

'We shall go to Bisham soon,' said my stepmother, watching me carefully. 'You must visit. I shall show you the improvements I've ordered.'

'I was not aware my father's house needed improvement.'

'Ah stepdaughter, all houses, like all young women, benefit from a little improvement. When you travel, as I have done, it is a lesson you learn. The great princes of Europe embellish their palaces in a way we English can only dream of. At the Burgundian court I saw magnificent tapestries of a kind we lack here, and so much gold on display that your eyes could easily be blinded. Wait till you hear my plans, then you can tell me what you think.'

'She is carrying a child,' I said bluntly.

Richard Nevill and I were lying in the privacy of my bed with the curtains drawn

'Blood of Christ!' swore my husband.

'It may be a girl,' I said hopefully.

'She definitely said she was with child?'

'Not exactly, but she meant me to understand that she was.'

'Your father has said nothing.'

'Perhaps she's not told him.'

'Yet she told you.'

I sighed. Of course she had told me. She was boasting, trying to make me feel inferior.

'I think she wanted to show me that she has succeeded where I have failed,' I said miserably.

'We have two daughters. That's not failure.'

'But she is certain she's carrying a son.'

My husband frowned. 'Is that possible? Can she tell?'

'Some say it is possible. There are midwives who swear to special ways of divining if an unborn child is a boy. But those kind of woman require payment for their services.'

'And you?'

I flushed and turned my head away. 'No,' I said, very low.

After Cecilia's birth he had asked me regularly if I thought I could be with child again but this past month he'd stopped asking. Perhaps he was as tired as I was of my failure to conceive or perhaps he had accepted that we would only ever have two children and they would both be girls.

I wondered if my mother had felt like I did. To my knowledge my father had never reproached her for not giving him a son and it was not until I became a wife and my father remarried that I realised he must always have wanted a son. I'd thought I was special but perhaps my father had looked at me and seen nothing but failure.

Perhaps that was what Richard Nevill saw when he looked at me.

We spent the summer months at Middleham but at the beginning of October travelled south once more. I was anxious for news of my stepmother. Despite her oblique suggestion in the spring we'd received no invitation to visit Bisham and I wondered if this meant she was occupied with childbirth.

'Nothing!' said Eleanor, admiring her reflection in a small circular mirror. 'If there was a child it has disappeared or else is sleeping. I saw her last week and she's as slender as a willow wand and just about as seductive. What can Burgundy have seen in her?'

She touched a small blemish at the side of her mouth.

'Are you examining your moral imperfections, Mistress Eleanor?' I enquired.

She laughed. 'No, I am ensuring I have no illusions about my beauty, Lady Nevill. Humphrey tells me I am the epitome of all things desirable and have no equal. But I like to see for myself that he's right.'

'And?'

She turned round and smoothed her gown over her hips in a way I'd seen no other woman do. Edmund said it was enough to make a man want to tear off Mistress Cobham's clothes and throw her onto the nearest bed even if he preferred a woman who was less of a serpent.

'When we marry he will have a peerless wife and be envied by all,' said Eleanor.

'Has he asked you?'

'Of course he's asked me. He's been begging me to marry him since the day I first showed him what a superlative wife I could be. We expect the pope's ruling any day. Then,' she smiled, 'you will have to call me, your grace.'

'A great step up for you,' I said a trifle enviously.

'Don't speak as if this fell into my lap like a bunch of wayside flowers thrown by a villager's child. I have worked hard for it.'

'What of Mistress Jourdemayne?'

'I don't give her a second thought and neither should you. She had nothing to do with my success. She was merely a wise woman who dabbled in love charms, nothing more.'

I kept my mouth shut. If Eleanor chose to forget the little ring imbued with devilish powers for which she'd paid good money, then so be it. I was certain she'd used it on Lord Humphrey to entice him into her bed and like the buried newt and the muttered spell at Ewelme, the ring had proved remarkably effective.

The Christmas festivities at the start of Henry's seventh year were celebrated at Eltham. Richard and I received our expected invitation and with the royal command for our attendance came a joyful piece of news – our cousin, Tom Beaufort, was to be released. After six years of captivity, Katherine's brother had given him his freedom and he would shortly join the earl of Warwick at Rouen. It was only when I considered the implications of letting an English prisoner go free that I realised a deal must have been done. Our enemy would have wanted something in exchange. This was not in any way an act of kindness, merely a hard-headed business transaction.

'And Cousin John?'

My husband scanned the message. 'I'm truly sorry, Alice. There's no mention of John. As long as we hold the duke of Orléans they'll not let John go. I think even your aunt knows that.'

'Could we not release the duke?'

'No, we could not. Orléans has royal blood in his veins and is Burgundy's enemy as well as ours. Think of the power he'd wield and the trouble he'd cause. Do you want your father dead and Henry's French kingdom torn from our grasp?'

I shook my head. Of course I didn't want that but I mourned the loss of the man who'd always been my "big cousin". His long imprisonment felt like a living death.

Two days before the Feast of the Nativity we set off for Eltham. Snow had fallen in the night and once away from the river and up on the heath the road became treacherous. Our progress was slow but at last our patience

259

was rewarded. Stretching ahead of us were the open gates of the park and a fairytale kingdom.

The avenues wore cloaks of gleaming white and the trees were adorned in their Christmas finery. The moat was frozen solid and as we walked our horses carefully across the swept wooden planks I caught my first glimpse of the royal palace. Icicles dangled precariously from overhanging eaves and all the tiny panes of glass glistened and sparkled in the mid-morning sun. There was no wind and no sound from the village, and the distant heath might have been in another country. It was breathtakingly beautiful.

Inside, the palace was overflowing with people, all wearing their best clothes. They were talking and laughing and greeting each other as if they'd not met for months. Amidst the melee I caught sight of one of my sisters-in-law and, by the stairs, my cousin of March's widow who'd recently remarried. Of Lady Warwick there was no sign but somebody said she was closeted with her husband.

At that moment a gentle hand touched my arm. It was my stepmother.

'Lady stepmother,' I murmured, greeting her with a small curtsey and an incline of my head.

'Stepdaughter.'

Eleanor was right. There was no child. She was as slender as the day I'd first seen her standing at the door of her father's house at Ewelme. Nor could there have been a baby born in the months since I'd last seen her. Somebody would have told me. I breathed a sigh of relief and smiled at her, feeling unaccountably generous.

In the days that followed my stepmother frequently asked me to sit with her and it was hard to rid myself of her company. She held onto my arm and talked about people unknown to me, women she'd met whilst in Rouen. She gossiped about the friends she'd made, telling me how much she admired the earl of Suffolk. 'A wonderful man and so brave.'

'Does my father admire him too?' I enquired, wondering if my stepmother spent her time ensnaring all men, the way she'd ensnared my father and the duke of Burgundy.

She smiled and for the first time I acknowledged to myself that she did possess a rare kind of beauty. Her skin was smooth and pale and she resembled a lily set amongst a host of gaudy gillyflowers.

'Your father is William's friend.'

So she called the earl of Suffolk, William.

'As was the duke of Burgundy once,' I remarked nastily.

She laughed. 'The duke is a handsome rogue. He is searching for another wife to replace the one he's just lost and wishes to amuse himself until he finds her.'

'Was that what he was doing with you, amusing himself?'

I knew the moment the words were out that I should not have spoken. It was not my place to champion my father in a dispute over his wife's honour.

She looked at me levelly. 'Life is difficult for a woman, stepdaughter. Perhaps you'd do well not to listen to rumours. If I believed all that was said about you...'

'Me? What could anyone have to say about me?'

She regarded me with a crooked little smile. 'There is

talk of you in connection with that good-looking young man, Edmund Beaufort.'

'He is my cousin.'

'And the duke of Burgundy is England's ally.'

'I've done nothing wrong.'

'Neither have I. But people love to gossip and mostly draw their own conclusions.'

'And what conclusions have you drawn about me, my lady?'

I sounded sharper than I meant to, but I was angry and also afraid. I was fully aware that my meetings with Edmund would not bear too much scrutiny and certainly his behaviour to me had occasionally bordered on the outrageous.

'From what I hear, Edmund Beaufort is a dangerous young man and, for a married woman, even more dangerous than the duke of Burgundy.'

'He has always been most pleasant to me.'

'In my experience, and you must accept that my experience is somewhat wider than yours, when a man is pleasant to a young woman who is not his wife, he wants something.' She put up her hand to stop my protest. 'What you have to consider, stepdaughter, is, what is it that Edmund Beaufort wants from you?'

'He wants nothing from me. We are friends. We are cousins. We have always been friends.'

'As I was saying, you must discover what he wants. And when you've done so you must decide if you are prepared to give it to him.'

At that moment the London players finished their entertainment to rapturous applause from around the hall. As they scampered away behind the screens, trailing lengths of silk and a couple of makeshift sheep, Sir Robert Babthorp called on Katherine's Welsh harpist to entertain the company. While the man plucked at the strings of his harp, my stepmother whispered to me how unfashionable the ladies' clothes were in England. She said amazing creations were worn by the ladies at the Burgundian court. Then she told me how the new style of headdress would suit the shape of my face. I was beginning to think she would never stop.

At last, in desperation, I excused myself saying the room was too stuffy and I felt a trifle unwell. Before she could offer to accompany me I fled from the hall past the guards and the watching servants into the shock of the outside air. With dusk fast approaching, frost had returned and the hard-packed snow at the edge of the path glittered eerily in the torchlight. I breathed a great sigh of relief and walked briskly back towards the main palace building. By the entrance, leaning against the porch wall was a man – Edmund!

'Escaped the dragon?'

I laughed. 'Yes. She's had me trapped ever since I arrived.'

He leaned forward and kissed my mouth and I remembered what my stepmother had said. His lips were cold. He must have been standing outside for some time.

'I've been waiting here hoping I'd get the chance to speak to you,' he said.

'We've been at Middleham.'

'I know where you've been.'

'Could we go inside the porch please, Edmund? It's freezing out here.'

He smiled and took my arm and led me inside. Once out of the biting cold, he pressed me down on a bench and then sat close beside me. His shoulder was nudging mine and his legs were touching the folds of my new velvet skirt. It occurred to me that I should move but the warmth from his body was comforting and I knew my stepmother's words were nothing but spite.

He picked up my hand and idly examined the palm. Slowly, he traced the lines with his cold finger which unaccountably felt as if it was burning hot.

'They say you can know a man's future from his hand,' he said. 'D'you believe that?'

'What about a woman's?'

He pressed his thumb hard into my palm. Oh I already know what is going to happen to you, my sweet Alice.'

A shiver ran up my arm and down into my belly causing a dangerously warm glow.

'And what is that?' I whispered, my mouth dry with fear and anticipation.

'This,' he said, taking me in his arms and kissing me properly.

I knew what he was doing was dangerous and I pushed him away.

'Stop it, Edmund! I'm not some maidservant you've cornered in the laundry.'

'I wish you were. Then I could do with you all the things I'd like to do.'

This time I removed myself further along the bench, well out of his reach.

'How is Katherine?' I said, hoping to distract him.

'Distant.'

'No progress then?'

'None. Unfortunately I've been away half the year helping my uncle.'

'And Katherine's affections have cooled?'

'Perhaps. Will you do me a favour, Alice?'

'I doubt it. What is it you want?'

He moved along the bench so that he had me trapped between him and the wall. At that moment the inner door to the palace opened and two men came out. They passed by on their way outside talking to each other and laughing at some joke. They failed to see the two of us tucked away in the shadows.

Edmund put his finger to his lips. 'Shh!'

I waited until the men had disappeared in the direction of the Great Hall.

'Who are they?' I whispered

'No-one of importance,' he said carelessly. 'Now, tell me, are you going to do me this favour?'

'That depends on what it is you want.'

'An introduction.'

'Is that all?'

'Yes.'

'An introduction to whom?'

'I don't know her name but I'm guessing you do.'

I doubted there were many women I knew whose names were not also known to my cousin but I was suspicious.

'Where did you see her?'

'I've not seen her but I've heard about her. And I know you've had dealings with her.'

The hairs on the back of my neck began to prickle and I heard the warning bell ringing loud and clear in my head.

'What dealings?' I said warily. 'What do you mean?'

'You know who I'm talking about, Alice.'

I shook my head. 'I know nothing, nothing at all and I've no idea what woman you mean.'

'Yes you do.'

'If you're going to carry on being like this, Edmund, I shall leave.'

I tried to get up but he put his hand on my shoulder and pushed me down.

'Let me go!' I hissed.

He placed his other hand on my neck and moved his face so close to mine that I could see the glittering hardness in his eyes. 'Shall I send word to my uncle that you've refused to help?'

I gasped. 'You wouldn't.'

'I would.'

'He's gone away. He cannot touch me any more.'

'He is a newly created cardinal and more powerful then ever. I left him talking with princes and planning a new war. You cannot escape him, Alice, you know that. Don't be foolish. Do what I ask and I shan't say anything.'

I began to shiver. The darkness was closing in and all the horrors I thought I'd outrun were returning to haunt me. At that moment I wished the man beside me was my husband. not Edmund. Richard's presence was solid and reassuring. I could always depend on him to protect me and I was beginning to be unsure how much I could depend on my cousin.

'I cannot.'

'Yes, you can.'

'He will have me arrested if I go back to her,' I stammered.

'Not if I'm with you. I shall protect you from him if you do as I ask,' whispered Edmund. 'I promise.'

'How can you possibly protect me from someone like him?'

He laughed. 'Because he needs me. Without me, his plan will fail.'

I shivered in fear at the memory of that day at Southwark when the bishop had threatened me with burning.

'Alice,' Edmund persisted. 'You have to help me. I cannot do this without you.'

I hesitated.

'Very well,' I said, my voice almost a whisper. 'What exactly is it that you want me to do?'

'Take me to the wise woman, to the witch or whatever name you call her. I need something from her.'

'Why me?'

'Because I can trust you not to betray me just as you can trust me to keep you safe from my uncle.'

Of course I should not have agreed to this plan but I was in such a muddle of fear that I clung to the one certainty I knew above all others – Edmund would never knowingly harm me.

How wrong I was.

# 19

It was our first night back at The Erber and the downstairs servants were still scrambling into their livery and putting the house to rights. We had left Eltham a day early and for some reason no-one had forewarned our steward.

'I suppose our luck cannot hold much longer,' grumbled Richard as he resorted to opening the door to my room himself. One of the grooms should have been on hand but there was no sign of anyone and both my maids had mysteriously vanished. 'Where in God's name is that boy?'

'You sent him to the yard for your boxes,' I said, wrinkling up my nose at the smell of stale air.

'So I did.' He stepped aside to let me enter. 'Your stepmother showed a remarkable fondness for your company. I trust she opened her heart to you. Mind you, people say she's a clever woman and that sort choose their words with care.'

'All she did was prattle: fashion, friends, gossip. Nothing of consequence.'

'And your father said nothing to you regarding his plans?'

'Of course not.'

Richard kicked the door shut with what seemed to me, excessive force. Whatever had or had not been said at Eltham had clearly annoyed him.

'You didn't think to ask?'

'It is not my place,' I protested.

'Well, if you cannot discover the truth there's nothing I can do. Before we married I was privy to the arrangements for the disposal of your father's property. You were his sole heir. Now everything has changed. Even if there's no child that woman will get a third of whatever's entailed as her dower. She's young. It could be years before I get my hands on your inheritance. By Christ! What a mess!'

I wrapped my arms round myself and shivered. The boy had failed to light the fire and the room was cold. Doubtless no-one had bothered to shake out the bed covers or examine the mattress for damp.

'Can you not ask him?' I said.

'That would be most unwise.'

'Why? He knows you married me to get what is his.'

Richard paused in the undoing of the laces on his doublet and shot me an unfriendly look. 'It was not a one-sided bargain, Alice. Our fathers worked hard to create a mutually satisfactory contract. There were advantages for both parties. The Nevills were high in royal favour and you needed to be cared for.'

'And you had designs on my father's title and his wealth.'

My husband gave a short laugh. 'At least one of us got what they bargained for.'

'And I must be grateful,' I said bitterly. 'I have a husband who provides for me but blames me daily for failing to deliver his expectations.'

'What makes you think I blame *you*?'

'How could you not?' I subsided onto the settle by the hearth and stared at a pile of cold ashes. 'No son, no earldom. Nothing. Cecily is a duchess, your other sisters are countesses; your brother Robert is a bishop and William is Lord Fauconberg with an exceedingly wealthy wife. Whereas you are nothing and I am the heiress who has proved worthless.'

I was thoroughly miserable. Since leaving Eltham I had worried myself sick about Edmund's uncle and what I'd promised my cousin but had no-one in whom I could confide. It was out of the question to tell my aunt of my troubles and Eleanor was far too busy arranging her glorious wedding to Lord Humphrey to have time for me. As for my husband – I wanted to tell him everything, to confess it all, but didn't dare. Any mention of Edmund would make him exceedingly angry which, when I thought of everything I'd done, was not surprising.

'Perhaps you wish to put me aside,' I muttered.

'Richard shrugged off his doublet and came and sat beside me. He took my cold hands in his. 'Is that what you think of me? That I care so little for the mother of my children that I'd abandon her?'

I turned my face against the front of his shirt so that he couldn't see my tears.

'I'd not blame you if you did.' My voice was muffled by the warm linen.

He was gentle with me, allowing me time to weep before he pulled me up and made me look at him.

He pushed the hair out of my eyes and stroked my wet cheeks. 'You are my wife, Alice. I have no-one other than you.' He gave a wry smile. 'I know you think I keep a woman in my rooms at Westminster but you are mistaken. If I need a woman in my bed, it is you I want, nobody else.

And if all we are blessed with is daughters then we must accept it as God's will. As for our future? We shall build it ourselves. We are Nevills and thanks to my mother I am well endowed with property.' He patted my knee. 'We'll not starve.'

'And the earldom?'

His face shadowed. 'That, we shall *not* discuss.'

Of course we would not discuss it. We never discussed anything of real importance. I was permitted to talk of velvets for bed curtains and suggestions for our daughters' education but not to share my husband's deepest concerns. It was Richard's brothers who were his confidants, not me. It was to them he turned when he was worried. Yet I longed to be more than just the wife he took to bed and the mother of his children. I wanted to be his friend and companion in all things. I wanted to be valued for myself not for what I might bring him.

And I had concerns of my own, ones that Richard knew nothing about, ones that gnawed at the edges of my mind and gave me no peace.

After hesitating for several weeks I sent a boy with a message for a Mistress Jourdemayne to be found somewhere in the squalid alleyways behind St Pauls. He returned with the unwelcome news that the woman had removed herself from the city to her husband's new house at Eye next Westminster.

'We have to make an expedition out of the city,' I said to Edmund on the morning of the day we'd agreed for our visit.

'Is that a problem?'

'We must be careful. I dare not risk being seen with you.'

He laughed. 'Is my reputation that bad?'

I glared at him. My misgivings about this adventure were growing by the hour and, more than anything, I wished it over and done with. I was angry with him for forcing me to take him to Mistress Jourdemayne and angry with myself for not being strong enough to refuse. I recognised that in capitulating to his demands I'd exposed a weakness in my character, one which would have saddened my Aunt Margaret.

I pulled up the hood of my oldest and most concealing cloak, repeated to myself the instructions on how to find Eye, and gathered up the reins. My mount was not my own but an elderly plodding creature from the stables, one which had seen better days. Beside Edmund's fine hunter I must have appeared a drab companion but the last thing I wanted was to be recognised as the wife of Sir Richard Nevill, important member of the king's council.

We rode out of the city to the west towards the old priory near Charing where the road divides. When we reached the great wooden cross we struck out on a path which passed by the low walls of a little church and then meandered on through empty fields. This was Abbey land but, being winter, there were few people about and I was glad of Edmund's company.

Eye was nothing more than a huddle of half a dozen dwellings clustered round a tiny crossroads. A small boy sitting cross-legged in the dirt pointed to one of the better houses when I asked the whereabouts of Mistress Jourdemayne. Edmund tossed him a coin for his trouble.

We walked our horses up to the sturdy wooden gate and dismounted.

The house was well proportioned, two storeys, timber-framed with a thatched roof. To one side were a couple of bare trees and behind them several neat rows of winter plants. I thought Master Jourdemayne must do well at his trade to afford such a house.

By the time Edmund had looped the reins to a post, the door had opened a slit and I knew we were being watched. I unlatched the gate and walked up the path. The door swung wide open.

'My lady,' said Mistress Jourdemayne, curtseying politely. 'I'd not thought to see you again but you be a mite welcome. Come in out of the cold.'

She looked much as she had the last time I'd seen her at Castle Baynard: small, neat and perfectly composed. She was wearing a cap and a large coarse apron which almost covered her from neck to toe. All the time I was looking at her she had her eye on Edmund. She nodded to him, taking in at one glance the cut of his clothes and the obvious lack of finery. From what I'd gleaned about her customers in grand houses like Castle Baynard she'd not be slow in recognising my cousin as a young man eager to make his mark but without the funds to do so.

The house was surprisingly clean and we were shown into what I supposed was a parlour. There was a small fire but no sign of any iron pots so it wasn't a kitchen. I had some idea how other people lived from my visits to the poorer tenants at Middleham but Mistress Jourdemayne's house was different. It smelled different. Above the usual noxious odours of unwashed bodies and stale cooking was the pungent scent of summer-dried lavender.

She watched me and gave the beginnings of a smile. 'I guess you've not come to admire my house, m'lady, but afore we settle to business, you'll take a cup of ale?'

'Thank you kindly, but no.'

She nodded and bade us sit down. The stool was hard but there was no sign of a cushion. Possibly such luxuries were unknown to Mistress Jourdemayne.

'Mostly my customers like me to attend them in their own houses,' she said in her strange country burr, settling herself on another of the small hard stools. 'But as you be here I take it my presence in your house be unwelcome. Your husband would not approve. This is not your husband, I'm presuming.'

'No. This is not my husband. He is a friend and he requires your help,' I said bluntly, wanting this visit finished as quickly as possible.

'A friend eh? And what shall I call your friend?' She laid great emphasis on that last word as if she knew that what lay between Edmund and me was more than simple friendship.

'You may call me the man who would go far,' said Edmund with a charming smile.

Strangely, his charm did not impress Mistress Jourdemayne. She gave him a long level stare and said, 'Far be not the most comfortable of destinations for a man. It seldom brings the rewards he expects.'

'I am assured you can help me in that regard.'

Her eyes glinted as if Edmund had placed himself exactly where she wanted him. I wondered if she knew the intricacies of the game of chess and then dismissed the notion as ridiculous.

'That depends on what you want.'

'There is a woman,' began Edmund.

Mistress Jourdemayne chuckled. 'With a man like you, there be always a woman.'

I could almost feel Edmund preen himself. "Too full of boyish pride," my mother had once said and maybe she was right.

Edmund smiled lazily. 'To me, she is a particularly desirable woman.'

'And she has refused you. I'm not surprised.'

Now Edmund's vanity was pricked. He needed to reassert his manly credentials and quickly before Mistress Jourdemayne marked him out as a charlatan.

'Naturally she desires me.'

Mistress Jourdemayne smiled like the consummate opponent she was. I'd seen her play this game before, with Eleanor.

'But she hesitates?'

'The matter is complicated.'

'For you, my friend, I suggest, matters will always be complicated.'

Edmund ignored her jibe. 'Mistress, we are not talking here of a virginal girl but of a woman of some experience. A young widow.'

'And you wish for something to overcome this young widow's natural misgivings, to make her compliant, to bend her to your will.'

'I'd not force her.'

'Of course not. A man like you never forces a woman.

He has no need. But deceit, false promises, trickery – those be different. They have legitimacy, do they not?'

'I'd not lie to her.'

'So my ever-truthful, far-travelling friend, what exactly be it you want? A love potion to slip into her cup? A veil to entrap her sensibilities? A charm to bind her to you for eternity?'

Edmund's eyes gleamed as Mistress Jourdemayne laid out the various mysteries at her disposal.

'Are there not words which need to be said?' I'd not meant to speak and the moment the words were out of my mouth I wished them unspoken.

There was an awkward silence.

'It's nothing,' I muttered. 'I was mistaken.'

Mistress Jourdemayne fixed her gaze on me. 'My lady, what you see in the past often lies in the future and for that you need the gift of foreseeing.'

I had no idea what she meant so kept my head down and said nothing.

'Foreseeing?' said Edmund with a small intake of breath. 'Can you foresee the future?'

She laughed, the throaty cackle I remembered from the dark room at Castle Baynard when Eleanor had traded a silver coin for something conjured up by the devil.

'Some things I know. Others be hidden.'

'But you have the power?'

'I may have.'

Edmund held out his hand. 'Tell me what you foresee for me?'

'It will cost you.'

'How much?'

'Three pennies of the old sort.'

'You value yourself highly, mistress.' Edmund raised his chin. 'But it's little enough to know the truth. It is the truth, isn't it?'

Mistress Jourdemayne gave a sly smile. 'The imprint of a man's destiny never lies. It's there for all who can read the signs.'

She took his hand, turned it over and examined the lines which criss-crossed his palm. The little window barely gave enough light to see by but the fire in the hearth provided a steady glow. After a little while she released his hand.

'Well?'

'A child born into darkness and a child born into the light.' She paused. 'One holds a key, the other, a sword.'

Edmund leaned forward and peered at his hand as if trying to see what she could see. 'What does that mean?'

'It means no good will come to either child.'

I gave a small gasp. This was dreadful. Horrible.

'And the key?'

'Keys unlock doors.'

'What doors?'

She shrugged. 'Who knows? A door a man might wish to open?'

Edmund frowned. 'Your words make no sense, mistress. You'd better look to your skills or you'll not get a penny from me. Look again. Tell me what will happen to me?'

She took his hand.

'Ah you? For you I see a castle and I see bloodshed and I see death wrapped in his black cloak.'

Edmund turned deathly pale.

'Soon?' His voice was half strangled in his throat.

'You have a long road to travel, my friend, and much mischief to make.'

He sighed in relief. 'And the woman? What can you foresee of her?'

She raised her gaze to his. 'I see betrayal.'

'Of me?'

'It is unclear.'

'Look closer. I must know.'

Mistress Jourdemayne sat back on her stool. 'You cannot command what lies beyond man's earthly understanding, my friend. Some matters can never be known. Be content with what I have told you because there be nothing more.'

For once I was glad of the long weeks of fasting and penitence as they allowed me to immerse myself in prayer and not spend my days thinking about the visit to Eye and what might come of it. I tried to banish thoughts of death and betrayal, of children born into light and darkness and the key which could unlock a door. To my great relief I saw nothing more of my cousin, not until Richard and I attended the Easter celebrations that year at the royal palace at Hertford. And it was there that the long awaited invitation to visit Bisham arrived.

One evening my father sent a note to our rooms mentioning a date when he and my stepmother would be pleased to welcome us to Bisham. I was overjoyed but Richard was grudging in his acceptance. He was annoyed because the lengthy parliament had once again delayed our return to Middleham and now a visit to Bisham would delay it still further. I had no idea what was being discussed at the parliament or why matters had taken so long to resolve and no-one of my acquaintance cared to enlighten me. It would have made no difference if they had but sometimes, looking back, I wonder.

I saw Edmund once or twice during the entertainments. He was mingling with the other guests, laughing with the husbands, flirting with the wives and making himself unfailingly pleasant to the elderly dowagers, as he always did. But he deliberately avoided me. I had no desire to be drawn into conversation with him so it was probably for the best. In truth I would rather not have seen him at all.

But Katherine was another matter. To my distress she didn't ask for me, not even once. I waited and waited but there was no summons. Isabel, Lady Warwick was constantly at her side, keeping her company during the endless formal feasting but I was ignored. Katherine's disregard made me realise that our years of friendship had finally come to an end and I was being disposed of like a worn-out glove. It was inevitable. After all, what was I to her but yet another young woman who had disappointed her in a world full of such disappointments. Change was coming and none of it was to Katherine's liking.

Our young king was nearly seven years old and the days of nursemaids and governesses were nearing their end. Arrangements were almost complete for his separate household and soon he would move into the world of men. He would have knights and esquires to guard him and boys from noble families as his companions. Isabel's husband was to be his master and would appoint an array of tutors and priests who would supervise his charge's continuing education. Naturally Henry would see his mother from time to time but their former closeness could never be recaptured. By the end of this year, Katherine would retire from his side and slide into the shadowy world of a widowed queen. I could imagine her distress and the loneliness she would suffer without her beloved son and those who surrounded him but there was nothing I could do to help other than pray she'd find contentment in some other way.

# 20

A PERFECT NEVILL WIFE 1428

Bisham looked exactly the same. It had not changed since the day nine long years ago when I'd last walked under the gatehouse with my father. It was as if the house had been under an enchantment, awaiting my return. Every window, every turret, every wisp of straw stirring in the dust looked exactly as they had before. In those far-off days, I'd been wrapped in grief at my mother's death but the passage of time heals all sorrows and now I could think of her without the familiar ache in my heart. I'd not forgotten her, she would always be my beloved mother, but I had other people who claimed my love: my husband and my two children.

My stepmother touched my arm, the way she was apt to do. 'Let me show you something,' she said in her low cool voice which I was finding increasingly irritating. 'I'd appreciate your opinion.'

I doubted she'd value my opinion any more than she'd value the opinion of one of her stable boys but I was too polite to say so.

We walked through the inner courtyard and round the side of the house to the tiny Lady's Garden. It had been created by some long-ago lady of Bisham and was the place where my mother and I would sit on sunny days. The bushes were a little more ravaged than I remembered and the branches of willow brushed the path all the way round creating a hidden refuge. Apart from some Lenten lilies, few flowers were in bloom but the wonderful scent of Our Lady's Tears drifted on the still afternoon air. Nothing had changed.

'Your father is a kind man and wishes to please me,' my stepmother began. 'He suggests we enlarge the garden. Open it up. Get rid of the bushes and trees which cause shade. Introduce a fountain, a pavilion and a wide flowery mead. He remembers the gardens I admired at the Burgundian court and how enchanting they were. He proposes removing those tumbling plants which he feels have no place in a garden designed to bring man closer to God. In other words he wishes to change it utterly.'

I could feel my heart squeezed tightly and my mouth go dry. I could say nothing to this wholesale vandalism of my mother's favourite refuge. Here was the turf bench where she would sit when the days were warm. That would be dug out and replaced with an elegant foreign pavilion of the type preferred by women like my stepmother. There would be low box hedges and circular pebbled paths and my mother's beloved rose trellis would be torn down. Riotous greenery and earthy splendour would be replaced by symmetry and strict order, suitable for the rigour of meditation and enrichment of the spirit.

I wanted to weep.

But my stepmother was talking and I was trapped as her persistent voice kept penetrating the veil of my misery.

'I have told him that would be a mistake. I am certain your mother would not want her garden altered. I believe we should leave everything just as it is. What do you think?'

I raised my head. She was looking at me, her lips beautifully curved.

When I said nothing, she took my hand in hers. 'Alice, you and I, we should be friends. We should not be enemies. You never know, we might even find love and affection. You were such an innocent when I first knew you, utterly determined to hate me. But look at you now! Fully grown into womanhood and already a mother.'

'I think,' I began and then could go no further because of the sudden churning in my belly.

'Is something the matter?'

I put my hand over my mouth. 'I'm sorry, my lady, I believe I am unwell.'

And with the gracelessness of a spit boy who has cleaned out the dregs of the household's cups, I vomited over an emerging bed of mint.

'Forgive me,' I cried. 'Forgive me. I thought I was done for the day. It came upon me unawares.'

I crouched on the ground with my stepmother holding me in her arms as I wept.

She sent her maid running for a basin of water and a cloth. while she stroked my forehead and murmured the kinds of words my mother used to say when I was a child.

'There, there; no need to cry, it's all over.'

When the maid returned, my stepmother gently wiped my mouth with the cloth, then the rest of my face and my fingers which were sticky with vomit.

I struggled to my feet, embarrassed at having disgraced myself.

'Is it what I think it is?' she asked, rising and handing the cloth back to the maid.

Dumbly, I nodded.

She reached forward and placed her arms around my unresisting body. Her skin smelled sweetly of rosewater and her cheek was soft. 'How pleased your father will be. Does your husband know?'

'No,' I whispered. 'I've not yet told him.'

She laughed. 'I think you'd better.'

I smiled weakly. 'I think so too.'

'And the garden?'

I looked around and thought to myself – it's only a garden. It's not forever.

'Everything changes. It must. It is how we are made: to improve, to alter. My mother loved her garden but I believe she, of all women, would understand if you wish to make changes.'

'And you?'

I placed my hand on hers and curled my fingers so that we were hand-clasped. 'I am not the girl I was and if, in the past, I have offended you or done you harm, my lady, I can only beg your forgiveness.'

And like that we wandered slowly back to the house and to our husbands.

'Don't tell her yet. She's not strong enough.'

The words drifted in from somewhere outside the room high in the tower at Middleham but I was enveloped in a haze of happiness and exhaustion and paid no attention.

''A boy!' the midwife had exclaimed. 'Just as I said it would be, my lady. God has blessed you.'

She had been saying for weeks that she thought I had a boy in my belly but I'd not believed her. And yet, here he was, a tiny squirming bundle. Richard, named for his father, born, like his sister, on the feast day of Saint Cecilia. Strong and healthy with a lustier cry than either of my daughters. Within hours he'd been borne away to the church to be baptised but now was safely back in his cradle while I reclined on my pillows, amazed at my cleverness.

I idly wondered what my husband had been going to tell me before his mother advised him to wait.

In the days that followed a stream of women came to see me, giving their congratulations and bringing little gifts for the baby. But the only person I wanted to see was Richard. This was our triumph, his and mine. This was *our* son, *our* family.

On the fifth day he came. By then I was feeling better and was lying on the day bed near the fire. He pulled up a stool and sat beside me.

'And how is my clever wife?'

I grinned. 'Suffering from the sin of pride, I regret to say.'

He leaned over and kissed me tenderly on my mouth. 'It's no sin. I could not be more proud of you. You are a perfect wife.'

I rested my head on his shoulder and thought how blessed we were. Three children!

'Tell me what's been happening?' I said, thinking how companionable it was to be here with my husband. 'Nobody will tell me anything and I am dreadfully bored.'

Richard took my hand and stroked my fingers. 'There is not much to tell. Duke Humphrey has been seen everywhere with his new wife and you can imagine what the gossips make of that. My mother, who I thought would disapprove, merely says Duchess Eleanor is a clever woman but it was a mistake to marry in May. Unlucky apparently.'

I chuckled. 'That will not bother Eleanor.'

'And my uncle, the Cardinal, has returned. He writes that he's raising an army for the Pope's crusade against the Hussites and wishes for my support.'

Any mention of Richard's uncle made my blood run cold. Even here in my room, safe behind the high walls of Middleham I could feel his bony fingers reaching out to grab me by the throat.

'He'll not come here, will he?' I said nervously.

'The council wish him to go to Scotland to renew our truce. They say we don't have the resources for a Holy War at this time.'

'Was that what you were going to tell me yesterday when your mother said I should not be told?'

He paused and all of a sudden I knew he was about to tell me something terrible.

'No. Not that. It was about your father.'

The fire crackled and a little cloud of smoke billowed out into the room. No, not my father! Please God, not my father!

'You must be brave, Alice, he said quietly. 'The news is bad. Your father is dead; killed by the French.'

'No! Please no! It's a mistake!'

Richard tightened his hold and pressed me hard against his chest. 'It's not a mistake. He told me at Bisham this would happen one day. He said death was the inevitable end for a soldier and he'd no wish to die in his bed.'

My heart felt bruised, damaged, broken. My father was the last link to those golden years at Bisham. The man whose safety we prayed for, whose homecoming we longed for, the first man who'd ever held me in his arms.

'When did it happen?'

'A month ago.'

'A month!'

'It was too much of a risk to tell you with the birth so near. Then my mother said to wait until you were stronger.'

I nodded, too damaged to think of all that time others had known and I had not.

'Where?' I whispered.

'In front of the walls of Orléans. Your father believed we must take Orléans in order to conquer the rest of France. Burgundy disagreed. Since their falling out your father told me he felt less blessed. He believed dark days were coming. And now they've come.'

I was numb. Cold. Too sad to weep for my father.

'How did it happen?'

'A stone ball fired from a cannon. Smashed into a wall of the tower. Your father was standing at an upper window. They found him amongst the rubble.'

'He'd rather have died with a sword in his hand.'

'Ah dearest, his death is no less glorious. He will always be remembered. In years to come when men talk of how Henry's French kingdom was won, praise will be heaped on your father. Everyone knows what a great commander he was. Possibly the greatest ever.'

'Where did they bury him?'

'The duke of Bedford has given orders for the body to be returned. We shall bury him with all honour at Bisham.'

'Bisham?'

Richard failed to hide the gleam of triumph in his

eyes. 'Bisham is ours, Alice. It is what your father would have wanted.'

'What of my stepmother? She might …'

Richard made a dismissive gesture. 'She's at Rouen. She's not seen him in months.'

My father had loved me. I knew that. But he would have loved a son more, and I, in my pride and foolishness, had denied him that. Now there was no-one but me. I would be the heiress my husband married. I would inherit everything my father possessed and Richard would be the earl of Salisbury. At last I'd given him what he most desired in this world – an earldom and a son. I was, as he'd said, a perfect wife. Alice, Countess of Salisbury, a perfect Nevill wife.

# 21

## THE PALACE OF WESTMINSTER 1429

It was hard to believe almost nine years had passed since Katherine's coronation. Yet here we were celebrating the coronation of Katherine's son with another day of endless ceremonial and feasting. Last time I was plain Lady Nevill, a nervous new wife, greatly afraid of displeasing her husband; and the young woman beside me, whose father was an impoverished country knight, spent the whole afternoon gazing enviously at her betters. Now she was a duchess and I was a countess. I was a countess whose two daughters were thriving and whose son had already taken his first steps and mastered four words. I was content. As for Eleanor? One could never tell.

The banquet lasted for hours. Dish after exotic dish passed through the hall, carried to the top table where the king sat on the dais flanked by an elderly Archbishop Chichele, and His most Worthy Eminence, our esteemed Cardinal of England. The title might have changed, the years added a few more lines and an enlarged belly beneath his splendid scarlet robes, but the hawk-like gaze of the one-time bishop of Winchester, Henry Beaufort, was as fierce and penetrating as ever. I sensed he was searching for me amongst the crowds and kept my head lowered.

Lord Humphrey was scowling, not only on account of having to share a table with his enemy, the cardinal, but also because, from today, he would no longer hold the title of Protector of the Realm. Eleanor said he'd been in a rage all week. Humphrey had not wanted the cardinal to be invited to participate in the coronation but his brother and the council had insisted. Apparently the cardinal had bowed to the council's wishes and taken his crusading army, not to crush the Hussites as the Holy Father wanted, but to help the duke of Bedford who was in sore need of more troops. Pope Martin was said to be furious, which was unfortunate as we needed him to smile on our claim to the throne of France, but the duke and the council were delighted. To show their gratitude they had honoured the cardinal by offering him a prominent position in today's ceremonies.

To my surprise the king survived his arduous day of oath-taking, anointing, crowning and homage-giving without a single yawn. He seemed to enjoy the lengthy processions and interminable masses and the gargantuan orgy of food, and even laughed when the king's champion made the traditional challenge to all-comers by riding up the hall on his black charger. At the end of the banquet Lord Warwick offered to carry the boy back to his rooms but Henry insisted on walking the length of the hall unaided, leaving the earl behind to carry his train.

Henry was scarcely eight years old, really much too young to be crowned, but events of the summer had necessitated this hasty coronation. Katherine's brother, encouraged by some ignorant peasant girl claiming she was sent by God, had managed to get himself crowned in the cathedral at Rheims. The idea of that imposter calling himself Charles VII, *le roi tres-chrétien*, was ridiculous.

But it was also dangerous. It was a direct threat to Henry's claim to the dual kingdom and made a mockery of my father's many victories.

'Do you think she really is a holy maid?' I asked Eleanor, resting my aching feet on the proffered footstool.

'Jesu, no! They say she wears men's clothes. And that, as you know, is in contravention of God's law. Although I've never understood why.'

'They say she cuts her hair short like a man.'

'How foolish,' said Eleanor smoothing one of her elaborately devised cornettes with a single practised finger. Her veil fell in a ripple of pleats from two points above her forehead and cascaded elegantly over her shoulders, a feat I never managed to achieve. The only time I'd tried, I resembled a bedraggled cow and my women had laughed behind their hands. My hair was too fine, my veils too plain and my senior maidservant too unskilled for this new fashion.

'Lady Warwick says this girl is doing the devil's work,' I remarked straightening my shoulders and trying to ignore the increasing discomfort in my back. 'If she was truly sent by God she'd be making peace. Instead she's inciting war.'

'Mmmm,' said Eleanor, reverting to stroking the furred trimming on her green velvet sleeve as she reclined on one of her couches, artfully displayed for all her visitors to admire. 'Bedford says she has suits of armour made specially by a master armourer and rides into battle ahead of the men. He believes she's a witch.'

I caught my breath at that forbidden word. Eleanor and I never talked of witches or of any kind of conjuring. She didn't care to be reminded of the young woman she'd once been and the dark steps she'd taken to achieve her present exalted position Whatever else we discussed, and our conversations were surprisingly uninhibited and wide-ranging, I made certain I never mentioned our secret encounters with Mistress Jourdemayne.

'Our priest says she's an abomination in the sight of God and must be punished,' I said firmly.

'Oh, have no doubt, my friend, she *will* be punished. If not by God then by Bedford or by Philip of Burgundy. She has sinned sufficiently to make their over-zealous bishops smirk with glee at the thought of such foul heresies. They'll enjoy tearing her to shreds. So you see, holy or not, she's a fool.'

Marriage to Lord Humphrey suited Eleanor. She had flourished like a flower in the sunshine since becoming his wife, her poise and her beauty growing by the day. Everyone said he loved her deeply and every woman of my acquaintance spent hours discussing how she had managed to net such a great prize when in reality she was a nobody.

Eleanor put out her hand and stroked my swollen belly. The feeling was not unpleasant.

'How long now?'

'Two months. The midwife says January.'

'And will it be another boy?'

I laughed. 'Richard says so.'

Eleanor closed her eyes and I could feel the heat of her envy. It lay like a burning wall between us, spoiling what would otherwise have been a perfect friendship. She was desperate to conceive a child. I was certain she used potions and other remedies but so far there had been nothing, not even the slightest hope. Poor Eleanor! As regular as the moon. A child would crown her success but without one Lord Humphrey might soon be wondering why he'd bothered to marry her. She'd been a stimulating and intriguing whore and what was the use of a barren wife? It was not as if Eleanor provided the powerful connections Anne of Burgundy had brought to her marriage with Humphrey's brother. Eleanor had brought nothing to Lord Humphrey but her own, beautiful, fascinating self.

'I suppose you and Sir Richard will attend the boy's second coronation.' Eleanor's voice was cool.

This was another tricky problem as neither Eleanor nor Lord Humphrey would be travelling to see Henry crowned in his French kingdom. Humphrey would remain in England as the king's lieutenant and keeper of the realm and naturally, Eleanor would stay with him.

'I'm not sure. Richard has duties in the north to deal with.'

'D'you think the boy is strong? I thought he looked fatigued.'

'It was a long day for a child of his age.'

'Yes, but he was pale. Perhaps he is sickening for something.'

The look on Eleanor's face was calculating as if the state of young Henry's health was of great interest to her.

'Children are often sickly, little childhood illnesses. It means nothing.'

'On the contrary, it means everything. If he were to die...'

'Eleanor!'

'Don't look at me like that. It was only an hypothesis.'

'It was treasonous.'

'Don't be silly. The boy is Humphrey's beloved nephew. He is the joy in both our hearts and we shall do everything within our power to keep him safe. When he returns from France Humphrey has promised to bring him to Greenwich to admire the improvements we've made. What use would I have for treason? '

What use indeed. I never understood Eleanor. One moment she was speculating as to the young king's death, the next telling me she was his most devoted aunt who would care for him as tenderly as a mother. But I knew, better than most, what Eleanor was capable of and I shivered at the thought of putting the boy into Eleanor's sole charge.

Next day when I was supervising the packing of my chests ready for our journey north I had an unexpected visitor. It was Lady Warwick who since Richard's ennoblement had made subtle overtures of friendship, sending me unexpected gifts of fish and late autumn fruits. Today she was looking less than pleased at having had to brave London's streets which were full of unsavoury detritus left over from yesterday's celebrations.

'I wanted to see you before you departed, Lady Alice.'

'I am honoured, Lady Isabel,' I said politely.

She looked round the room, noting the tapestries Richard had imported from Bisham. She must have newer and finer ones in her rooms at Caversham but I was particularly fond of these old ones, remembered from my childhood.

'I thought you should know that your late father's wife is planning remarriage,' she said, her eyes widening slightly at the expensive new silk hangings on my bed. Richard had commissioned them to please me after the birth of our son and I dreaded to think how much they had cost him.

'So soon? I had no idea.'

There had been half a dozen letters from my stepmother in the year following my father's death, each one more solicitous than the last. I thought we were slowly becoming friends now that we no longer needed to bicker for the crumbs of my father's affections. She told me how much she'd been honoured by his offer of marriage, how kind he had been to her during their six years together and how well he'd provided for in her widowhood – too well according to Richard. But nowhere had there been mention of a new husband.

'Do I know him?' I asked wondering who could possibly match up to my wonderful father.

Lady Warwick's eyes finally came to rest on the little silver box with the Montagu crest which my mother had used as a workbasket for her embroidery silks.

'William de la Pole. Earl of Suffolk.'

Lady Warwick's voice betrayed her thoughts, even if her face remained perfectly composed. She didn't like him. That much was clear.

'He's the great-grandson of a wool merchant,' she remarked as if that was all there was to say about my stepmother's choice of second husband. Not surprising when Isabel Warwick was the great-granddaughter of a king.

A wool-merchant's great-grandson indeed! I wondered why my stepmother had not told me. 'When do they wed?'

Lady Warwick shrugged. 'He was taken prisoner at Jargeau so they'll have to wait for the ransom to be decided. But have no doubt, Lady Alice, they *will* marry. I have it on excellent authority.'

I smiled sympathetically. 'My stepmother's own grandfather was a low-born scribbler so perhaps they are well matched. They've know each other a long time. Perhaps...'

I stopped, remembering my suspicions about my stepmother's feelings for this wool merchant's great-grandson. Had she been unfaithful to my father? She would not have been the first wife to cuckold her husband with his friend, nor the first wife to put another man's child in the family cradle.

Lady Warwick's eyes saw further than I expected. She patted my hand in a motherly way and said, 'Don't imagine things you cannot know, my dear Lady Alice. Remember your father as the great man he was and forget everything else. I'd not have you distressed.'

I thanked her but with her next words I realised she had not come in friendship to tell me about my stepmother but to issue a warning.

'A mésalliance is always unwise, never more so than when it touches on the honour of the king.'

I held my breath, waiting for what she'd say next.

'I doubt your husband has told you, Lady Alice. Parliaments are such tedious affairs husbands rarely bother their wives with details. But I thought you should know. It could be you're close to someone to whom such information might prove useful, someone who is unaware of the danger.'

'I'm not sure I understand you, Lady Isabel. My husband has said nothing.'

'As I thought.' She smiled, barely raising the corners of her lips and the smile did not reach her eyes. 'In the parliament, some eighteen months ago, it was agreed that a law should be drawn up to preserve the honour of the most noble estate of queens of England. This has been done and the law says that no man can make a contract to marry himself to a queen of England without special licence and assent of the king.'

I gave a sudden gasp when I realised what she was saying.

'So her grace, the king's mother could remarry if she wishes?'

She raised a hand. 'Wait! You've not heard everything. To give assent the king must be of the age of discretion.'

'But that would mean …'

'Exactly Lady Alice, a very long wait indeed. And no guarantee of success at the end. Grown sons are notoriously suspicious of men wishing to marry their mothers. They assume the worst and they are usually right.'

'Perhaps a couple wouldn't wait. Perhaps they'd forego royal assent and pay the fine.'

She laughed. 'You're over-hasty, Lady Alice. Nowhere is there mention of a fine. If a man acts contrary to this law he will forfeit everything he owns for the whole of his life. He will lose his lands, his tenements, his goods and his chattels, both those which are in his own hands and those held by others for his future use. In other words he would be ruined.'

This was terrible news. Edmund wanted to marry Katherine but if he succeeded he would have nothing and she would be disgraced. The journey to Eye had been a mistake but at the time I'd not realised how terrible the consequences could be. Mistress Jourdemayne had seen a life of mischief-making for Edmund but nowhere had there been warning of utter ruin. I prayed the charms Edmund had purchased that day still lay unused in a locked coffer and I prayed that if not, Katherine would have the strength to resist.

# 22

## WALTHAM ABBEY 1430

Someone opened the door letting the dank chill of a late November morning drift into my room. Twelve months had passed since we'd last been at The Erber and I'd almost forgotten how unpleasant the city could sometimes be. It was not just the cold but the dampness which Richard said came from river water lapping at our outer walls when the tide was high. I shivered and reminded myself to ask if the nursery fires had been lit.

'A lady to see you,' whispered my maid, looking as if she was about to expire with cold.

'Does she have a name?' I asked, exasperated by the chaos around me.

'I think it may be the duchess, my lady.'

'Duchess Cecily?'

'No, my lady; t'other one, the duchess of Gloucester.'

Unexpected and a trifle overdue but Eleanor would have come to offer belated congratulations. She must have been busy because I'd not seen her since the birth of our second son, little Thomas.

'Tell one of the men to bring more logs and have the kitchen send up some cakes. And don't forget to remind the men in the ewery about the wine.'

With the king's party still in France and not likely to return for several months, our servants had clearly forgotten what was required in a noble household. Just because no important visitors came did not mean I would tolerate this muddle. The steward had been lax in our absence and that was another unpleasant task ahead of me; he would have to be reprimanded. With Richard absent in the North for weeks at a time, raising troops for the duke of Bedford's campaign in France, all domestic responsibilities at The Erber fell on my shoulders. I now had some sympathy for my mother-in-law who had carried out these duties as well as supervising the care and education of nine children whereas I had only four. I placed my hand carefully on my belly and smiled to myself. In a few months, God willing, there would be five.

I heard footsteps and as my maid opened the door I saw Eleanor. She was shrouded in a heavy dark cloak which almost obscured her face. From what little I could see, she was not smiling.

'Send them away,' she said quickly, not bothering to make a proper greeting. She eyed the two women huddled near the fire with intense dislike as if they had personally offended her. 'I need to talk with you; alone!'

I raised my eyebrows but knew better than to start arguing.

'You may go down to the hall,' I said to my poor companions who had only just managed to make themselves comfortable. 'I shall send word when I need you.'

As soon as the door closed, Eleanor subsided onto a stool.

'What's wrong?' I asked, crouching down beside her. He face was the colour of cold ashes and although her fingers were perfectly steady, her eyes were wide with fear. She looked terrified.

She grasped my hands. 'Can you not feel it?'

'Feel what?'

'The danger, you fool. Out there! They could come at any moment and if they come for me, you can be certain they'll come for you.'

'Mother of God, Eleanor! What d'you mean?'

I felt my belly twist and my veins fill with ice at the enduring fear of something unknown, some unnamed menace confirming my childhood fears.

'They have her in the Fleet,' whispered Eleanor. 'She's been taken. And not just her. There are six others.'

'Who? Who's been taken?'

'Mistress Jourdemayne.'

'Holy Mary!' Fear clutched my breast. My first instinct was to run. 'What's the charge?'

'What d'you think?'

There was only one reason why a woman like Mistress Jourdemayne would come to the attention of the authorities and it would not be a failure to sweep away rubbish from the front of her house. In my head echoed Bishop Beaufort's words from that long ago day at Southwark: sorcery, denial of the sacraments, dealings with the devil, heresy!

'Witchcraft?' I whispered, almost unable to speak as the full horror of our predicament swept over me.

'It is claimed they cast a horoscope. Plotted the king's death,' said Eleanor flatly.

'Mistress Jourdemayne would never do such a thing.'

'Those who employ her might. D'you not understand?

Can you not see what is going to happen? If she speaks about us and our meetings, we are implicated.'

'But we are innocent.'

'Doesn't matter.'

Oh Jesu! This could not be happening. I'd done nothing. Then I remembered what Eleanor had said a year ago? "If the boy should die." I was entirely innocent but was she? And if they started asking questions they'd soon discover about Ewelme and the ill-wishing of my stepmother.

Eleanor grasped both my arms so tightly that I cried out in pain. 'Listen to me!' she said. 'Nobody knows of our meetings. Not a soul. No-one was present. Just you and me and her. There were no witnesses and I've said nothing.'

'Nor have I,' I said quickly. 'I've told no-one, but …' I paused. 'The cardinal knows. I told you. At his palace at Southwark. He had me in for questioning and threatened me. He knew about our meetings with Mistress Jourdemayne but I swear to you, Eleanor, I told him nothing. He already knew. Someone else had told him.'

Racing through my mind was the thought that this might have to do with Edmund and our visit to Eye, but that had been nearly three years ago. All my cousin had wanted was a love charm, a potion, something to lure Katherine into his arms and into his bed. There'd be no reason for Edmund to harm the king. Getting close to Henry was part of his plan. But would someone who disliked Edmund, implicate him in a plot? I tried to think. Who would benefit from the death of Katherine's son? Who would take his place? The childless duke of Bedford was the heir. A happy marriage with Anne of Burgundy but people whispered that she was barren, that the duke

302

was unmanned, often sick and weary, that his brother, the protector, had ill-wished their marriage. And who came after Bedford? Lord Humphrey.

I stared at Eleanor, wondering about her husband with his heretical books and scholarly friends? Could it be him? And what of the cardinal? Would he want Henry dead to promote a Beaufort claim to the throne? Impossible!

Or was it.

'Where is the cardinal?' I whispered.

'In Ghent, soothing Burgundy's ruffled feathers or he may have returned to Rouen. Bedford has informed the council that Rheims cannot be recaptured and the cardinal must crown the boy in Paris.'

'So he's not here.'

'No, our armies have to secure the way to Paris first.'

I tried to imagine the chaos across the Narrow Sea and hoped for all our sakes that Katherine's son was safe in Rouen.

'Eleanor, why did you come?'

She shrugged. 'To warn you. Though why I bothered. You've not been much help.'

'There's nothing I can do,' I said. 'You got us into this mess in the first place. It was not my idea to seek out a known witch.'

Eleanor tipped back her head and laughed. 'But it worked Your husband has what he wanted. And I? I have everything a woman could desire.'

We were sniping, both brittle with fear, unwilling to accept the other was not to blame for our hideous dilemma.

A knock at the door made us both jump. It heralded the arrival of a man bearing a basket of logs closely followed by two boys, one from the kitchen, the other from the ewery. While they went about their business, stirring the fire to life and setting food and drink on the table, Eleanor and I sat in silence.

As soon as they'd gone we looked at each other in despair. We both knew there was nothing to be done until someone made a move and if we kept our heads down and said nothing, perhaps we might yet be safe. At the moment the whereabouts of the cardinal was the least of our worries.

The days crawled by, the hours of daylight grew less and soon it was Christmas.

'A kiss for my wife,' said Richard, seizing me round the waist and placing his mouth on mine. He tasted of the wine he'd just drunk and I felt the urgency of his embrace. He had arrived in time for the start of our nativity celebrations but was leaving after just three short days. He had to see a tenant near Southampton who had failed to provide armed men for his lord and needed reminding of his duty. He promised to be back for Twelfth Night.

'Will they miss us if I carry you off to bed?' he whispered into my ear. 'It's been a long time.'

'You were in my bed last night, my lord,' I said, wishing he wasn't leaving. 'The distance to Southampton is not above sixty miles, a gentle trot to my lord of Salisbury. If the roads are clear and the snow holds off, you'll be back in six days.'

'I know, but putting my arm around you like this has given me ideas. You feel very comfortable.'

'You mean plump?'

He took my hand in his and placed it on my belly. 'No. I mean you are a woman to be prized above all others and you are entirely mine, my beloved little Alice.'

'Not so little,' I laughed.

'Comfortable,' he said, smiling. 'But if you'll not oblige me, my lady, then I'd better get to the yard and collect my men. Will you give me a blessing?'

He knelt down and I placed my hand on his familiar dark head. I loved the springy feel of his hair and the way it moved at my touch. I murmured the words and then bent and kissed him.

'May Our Blessed Lady keep you safe,' I whispered. 'And come home to us soon.'

I didn't want him to go but steeled myself to watch him ride out at the head of his men and disappear into the chill of a late December morning. When Richard was with me I could forget my fears and feel safe but now he was gone. I was alone. I turned back into the warmth of the hall where boughs of winter greenery arched over the doors and brightly coloured ribbons strung above our heads seemed a little less glorious than they had a few hours earlier.

Next day some travelling players came into the inner courtyard to amuse the household. Joan stood by my side with her thumb in her mouth, watching the antics with a solemn little frown, but I took one look at the fire-breathing dragon and ordered the nursemaids to return the younger children to the nursery. Cecilia went obediently but Dickon refused and had to be bodily removed by one of the grooms. As my son's howls echoed through the air I thought they boded well for his future. Men needed to be bold and determined and kick against authority, otherwise they'd not be men.

A cough from behind me. It was our steward.

'There's a man come to see you, m'lady. Says it's urgent.'

I sighed. 'Who is it?'

'He didn't say, m'lady, but he wears the cardinal's livery.'

'The cardinal is in Rouen,' I said, trying to quell the wriggling fear in my belly.

'I'd not know, m'lady. The man's not come far. Maybe his eminence has returned.'

I passed Joan into the care of her governess and walked reluctantly back into the house. The cardinal's man did not look like someone who had travelled from across the sea. He had the air of a man who has simply strolled down the street to deliver a request. He bowed and passed me a note.

I recognised the seal and the familiar flourishes of the cardinal's hand. The words were few but nonetheless terrifying.

*"I charge and require you to place yourself at my disposal. You are needed to serve God and the king."*

'What does the cardinal want of me?' I asked.

The man gave a brief smile. 'Tomorrow you are to ride with him to Waltham, m'lady.'

'That is impossible. The earl, my husband, is absent. I must remain here until he returns.'

The man was unperturbed. 'His eminence said if you were unwilling I was to remind you of your last meeting with him.'

It seemed the cardinal remembered our meeting at Southwark every bit as well as I did. I tried not to show

how afraid I was but my heart was pounding and every one of my senses was alert to danger.

'Very well,' I said. 'I must arrange an escort and have my maids get ready. When does his eminence wish to leave?'

'At first light, m'lady. His eminence commands that you bring only one maidservant and no men. He will provide an armed escort so you need have no fear.'

No fear! As if putting myself in the cardinal's power would bring me anything but fear: belly-churning, knee-trembling, unimaginable fear. And why Waltham? What business could the cardinal have there? The abbey possessed a famous Holy Cross but I doubted this visit was to pray at the shrine.

A pale grey light was emerging from behind the rooftops across the river when the cardinal's entourage arrived. This was not the usual grand display of wealth and power with hundreds of liveried servants and outriders and the cardinal seated on his white mule, but a small group of lightly armed men in dark cloaks intent on speed. I kissed the cardinal's ring as he sat on his horse and was then hoisted unceremoniously onto my own mare. My maid rode pillion behind one of the cardinal's men and my chest was strapped to a pack horse.

We barely stopped all day, riding at pace through the valley of the River Lea. Everything was shrouded in a low thin mist and the dampness seeped into my cloak and chilled my face, my gloved hands and my aching bones. The cardinal did not speak and when we halted for a bite of food at midday he ignored me. With every mile we covered I became more and more apprehensive, more fearful as to what awaited us at Waltham.

The abbey at Waltham was vast, bigger than I had expected and even at a distance and softened by the gathering shadows, the walls looked menacing. We passed over a bridge and under the abbey gatehouse, surprising a party of pilgrims streaming into the abbey precincts. It was almost dark and every torch was lit which would have provided a warm welcoming feeling if I'd not been so terrified. I was helped from my horse and quickly escorted to a small room set aside for the more exalted of the abbey's visitors. Hot water was provided and I was told the cardinal would sup with me in private.

By the time I had changed into a fresh gown and washed my face I'd gone beyond being frightened and just wanted to know what was to be done to me. Perhaps Edmund had betrayed me to his uncle but I tried not to think of Mistress Jourdemayne imprisoned in the darkness of the Fleet and what she might have said. A knock at the door announced the cardinal's valet who was to escort me to the cardinal's private chamber.

This time the room was plain but the cross on the wall was heavy with jewels and the jug and cups at the cardinal's left hand were of best quality embossed silver. The napery on the table and the plaster on the walls were both spotlessly white. The only splash of colour was the cardinal's red robes.

'Come in, Lady Salisbury.'

There is nothing so sinister as an enemy's smile, especially when you have no idea what his next move will be. I bowed my head and perched nervously on the hard wooden stool which was what the abbey provided for its visitors. We waited while two of the cardinal's men brought dishes of food and poured some wine before retiring and closing the door behind them.

'I will not bore you with pleasantries, Lady Salisbury,' said the cardinal in his familiar oily tone. 'They are not appropriate. Tonight's dealings are urgent. Do you understand?'

'Yes, your eminence,' I said in a voice which was barely above a whisper.

'A task of great importance must be undertaken without delay and I have chosen you as the instrument of God's will.'

I gulped, fear gnawing relentlessly at my belly. For a moment I feared I might faint.

'Her grace, the mother of the king is, at this moment, here within the abbey precincts. She rests with her household in the royal lodgings. Tomorrow she will leave for the bishop of London's house at Great Hadham.'

I had no idea where Great Hadham was or why Katherine should wish to go there. Perhaps this was one of the houses assigned to her in her widowhood.

The cardinal fixed me with a steely glare. 'Lady Salisbury, we have only this one opportunity to prevent a tragedy of unimaginable proportions from engulfing the Crown. Whatever happens you must proceed with all haste. There can be no delay. What needs to be done must be done tonight. I know the responsibility I have laid on your shoulders is a great one but I advise you not to fail me in this matter. You are well acquainted with her grace, the king's mother, are you not?'

I moistened my lips, thinking there must be more to this, something he'd not yet told me. 'Yes your eminence, I am acquainted with her grace. It was at your command that I befriended her.' I paused remembering the first time I saw Katherine, how our friendship had grown and how her feelings for Edmund had come between us.

'Your eminence, I fear her grace no longer has need of my friendship. It may be I have offended her in some way, perhaps something I said.'

The cardinal waved away my comments as an irrelevance.

'This is not a game, Lady Salisbury. I am not interested in whatever disagreeable words passed between you and her grace, nor do I need reminding of your past misbehaviour. The orders I am about to give you are for the protection of his grace, the king. It is essential that nothing, absolutely nothing, either now or in the future, is allowed to damage the reputation of the Crown or the king or those whose duty is to him and him alone.'

He glared at me as if it was I who would threaten the Crown's reputation. Under my breath I began to pray. I was numb with fear. This *must* have something to do with the taking of Mistress Jourdemayne. Eleanor had warned me of what might happen if they came for us; of what was done to those who meddled in potions and mysteries, to anyone who denied God's holy word by invoking the power of the devil. And now that moment had come.

The cardinal leaned closer and said, 'This evening you will make your way to the royal lodgings and beg an audience with her grace, the mother of the king. You will go alone. Do you understand?'

I nodded mutely, too terrified to speak.

'I shall not ask what means you employ to enter into the presence of her grace, that is your affair. But you must not fail. Do not allow yourself to be fobbed off with excuses. It is vital that you see her tonight.'

'What am I to say to her grace?'

The cardinal spread his hands out as if the question had no meaning. He shrugged. 'Whatever you like. Talk of your children, the chill of the abbey rooms. Whatever. It matters not. What does matter is that you pay great attention to her person. Study her carefully with a woman's eye and when you return you will tell me what you have seen.'

'Is there something in particular I am to look for?'

His smile was no more than a curved thread of his bloodless lips. 'When you see her, I think you will understand.'


I had no appetite and as soon as the meal was finished the cardinal called for one of the abbey's lay brothers to escort me to the royal lodgings. I paused to collect my cloak and then set off along the covered walk, caught between low frosted hedges and the encroaching dark. My companion was a silent little man who paid me no more attention than if I'd been a dog trotting at his heels. At the door I gave my name and explained to the guard I had come on the cardinal's instructions to visit her grace, the mother of the king. He must have thought it odd that I was alone but he ordered the door opened and I was admitted into a high-ceilinged hall. The fire in the hearth was a bed of glowing ashes and to one side, the usual trestles and benches had been neatly stacked. The evening meal was long past but a few servants still moved quietly about their business.

The man who had admitted me led the way through a large empty chamber and into a further one where I recognised one of Katherine's musicians engaged in conversation with the maid, Guillemot. The young woman's eyes widened in alarm when she saw me. I made to speak but she scuttled away as if I was plague-ridden.

'Please to wait, m'lady,' said my escort. 'I shall inform her grace of your arrival. But,' he added as if on an afterthought, 'her grace may have retired for the night.'

'This early?' I remarked, disbelieving every word he said.

He bit his lip. 'Her grace is weary these winter days, m'lady. But I shall ask.'

He disappeared to whatever lay behind the door while I sat down to wait on a bench.

After a long time he reappeared with Guillemot at his side. She curtsied low as if I was a duchess come visiting and said, 'Her grace regrets she cannot see you, my lady. She is sick.' As the words tumbled out, her face flushed a rosy red at the blatant lie.

I stared at her severely until she lowered her gaze.

'I would have you go back and inform her grace that if she does not admit me into her presence tonight, she'll likely have the cardinal walk into her bedchamber unannounced. Remind her that I am her friend in all things and shall do my utmost to protect her.'

Guillemot's mouth trembled, she hesitated, then turned and fled. I had no idea why Katherine was reluctant to see me or why she'd instructed little Guillemot to lie.

There was a mystery here, lurking just out of reach, one I could almost touch, but not quite. What it was, I had no idea.

Eventually Guillemot sidled out again looking even more apprehensive. She stood aside to let me enter and as I brushed past I heard the slight sigh of her breath. The room was in shadow, a single stand of candles shedding a small soft light in a far corner. Katherine was seated in a chair before the fire with a heavy furred robe draped over her shoulders. She was wearing a plain loose woollen gown.

'Your grace.' I greeted her as I had always done with a deep curtsey.

She said nothing and made no move, continuing to stare into the flames.

'Your grace?' I said a little louder, wondering if I should rise.

'You may approach,' she said quietly.

As I stepped closer I saw what it was she'd been trying to keep from me. Her dark green velvet robe with its voluminous sleeves and furred lining hid most of the damson-coloured gown beneath, but no amount of artfully draped clothing or dim lighting could disguise what the cardinal must already have suspected: Katherine was carrying a child. And from the size of her swollen body she must be hastening to Great Hadham for the birth.

I was so shocked my mouth dropped open.

This was the queen dowager, the mother of the king! A widow who was indisputably great with child. Not even the most fervent believer in holy miracles could accept this as her husband's work. King Harry had been dead eight years. I'd heard tales of women carrying a child in the womb for more than a twelve month, but not this. Not for eight years!

Katherine said nothing. Unlike Guillemot she neither blushed nor seemed distressed but of course she must have known the day might come when her condition would be discovered. She was fortunate there'd been no need for her to attend court. To appear like this, however well disguised, would have set every woman's tongue wagging and retribution would have swiftly followed.

'*Bien*!' she said levelly when silence threatened to suffocate the room. 'Have you seen enough?'

'Oh Katrine, your grace. I didn't know.'

'Of course you didn't. I made certain of that. No-one was to know. With my son and his advisors in France it was easy. People take scant interest in what I do or where I go. I trust no-one and my household is sworn to secrecy.' She gave a deep sigh. 'I thought they were loyal but it seems one amongst them is not.'

'They love you.'

'Perhaps they do but we both know that for some, love is not enough. However, I am used to disappointment.' She regarded me as if I'd been a particular source of disappointment. 'So, my faithless friend, I hear you travel with the cardinal.'

'Yes, your grace. I do but please understand I have no choice in the matter.'

'You are here to spy for him. He wishes to expose my secret.'

'He has power over me,' I whispered, 'or I would never betray your grace. It grieves me to do so.'

'*Bien sûr,*' she said with a little movement of her head. 'No-one is disloyal by choice. But I had thought better of you, Lady Salisbury.'

She smiled sadly.

'The cardinal is unsure,' I said quickly. 'He has only suspicions.'

'But you will tell him what you have seen and then he will know for certain.'

She shifted as if to ease the ache in her back. The last two months could be very uncomfortable as I knew only too well.

'Who...?'

'Do not ask me that,' she spat. 'You of all people have forfeited the right to ask me anything.'

I knew the child must be Edmund's. There had been no-one else. There'd been no rumours, no whispers of other flirtations, nothing. My cousin had admitted to wanting her with an unquenchable passion and the last time we'd spoken privately together, Katherine had admitted to being tempted.'

'Doe he know?'

'Did you not hear. Nobody knows! Nobody!'

So she'd not told him. Or was it *he* who had told *her* there was no prospect of marriage between them no matter how much he loved her. He would have taken her to bed and *then* told her. After he had compromised her and held her heart, he would have told her. He'd have cradled her in his arms and sworn undying love. She would have wept and said she was his, no matter what, just as once upon a time I would have done the same.

Perhaps together, Edmund and the cardinal had

discussed the problem of what to do. The new law had swept away their plan for Edmund to move closer to the throne. Now there was no prospect of marriage. A child would not change Edmund's mind. He knew the penalty for marrying Katherine and he'd be a fool to pay it. No man would choose to lose everything for a woman, no matter who she was. If Katherine was suffering she would have to suffer alone.

'If there is anything I can do for your grace,' I began.

'You have done quite enough, Lady Salisbury. And since there is nothing more to be said, you'd better bring the cardinal to me. I'm sure he is anxious to see for himself and if he is to come, I would rather it was now.'

She turned her head away and sat watching the flames, taking no notice of me as I rose and made my farewell.

The sound of the Compline bell echoed through the abbey precincts as the cardinal swept into the rooms of the queen dowager, his crimson robes snapping behind him like an angry serpent's tail. He frowned with disapproval at the obvious lack of grandeur, noting the meagre estate in which Katherine lived. "Hiding her shame" were the words he'd used when I'd told him of my discovery.

Katherine had changed into a low-cut gown of green damask and was wrapped in a robe of deep blue velvet with fur trimmings at wrist and hem. She looked weary.

'You will forgive me, your eminence, if I do not rise to greet you but I find myself somewhat inconvenienced, as you see.' She looked at him out of a pair of steady dark eyes.

I was permitted a chair at the side of the room but Katherine's servants were sent away. Even faithful

Guillemot was dismissed. The cardinal's conversation with the queen dowager was to be private and I the only witness to the words he delivered in his low, disdainful voice. He spoke of untrammelled lust, licentiousness, uncurbed carnal passions, fornication, betrayal. He was merciless and tore her apart, knot by knot, thread by thread, until, like a richly prized tapestry of rare and precious beauty, Katherine began to unravel. Her face paled, her lips trembled and she crumpled under the torrent of accusations. Tears spilled from her eyes and yet still the cardinal persisted.

'You have removed yourself from the grace of God and can have no hope of forgiveness in this life.'

He spoke of a child born into bastardy and a mother forever marked as a harlot. He talked of Katherine's mother, the unspeakable Queen Isabeau whose hands had seized the reins of power, soiling the Valois name with her trail of greedy lovers. He made sly suggestions of how it was "like mother, like daughter" and finally, when Katherine was weeping in terror and despair, he spoke of the irreparable damage she had done to the Crown.

King Harry of blessed memory, in furthering God's purpose had honoured her with his hand in marriage, plucking her from the mire of her father's divided realm. He had raised her to greatness but as a result of her perfidy, questions would undoubtedly be raised about the legitimacy of her son. The word, "adulteress", reverberated round the room as Katherine cowered beneath the onslaught of the cardinal's words.

'What does God want of me?' she wept. 'I am trapped by my woman's body.'

Deciding he had reduced her to a state where his will could be imposed on hers, the cardinal changed tack like a ship's captain seeing advantage in a sudden contrary breeze.

'There is one way,' he purred, his voice now low and caressing.

'Tell me,' she said eagerly. 'I will do anything to help my son.'

'You must marry.'

I watched the hope in Katherine's eyes die. 'C'est impossible. I cannot. You know I cannot. The English parliament has forbidden it.'

The cardinal gave a small complacent smile. 'It is true the law forbids a widowed queen to remarry unless...'

'A man who breaks this law loses everything,' she whispered, tears welling up in her eyes again. She knew. Edmund had told her. Before he deserted her, before he destroyed her, he had told her why he was leaving, why they could not marry.

The cardinal paused for a moment, gauging Katherine's malleability.

'The law applies only to Englishmen,' he said smoothly.

'None of my countrymen will have me,' she whispered. 'You know that. They look at me and see treachery. When Harry made me his queen they spat at my feet for giving myself to a foreign invader.'

The cardinal was like a boy herding geese, his little stick pushing and prodding the feathered beauties this way and that while keeping one eye fixed firmly on the open goose pen.

'Regardless of what your countrymen may think of

you, your grace, the council would in no wise permit you to marry a Frenchman.'

'So marriage is impossible.'

'To marry a perceived enemy of the English Crown, yes, that would be impossible. But,' he paused, 'I believe there *is* a way.'

Katherine raised her head, her eyes alight with hope.

The cardinal continued. 'You have in your household, I believe, some Welshmen.'

It was disingenuous of the cardinal to pretend he didn't know. He would have a complete list of every servant in Katherine's little household, from her steward to the boy who scraped the pots in the kitchen. He would know their names, their provenance, the strength of their loyalties and probably the content of their dreams. There would be nothing he did not already know.

Katherine's head drooped. She spoke in a whisper. 'Yes. I have three who served my late husband and who now choose to serve me.'

'Good. Shall we summon… let us say, Master Tudor?' He turned to me. 'If you would be so kind as to ask her grace's maid to fetch Master Tudor please, Lady Salisbury.'

After giving Guillemot her orders I sat in an increasingly uncomfortable silence, disturbed only by an occasional hiss from the fire. I knew little of the Welsh. Richard's business was mostly in the North and we seldom came across any Welshmen. I'd heard they were a fierce race of pagans who greatly mistrusted the English. Some women of my acquaintance believed they were nothing but animals.

This particular Welshman was middle-aged, of slender build with dark curling hair and a closed expression on his face. As he made a reverence to the cardinal I saw his hands were surprisingly delicate but on the tips of his fingers there were scars.

'Owain ap Meredyth ap Tydier.' The cardinal spoke fluently in what sounded like a foreign tongue. Was this Welsh?

Master Tudor eyed the cardinal suspiciously.

'Your eminence asked to see me?'

'I did. Tell me, Master Tudor, are you married?'

If the man thought the cardinal's line of questioning peculiar, he chose not to show it.

'Not as you'd notice, your eminence.'

'And why would that be?'

Fresh sweat gathered on Master Tudor's forehead. He could have no idea what the cardinal wanted. He knew only the breadth and depth of the cardinal's power and the inadvisability of crossing him.

'Marriage is a serious business, your eminence. I've not had time to find a wife.'

'But you are not otherwise inclined?'

Master Tudor flushed a deep embarrassed red. '*Sodomiaeth*? No! Who is it who has accused me of that vileness?'

The cardinal raised his eyebrows at the vehemence of the Welshman's answer. I knew nothing of the Welsh tongue but could guess at the meaning and turned my head away in disgust. The existence of catamites was well known to women, whispered about in private but never mentioned in public.

'Peace, Master Tudor! Your colleagues say only good things about you and that is to your advantage. I have summoned you this evening because I wish to put to you a proposition, one which I think you should consider most carefully. Yes, very carefully indeed.'

The Welshman's eyes were wary and he rose slightly onto the balls of his feet like a man preparing to flee.

'You are loyal to her grace, the king's mother?'

'I would die for her.'

The cardinal smiled. 'That will not be necessary, Master Tudor. However, her grace is in need of someone to do her a very great service and I think you could be the man.'

Master Tudor shot a glance from his dark-lashed eyes at Katherine and then lowered his gaze. 'I am sworn to her. I will serve her grace in any way I can. '

'No matter what is asked of you?'

'No matter what is asked of me.'

'Good, good.' The cardinal leaned back in his chair and folded his hands across the great scarlet mound of his belly. 'Then, prepare yourself, Master Tudor. For today is your wedding day.'

'*Annwyl Crist!*' The man took a step back. 'Pray forgive me, your eminence. You took me by surprise. Is there some young woman her grace wishes me to marry?'

The cardinal smiled. 'No, Master Tudor. There is not. Her grace wishes to marry you herself.'

The silence was so profound I thought I could hear Master Tudor's heartbeats as his eyes widened, first in disbelief and then in horror.

'But your eminence. That is *amhosibl*. Impossible. I…,' he stumbled for the right words. '*Yr wyf yn dim.* I am nothing. A grain of sand beneath the foot of her grace. *Anheilwng*, unworthy, even to touch the hem of her robes.'

For several minutes, as the candles guttered and the darkness deepened, the cardinal let Master Tudor babble on in his garbled mixture of English and Welsh until at last, he ran out of words. By then, tears were streaming down his cheeks and he had sunk to his knees.

Katherine's face was unreadable. Like a wild animal backed into the corner of a thicket with no seeming way of escape, I could only imagine her thoughts. How could she, the daughter of one king, wife to another and mother to a third, how could she possibly give herself in marriage to a servant! It was unthinkable. If she married Master Tudor she would be brought down to the level of the lowest of men. But if she did not, she would be branded a harlot and would ruin her son's sacred inheritance.

I shivered and wondered what Master Tudor was really like beneath his humble demeanour. There was no sign of him being violent but with servants one never knew. Katherine could not marry him. It was disgusting. She would be the butt of jokes wherever she went and would have no standing of any kind. No-one would welcome her into their house. Their friends would snigger and make lewd remarks.

'There would be no need for the marriage to be known,' said the cardinal calmly. 'You and she could live quietly at Great Hadham or at another of her grace's houses. Obviously you would not come into the king's presence. There would, in fact, be no need for anyone to know the truth. The child would be raised away from the royal court. If it is a boy he might be placed within an enclosed order where he'd be trained to serve God. As I am sure her grace understands, sometimes a child must pay for the sins of the parents and a woman caught in adultery has much to repent.'

The man lifted his face. 'Your eminence, I cannot.'

'You see, Master Tudor,' continued the cardinal. 'The simple truth of the matter is that the king's mother cannot be permitted to give birth to a bastard child. A solution must be found and you, however much you protest, are part of that solution. There is no other way and you have no choice. None at all.'

Later that evening I stood witness to the marriage of Katherine of Valois, widow of Henry, late king of England, and Owain ap Meredyth ap Tydier. Throughout the ceremony Katherine's face was as pale as the Christmas roses blooming in the abbey gardens while Master Tudor quivered like a leveret in the grass. He swayed on his feet and was almost unable to speak the necessary responses. His hands shook as he slid the ring provided by the cardinal onto Katherine's finger and the thought crossed my mind that he might faint. But he remained upright, looking for all the world like a man on the scaffold preparing to meet his maker.

There was a brief nuptial mass after which the cardinal reminded both parties that the marriage must now be consummated.

'The union of man and woman in marriage represents the union of Christ and His Church and thus should not be treated lightly.' He pursed his lips, lowering his gaze to Katherine's belly. 'The circumstances are unfortunate but this must be done and done tonight. There must be no possibility of this marriage being undone.'

I escorted Katherine to her bedchamber. She walked as if in a trance, seemingly unaware that I was at her side. Waiting for us was Guillemot who silently helped Katherine out of her clothes. Under the circumstances, I turned my face away from her nakedness, not wishing to see the result of Edmund's stupidity.

'Leave it,' ordered Katherine as Guillemot prepared to braid her mistress's long dark hair. 'I shall wear it loose.' She gave a short laugh. 'If I am to be honoured as a bride it is better I appear as one'

'Katrine, this is wrong,' I whispered. 'You cannot allow it. You will damage the child.'

Slowly she raised her head to look at me. 'I doubt I'm in danger of rough wooing. And the child is damaged already. Go away, Lady Salisbury, Your part in this tragedy is finished. You are of no further use.'

Clothed in one of her many embroidered silk nightshifts with her hair falling to her waist, Katherine looked about fifteen. Even the red-rimmed eyes and swollen belly did nothing to detract from her virginal appearance. She was all purity and innocence. With a velvet robe draped over her shoulders she knelt at the foot of the bed and together we waited.

The arrival of the cardinal and Master Tudor escorted by two of the cardinal's men, prevented further words between us. The Welshman was clothed in a borrowed nightshirt and a cloak which I'd last seen wrapped round the shoulders of Katherine's steward. He looked deeply unhappy. The sharp aroma of *eau de vie* wafted across the room, several cups doubtless drunk to stiffen Master Tudor's resolve.

The cardinal looked benign. He murmured prayers over the heads of the married couple, blessed the bed in which they would lie and prayed for a fruitful marriage. Guillemot took the velvet robe and I helped Katherine climb the steps into her bed and gently pulled up the covers. On the other side, the cardinal's men practically shoved Master Tudor up and beneath the sheets. He looked sick with fright.

Katherine put out her slim white fingers and laid them on her new husband's hand where he grasped the fur cover like a drowning man seeking salvation. In that one small gesture I knew that whatever the future held she would be kind to him. It was not what the cardinal had sought nor what either party to the marriage could imagine but in the years to come it might be that people would look favourably upon the marriage of Katherine of Valois, widowed queen, and Owain Tudor, servant. It was more of a mésalliance than the one Lady Warwick had envisaged but it might bring a degree of happiness to both parties, enriching the years ahead for them both. But for Katherine's unborn child there could be no future.

That night, before I was allowed to retire, the cardinal had me brought to the chapel in the abbey's church and there at the shrine of the Holy Cross had me swear to keep secret all details of our night's work. As I kissed the cold black stone, worn smooth by the lips of a thousand pilgrims, I felt the weight of God's hand in everything that had happened, not just in the begetting of Katherine's child but in this furtive marriage.

There was nobody with whom I could share this

secret other than Katherine and I doubted I would see her again. She despised me, regarded me as the cardinal's pawn, a woman whose loyalty could be bought and who had betrayed her in her hour of need. The Katherine I had known was a forgiving woman but my disloyalty was beyond forgiveness.

Before we parted next morning, the cardinal surprised me. As I knelt to receive his blessing, he raised his hand but then paused.

'I misjudged you, Lady Salisbury. I took you for a foolish young woman but it seems the passing years have endowed you with the benefit of wisdom. You smoothed the path for her grace and your presence reminded her of her obligations. I thank you for your help.'

As he leaned over me he whispered, 'But my memory is long and I never forget a person's sins.'

Within a heartbeat the blessing was given and the cardinal disappeared, leaving me to make my lonely way home to my children. I was accompanied by a small party of the cardinal's men whose job was to keep a sharp lookout for any malcontents bent on harm. But I knew a greater harm had already been committed, a harm against two people now making their slow way north to Great Hadham. Theirs was the tragedy, not mine.

# 23

## ROUEN 1431

Spring came early that year and with the warmth came new life. Not just soft green shoots beneath hedgerows or spindle-legged calves in farmers' byres, but here in my birthing chamber at The Erber. To Richard's joy our child was another boy and we named him John. Breathing in the scent of the tiny bundle in my arms I wondered about Katherine's child. There'd been no word from Great Hadham but that was not surprising as the birth would of necessity be shrouded in secrecy. Talk of the whereabouts of her grace the king's mother was non-existent as even the most devoted collectors of tittle-tattle amongst those of my friends left in England were uninterested in her doings. She had been swept into the shadows almost as if she had never existed.

As my neighbours sat gossiping around my bed, supposedly admiring my handsome newborn son, all talk was of our capture of the girl they called the Maid. I'd first heard of her two years earlier after her appearance at the siege of Orléans. People said she claimed to be sent by God to chase the English out of France but of course common French soldiers are a credulous lot and will believe anything they're told. Instead of giving her a whipping at the tail-end of a cart as she deserved, they gave her a suit of armour and a white horse and placed her at the head of their army. Oddly, she had some little success but that was just happenstance.

Inspired by the boasting of this half-witted girl, Katherine's brother managed to get himself to Rheims to have a crown put on his head, an event which had caused gales of laughter amongst my friends.

I lay back against my pillows, listening to them talk.

'Bedford paid the Burgundians good money to hand her over.'

'I hear she's been taken to Rouen to be examined.'

'To what end?'

'To see if she is – how shall I say,' a small giggle, 'intact.' You mean…?

'Yes, my dear, to see if she's a virgin. She swears no man has touched her.'

'The men say she's no maid but a creature in the form of a woman.'

Gasps of horror and a scream from somebody's sixteen-year-old daughter.

'My husband says she's naught but a French whore.'

'Truly?'

The woman lowered her voice to a mere whisper as everyone leaned in closer to hear the juicy details. 'The English lords go to her cell, three or four at a time. They grab her and insinuate their persons under her clothes.'

'*Nom de dieu!*'

'I thought she wore boy's garments?'

'Ways and means, my dear. Use your imagination.'

There was a prolonged pause while imagination was permitted to run riot. A prison cell, one defenceless young woman, a group of men, intent on… what? It was enough to turn the stomach of the most hardened of women.

'What is the charge?' barked the senior dowager present whose imagination appeared sadly limited.

'If the cardinal has his way it will be heresy.'

I flinched at the word but nobody noticed.

'And who is to conduct the questioning?'

Everyone turned to me as the most reliable source of information.

'My husband says the bishop of Beauvais, Pierre Cauchon.'

Heads nodded as if every woman present was personally acquainted with the good bishop. All I knew of him was what I'd learned from Richard, that he was a fervent supporter of the English.

'Now we have their Maid our army will make short work of any resistance,' said one woman with great confidence. 'Then my husband can make arrangements for my journey to France for the coronation.'

There followed a flurry of discussion about where the young king's coronation would take place – the majority favoured Paris – and whether Burgundian headdresses were truly flattering for older woman. Many of my neighbours were still wedded to jewelled crespines over the ears and decried the fashion of showing more and more of a woman's unadorned hair.

'Your good-looking cousin left from Dover last week, Lady Alice,' said one of my more well-informed neighbours.

'My cousin?'

'Edmund Beaufort. Two thousand men he and his brother had, or so my sister's husband says.'

Looks were exchanged between two of my acquaintance who liked nothing more than the thought of a well-muscled man no matter that he was a pikeman.

'Who is to lead them?'

'Lord Audley and Lord Fitzwalter. I believe.'

'I wish Edmund Beaufort would lead me,' giggled the plump redhead sitting in the corner. 'I'd follow *him* willingly.'

This led to gossip about somebody's husband and the wife's fourteen-year-old maidservant discovered in a hayloft together. Once even ounce of enjoyment had been squeezed from that particular situation my neighbours rose like a flock of pigeons, fluttering, cooing and promising to come again. Kisses were blown, farewells were made, and then, still chattering and laughing, they swept out of the room and down the stairs.

So Edmund had gone to France. I could not help but wonder if he knew about Katherine's child and if he did was he full of remorse for the way he'd treated her. Whatever my cousin *did* know I was certain he'd not have heard about Master Tudor's part in the dismal affair. That was to remain a secret from everyone.

I lay there, sleepy, listening to the familiar sounds of The Erber and the river boats beyond, wondering when Richard would go to France and if he might take me with him for the coronation celebrations. The delight I took in our children was a continuing pleasure but what woman would willingly refuse an invitation to see Paris.

The port town was less than an hour's ride ahead when we began encountering men encamped on both sides of

330

the Dover road. Everywhere I looked there were tents. According to the captain of my escort, who was a local man never slow to give his opinion, they'd sprung up overnight like mushrooms in a damp meadow.

'God willing t'won't be long afore they be gone, m'lady. They'd best be takin' their trash along wi' them. But I'll not complain if they teach them French churls a lesson or two.'

This was my husband's army, mustered to provide a retinue for the cardinal's journey to Paris. Fortunately the cardinal was nowhere to be seen, having elected to remain in Rouen to oversee the trial of the young woman they called the Maid.

As well as dust from the road and the smell of thousands of unwashed men, a scent of cherry blossom drifted across from a nearby orchard. This was a springtime adventure under a sky of sweet English softness. We had left Canterbury early that morning and as we'd passed under the city walls I spared a thought for our children, safe and well cared for in the nursery at Middleham. Three weeks earlier the wet nurse had been dispatched with our youngest who would by now have joined his brothers and sisters: five young Nevills growing up together in safety amongst the hills and dales of the North Country while their parents were bound for the war-torn plains of Northern France.

As soon as we arrived at Dover Richard went down to the quayside to supervise the loading of our baggage while I navigated the stony path leading up to the castle where we would lodge until it was time to embark. Even with a slight onshore breeze the day was unseasonably warm yet I could not help shivering. This was my first sea voyage and

I was nervous. I'd heard too many stories of shipwrecks and pirates and sea monsters rising out of the deep, to be entirely comfortable with the idea of setting foot on board ship, no matter how many times Richard said there was no danger, none at all.

The castle was vast, sprawled on a headland overlooking the town with a wonderful prospect of the sea between here and France. Inside, it was crowded but there was nobody I recognised. A clean-looking young woman showed me to our room which turned out to be small and cramped but no worse than some of the other places we'd stayed at on our journey through Kent. With so many people making the crossing it was not surprising the best rooms had already been taken. Luckily the wind was set fair and we were expecting to sail within two days so our sojourn here should not be long and once in Rouen we'd have better accommodation. Nobody had yet said how long we would stay there before setting out for Paris or if perhaps we were to go to Rheims for the coronation. I knew nothing of Rheims other than that kings of France were always crowned there in the way that English kings were always crowned in the abbey at Westminster. I supposed the duke of Bedford and the earl of Warwick would decide.

My maid removed my dusty outer clothes and quickly helped me into a fresh gown. A splash of rosewater along my neckline and a session in front of my travelling mirror to repair my face and adjust my new hat, completed my preparations. The ivory-coloured chaperon with its tiny pleated veil had been a gift from Richard. It covered scandalously little of my hair but he assured me it was the latest fashion in Burgundy and perfectly proper.

'I feel half-naked these days.' I remarked to my maid.

She smiled and murmured how delightful I looked.

The knock at the door took me by surprise. The girl hurried across the floor to see who it was, leaving me gazing with pleasure at my reflection.

I turned on the stool to see Guillemot. She was the last person I expected to see in Dover Castle but I schooled myself to show no surprise; she was after all only a servant.

She curtsied. 'My mistress, her grace, the queen dowager is asking for you, my lady.'

My stomach turned over. Katherine! Here! Memories of Waltham and the cardinal's threats rose up into my throat, making me want to vomit. I willed myself to be calm. Richard had said the cardinal was in Rouen. I was perfectly safe.

'The king's mother is here?'

'Yes, my lady. We are bound for Rouen.'

I'd not expected to see Katherine again and certainly not on her way to Rouen where she could hardly avoid meeting the cardinal. But when I thought about it, I supposed it was no surprise. He would want to keep an eye on her and she would want to be present at her son's coronation. For Katherine, this would be a homecoming, bittersweet in many ways, but an opportunity to see her family, those who were loyal to the English. Obviously she'd not see her brother. He was our enemy.

I made a final adjustment to my hat, pulling it a little forward, then followed Guillemot out of the room, up a flight of worn steps into the old part of the castle where some bygone king had seen fit to fashion a magnificent set of royal chambers. No expense had been spared and I promptly regretted our tiny windowless room.

Katherine smiled as I entered. She was sitting with a small piece of embroidery in her lap listening to a boy who was plucking the strings of a gittern and singing a mournful song.

For a while we made greetings and polite conversation but at no time did she mention either our previous meeting at Waltham or the secret we shared. Perhaps, like me, she wanted to forget although for her that was surely impossible. Every day she would be surrounded by reminders: a husband who was not the father of her child, and a child begotten in sin whose father had callously abandoned her.

'I thought that as you are also travelling to Rouen, you would favour me with your presence on board ship?' she said lightly. 'The captain assures me that my cabin has room enough for two and from what I remember of our happy times together at Kennington, you are a congenial companion.'

So this was to be the pattern of our meetings. We would not talk of the child or of her marriage to Master Tudor and there would be no mention of my cousin, Edmund. We would both pretend nothing untoward had happened: Katherine was still a grieving widow, the mother of a single perfect son and Edmund Beaufort, with his dangerous attempts at seduction, had never intruded into either of our lives.

'I should be delighted, your grace,' I murmured, though in truth, even without our shared secret, I had no desire to spend an awkward few hours with Katherine in a stuffy little cabin while we were tossed unceremoniously around on the waves. If I was going to disgrace myself by vomiting into a basin, I would rather be alone with my maid or with the other women, not with the mother of the king.

The few hours on board which I'd been promised, stretched to a whole day and darkness was falling when we heard the welcome sound of someone shouting "Have a care! Honfleur ahead!" Despite the constant slap of waves against the hull and the unaccustomed movement of our little world, I had proved a stalwart sailor and had not vomited once. Guillemot reported that the ladies in the other cabin were in a sorry way: prostrate and groaning on the bed while the place stank like a privy pit.

Guillemot was allowed out on deck to watch our entry into the harbour, leaving the two of us alone. Katherine turned to me and said in the lowest of voices. 'As you have been kind enough not to ask and because I know you can keep a secret, I shall tell you. The child was a boy.'

For a moment I wondered what she meant by telling me, but before I could reply, Guillemot returned and began laying out Katherine's clothes in preparation for the very public return of the king's mother to the land of her birth. The young king awaited his mother at Rouen but here the garrison and townspeople of Honfleur would welcome Katherine as the key which had unlocked the door of the entrance gateway into France.

'Nonsense!' my Aunt Margaret had said when I'd told her what people were saying of Katherine. 'It was the murder of Philip of Burgundy's father, John the Fearless. That killing was what gave Harry the opportunity. It drove the son into our arms. Katherine was merely a symbol. Valuable but not sufficient in herself.'

Once we arrived in Rouen I quickly discovered there was only one topic of conversation. Katherine and I could have been two fabulous creatures on chains, exhibited for people's delight, for all the population cared. The great feast organised by The duke of Bedford for the English king to welcome his mother was of little importance. All anyone wanted to know was what news there was from Bishop Cauchon's last questioning of *La Pucelle*, as the people here called the Maid.

Gossip was running wild round the castle. She saw angels, she heard voices, she talked with the saints. Saints? Which saints? Why, Saint Michael, Saint Margaret and Saint Catherine of course. But had she not said her voices came directly from God?

The tree of fairies in *La Pucelle's* home village, where girls danced half-naked at the foot of the oak and wove garlands to hang on its branches, was endlessly discussed. Had the bishop really said the spirits amongst the leaves must be demons and that the Maid erred in her thinking? Could she not recognise a diabolical presence for what it truly was? Surely everyone knew witches celebrated their Sabbaths underneath the oak.

Men grinned when they heard *La Pucelle* had been taken to an underground room and shown metal instruments with teeth and blades and pincers. They wanted to know exactly what the bishop's torturers had done to the whore. Which parts of her body had they pinched and nipped and cut? Had she confessed when they'd pulled her limbs?

'What are they doing to her?' I asked Richard, my stomach turning over at the thought of those sinister tools of torture.

'Trying to save her soul'

'Is that possible?'

'No, it is not possible because we all know she cannot be allowed to live. She is far too dangerous. They must find her heretical in her thoughts and in her deeds.'

'Even if she is innocent?'

My husband gave me an odd look and came and sat beside me. He took my hand in his and idly stoked my fingers. 'Do you think a young woman who dresses like a man, who believes God directs her every step and who sets herself up higher than the most venerable and learned of churchmen, can be judged by these very same churchmen, as innocent.'

'No, but...'

'Alice, listen to me. She refuses to submit to the authority of the Church. She defies them at every turn with her twisted arguments.'

'Does that make her a heretic?'

'The Church suspects her guilty of heresy and blasphemy. Who am I to argue with that judgement?'

'So they will burn her.'

'The pyre is being built.'

'Here?'

For some reason I'd thought they would take her elsewhere for burning, to her home village or to Paris; somewhere I wouldn't have to smell her roasting flesh and watch her body consumed by flames.

'The Abbey of Saint-Ouen.' He must have read the horror in my eyes. 'Dearest. she is our enemy. Why do you think the cardinal is in Rouen if not to stiffen Bishop Cauchon's resolve. The cardinal would happily have her spit-roasted for his dinner and not simply for the pleasure of saving her soul. He'll not allow an appeal to Rome so Cauchon has no choice. He will hand her over to the executioner.'

At Richard's mention of the cardinal's part in all this, I felt the accustomed fear churning in my belly. The cardinal would have burned me too, given the chance. If I'd not proved useful to him he would have turned me over to the king's executioner just as the bishop would do to the Maid. It had taken the bishop and his inquisitors four months of ceaseless questioning to uncover her true nature but now she was exposed as the heretic that she was. I wondered if, like me, her folly began with an innocent desire to do good and if, like me, she truly regretted the sinful acts she'd done. Had she been caught up in someone else's web of evil, unable to extricate herself until it was too late. Would I look at her and see myself.

From one of the highest rooms in the castle, I peered out at the river far below. Before she was handed over by her captors to the English, I'd been told the Maid had tried to escape. She had jumped from the window of a great tower just like this one. Had she truly thought God would allow her to fly like a bird or was she tricked by the voices in her head. As children we'd been warned about demons who crept into people's minds and how prayer would be our armour against these tools of Satan. We must always, the bishop had thundered, be on our guard against the evil one trying to corrupt us. Clearly The Maid had not been sufficiently vigilant.

He was wearing soft-soled shoes so I didn't hear him coming. It was the warm breath on the back of my neck

338

and the familiar voice whispering in my ear that told me he was there.

'I didn't know if you'd come.'

Warily I turned to face my cousin. 'What are you doing here, Edmund? Why are you not with your uncle?'

He knew better than to touch me, not now after all that had happened between us, but he came as close as he dared.

'They have her surrounded by guards,' he said in a low voice. 'I can't get near.'

'For pity's sake, why would you want to? She is our enemy.'

'Ah Christ, Alice! Not the Maid – Katherine. She won't even look at me. It's as if I do not exist for her any more.'

He didn't know. Clearly his uncle had told him nothing of what had happened at Waltham this last winter, of the child, the Welshman, the enforced marriage. I hesitated for a moment but knew I'd not be the one to tell him. All I could do for my cousin and for Katherine was to warn him off. It was little enough after the part I'd played in this whole sorry affair.

'Leave her alone, Edmund. There's nothing you can offer her any more. Pursuing her will only bring misery to you both.'

'I don't care,' he said, pulling off his hat and running his fingers distractedly through his hair. 'I'd suffer the fires of Hell to be with her just one more time.' He began pacing the floor banging his fist on the walls. 'It was a mistake! We parted badly but I regret what I said. Afterwards I sent her a letter but she sent it back unopened. I sent another and another but each one was sent back. Alice, she needs to know how much… how much I regret what I said at our last meeting.'

'Let her be. Edmund.'

He sank down onto the stone bench and put his head in his hands. 'I cannot. She has cast a web around me. I am caught fast. I've tried other women but it's no good. Alice, you are the only person who can help me.'

For the length of one hot summer when I was young, I had worshipped this cousin of mine, seeing him through a distorted glass of girlish adoration. In Quarry Wood he had been my hero, brave and resourceful, leading me through dappled sunlight to our secret bower in the undergrowth. If I'd been a little older, a little wiser, known a little more of the nature of men, he might have succeeded in seducing me, but my very innocence had come to my aid. Edmund was no hero, not then, not now. He was what he had always been: totally unscrupulous when it came to getting his own way and I didn't trust him an inch.

'There is nothing I can do for you, Edmund,' I said firmly.

'You could carry a letter. Give it to her. You could explain. Tell her I must see her.'

Deliberately I removed his hand from my sleeve. 'Edmund, hear this. I want nothing more to do with your plans. They are ill-conceived. You will have to find someone else to help you because I will not. Now I must go.' I gave a small smile to show I bore him no ill will. 'I wish you a good day, dear cousin.'

I left him quickly, hurrying as fast as I could down the winding steps, fearing he would follow, but when I reached the bottom no-one was coming after me. There were no footsteps and the stairway remained silent. The

340

echoing chamber at the foot of the steps was empty except for the forlorn figure of Guillemot standing by the far wall. I thought she was waiting for me but as I passed by she merely curtsied politely, her head bent. I gave her not a second thought.

Two days later they burned the Maid. Isabel Warwick came for me soon after dawn and told me to prepare myself.

'We are required to be present, my dear. Orders from my lord and from the cardinal. She must have seen the look of naked horror on my face because she patted my hand. 'Don't worry, we'll not be down in the square. That'is for our men and for the townsfolk. They're the ones who are clamouring to see her burn. There is a little covered gallery overlooking the market place. We shall stand there. I hear it commands a good view.'

'I thought she'd recanted. Everyone was saying so. They cannot burn her if she's submitted.'

Isabel said quietly, 'I too thought Bishop Cauchon had saved her soul for Christ. But alas, it was not so. I fear the devil will always find a way. When the bishop was called back to her cell he found her once more dressed in men's clothes. She claimed her voices had told her she'd damned her soul to save her life. She told the bishop she had truly been sent by God. So...'

I placed my hand over my mouth to stop myself from crying out. Why had she done that?

Isabel sighed. 'Naturally there was nothing more the bishop could do. She had condemned herself out of her own mouth. A relapsed heretic must be abandoned by the Church. She is to burn.'

'Will there be many present?'

*Jhesus Maria*! Yes. They are flocking through the gates in their thousands. There's not been a burning here for years and folk are hungry for a spectacle. The king's father, he was a great man for burning heretics as I'm sure you know. 'She lowered her voice. 'A man who condemns a close friend to burn is a man to be greatly feared. People here regarded him as a terrifying figure. They need to know the English lords have not lost their appetite for punishing their enemies.'

I closed my eyes and wished I was anywhere but in Rouen. I thought of Bisham: a sweet English spring, wrens singing in the hedgerows, glossy golden celandines, rose-red campion and starry white stitchwort, buttercups sprinkling the meadows, apple blossom, waving grasses. I refused to think of the heat, the jostling crowds and the smell of evil.

She came in a cart, a small figure with a cap on her head, looking more like a child than a young woman caught in the devil's grasp. But, as Isabel said, looks can deceive. High above the crowd, the English soldiers held her tightly as she was bound with chains to a wooden stake. One of the abbey's brothers who'd been appointed her last adviser and friend as was the custom, stood nearby. Even from this distance I could see her lips move in prayer as if seeking salvation at this her last hour.

The brother was murmuring words of comfort and one of our men thrust a little cross made of two twigs into her hands. The people in the market square howled like a pack of wolves baying for blood, pushing and shoving to get a better view. I held my breath. Sunlight crept over the rooftops and glinted on silver and steel as a hush descended on the crowd. The executioner stepped forward and thrust a burning faggot deep into the pyre. For a moment nothing happened. Then the brushwood caught light and little tendrils of smoke began curling up around her slight frame. With a sudden explosion, a sheet of flame shot skywards and within the space of a heartbeat she was engulfed in a fiery inferno. Above the crackling and roaring of the flames and the noise of the crowd I could hear her voice cry out, 'Jesu! Jesu! Jesu!'

People were shouting and jeering, some weeping, some praying. The din seemed to last for an eternity until at last the market square fell silent. There was no sound from the crowd and no movement from within the dying flames. The executioner raked back the fire and there, exposed for all to see, were the charred remains of what had once been a human being. I gagged, thrust my hand over my mouth, and nearly vomited. Nothing was left but the naked, half-burned body of a young girl still chained to the stake. The evil that had infected her had been burned away.

'See! She were a maid after all,' said a voice behind me. 'And you believed she were a man.'

'They'll burn her twice,' remarked Isabel quietly.

'Is once not enough?' I said, choking as a noxious smell drifted in our direction.

Isabel looked at me pityingly. 'Have you not seen a burning before, Lady Salisbury? They burn the body a second time to get rid of every scrap of flesh and bone till nothing's left but ash. That will go in the river to frustrate those who crave a relic of today's work. Next they'll be saying she was a saint.'

We had been taught as children, that every soul could be saved for God. Why not her?

'I wonder where her soul is?'

'That is a question for the scholars, my dear. At least she is dead and gone and that's a mercy. She'll not trouble us any more.'

'She seemed so... innocent.'

Isabel took my arm and guided me into position as the ladies took up their places in the procession.

'If your father was alive she'd have conjured up an abomination to have him dead. Think on that and you'll realise she was no innocent. She was the embodiment of everything that is evil.'

The heat in Rouen that year was stifling and like every other woman I found myself longing for a good English shower of rain. My stockings stuck uncomfortably to my legs and even sitting still, sweat gathered between my breasts, round my waist and down the back of my neck. No matter how many times I splashed my face with water I could not keep cool. Summer dragged on with no respite and no word of a date for the coronation. Rheims was sympathetic to the enemy and our route to Paris by river was made dangerous by ambushes.

I saw Edmund twice: once accompanying the cardinal through the inner courtyard of the castle, and once talking to Guillemot down near the laundries where he had no business to be. I almost laughed at the way he'd got her trapped against a wall, talking rapidly, making the most of his brute male power to terrify the poor woman. But he'd get no joy from Katherine's maid. She was as loyal as a dog to her mistress and if Katherine had no wish to see Edmund, Guillemot would not be the one to let him through the door. He might try persuasion or threats, both of which he'd used on me in the past, but Guillemot would stand steadfast no matter what he did.

On one occasion I found myself required to attend Katherine at a reception for visiting dignitaries from Burgundy but this was a strictly formal affair which gave us no opportunity for private conversation. Her skin was pallid and despite the skilful application of powder and paste, I could see dark smudges beneath her eyes and new lines down the sides of her mouth. I thought she looked tired and unhappy and wondered if she was sickening with some ailment. If we'd been in England, by now I would have left London and gone north to Middleham away from the stink and disease of the city. Here I was trapped. Beyond the fortress walls, Isabel said our armies were achieving great success. The mighty Château Gaillard had been retaken and in October the vital town of Louviers fell after a long and bloody siege. At last the way to Paris was open.

But joy at our victories was tinged with sadness when I discovered that my cousin Tom Beaufort was dead, killed at Louviers. He was fourteen when he'd ridden off to war and sixteen when captured at Baugé. He'd suffered six years of imprisonment and it seemed cruel to die so soon after his release. I sent a note to Edmund, consoling him on the loss of a brother and a letter to my Aunt Margaret at Syon. Not content with depriving her of her second husband, this war was swallowing up her sons and I prayed she would not also lose John and Edmund.

Perhaps it was the loss of my cousin or the slipping of the seasons from summer into autumn or simply lack of sleep, but I began to worry about my children. For three days I fretted, imagining all kinds of dangers from unguarded wells to neglectful nursemaids. Were the stairways at Middleham safe? What if the wet nurse tripped while carrying little John? What if Dickon pushed Cecilia into the pond? What if an outbreak of sickness arrived in the castle? By the end of the week I was so concerned I asked Richard if I might go home.

'Do you not wish to stay for the coronation?'

'I do but ...'

'You'd see Paris,' he said slyly.

'I would rather return to England.'

He frowned. 'Has this to do with Edmund Beaufort?'

My surprise was genuine. 'Of course not.'

Richard had put on his stern face, the one I'd seen too much of in the early years of our marriage. 'You were seen talking with him the other day.'

I reached out for his hand and smiled into his eyes. 'You have no reason to be jealous.'

He smiled back. 'I'd prefer my wife to be more circumspect.'

'I shall try harder to be a perfect Nevill wife.'

'And what should a perfect Nevill wife do in this situation?'

I placed my hand on his chest. 'First see to her husband's comfort.'

'And you think I am sufficiently comforted?'

'I think I am a distraction.'

He kissed the top of my head. 'You are.'

'But a perfect wife should also attend to her husband's children and to his business affairs when he is absent.'

'Is something amiss?'

'No, but it has been five months.'

'It may be another five months before we're finished here.'

'So have I your permission to go to Middleham?'

'If you must.'

'I think I should.'

He pulled me into his arms. 'I never thought to hear you say you prefer Middleham to Paris.'

Of course I could not tell him the real reason I wanted to leave. It had nothing to do with our children but everything to do with Rouen. I thought if I went to Middleham my nightmares might cease. Most nights since the burning I had dreamed of fire. In the sultry heat of a Rouen summer, sweating with fear in a bed of damp sheets, flames crept closer and closer and my throat filled with smoke. Heavy iron chains bound me tight to the stake and however much I struggled I was unable to move. I screamed with terror but once choked awake, there were no screams. I was gasping for breath and my cheeks were wet with tears.

Only with Richard beside me did I feel safe. The nights he came to my bed I slept wrapped in his arms and woke peacefully to a new day. But Richard was rarely there. His duties took him away from Rouen and I was left to face my demons alone.

Like all apparitions they were creatures of darkness, disappearing as sunlight crept slowly across the floor. But on a bright sunny afternoon one of my past demons caught me unawares. My mind was full of plans for my journey home, balancing the competing needs of visiting my aunt at Syon against travelling north to Middleham to see the children. I came into my room to find my stepmother standing amidst the chaos of half-packed chests, lost in admiration for my new bedcover. I'd not seen her since my father's death and was a little surprised at how well she looked.

'An intriguing pattern.' She smoothed her hand longingly over the gold thread embroidery as if she'd like to snatch it up and carry it off. 'Where did you find a seamstress to devise such an elegant design?'

'Lady Warwick knows someone.'

She shrugged as if this was to be expected. 'Isabel Warwick knows everyone. She has a nose for that kind of thing. I tell you she is worse than a terrier for digging out snippets of gossip. Has she told you I am to be married?'

I blushed. 'She has.'

'Hmm!' My stepmother's lips pursed in disapproval at having her news no longer the surprise she wanted it to be. 'I expect Lady Isabel looks down on my choice of husband. But William de la Pole is more skilled in diplomacy than her own husband. Lord Warwick might represent all that is ancient and revered, everything we have been taught to admire, but times are changing: a new king, a new kingdom and those who will prosper will be new men, men like my William.'

I disagreed but kept my own counsel. I suspected that in this imagined new world of my stepmother's, those who would prosper would not be new men but, as always, powerful and cunning men.

She gave a final stroke to the peach-coloured satin and came over to take me in her arms.

'We shall marry once the king has been crowned,' she purred in the manner of a woman who has finally got exactly what she always wanted. 'I trust you wish me well.'

I kissed her perfumed cheek. 'Of course I do. My aunt believes it wise for a young widow to remarry no matter how dear her husband was to her and I know my father was ever close to your heart.'

'He was,' she sighed. 'A good husband. But he made no pretence of where his duty lay.'

So there had been some dissension in their marriage just as I'd thought. Perhaps after the incident with the duke of Burgundy my father had been less in thrall to my stepmother.

'And is William de la Pole different?' I asked artlessly.

'Yes, very different.' She gave a little smirk of pleasure. 'Oh how I wish you were not going back to England. I'm surprised Richard has agreed to your leaving but of course some husbands seem not to care if their wives run off to hearth and home.'

'I am hardly running off,' I said looking at the vast array of chests.

'And such a shame to miss the coronation! But you will be company for the queen dowager.'

'The queen dowager is leaving?'

'Yes. Did you not know?' She lowered her voice. 'Lord Warwick is not best pleased. As the mother of the king he expected her to attend the celebrations in Paris. But she says she is unwell.'

She looked to see my reaction but where my

stepmother was concerned I had long ago learned to give nothing away. She picked up a piece of crimson ribbon lying half out of a box and ran it though her fingers.

'Pretty! In my opinion it is not sickness at all but a desire to avoid that mother of hers. Did you know that the queen dowager's brother is a bastard?'

I raised my eyebrows. This was a piece of gossip I'd not heard before. 'Are you certain?'

'Oh yes! Though mind you Queen Isabeau betrayed her husband with so many men it's hard to know who the young man's father is. People say it was the old king's brother.' She shrugged. 'But we do not say this in front of her grace. She cannot help her mother's nature. I can tell you, my dear, because I know you can keep a secret.' She smiled and gave me a tap on my nose as if I was a little girl.

So Katherine was returning to England. How odd! There was no good reason for her to go. If she was sick, she had her personal physician and if she needed further advice, the best doctors in the world were to be found in Paris. This was her home, the country where she'd lived as a child and must surely be more comfortable to her than England.

But of course – the child! For a moment I had forgotten. She never talked of him but she must surely want to satisfy herself that he was well cared for. I thought again of the scenes at Waltham and Katherine's serenity in the face of impending disaster. In Rouen she was unquestionably the queen she had once been: perfectly poised, beautifully clothed, a royal lady to her elegant fingertips. But that night last Christmas she had shown me a different side of her nature, one perhaps a little more akin to that of her mother.

She had made no protest when the cardinal had ordered her to bed with the lowly Master Tudor. I recalled how she'd talked of rough wooing and how she had laid her fingers lovingly on the Welshman's hand as if she could not wait to have contact with his bare skin. Despite the mound of her belly she had looked virginal yet seductive, her face glistening with sweat in the candlelight as she had turned to the man who was now her husband. Sweet Mother Mary! Surely she was not in thrall to Owain Tudor?

Edmund had once hinted that Katherine not only permitted but enjoyed certain intimacies. This tallied with Aunt Margaret's belief that Katherine was unable to control her desires. And Isabel Warwick had once told me how the bishops were worried in case the new law relating to the remarriage of queens might prevent the marriage of a couple who had already indulged in fornication. The bishops had observed Katherine over several years and knew her as well as any. Did they suspect what I now suspected?

I waited for the summons and sure enough by the end of the day one Katherine's young pages brought me a message: the queen dowager wished to see me.

It was unusual in Rouen to see Katherine without an accompanying flock of ladies but this evening's visit was exceptional so apart from Guillemot keeping guard at the door, she was entirely alone. She was wrapped in a dark robe and her eyes were red as if she'd been weeping but otherwise she seemed perfectly composed. Her hands lay in her lap, a needle placed to one side on top of a small piece of exquisitely executed embroidery.

'Your grace,' I began, uncertain if I'd been invited as a friend or a counsellor or in my capacity as Countess of Salisbury.

Giving myself time to assess the situation, I sank into a perfect curtsey. Katherine's chamber had become more formal since we'd arrived in Rouen and failure to achieve the correct depth when curtseying was now met with glacial stares from female onlookers. It was, of course, the influence of the Burgundian duchess of Bedford. Meals were eaten in silence with the king and his mother, served on bended knee by a procession of liveried servants. And afterwards, the only dance permitted was the stately bassedance. The English carol with its leaping steps and joyful enthusiasm was forbidden and perhaps with my cousin in his present mood, the lack of opportunity for accidently collapsing against a woman's breast, was advisable.

'Lady Salisbury, I thank you for coming,' she began, her voice trembling a little. 'When I heard you were returning to England I thought …' She paused and raised her head, looking me straight in the eye. 'You understand, I cannot do this alone.'

I was mistaken. She was far from being perfectly composed. Her fingers began twisting the cloth of her skirt into little knots and I noticed her biting her bottom lip. I was unsure what she wanted from me but it was clear she was suffering some inner torment. At Waltham I'd been unable to help her, constrained as I was by the cardinal's presence. Perhaps now I could make amends.

I spoke softly. 'I will do whatever you ask of me, your grace. If in the past I have appeared less than faithful I would ask you to forgive me. Let me now prove myself a loyal and trustworthy friend.'

She smiled and held out her hand. I stepped forward and placed my lips to her fingers. Her skin smelled of a deep exotic fragrance quite unlike the sweet, light rosewater she commonly used.

'You will accompany me on the journey home to England?' She was pleading with me not ordering me.

'I shall be honoured, your grace.'

'You will be my companion? You will not leave me unguarded?'

A sliver of fear vibrated in the air. There was no reason for fear yet Katherine was afraid, so afraid she was asking me for protection. It could only be a matter of weeks before the coronation took place yet something had frightened her so badly that she was prepared to abandon her duty to her son and take flight. Oddly, she perceived safety, not as her mother's house in Paris or some other place under the protection of the duke of Bedford, but as England.

Then I remembered Guillemot talking to Edmund down in the laundry and suspected where the source of Katherine's fear might lie. Had the stupid young woman given in to Edmund's demands to gain access to her mistress?

'Your grace, if you wish me to protect you, I need to know what we have to fear? Is there someone who wishes you harm?'

She shot me a look of pure terror. 'Oh Jesu! Save me from myself. I am unworthy.'

I wanted to comfort her, put my arms around her in the way I'd once done, but we had gone far beyond those days of simple friendship. Bluntness was what was called for here.

'Your grace, if we make haste we can leave tomorrow. There is a ship bound for England. She sails on the morning tide. I can ask my husband to make arrangements if that is what you wish.'

'Yes,' she whispered. 'That is what I wish.'

'What of his grace, the king?'

She moistened her lips with her tongue and touched the corner of her mouth with one hand.

'Alice.' She beckoned me closer, this time calling me by my given name. 'He came to me. Guillemot brought him. I would stay if I could but I cannot. I must not.' She let her head droop and whispered, 'I do not have the strength to resist.'

One look at her face, white as a winding sheet, and I knew the truth. It was not her son she was leaving but Edmund. She was frightened of him and frightened of what he might make her do. That was the reason for this precipitous flight. I smiled, wryly. A widowed queen and a terrified countess, both trying to escape their demons by running for the perceived safety of England, both hoping that salvation lay far from the crowded streets of Rouen, far from the men who would do them harm.

# 24

## CONFESSION 1432

It was six months after I left France and a week before the garter celebrations at Windsor when Eleanor arrived unannounced at Bisham. She'd been visiting Oxford on behalf of her husband, inspecting the work of an illuminator of manuscripts from Padua, when she'd heard some alarming news: Mistress Jourdemayne had been taken from her prison at the Fleet and escorted under guard to Windsor Castle for further questioning. This could only mean the Church was involved.

'And that is not all,' Eleanor said, making herself comfortable on my best velvet-covered settle, 'There are others.'

'Other what?'

'Prisoners. A friar called John Ashwell, and a clerk by the name of Virely.'

I shook my head. 'I've not heard of either man.'

'Of course you've not, why would you. But I can assure you these men are well known to those of us who seek out deeper truths. Doubtless the fools were caught boasting of their work. Now all three are all to be examined on a charge of sorcery. Of course the bishops have no proof.'

'Then why are they being held?'

Eleanor raised her shoulders in an elegant shrug. Even on the scaffold, I thought Eleanor would retain her elegance to the last. 'Perhaps the bishops hope the cardinal will return. He has a certain way with prisoners, you understand.'

My belly turned to ice at the cardinal's name. Some nights I was tormented by dreams of burning, where the cardinal thrust me onto the pyre and twisted the chains which bound me to the stake. When I tried to escape he had Edmund hold me down while he screamed in my face, "Heretic!"

'I cannot bear this,' I said bleakly.

She put her hand on my arm. 'Bear up! Not all the news is bad. I believe the cardinal will not return,'

I jerked my head up. 'How can you be sure?'

She grinned impishly. 'He arranged to have his treasure shipped overseas so that he could live in comfort in Ghent. But I suggested to Lord Humphrey that it might be a good idea to seize the cardinal's chests.'

'Eleanor!'

'Don't look at me like that. I did nothing but whisper a few words in my husband's ear. Now I hear that writs have been issued against the cardinal, and Lord Humphrey has organised the removal of all his supporters from the council. So I doubt the cardinal will return to cause us more trouble.'

This sounded to me like yet one more move in the endless game between the cardinal and Lord Humphrey. I feared next year might see a reversal in Lord Humphrey's fortunes. Then the cardinal would return.

As was usual for the Garter celebrations, the royal castle at Windsor was crowded with people. I received a sour look from Lady Percy. Now that I too was a countess she was my equal but that was not the true source of her displeasure. On his return from France in February Richard had been rewarded for his good service by being made warden of the east march much to the fury of Henry Percy who had doubtless vented his anger on his wife.

'Have you heard?' whispered Isabel Warwick. 'I can scarce believe it but my lord insists it is true.'

Isabel had drawn me aside into one of the little window embrasures in the public rooms at Windsor. She turned her back on the other ladies who were waiting for the summons to dinner, thus creating an illusion of privacy.

'Heard what, Lady Isabel?' I asked, thinking what a gossip Isabel was becoming.

'About her grace, the king's mother. I was shocked to the core, I can tell you.'

I stiffened involuntarily. 'Is she here?'

'No, nor likely to be.'

'Why? What has happened?'

Isabel stood on tiptoe because she was half a head shorter than me, and whispered into my ear.

'She has married her master of the wardrobe.'

'Her what?' I said trying to look surprised.

'One of her household men. A servant!'

'That cannot be true,' I said, crossing my fingers against the lie.

'Oh, but Lady Alice, it is. Imagine! She who was once King Harry's queen! Marrying a servant. It's disgusting. Of course I blame her mother. My husband says Isabeau was worse than a common harlot in her day. And now the daughter has proved to be the same.'

How had the news got out? Katherine's marriage was supposed to be the deepest of deep secrets. The cardinal would have said nothing and neither would Katherine. But someone had talked.

'Are you quite certain, Lady Isabel?' I said. 'Her grace has always struck me as a woman fully aware of her royal responsibilities.'

Isabel, now that she had started on her story, was like a runaway cart. The words kept tumbling out. 'There is a child, Lady Alice. A child! Think on that! A child! Conceived in sin of course. I cannot see how it could be otherwise. But how was it done? Why was she not stopped?'

'A child?'

'A boy. *Jhesu Maria*! Half-brother to the king!'

'And the man?'

Isabel put her hands to her forehead. 'Some Welshman. As if it could not get any worse.'

'A Welshman! And they are definitely married?'

'Oh yes.'

'Has the king been told?'

'Lady Alice, how does one tell a boy that his mother has dishonoured herself by marrying a servant. Oh *Sweet Jesus*! She might as well have coupled with a common soldier as with a Welshman.'

'What will happen?'

Isabel shrugged. 'There is nothing to be done. Marriage is a binding sacrament. Do you know, when Lord Humphrey was told, he laughed. Laughed! As if the idea of the king's mother marrying a servant was amusing. But the council will not be amused. They will have her retired quietly. Far away from court and with luck no-one will be any the wiser. If there is an occasion where she must appear in public it will be brief and carefully supervised.'

'And the Welshman?'

'Oh mercy, no! He will not appear. Not at all. Impossible! Lord Warwick suggests the man is granted the rights of an Englishman to give a cloak of decency to the whole sordid affair. But that is all. And to think I once accused your cousin, Edmund Beaufort, of having an interest in her while all the time the harlot was indulging in God knows what with one of her household servants. It beggars belief.'

'Indeed,' I said, thinking how lucky Edmund had been. The child, I was sure, was his and yet he would walk away with his reputation untarnished. As for poor Katherine, hopefully she would make some sort of life for herself with Owain Tudor. Her position was precarious but I could wish her nothing but contentment. I had promised I would pray for her and I would.

But Isabel had more secrets to impart. She placed her hand on my sleeve to prevent me leaving. 'Apparently the king's treasurer visited her grace in the early winter, before he set out for Rouen. His squire was told by one of the maidservants that her mistress was vomiting each morning but the stupid youth thought nothing of it. Now it is clear why she hurried back to England. Her hunger for the Welshman was so great she could not even wait for her son's coronation. It is utterly degrading.'

I placed my hand on my belly. In the early winter I too had been vomiting in the mornings. My condition was the inevitable result of our last few days in Rouen when

Richard had come to my bed. Katherine's haunted face, her fear, her insistence that we should leave at once. It all made sense now. It wasn't Owain Tudor she hungered for but Edmund and if now she truly *was* carrying another child, it wasn't Owain Tudor's child but Edmund's.

Once the celebrations were over Richard and I travelled back to Bisham, past the familiar landmarks of my childhood: the old wharf at Maidenhythe which had been a source of great delight to a small girl; past Cookham, to the bridge which spanned the river at Great Marlow where we used to stop and watch boats pass underneath; and finally to Quarry Wood – *my* Quarry Wood where I'd wandered happily with my mother and where my cousin, Edmund, once tried to seduce me. Down by the river the trees trailed their lower branches almost into the water while higher up the slope a pale green haze of leaf bursts signalled the start of a fair summer to come.

Bisham, a half day's journey from Westminster, was now Richard's favourite house out of all our manors, the one where he brought guests he wished to impress with his importance. But in years to come, once he had control of his mother's Yorkshire lands, I knew we would move north to Middleham and to my surprise I found the idea not unpleasing.

As we entered the house we were met by a tidily dressed row of small children. Joan, at seven, could be relied on to do her duty but I was pleased to see Cecilia and Dickon out of their short clothes at last, no longer looking like babies. Cecilia managed a wobbly curtsey but forgot what she was supposed to say whereas Dickon stepped forwards confidently and made a commendable bow and a bright, 'Greetings lord father. Greetings lady mother.' Tom, his hand held firmly by one of the nursemaids regarded us with great suspicion until I smiled at him; then I received a beaming smile in return. While little Johnny, safe in his nursemaid's arms, stretched out his hands and shouted 'Bah!'

'Noisy little beggars, aren't they,' remarked their father. But he duly enthused over how much they'd grown and commented favourably on Joan's progress in the schoolroom.

That evening he stood with his arm round my waist feeling the gentle swell of our next little Nevill safely tucked up in my belly.

'We're part way to creating our own dynasty, sweetheart. Three sons, two daughters and another, God willing, soon to be safely born. My mother brought up nine of us. Perhaps we shall do even better.'

I thought of my own poor mother who'd endured year after year with only a single daughter to show for her endeavours, and realised once again how fortunate I was.

That evening I celebrated our return to Bisham by tempting my husband into bed with whispered promises of what I would do for him. We might have been married ten years and have five children but I'd not forgotten the duties of a wife. And some duties were certainly more pleasurable than others. Lying clasped in his arms, listening to his steady heartbeat, it was easy to forget everything else: past worries and fears for the future. But as always, my demons were waiting patiently for me to be alone.

The following evening Richard entertained members of his council. Waves of laughter from the hall floated up the stairs and I knew from experience this would last well into the night. After the food and drink would come music, a few verses, maybe a song or two, and it would be gone midnight before any discussion of important matters would take place. Rooms were ready for our guests and there was no need for me to be present. I had greeted the men on their arrival and then retired to my rooms.

My bed companion for the night was the daughter of one of Richard's friends, a pleasant young woman of sixteen, who would shortly return to her father's house for her wedding. I would be sad to lose her but she was certainly ready for marriage. She helped me undress, telling me how much she had learned under my care and asking, in an agony of embarrassment, what she should do if she found her husband's attentions unpleasing.

'From what your mother says, he is an amiable young man so you've no need to worry.'

'But you and Sir Richard are so happy together. What if it is not like that for me?'

I smiled. 'Place your husband's needs and desires above your own and you will have a good marriage. Be patient and trust in the Blessed Virgin to guide you and most of all, do not let yourself be led astray. Be steadfast and remember that once you are married your husband is your life and only you can make a success of your marriage. Nobody else.'

She kissed me and together we said our prayers.

All will be well, I told myself. We are at Bisham. Richard is in the hall. My bed companion is a good young woman. Nothing can happen.

But in the hours of darkness they came once more. First the disquiet, the fear bubbling beneath the surface, the sense of a brooding presence coming closer and closer. The air vibrated with the sound of far-off drums, a trumpet call, men marching. A voice whispered, 'They are coming for you. Best go now while you have the chance.'

I tried to run but my feet were stuck in stinking black mud and however much I struggled I was unable to move. I reached out my hands but where there should have been firm ground my fingers met a thick sticky liquid. It covered my hands and began sliding up my arms. It was blood!

She stood there with her shaven head and young girl's face, her bound hands outstretched, pleading. *'Aidez moi! Aidez moi!'*

The smoke came slowly, creeping over my legs, my waist, my arms and into my face. I couldn't see and I couldn't breath. I was choking. *'Aidez moi! Aidez moi!'*

Now the fire: crackling, roaring, burning, howling, screaming.

'Burn the witch! Burn the witch!'

Hands grasped my shoulder. Someone was shaking me.

'My lady! Wake up!'

There was no time. I had to escape. I had to run. I screamed with all my might and tried to push the hands away. And all the while voices were saying, 'What's the matter with her? Should we fetch help? A priest? What shall we do?'

Flames were coming closer and closer and the cardinal was whispering, 'This is your punishment.'

'Send for Sir Richard,' said a distant voice.

'Such a foolish act,' continued the whispers. 'So unnecessary. But you must pay for your sins. You will burn in the fires of Hell for what you did.'

'No!' I screamed. 'I beg you. I'm not ready. I have children.'

'Burn her!'

Then suddenly, breaking through the swirling clouds of terror, my husband's voice, 'Alice! Wake up!'

A pair of arms lifted me so that my head lay against something which smelled of a man's warmth and I stopped fighting. I opened my eyes and there he was, his face creased with anxiety.

My women hovered behind him, dressed in their nightshifts, white with fear, too frightened to move.

'What's been going on?' demanded my husband.

'My lady suffered a bad dream, my lord.'

My bed companion gave a little bob. 'My lady often cries out in the night, my lord. But this was worse than usual.'

There was a murmur of agreement. 'She says it is nothing, my lord, just a bad dream.'

'A bad dream which makes her shout out in terror? How long has this been going on?'

They did not want to admit how long it had been while they had said nothing. This was women's business.

'Since we returned from Rouen, my lord.'

'No, no! My lady was crying out when we were in Rouen, I remember. It was in the summer.'

'It has been like this since they burned the Maid, my lord,' admitted my bed companion.

'And how often does she wake screaming?'

They shuffled their feet, unwilling to admit to the truth.

'Most nights, my lord.'

'Are you telling me that most nights the countess cries and screams in her sleep and I was not told.'

The silence was almost worse than the dream which was fading fast now that the candles were lit and Richard was holding me.

'I told them not to tell you, my lord,' I said, not wanting my women to suffer on my account.

'Why do you scream?' Richard turned his attention to me. 'What is it that frightens you?'

When I said nothing, he stood up. 'Very well. If you'll not tell me here in your own chamber, we shall we go to the chapel. You can answer me there.'

He was angry.

'I cannot tell you, my lord,' I said, very low.

'Why not?'

'Because…'

'Yes?'

'Because you will think me unworthy to be your wife,' I whispered.

He stared at me in disbelief.

'Very well.' He turned to one of my women. 'Give me that cloak.'

Wordlessly she handed him my old cloak which someone had discarded on the perch by the door to the wardrobe. He wrapped the cloak around my shoulders and then lifted me up in his arms as if I was nothing but a bundle of feathers.

'By Christ, Lady! There's no weight to you at all. You're naught but thistledown.'

He cradled me as if I was a child, carrying me down the steps, through the hall past a dozen sleepy-eyed servants, and out into the breaking dawn. He walked across the courtyard, under the arch and round to where my mother's little garden still lay, undisturbed, just as I remembered. My stepmother had preserved everything as it had always been.

Richard kicked open the gate and walked towards the old turf bench. He set me down on my feet on the path. The seat was damp with dew so he took off his robe and folded it up into a cushion. Then he sat me down, still wrapped in my cloak.

'Comfortable?'

I nodded.

He sat down beside me, dressed in only his nightshirt and took my unresisting hands in his and despite the early morning chill his hands were warm. He looked like a man determined to have answers to his questions.

'Now, tell me what this is all about.'

I opened my mouth but before I could speak he placed a finger on my lips.

'Remember this, Alice. You have been my wife for more than ten years so I know you very well. Do not be tempted to lie to me. Do you understand?'

I nodded again and whispered, 'Yes.'

This was the ultimate test of love, the giving of every part of oneself to the other, with nothing held back. It was what my Aunt Margaret had counselled to bring myself closer to God. Hiding from the light did not bring peace. I was a grown woman and could not longer creep into my mother's arms when I felt afraid. I had to stand on my own two feet and face my fears and if I truly loved Richard Nevill I must place myself in his hands and trust that when he knew the truth he would still want me for his wife for without trust, love was a paltry thing not worth having.

I looked up into his eyes and prayed that this brave and resolute man, this man I called my husband, even if he did not love me, valued me and could find it in his heart to understand and to forgive.

So I told him. I told him everything.

'I wanted to please you,' I began in a low voice, remembering those early days of our marriage when my sisters-in-law poked fun at me and I knew my husband would never want me if I could not bring him my father's earldom.

I told him how I'd been introduced to a wise woman who said she could help me and how after some hesitation I had stupidly followed her advice, not realising how dangerous it was to meddle in such things.

'It would have gone no further but your uncle – the bishop as he was then – found out what I'd done and threatened me.'

'Threatened you! How?'

'He said I would burn.'

Richard swore softly under his breath. 'And you believed him?'

'He was a bishop. Naturally I believed him. He was an important man.'

'What did he expect from you?'

Out came the story of how the bishop had wanted Edmund to get close to the little king's mother and how he'd used me as bait for his own purposes. 'I think he had marriage in mind all along but his plan went wrong.'

'The law concerning the remarriage of English queens.'

'Yes.'

'And the rest? I presume there is more?'

I told him how Edmund had threatened me and how, against all my instincts, I'd helped him purchase a love potion.'

'Young women often buy charms and potions to make young men fall in love with them,' I explained. 'We think nothing of it. When I was a girl we put may blossom under our pillows. I'm sure your sisters did the same.'

'Foolish nonsense,' muttered Richard.

'After that I thought it was finished and I was safe but one night the cardinal 's man came for me. He said I was needed. The threat was veiled but always there.'

'When was this?'

'A year and more ago. It was Christmas and you'd gone away on business.'

'What did my uncle want with you?'

As by now half the court would know about Katherine and Master Tudor there was no reason for me to keep silent any longer so I told him the rest of the story, about my visit to Waltham and Katherine's secret marriage.

'And the child?'

'I believe it is Edmund's but he'll not acknowledge it. Everyone will assume it is Owain Tudor's child.'

'And all this happened because you wanted to please me?'

I gave a little shrug. 'I suppose so.'

He sat for a while, saying nothing, staring at a rose in bud as one of the stable cats padded quietly along the path.

When he spoke it was in a sombre voice. 'Most certainly the earldom and the Salisbury manors added to my worth in the eyes of others but whatever their value I'd not have wanted you to imperil your soul or your life for them.'

'They were the reason you married me.'

'Yes, they were.'

'You wanted them.'

'I did and I do. I cannot see how I could be the man my parents intended me to be, without them. But Alice, dearest, title and property were only half the bargain my father struck with yours. The other half was you.'

'You told your sisters you didn't want me. I heard you.'

He gave a wry smile. 'Perhaps when we were first wed I did not care for you overmuch. You were a girl, just little Alice Montagu. But now you are my wife, my helpmeet, the mother of my children and I value you above everyone.'

I could feel tears gathering in the corners of my eyes and tried to blink them away, ashamed to weep in front of my husband.

'And all this?'

'Nobody will harm you, sweetheart. You are my wife and I would not permit it.'

'The cardinal?' I whispered, fear still thumping in my chest.

'Him most of all. Lord Humphrey is determined to keep my uncle out of England and even if he returns, his influence is not what it was. If he moved against you he would have me to reckon with.'

'And my cousin?'

Richard put his arm round my shoulder and held me close. 'One day there will be a reckoning between Edmund Beaufort and myself but that time has not yet come. I have his measure so I'd not have you concern yourself with him any more.' He put his mouth on mine and kissed me gently. 'Remember, you are my entirely beloved wife.'

We stayed like that for a long time while the sky turned from pale grey to a wash of lemon and finally to the purest of blues, the colour of the song thrush's egg. From the village church by the river came the sound of a clanging bell and in the priory nearby the brothers began chanting the second office of the day. In the bushes behind us a solitary wren was calling for its mate and in the courtyard half a dozen wagons were rumbling under the gatehouse, making their slow way round to the kitchens where the boys would be waiting. I could feel a peace I'd not known for a long time seep into my bones as from beyond the walls, down in the water meadows, came the voice of a young girl singing and the answering low of a cow.

# EPILOGUE

## MIDDLEHAM 1459

The young man had come up from Kettlewell, passing over the moor and along the path through Coverdale. He had lost count of the days since he'd left Ludlow but reckoned it must now be well past All Hallows. In Preston he'd seen women with soul cakes to appease the dead and criers ringing their bells in the streets like they did back home, and that was several days ago.

As he approached Middleham he kept well out of sight and once more the night became his friend as he searched for the secret path hidden deep in the undergrowth. He'd been shown the way before they left – "Just in case, lad," his father had said, not needing to elaborate. They both knew how dangerous their lord's plan was, and the penalty for failure.

Afraid of a last-minute mishap he dismounted and led his horse carefully through the boulder-strewn grasses, wishing there was a torch or even a sliver of moon to light the way. But there was nothing, just acres of unrelieved blackness, more treacherous to a tired man than the shake holes at Caseker Scar.

Once he reached the foot of the castle wall he tied his exhausted mount to the bole of a tree and felt around for the footholds carved into the stone. At first he thought he'd mistaken the place but eventually his fingers felt one cleft and then another where someone had chipped away a slot just wide enough for a man's boot. He muttered a prayer, took a deep breath and began the long wearisome climb up the wall to the unshuttered window some thirty feet above his head. There was no knowing what kind of reception he'd get if his pursuers had managed to outpace him but at Skipton no-one had heard owt so he reckoned he was safe.

'What the…!'

He clamped his hand over the old man's mouth.

'Only me,' he whispered.

'Christ's balls, lad! Ye nearly had me stricken, comin' in like that.'

'Where's the mistress?'

'Abed.'

The old man tried to grab an arm but it was too late, the young man was already gone.

The lady of Middleham woke to a rumble of thunder over the moor far away to the south. The men had said there'd be rain by morning and it sounded as if they'd be proved right. Was that a scratch at the door? She reached under the pillow for the blade she always kept there, then slipped out of bed with the knife in one hand and the other grasping the front of her night-robe as she approached the door.

'I thought you were an intruder,' she said in relief as the young man dropped to his knees.

There'd be no written message, she knew that. It would be far too dangerous if the lad was caught.

'M'lord says you must leave, lady. It's not safe to stay.'

Fear clutched at her heart. 'What happened?'

'We were betrayed. M'lord says they'll make for Calais or, failing that, Ireland. He begs you not to delay. He says if you're caught, they'll burn you.'

They'll burn you! In that instant she was back in Rouen, a whole lifetime ago: the summer heat, the baying crowds; the fire, the smoke, the young woman screaming "Jesu! Jesu! Jesu!" as fames engulfed her slender body.

'We must leave at first light,' she said.

'Forgive me, lady, but we should leave now.'

She didn't argue. 'Horses?'

'I've been to the stables and I have food.'

She lifted up a bundle sitting on top of a chest. 'And I have my things. Give me a moment to dress and I'll be with you.'

She deliberately chose an everyday gown of an undistinguished brown homespun, a thick grey kirtle, her warmest cloak and a pair of comfortable old riding boots. He gloves were plain leather gauntlets not the sort a countess would wear but if they'd stripped Richard of his title she was no longer a countess.

As a girl she'd been taught that a woman could not outrun her destiny but in the long years of their marriage, Richard had shown her that Nevill's make their own destiny, answerable to no-one but God. So she gathered up her belongings and went quietly down the back stairs to the stable yard to join her companion. As they rode out into the night with their horses's head turned resolutely to the west, she didn't look back. If her husband's enemies came to Middleham, they'd find her gone.

# Author's Note

The marriage of Katherine of Valois and Owain Tudor is part of our national story but there is no certainty in anything to do with their marriage or the birth of Katherine's two "Tudor" sons. The elder of these two sons, Edmund Tudor, married Margaret Beaufort (Edmund Beaufort's niece) and it was their child, Henry Tudor, who defeated Richard III at Bosworth and took the English throne as Henry VII.

Some time after 1431 Edward Beaufort married a daughter of the Earl of Warwick's first marriage.

Katherine died in 1437

In 1441 Eleanor, Duchess of Gloucester was accused with Margery Jourdemayne and others of treasonable necromancy. Eleanor was forced to do public penance and afterwards, imprisoned for life. Mistress Jourdemayne was burned at the stake.

The story of the Nevill family continues in the next book *Fire and Fleet and Candlelight*.

# Acknowledgements

I could not have done this on my own so I should like to thank those whose support is invaluable from the historians who have laboured long and hard to unearth the truth of our past to the helpful ladies in my local library at Ilminster who are never too busy to find the books I need for my research. And as always my thanks go to Richard and to our daughters, Natasha and Alex, and to Jackie, Jane, Kat and Ken of the writing group without whom I would be truly lost.

These are just a few of the books and sources I studied while exploring the story of my fourteen times great-grandmother Alice Montagu who married Richard Nevill.

| | |
|---|---|
| John Ashdown-Hill | Royal Marriage Secrets |
| Helen Castor | Joan of Arc: A History |
| K L Clark | The Nevills of Middleham |
| R A Griffiths | The Reign of King Henry VI |
| G L Harriss | ODNB online: Henry Beaufort |
| Brian P Levack (ed) | The Witchcraft Sourcebook |
| Jonathan Sumption | Cursed Kings: The Hundred Years War IV |
| Bertram Woolfe | Henry VI |
| JH Wylie & WT Vaughan | The Reign of Henry the Fifth, vol 3 |

# Coming Soon

## FIRE AND FLEET AND CANDLELIGHT

It is 1453 and England is in a state of turmoil. On the throne sits Henry VI, a weak and unstable king, surrounded by men who hunger for power. The years of prosperity are over and apart from the town of Calais, France is lost.

In the North the Percy brothers are conducting a private war against the Nevills while in the South West the Earl of Devon's son is pursuing his own deadly blood feud against the Bonvilles.

Caught in this maelstrom is Kathryn Nevill, young daughter of the Earl and Countess of Salisbury, who, one sunny day in August while returning home from a wedding, comes face to face with a shocking act of violence. When her father finds her a husband she sees a way to escape these horrors only to discover that her new world is steeped in its own particular brand of murderous savagery.

*Fire and Fleet and Candlelight* is a tale of love and loss, of family loyalty and unimaginable tragedy but ultimately a story of fortitude and hope.

# About the Author

Caroline Newark was born in Northern Ireland and as a child she wanted to be a farmer's wife, have twelve children and live in a cottage with roses round the door. Instead she became a teacher, a lawyer, a dairy farmer and cheesemaker. But other remnants of that early dream survive – she has two daughters, five grandchildren and lives with her husband, Richard, in a house in a village in the West Country with roses and honeysuckle just outside the back door.

In 1997 after her mother died, Caroline found a small, red leather-bound book lying in a drawer in a bureau. Inside were details of twenty-one generations of her mother's family starting in 1299 with a marriage between the Royal Houses of England and France. With one book for each generation, Caroline has imagined the lives of these women who lived in our past.

Website: www.carolinenewark.com
Contact: caroline@carolinenewark.com
Follow: Caroline Newark on Facebook

 **Matador**

For exclusive discounts on Matador titles,
sign up to our occasional newsletter at
troubador.co.uk/bookshop